THE
LEGEND
OF THE
THIEF

THE
LEGEND
OF THE
THIEF

by Mandi Grace

FORWARD

Once upon a time, a seventeen year old girl decided to try her hand at writing a retelling of the legend of Robin Hood, only to become entangled in the world she had created for a solid eight years. Once upon a time, that same girl did an internet search on how to self-publish and immediately did exactly that with her first Robin Hood book, Lucy's Legend: A Robin Hood Story.

For those of you who might have read the original, THANK YOU. That young girl is still floored that anyone reads her books at all. For those of you who have no idea what I'm talking about, let me explain…

When I started self-publishing I did so under the name Amanda Grace. The series I lovingly refer to as the OG Robin Hood series, five books in total, were all under that name. Lucy's Legend is the one that started it all. Only the second complete novel young me had ever written, it was my first foray into publishing and I most definitely would not be where I am today without it.

Eventually I switched over to writing under Mandi Grace, but I left my old books behind me for several years. The sequel Robin Hood series (Return to Sherwood) was my only Mandi Grace work. And then one day I decided to move all of my books under one name—and while doing so, revisit and rewrite the old ones to give them a more polished story and brand new covers. This is what you hold in your hand today.

Rewriting Lucy's Legend and turning it into the Legend of the Thief was an interesting, sometimes frustrating, always magical adventure. It was emotional and nostalgic to revisit my beginnings; it was horrifying to see how truly atrocious my writing used to be; it was liberating to accept young me and her work and be at peace with it. The whole crazy experience was filmed and is on my YouTube channel if you desire to watch the highs and lows of rewriting a book nearly a decade after its first conception.

This new Legend of the Thief is twice as big as the one seventeen year old me wrote and, I hope, twice as good.

to the seventeen year old with a dream.

to Lucy's Legend.

Prologue

MARI-LU DANCED ON her toes, reaching up to grasp Aunt Lucy's hand and tug imploringly. "Please, Auntie Lucy, please?"

Aunt Lucy, graceful as always to Mari-Lu's young eyes, lifted a wrinkled hand and placed it on Mari-Lu's small head. There were seventy years that spanned the gap between little Mari-Lu and her great-grandmother—the woman everyone in Nottinghamshire referred to as their Aunt Lucy, though she was actually an aunt to only a few. Mari-Lu had adopted the name, as it was far easier to say than 'great-grandmother Lucy.'

"Please!" Mari-Lu let her big blue eyes—so reminiscent of Aunt Lucy's old ones—get as wide and innocent as she dared, her seven-year-old heart skipping a few beats as she waited for Aunt Lucy to agree to her request.

Not far from the imploring child and her great-grandmother was the mother of the young one, Marian, wife of Robin—not THE Robin Hood, of course, but rather his grandson.

Marian sat in the soft green grass with her back to an aged, smooth stone carved with an inscription. The inscribed stone stood straight and proud in the center of an old meadow, and it was there that Marian had brought her daughter to hear Aunt Lucy's story. Aunt Lucy lowered herself to a fallen log and Mari-Lu perched at her feet, still holding her hand and imploring. Marian could remember when she was a child, not so long ago, and would beg Aunt Lucy in the same fashion, entreating her to

1

tell the story one more time. Of all the members of the original gang who had sequestered in Sherwood Forest and fought the good fight all those years ago—the ones who had lived long enough for Marian to know them anyway—Aunt Lucy was the best story teller.

That may have been part of the reason Aunt Lucy was the keeper of the family history and the one who entertained the village children with stories of the great Robin Hood and the days of Sherwood, though she rarely told the entire tale in one sitting.

"Please, please, please!"

Finally, the graceful Aunt Lucy spoke through the little girl's pleas, her voice gentle, "What do you want to know?"

At last being given the invitation she wanted, Mari-Lu scrambled into Aunt Lucy's lap. "The whole story!"

"It's a long one," Aunt Lucy warned.

Mari-Lu had heard pieces of the story before; anyone who lived in Nottinghamshire had heard Aunt Lucy telling her tales. You could not escape such things so close to the very places Robin Hood had lived, where his story was born. Robin Hood himself had enjoyed spinning tales of his youth until his death four years prior. But the entire story? That would be a rare treat indeed. Even Marian leaned forward to hear what Aunt Lucy might say.

Aunt Lucy brushed a lock of little Mari-Lu's brown hair out of her eyes, and Mari-Lu reached up to mirror the movement with Aunt Lucy's grey hair. Her face was wrinkled and weathered compared to the vibrant glow of youth of Mari-Lu's, her skin thin and papery where Mari-Lu's was soft and supple. Yet Marian knew that the elderly Aunt Lucy had once been a strong young woman whose heart and courage had been tested to the fullest extent.

"Please, Aunt Lucy," Marian could handle the suspense no more than her daughter could. "Tell her your story."

"But where do I begin?" Aunt Lucy smiled, her gentle voice carrying across the empty meadow. "This tale does not begin with me."

As Aunt Lucy opened her mouth to speak further, the story transported Marian to memories of her childhood and hearing the tales from Aunt Lucy and Robin Hood, and even great-uncle Mark when he'd been in a story-telling mood. Her daughter hadn't known the original members of the gang, and would grow up with only memories of Aunt Lucy, which saddened Marian. They had all been remarkable in their own ways, and she was eager for her daughter to hear their stories.

Mari-Lu stared transfixed at Aunt Lucy's face, as arrested by the story as any child could be.

"See, this story begins not with me, but in the village of Wetherby a few miles outside of the city of Nottingham, with a girl named Marian."

Mari-Lu clapped her hands. "My mama!"

Aunt Lucy laughed and so did Marian. Mari-Lu might have heard pieces of the story before, but she was only seven after all, and the passage of time was not a concept with which she was familiar.

"No, sweet child, your father's grandmother. The wife of a legend. But I am getting ahead of myself. When this story begins, Marian and the great Robin Hood were only children. Neither was great. They were ordinary children, much like yourself, who loved to splash in the stream that ran past the village of Wetherby and on into Sherwood Forest. Marian loved to braid flowers in her hair and Robin loved to skip stones across the stream."

"I like those things, too!" Mari-Lu giggled.

Aunt Lucy smiled, resting her aged hand atop Mari-Lu's head once more, her faded blue eyes smiling down into the young ones whose color reflected what her own might have been in youth. "Robin and Marian were never alone. Robin's faithful servant and dearest friend Much was always with them, as well as Marian's little brother Mark."

Hearing Aunt Lucy speak of Uncle Mark brought a moment of sadness to Marian. Aunt Lucy was the last living member of the gang and that was a tragedy.

Many among the first generation of their chosen family had died before Marian was born, and others before she was old enough to remember them. Of those she could recall with fond memories, Uncle Mark was one she remembered the best apart from Aunt Lucy and Robin Hood himself. Marian had been eight when Uncle Mark died though she still could vividly picture his twinkling eyes and the sound of his boisterous laugh. She could still recall how Uncle Mark used to interrupt Aunt Lucy's stories to add what he thought were more relevant details and it had always made Marian laugh.

Robin Hood himself had always listened to Aunt Lucy's stories with the utmost attention, never interrupting or adding anecdotes, though when Aunt Lucy wasn't telling the tale, he was more than happy to tell it himself. The flavor of each of their accounts reflected their own view of what their lives had been like when they were young and Marian appreciated all of it.

Robin Hood she had the most memories with, as did every young person in Nottinghamshire. Robin Hood and Aunt Lucy were staples in every childhood, not only for their storytelling abilities but also because they had both always made a point of caring for the poor in Nottingham and the surrounding villages even after the events of the story Aunt Lucy was now telling.

But Mari-Lu could only vaguely remember Robin Hood, and knew nothing of the rest of the Sherwood gang. They would always exist for her only in Aunt Lucy's stories, which made today even more momentous in Marian's eyes.

"Robin was the only child of the Earl of Locksley, and Marian was the eldest of the two children of Sir Godfrey, Sheriff of Nottingham. Everyone who knew them as children believed they were destined to be together. The Earl—Sir Edward—and Sir Godfrey had always thought of themselves as brothers, so close was their friendship in their youth. Though he was the Sheriff and the castle of Nottingham belonged to him, Sir Godfrey preferred to live in the village of Wetherby just a few miles outside of the city, raising his children where he himself had grown up. He spent time in the castle for business however, and the four children—Marian, Mark, Robin, and Much—spent a great deal of time there themselves."

Aunt Lucy dropped her voice to a conspiratorial whisper, and Mari-Lu leaned closer to hear her. "They discovered many secret passages and entrances, places that were dark and small where they could play without being disturbed. The children were adventurous and loved finding new secrets in the castle, and many years later those secrets were used to save lives."

The melodic voice stopped, and Marian glanced at Aunt Lucy. Her eyes were closed now as she stroked Mari-Lu's hair. Mari-Lu's eyes remained glued to Aunt Lucy's face, waiting with anticipation for whatever would come next.

"I never knew her personally." Aunt Lucy's voice was soft and reverent when she spoke. "But I imagine she might have been a lot like you," she opened her eyes and smiled down at Mari-Lu. Mari-Lu grinned back up at her.

"Do you know we named you after her?" Marian asked her daughter. Mari-Lu's head swung around to see her mother.

"My name isn't Marian, mama, yours is!" Mari-Lu laughed.

"Yes, but the Mari in Mari-Lu is for Marian. The Lu, if you'll notice, is for Lucy. You were named for two of the greatest women Nottinghamshire—and perhaps all of England—has ever known. One a martyr, the other an unsung hero."

"Nonsense," Aunt Lucy laughed. "I am neither, so you must be referring to Marian in regard to both."

"She'll see soon enough if you'll finish your story," Marian replied.

"I'm Marian and Lucy," Mari-Lu giggled.

Marian knew her daughter wasn't old enough yet to fully understand what it meant to carry on the names and heritage of Marian and Lucy. Marian herself was proud to carry the name of Robin Hood's beloved wife. Names meant a great deal in their chosen family.

Aunt Lucy began again, and Marian found herself transported back into the story of Robin Hood. How many times had Marian sat at Aunt Lucy's knee and listened to her tell this tale? A story of love and hate, of sorrow and joy, of death and life.

"… Marian loved everyone so deeply and passionately. She loved her country. She loved her brother Mark. But most of all, she loved her father. And she was everything to Sir Godfrey. Though her mother had died giving birth to her brother Mark, happiness and peace had ruled Marian's childhood. The laughter of Marian, Mark, Robin, and Much as they explored Nottingham castle or made their own castles in the mud on the banks of the stream, warmed the hearts of all who knew them. They were happy and carefree, as children ought to be. Yet as Marian drew near womanhood, shadows began to obscure her sun..."

Chapter 1

MARIAN LISTENED TO her father and the Earl of Locksley arguing the merits of the king's intention to march to Jerusalem in a Holy Crusade. Her father, Sir Godfrey, staunchly defended the king, while the Earl proposed it was folly. Marian wondered if either would hear her own opinion on the matter.

She was, after all, a woman. Today was her sixteenth birthday, in fact.

It was dusk, and Marian was ready for the day to be over. She wanted more than anything at that moment to have the Earl and his son leave so that her father would stop frowning. The crease in his brow was a sorry sight to end a birthday with, and the stress of the arguing men wasn't much better. The two men were sitting beside the hearth, the light of the fire reflected in their passionate eyes. Fourteen-year-old Mark was sitting nearby, hanging onto the conversation and nodding or agreeing with everything their father had to say. Robin was leaning against the door frame, silhouetted by the setting sun behind him which Marian could see through the open door. The oranges and reds painted behind Robin and beyond the rooftops of the other houses in Wetherby reflected the irritated atmosphere of the room.

"Our king isn't named 'the Lion-Heart' for nothing," Sir Godfrey said.

"It's not our place to invade Jerusalem and claim it," the Earl countered.

"I think he's brave!" Mark said.

"I think it's glorious," Robin added from the doorway.

"I still believe it is folly," the Earl said, shaking his head at his son. "What will we do with Prince John at our head in the king's absence?"

"He won't be in charge," Sir Godfrey countered. "I believe the King is naming William Longchamps his regent..."

Robin pushed away from the door frame as Sir Godfrey and the Earl got into a more heated debate, walking across the room to grab Marian's hands and pull her toward the door.

"Let them discuss the boring details," he quipped, shutting the door on the debate and the enthusiastic audience the two men had in the form of Mark. "I'd rather not hear them."

"Oh, Robin, how can you talk so? Your father is truly worried."

"And yours doesn't care."

"That's not it at all. He just trusts the king's judgment."

"And you? I know you have an opinion on the matter."

"I think men are too quick to go to war."

"Come on, Marian! Leave the gravity to them," Robin gestured toward the house they had just left. He took her hand and pulled her down the dirt path that led out of the village. Once beyond the houses, he grabbed her shoulders and pointed her toward the setting sun and the vibrant colors accompanying it. "There. Enjoy that beautiful sight."

Marian remained pensive despite his best efforts.

9

"Kiss me, Marian, love."

"Robin!" Marian swatted at his arm and he jumped backwards out of her reach with a laugh. But he sobered almost immediately. "I plan to join the king, you know."

"Would your father allow it?"

"I don't need his permission. I can make my own decisions."

"Yet I wish you wouldn't join the Crusades. Why would you want to go?"

"For the glory of it!" Robin grabbed her hands again, his eyes bright with an emotion Marian did not like.

"For the war of it," Marian countered, pulling her hands free of his grasp. "That's all you men think about. War, and riches."

"We men have three loves," Robin winked. "We also love women." Robin grabbed her hands once more, and Marian didn't pull away. "I, though, I only have one love."

Robin lifted Marian's hands to his lips for a moment. "Wait for me, Marian?"

Marian lifted her chin "I'll do no such thing, Robin of Locksley."

"My heart is always yours, Marian my love." Robin lifted her hand and kissed it once more. Then he looked up and winked. "Wish me luck!"

Then he set off into the night toward his own home in the village of Locksley, not bothering to wait for his father.

"Oh, Robin."

Sir Godfrey and the Earl were still in a heated discussion inside the house, with Mark undoubtedly having his wild imagination fed with ideas of war and glory.

Marian went inside, sat at her father's feet, and listened with forbearance to his discussion with the Earl until the latter finally left. Mark came to sit beside her with a mischievous grin once the Earl was gone.

"What did you and Robin talk about?"

"We spoke of nothing important, Mark. It doesn't matter."

"Did he not tell you then?"

"Tell me what?"

"He's joining the king on his Crusade!" Mark's face was alight with excitement, but Marian heard her father sigh and glanced up at him. He was watching Mark, his eyes filled with intensity.

"Isn't it marvelous?" Mark went on, "I wanted to go with him, but he wouldn't let me. He actually had the gall to say I was too young and insist I stay here. I'm not that much younger than he is! We are only four years apart!"

"Only four years," Marian rolled her eyes. "I am grateful Robin had the sense to tell you not to go. But I wish he would not go himself."

"I think that is unavoidable," Sir Godfrey said. "Sir Edward believes he will leave soon."

"I wish he wouldn't."

"Oh, Marian!" Mark shook his head. "You should be proud of your Robin."

"He isn't *my* Robin," Marian snapped. "And how can I be proud that he is eager to run off and kill people? I do not believe in what he is doing."

"But you support the king, don't you?" Mark demanded.

"I suppose," Marian sighed.

"You're just worried about Robin," Mark said. "Don't worry, sister dearest, he will come back to you."

"I didn't say I wanted him to come back to me."

❮❯

"It would be three years before Marian would meet Robin again," Aunt Lucy said. Mari-Lu watched her, hanging on every word. "He made good on his intentions and left that night with his manservant and childhood friend Much. He joined the Crusades, and became quite the expert swordsman and archer. He gained much fame among the soldiers and even became a trusted friend to King Richard the Lion-Heart…in England, however, things did not go as smoothly…"

❮❯

A young Lucy, only fifteen years of age leaned against the smooth stone of a windowsill, staring up at the night sky. She could hear laughter rising from the streets below, could hear a dog howling in the distance. She enjoyed living in London, but her favorite thing was being out in nature with Friar Tuck. He would take her wandering through the woods to teach her about the various plants and herbs; those were the days she could climb trees and splash in streams. If her parents went with her she would practice her sword work with her father, or have an archery contest with her mother. Here at court, however, she had to be prim and proper, always. Sometimes she felt she had two selves— the one in the forest, and the one at court. But both Lucys had one thing in common: they loved watching the stars.

Behind her, Lucy's mother was sewing by the hearth. Friar Tuck, a withered grey monk with a bald head, sat near her mother, reading by the light of the fire. Her father was on the other side of the manor having dinner with Longchamps tonight. Lucy had never met any royalty herself, but her father was an acquaintance with many powerful people in court, and William Longchamps was almost royalty after all, given he was now the King's Regent while King Richard was off on his Crusade.

"Come away from the window, love, you'll get cold," Lucy's mother said.

Lucy reluctantly pulled herself away from her favorite view and moved to sit at Friar Tuck's knee. "Will you read to us, Friar Tuck?"

Friar Tuck cleared his throat, and then began to read from the book in his hand. It was a passage of Scripture that he had painstakingly transcribed himself, translating it from Latin into French, the language of the nobility he spent his days with, including Lucy's family.

Suddenly the door crashed open and smashed into the wall with a loud bang. "We have to leave!"

Lucy's mother dropped her sewing as Lucy's father ran into the room.

"What is going on?" Friar Tuck asked.

"Assassins! They've killed Longchamps, and others, they're coming for me!"

"Who is coming for you?" Lucy's mother demanded, hurrying to her husband and trying to calm him.

"Prince John most likely. I don't know. But there are assassins in the manor killing anyone who has been opposing Prince John's attempts to gain power in court. He's coming for me."

"What do we do?" Lucy asked, her heart beating wildly in her chest.

Her father looked at her for a moment and seemed to consider, then he strode forward, grabbed her by the shoulders and pushed her roughly toward Friar Tuck. "Get her out of here. Keep her in hiding. Don't let her whereabouts be known."

"What will you do?" Friar Tuck asked.

"Give the assassins someone to follow. Now run from here!"

Lucy tried to dart forward to hug her father and beg him to stay, but her mother grabbed her. "No! He's right...if there are killers in the manor, we need to flee."

"I'll lead the way," Friar Tuck said as Lucy's father ran from the room. It was the last Lucy ever saw of him.

The flight to Friar Tuck's humble abode in the forest outside of London was a quiet one, filled only with the sobs of Lucy's mother. Lucy herself was far too confused to know what to feel. It had all happened so fast.

News reached them the next morning that William Longchamps was indeed dead, as well as several other nobles including Lucy's father. Poison, old age, many things were publicly claimed to be the cause, but Lucy knew what her father had said. Prince John had sent assassins.

It was only a week after her father's death that her mother succumbed to her grief and died.

Lucy remained with Friar Tuck, orphaned and alone and unsure how the world had come to this at all.

«→»

"That's awful!" Mari-Lu cried, staring up at Aunt Lucy with wide eyes.

"Yes, it was," Aunt Lucy agreed. "And things only continued to get worse. Over the course of six months after Prince John's rise to power, taxes rose steadily. Prince John, and his local

15

Sheriffs, claimed this was because King Richard was so caught up in the Holy War and needed funds. In the meantime, any standing armies still in England were 'reorganized' as Prince John called it, and he slowly replaced any Sheriffs and other nobles not loyal to himself with those more willing to do his bidding…"

Chapter 2

"THIS IS GETTING ridiculous!" Mark grumbled, looking over the meager fare Marian had brought home from the market.

"We have far more than most people, so don't complain!"

"Someone has to start doing something."

"We can start by taking some of this food to Widow Mary and the others in Wetherby and Nottingham who don't have enough food."

"That is not what I meant," Mark sighed. But he agreed it was a good idea, and so share their food, they did.

As the taxes increased, the poverty did as well, and with it the unrest. Prince John's idea of keeping the peace was executing anyone who spoke against him or his new taxes and laws. One such person who chose to speak out was Robin's own father, the Earl of Locksley. And for his courage, he was executed, leaving Robin the Earl.

Marian clung to her father's arm, watching as the servants of Locksley manor quietly shoveled dirt onto the grave of Robin's father. The funeral had been simple and quiet, despite his place among the nobility, because he'd been executed as a traitor.

Sir Godfrey's tears flowed freely, and he sagged into Marian who did her best to hold him upright.

"This is wrong," Mark said quietly from Marian's other side.

Marian agreed; it *was* wrong, on so many levels. Starting with the fact that Robin should have been here to be with his family and his father. He might not have been able to prevent it, but he could have supported Sir Godfrey—could have supported Marian—in the grief over the Earl's death. But Robin was still on the Crusades with the king, so Sir Godfrey, Marian, and Mark were left to be devastated and grieve alone.

Marian grabbed Mark's hand, though she still had her other arm wrapped around her father's waist to hold him up. Mark squeezed her fingers, and Marian knew she'd do whatever she had to in order to prevent her family from suffering the same fate as Robin's father. She couldn't stop Prince John and his loyal supporters from causing suffering to the rest of England, perhaps, but she could protect the two people she cared about. And she could protect herself; Robin might have abandoned them, but she decided that day that she didn't need him.

Sir Godfrey was less outspoken than the late earl had been, but it was not long before he was removed from his office as Sheriff of Nottingham and was replaced by a Sir John from London. Sharing the name of Prince John himself, which the good people of Nottingham soon refused to utter if they could help it, he was simply, horribly, the Sheriff of Nottingham. He took up residence in the castle in the city of Nottingham, while Sir Godfrey continued to live in Wetherby with Marian and Mark.

Though Sir Godfrey was grieved by the events taking place in Nottingham and the rest of England, he maintained hope that King Richard would return and set all to rights.

"Set all to rights?" Marian glared at her father across the table as the family was eating dinner. "The king can't bring the Earl of Locksley back from the dead, or William Longchamps, or any of the other unfortunate victims of Prince John's murders! This is what we get because the king—and even Robin—desired war above peace."

"Robin is fighting for our king and country!" Mark objected.

"Marian, you simply do not understand these things," Sir Godfrey said. "You think in such simple terms; war, peace. But what of duty? Honor? Fealty? King Richard is fighting to defend our faith in the Holy Land and you think less of him for it?"

Marian was quiet; she did think less of him for it, but her father would never agree with her. She had no desire to argue with him, but he was wrong; she did understand one thing quite clearly. Her people were in trouble.

◄►

Aunt Lucy hugged Mari-Lu, her eyes closed and a wisp of a smile on her face. "Marian was so passionate. She wanted—she needed—to do something. Unlike her father, she could not sit back and be silent, to simply watch and wait and hope for the king's return."

Aunt Lucy's voice grew soft as she continued, "The new Sheriff of Nottingham brought his own soldiers with him. Among these was a young lord named Sir Guy of Gisbourne. He was clever, hard, and ruthless. In short, he was exactly what the Sheriff of Nottingham needed. Taxes continued to rise, and the King grew ever more entrenched in the Crusades in the Holy Land."

"What was he doing there?" Mari-Lu asked.

"That is another story," Aunt Lucy laughed. "I will tell you that story someday, too. But for now, the people of England were suffering. Anyone who spoke against Prince John would be hung—usually on some false accusation or another. Prince John and his cronies never said they were killing people for supporting the king, but everyone knew the truth…"

❮❯

Marian clenched her teeth, willing herself not to shout at the new Sheriff, or better yet, punch his smug face.

The Sheriff was making rather a habit of inviting Sir Godfrey and his children to the castle for extravagant dinners. Marian was sure it was his way of rubbing their noses in his treachery. People were starving, and he sat there eating at a table filled with more food than they might see in a month. The good and beloved previous sheriff, Sir Godfrey, forced out of his position and then further forced to the indignity of sharing a table with his successor.

It was almost more than Marian could bear.

Beside her Mark was digging into the Sheriff's feast with gusto, but Marian refused to eat. Across the table sat Sir Guy of Gisbourne, the Sheriff's right hand.

Though many declared him to be handsome, Marian saw nothing in him. She preferred Robin's blond hair to Gisbourne's dark locks; Robin's sky blue eyes over Gisbourne's brown ones.

The young lord of Gisbourne always wore dark clothing and black leather, even his stallion was a beautiful black. He was stern, and Marian had never yet seen him smile. Contrasted to Robin's easy manners and ready smile, Marian was disgusted with Sir Guy of Gisbourne.

"I think this was a productive night," the Sheriff grinned, taking a long drink of his wine. "Marian, dear, have you enjoyed yourself?"

"You know perfectly well I have not," Marian snapped.

At the end of the table, her father winced, giving her a sharp look. Marian did not care that her father feared the Sheriff; she was not going to be cowed by such a hateful man.

The Sheriff laughed. "You are the most entertaining company I have had since moving here, Lady Marian. I do believe everyone around here is too afraid to speak their minds." He glanced around as though expecting to see trouble over his shoulder and then lowered his voice, "As if they all think something bad will happen…but not you."

"You can kill me if you like. I will speak my mind."

"Oh I have no desire to kill you. You are my favorite entertainment, Lady Marian. But I believe we've had enough for one evening. Don't want to have too much of a good thing, after all. I'll have my guards escort you home."

The Sheriff rose and Gisbourne followed him. As soon as they had left the room, Sir Godfrey leaned forward. "Marian! Don't anger him."

"You heard him. I amuse him."

"You are going to get yourself hurt. I won't stand for it. I'll not have you end up on the gallows like everyone else who speaks against him or Prince John. I need you to be safe."

The door opened again and Sir Godfrey immediately stopped speaking as several of the Sheriff's soldiers entered to escort Sir Godfrey and his children back to Wetherby. He was quiet the whole way back to the village, while the Sheriff's soldiers accompanied them, but as soon as they were safely in their own home and alone, he began again.

"You have to be smart, Marian. What example are you setting for your brother that you talk back to such dangerous men? You could get yourself killed!"

"I am not afraid of him."

"How many people have to be murdered for you to learn to fear Prince John's men? Hmm?" Sir Godfrey took Marian's hands in his own, his eyes imploring. "I need you to be safe, child. I cannot bear to lose you."

Marian sighed. "I'll try not to draw his attention so much."

It wasn't a promise Marian expected to be able to keep. The Sheriff always irritated her into voicing her opinions and she didn't expect that to change simply because her father was worried about her.

The next day while Sir Godfrey was in Nottingham, Marian approached her brother Mark as he was practicing archery behind their house.

"Mark!" Marian grabbed his shoulders, startling her brother. "I need your help."

"What do you need, sister of mine?"

"You have to be serious and you cannot laugh."

"I am completely serious and I will not laugh."

"I need you to teach me how to use a bow, and maybe a sword, too."

"Marian! You hate warfare. Why would you want to know how to use weapons?"

"Because someone has to protect our people! Father is right, you know. A lot of innocent people are dying. The Sheriff, Gisbourne, Prince John...they all think they can kill anyone who opposes them. It isn't right. Someone has to stop them."

"And you think you are the one to do it?"

"Mark, have you seen the suffering, or are you completely blind?"

"I have seen it. You know I have. People are starving because the growing taxes mean they can't buy food. Those who can't pay the taxes at all are being thrown in prison. Good people are suffering for it. And the unjust murders…Sir Edward, the Earl. Does Robin even know yet that his father died defending our King? But what could we do, Marian?"

"I've been thinking about that. I think…" Marian hesitated. She knew her idea was reckless. It was the exact opposite of what she had promised her father. "I think we should stop the executions. With a jail break, or the executions themselves. I don't know."

"Marian!"

"I know, I know. But we could do it. You already know how to fight; you can teach me. And we know the castle better than anyone—every secret passage. We could do it. There's a passage that goes directly to the dungeons, Mark. We could help people."

"And do what with them? As soon as we fight back, we're dead men. And if we manage to rescue someone, what then? They live here? They'll be found!"

"I don't know! I don't have all the answers yet, but we have to do *something*. And you can start by simply teaching me. We'll figure out what to do with our skills after that."

"Father won't like it."

"We won't tell him."

"I don't know…"

"You wanted to go to the Holy Land with Robin and fight for the King. Well, why don't you want to defend the King here, in England? Defend his people, Mark."

"So, what? We become crusaders in Nottingham? There are only two of us."

"Mark, we have to do something!"

Mark sighed. "I'm going to regret this...but okay. Let's do it."

So Mark began to teach Marian everything he knew of the sword and the bow. Together they began to use the secrets of the castle to spy on the Sheriff and his men, to watch Gisbourne training soldiers in the courtyard beyond the castle wall. They learned to be stealthy and follow the Sheriff's soldiers as they went about business in the streets of Nottingham.

← →

"Marian's not being safe at all," Mari-Lu said.

"No, she was not," Aunt Lucy agreed. "Marian was not the sort to sit by and watch horrible things happen—if she could do something, she would. And so she did..."

Chapter 3

IN THE NORTH of England, a soldier was beating a man for his inability to pay Prince John's outrageous taxes. The soldier's hand came down again, striking the young man across the cheek and sending him sprawling into the dirt beside his daughter. Once more the hand raised and then came down on the child.

"You cannot pay the King's tax?" the soldier taunted as the child fell beneath his blow. "You'll regret your insolence."

The young man struggled to rise, but the soldier's boot connected with his face and he fell backward once more. The child was crying from the sting of the soldier's blow, and the terror of watching her father being beaten.

"The King is fighting a Holy Crusade, or hadn't you heard?" the soldier laughed. "And you won't help your king and your country by paying for his war?" the soldier's boot hit the man's head again and he groaned.

The child looked on in horror.

As the soldier's leg swung backward for another kick, an arrow sprouted in his leg. With a cry of pain he stumbled backward, and then another arrow hit his other leg and he fell. A hooded figure dashed forward, bringing the hilt of a sword crashing down on the soldier's helmet, and he collapsed, unconscious.

Pulling back her hood, Lucy scooped up the child. "It's okay, it's okay. You're safe, little one. Let me see your cheek. Did that hurt? Hold still, I have a salve that will take some of the sting off, I promise."

Lucy pulled a small bottle from her belt and put a dab of liquid on her finger before spreading it on the little girl's cheek. It was medicine of Friar Tuck's making, concocted from the herbs he grew in the garden behind his little hovel in the forest outside of London.

The little girl's tears were gone, and she watched Lucy with wide eyes. Lucy smiled at her, and then moved to inspect the man. His face was bleeding, but he was alive. She rolled him onto his back and he groaned, opening his eyes and staring wildly around.

"Easy. The soldier is unconscious for now. You're safe. You'll need to get far from here. Can you sit up?"

Lucy helped the man upright, and then pulled a small pouch off of her belt. "This is money, so you can pay for inns and provisions as you travel."

"I can't take your money!"

"You can. Take it, and take your daughter, and run. Go to Scotland, hide in the forest, do whatever you like but do it far away from here."

Lucy pulled the man to his feet. For a moment he was unsteady, but as the little girl ran over and wrapped her arms around his waist, he seemed to gain his balance once more.

"What can I do to repay you, for saving me and my daughter?"

"Live," Lucy said. She pulled her hood back over her head, backing away from the man and his little girl. "Please, get far away from here. Stay safe."

Some distance from the farmhouse where she'd rescued the man was a wooded area and Lucy took off running toward it, not stopping until she was within the trees and out of sight of any prying eyes. She slowed her pace, and then leaned against a tree to catch her breath. She'd stashed her bag in these trees before rescuing the man and his daughter, and it took her several minutes of looking through the trees and bushes to find where she had placed it.

Pulling her quiver from her back, Lucy inspected her arrows. She would need to make more if she continued to leave them behind in her victims. She had intended to collect them, but every time she got involved in a fight like today, she seemed to forget everything she'd told herself she would do. Everything always happened so fast.

Lucy sat down, setting the quiver aside, and grabbed her pack to inspect its contents. She still had some bread and a few apples, but she would need to restock soon. Next to the food she had a small leather bound book, the parchment held between the covers carefully handwritten in a familiar script.

Friar Tuck.

Lucy could feel the pricks of pain behind her eyes as tears threatened to fall, but she brushed them aside. She had taken one of Friar Tuck's carefully translated passages of Scripture with her when she'd run away.

Not long after her parents' deaths, Lucy had decided she couldn't hide with Friar Tuck and let the world burn down around her. Her parents and so many others' lives were being ruined by Prince John and his followers, but Lucy knew she could do something about it. Her father and mother had instilled in her great knowledge and skill with the sword and bow, and she could make use of it. And so she did.

It was a lonely existence living on the run, looking for trouble, but Lucy had found the quiet life of a monk to be equally lonely. Living with Friar Tuck had been simple and familiar, and she knew he loved her deeply, but being so close to London only reminded her of her parents. She couldn't stay and face those memories…

⟪→⟫

"You ran away from home!" Mari-Lu stared up at Aunt Lucy's face.

"I did."

"How'd you know how to save that man and his daughter?"

"I was simply passing through when I saw the man being beaten and decided to do something about it. That was how I lived in those days, wandering from city to city, from farm to farm, stopping anything unjust that I witnessed but never staying long."

"What happened next?"

←→

Marian let the fletching of the arrow sift through her fingers as she prepared to nock it to her bowstring. The sun was obscured by stormy clouds overhead as Marian cautiously raised her bow and squinted at the target Mark had set up for her some yards away. It wasn't a great distance but Marian wasn't a great shot so she didn't question it. Mark watched her quietly while she eyed the target, and then let her arrow fly.

It hit its mark, though it wasn't a bulls-eye. Marian grabbed another arrow, determined to improve.

"That's better," Mark commented.

Marian remembered when she first started training with Mark and she couldn't even hit the targets he set up. The frustration she felt as he'd moved the targets closer and closer to her until she hit one spurred her on to keep trying harder. She wanted to be able to physically protect herself and her family, and the inability to accurately hit the target was hindering her.

Marian drew her bow back, feeling her arm and shoulder muscles respond to the pressure. She wore one of Mark's bracers to protect her arm, until her own would be finished. She'd already visited a tanner in Nottingham to request he make some—he had been a little surprised at her request, but because she was the respected daughter of a nobleman, and more specifically the daughter of the beloved previous sheriff, he had complied and started working on them directly.

Marian was impatient with her training, but wise enough to know that her tutelage under Mark's direction was progressing slowly, and until she was proficient they both agreed it would be wiser for him to do the actual rescuing of the innocent that they planned to do in Nottingham.

In the meantime, Marian sewed an outfit for Mark to wear as a disguise—a shirt and trousers of dark browns and greys so Mark would blend into the darkness of night, creating a hood and mask for him as well.

"You must always wear the mask and hood, Mark. Always. Never fight the Sheriff's men if you are not in this disguise."

"You worry too much, sister of mine."

"Promise me you'll do as I ask."

"I promise."

The Sheriff's men roamed the streets of Nottingham and the surrounding villages, taking money and food in the name of the king's taxes and arresting and beating up anyone they liked— whether they could pay the taxes or not. Word soon came from Prince John that debtors would be hanged.

The first time Marian walked through the market at Nottingham Square and noticed the freshly built gallows in the center of the market, she was horrified. That horror was amplified when the first body swung from it.

Not long after, while in the secret passageways in the castle, Marian heard the Sheriff suggest Gisbourne hang one of the citizens of Nottingham—not because he couldn't pay his taxes or because he was loyal to the King or outspoken against the Sheriff or Prince John, or any of the other usual reasons. He was simply bothered by the man's presence.

That night, Mark's disguise was put to its first test.

"He wants it done tonight," Marian told Mark. "He doesn't want a public execution, because he doesn't have a reason for this one. Not that any of the executions have valid reasons, but at least he can blame most on things like not paying taxes. He told Gisbourne this man bothered him and that was reason enough. He wants it done tonight so the people can't object or try to stop it. It's happening now, so I came home as soon as I could."

"We'll stop it, Marian, don't worry," Mark said.

"This is madness!" Sir Godfrey shook his head, watching Mark put on the hooded cloak and the mask that Marian had made to hide his face.

"They are going to execute James," Mark said. "He's done nothing wrong. You heard Marian; the Sheriff is bothered by him? What does that have to do with anything? We can't let this happen, father."

"Mark will be fine," Marian said, wrapping her arms around her father's shoulders. "Don't worry. We've been practicing this."

"I know. And I wish you had told me what you were up to before now, so I could have told you how foolish and stupid you are being. What happened to staying safe, Marian? To not putting your brother in harm's way?"

"What happened to defending the weak and the innocent?" Marian retorted. Marian moved to her brother, straightening the mask on his face. "Be careful, Mark."

"I will be. I'll be home before dawn."

When Mark reached Nottingham Square, James was already swinging; the two soldiers overseeing his execution were laughing to themselves as they watched him struggling to breathe.

"We'll soon be in bed," one said.

"And no one the wiser," the other chuckled.

There was a flash of moonlight on metal and one soldier dropped to the ground, a sword in his neck. Mark pulled it out swiftly and caught the blow of the second soldier, who had withdrawn his own blade when he saw Mark.

"Who are you?" the soldier hissed.

Mark didn't respond, but he fought back. Every strike and parry meant more time that James swung, losing air and slowly dying. He relied on every lesson his father and the Earl had instilled in him as a child, every sparring session with Robin before he'd left England, and every session he'd had recently with

Marian, letting his muscles relax into their memory of fighting as he struck and dodged and struck again.

It wasn't long before Mark's blade sliced into the soldier's hand, and he dropped his sword. Mark swung his own blade deep into his enemy's chest and then ran toward the gallows, cutting James free. He lay in Mark's arms gasping for breath for several moments.

"Thank…you…"

Mark patted his shoulder. "Are you alright? Can you breathe?"

"My neck'll be bruised no doubt," James said, coughing slightly and rubbing his hand against his throat where the rope had been digging into his airway. "I think I'll live, thanks to you."

"Get far away from here," Mark replied. "Away from Nottingham. I doubt you'll be safe here."

And with that, he ran back into the night.

The next day, news of the Hooded Rescuer filled the streets of Nottingham.

«→»

"The Hooded Rescuer?" Mari-Lu asked.

"Yes," Aunt Lucy said. "It seemed that before James had fled Nottingham, he had gone home and told his wife what had happened. She, in turn, had spread the word. Someone in Nottingham was opposing the Sheriff and saving the innocent.

34

And because Mark had been wearing Marian's disguise when he did it, his identity was unknown. So the people adopted a nickname for him—the Hooded Rescuer. The hope that sparked in the city because of that first rescue was palpable and Marian could not have been happier with their success."

"Did she help save people, too?"

"Not yet. She was still learning to use weapons, because unlike Mark she hadn't grown up knowing how to use them."

"But your parents taught you," Mari-Lu said.

"Yes, mine did. Not everyone's parents are the same, Mari-Lu. Marian was starting from scratch, but she was a quick learner and she was determined to be proficient. She was convinced the people of Nottingham needed protecting, and she knew she could do it. Yet she was willing to protect them through Mark's assistance until she could do it herself. A year after the king had gone on his Crusade and Robin had left, Marian and Mark had fallen into routine. She used the secret passageways to spy on the Sheriff and Gisbourne to learn about executions of innocents, and she brought that information to Mark. Together they rescued many people from the Sheriff's grasp, all of whom had to flee Nottingham afterward.

Mari-Lu's eyes were glued to Aunt Lucy's face as the story unfolded.

"As the Sheriff and Gisbourne murdered and acted out their treacherous deeds, the Hooded Rescuer appeared more and more. Nearly every execution seemed to be foiled by the mysterious man in brown, and oh how it angered the Sheriff…"

←→

"I'm going to catch that little rat and hang him in Nottingham Square for all to see! I'll hang him in his little disguise, too, so the people know exactly who I've killed," the Sheriff grumbled.

"You'll have to catch him first," Marian responded.

The Sheriff had begun to send for Sir Godfrey more and more on one false pretense or another; sometimes for dinner, sometimes so he could merely shout in his face about all the things that were bothering him, such as the Hooded Rescuer whom the Sheriff was sure was in league with Sir Godfrey somehow or other, given that Sir Godfrey was the most prominent noble in Nottingham who still had the people's respect.

During these visits, Gisbourne became quite fascinated by the beautiful Marian. The more he saw her the more he wanted to see her. He was watching her now, as the Sheriff turned toward her.

"I have a castle full of soldiers, I have Lord Gisbourne's prestige as a warrior, I have my own wits. How can you think I won't catch the traitor?"

"You don't even know who he is," Marian replied. "And a traitor, you call him? He's defending the innocent against a tyrant.

36

You have betrayed every ounce of humanity that may have once been inside you."

Though Sir Godfrey remained silent and resigned in the face of the Sheriff's many rants about the Hooded Rescuer and other things, Marian did not. Her fiery responses to the Sheriff's accusations that Sir Godfrey must know who it was intrigued Gisbourne. Marian was unafraid, and he found that most fascinating.

The Sheriff always sent them home again, unbound but escorted by Gisbourne and a soldier or two. The Sheriff seemed to find as much enjoyment in these shouting sessions as he had once found amusement in Marian's dinner conversations.

On their walks back to the village of Wetherby, Gisbourne would try to engage Marian in conversation. Her short replies only served to pique his interest further.

"Have you always lived in Wetherby?" Gisbourne asked.

"Yes."

"Do you like it here?"

"Yes."

"How old are you?"

Silence.

"Has your father always been sheriff?"

"Yes." A short pause and then, "Until your precious Prince John threw him out." The venom in Marian's voice did not deter Gisbourne.

"You seem well respected here. You don't by any chance happen to know which of your fellow villagers The Hooded Rescuer is, do you?"

Silence.

"The Sheriff is anxious to meet him."

"Isn't that nice." Marian's sarcasm made Gisbourne smile, which in turn made Marian even angrier. She came away from every encounter disliking Gisbourne more and more, while on his part he grew more intrigued and even fond of Marian with every passing day.

One day, after being escorted home by Gisbourne and left in peace at their doorstep, Mark crossed his arms. "It isn't fair."

"What?" Marian asked, watching Gisbourne's silhouette retreat into the distance as he wandered back to Nottingham.

"You tell me I'm not allowed to speak to the Sheriff when he is shouting horrible things at our father. You tell me that you absolutely forbid it. But you get to yell at him?"

Marian glanced at her brother. Their father had already gone inside. He often needed space to recover from the Sheriff's interrogations. Today the Sheriff had been particularly rude, and Marian had matched his fire, which is likely what Mark was referring to now. "I'm trying to protect you."

"You don't have to do that!" Mark complained. "I could tell the Sheriff he's an idiot as easily as you can."

"Well I am going to try to protect you anyway. You're my little brother and I feel responsible for your safety."

"I am just as angry at the Sheriff as you are; I should be allowed to spew some of my anger onto him as you do!"

"No, you should not. You *will* not."

Mark rolled his eyes. "Someday I will have the courage to defy you."

Marian smiled. "I doubt it. Besides, you get to do all the fighting off of the Sheriff's men, at least for now. You can let out your frustration there, as long as you always have your disguise."

Some time later, Gisbourne found himself alone in the face of the Sheriff's frustrations.

"This man is going to ruin me!" The Sheriff slammed his fist on the wooden table, and Gisbourne's face twitched. Whether he was controlling a laugh or a wince, the Sheriff couldn't tell.

"I'll have him beheaded for you in no time," Gisbourne replied. "The Hooded Rescuer is a nuisance, nothing more, and we will deal with him."

"He's giving the people a reason to revolt!"

"He's also predictable," Gisbourne said. "Let it be known you are going to hang someone, and he will show."

"I know!" the Sheriff yelled.

"So set a trap," Gisbourned remained calm in the face of the Sheriff's anger. "I'll handle him."

The Sheriff nodded. "Do that." A moment's pause and then, "Hang goody-two-shoes. The previous sheriff makes me nervous, and he's always looking down his ugly nose at me. He thinks he's better than me because the people love him. Well he's not!"

"Of course not, sir," Gisbourne said calmly, though the Sheriff was yelling. "I'll hang him, and behead the Hooded Rescuer in one night."

"Good. Let's set our trap and you can rid me of two nuisances."

Chapter 4

MARIAN WAS NEARLY asleep when her walls began to dance with shadows and light. Sitting up, she realized there were voices outside, and the shadows cast on her walls were from torches the people outside must be carrying.

Marian slipped out of bed and crept into the main room of her house. Someone pounded on the front door.

Mark was at her side instantly. "Who is it?" he whispered.

"I do not know."

Sir Godfrey entered the main room of the house from his own room and moved toward the door, squeezing Marian's shoulder as he passed her. "Who is there?" he called out.

"The soldiers of Nottingham, old man," a gruff voice called from beyond the door. "By the orders of Lord Gisbourne, you are to be brought into custody."

"What have I done?" Sir Godfrey asked calmly as he swung the door open to speak to the soldiers outside. Mark and Marian clasped hands and huddled in the doorway behind him.

"You've disturbed the Sheriff," the soldier laughed. "Though no one has told me, I do believe the gallows in Nottingham Square are for you tomorrow morning. Now, come with us quietly or we'll take you by force."

"There's no need for violence," Sir Godfrey said. He turned to Marian and Mark. "Goodbye."

"Father, you don't have to go with them," Mark hissed.

"Tonight, Mark, you become the man of our house. Don't take that responsibility lightly."

"Come on, old man!" the soldier grabbed Sir Godfrey's arm. "Let's go."

"Father!" Mark reached for him as rough hands dragged Sir Godfrey away from the house.

Marian yanked her brother inside, slamming the door.

"Marian! We can't let him go like that!"

"I know! Quick, the disguise!"

Mark hurried into his own room to put on the Hooded Rescuer disguise, his fingers trembling as he worked to fasten his cloak.

"We cannot let father die," Marian hissed as Mark came back into the front room.

"I know, I know…but, how do I rescue him?"

"I am coming with you this time; we have a long night ahead of us, I'd wager."

Marian spent the remainder of that night planning the escape, while Sir Godfrey spent the night locked in a cell in the dungeon of the castle, heavily guarded, wondering how it had come to this.

The next morning, before the sun rose, he was taken to the gallows in Nottingham Square. Gisbourne was alone in the Square, and he dismissed the soldiers as soon as they'd brought Sir Godfrey. Gisbourne led him up onto the platform and looped the noose over his head.

It was then that Gisbourne heard the sound of a horse approaching and he knew that his trap would work.

Turning quickly, he saw the Hooded Rescuer leaping off of his horse. Before the man hit the ground, Gisbourne pulled a dagger from his belt and with a flick of his wrist buried it deep in the man's side.

He doubled over, but to his credit he did not cry out. Perhaps he was made of sterner stuff than Gisbourne had given him credit for. Before jumping down from the gallows, Gisbourne shoved Sir Godfrey past the floor of the platform, so that his legs swung over the open air in the center.

Once on the ground, Gisbourne drew his sword to slice off the head of the brave but ultimately stupid villager.

All at once the Hooded Rescuer straightened, yanking the dagger out of his side and throwing it at Gisbourne. Instead of beheading the nuisance as he had promised the Sheriff, Gisbourne was forced to use his blade to deflect the dagger.

The Hooded Rescuer was struggling to mount his horse. Gisbourne charged forward, sword at the ready, but he was too late. The horse set off at a gallop as the wounded Hooded Rescuer swung his leg over it's back.

Gisbourne hesitated a moment, indecisive; he could run after him on foot, hope to raise the alarm before he escaped Nottingham—but trying to keep up on foot would not be easily achieved—or he could run back to the castle stables and get his own horse, but by the time he was saddled the Hooded Rescuer would be gone. Gisbourned sighed, turning back toward the gallows, knowing he'd simply have to face the Sheriff's ire. The trap hadn't worked. Next time he'd have to have more soldiers with him to capture and kill the Hooded Rescuer.

With a cry of surprise, Gisbourne realized the gallows were empty as he turned back toward them. Spewing curses into the grey morning light, Gisbourne angrily sheathed his sword. The Hooded Rescuer had help!

«→»

"How did they do it?" Mari-Lu asked. "Did Marian get Sir Godfrey? Did they have help?"

"Yes, of course," Aunt Lucy grinned. "They did have help."

"Who helped them?" Mari-Lu demanded.

"I have no doubt any and all of the residents of Nottinghamshire would have been willing to help Marian and Mark save their father. But Marian did not want Mark's identity as the Hooded Rescuer to be known. Only their father knew who the Hooded Rescuer truly was."

"Then who helped them?" Mari-Lu demanded again, her little brow furrowed in concentration as she tried to imagine who might have saved Sir Godfrey.

"To answer that question," Aunt Lucy smiled mischievously, "we must go back in our story, to a week before Sir Godfrey's hanging…"

←»

Marian was returning from the market in Nottingham Square, though her basket did not hold much. With the ever growing taxes meant to enrich the Sheriff of Nottingham, she could afford very little. But they were still better off than most people in Nottinghamshire.

As she neared her home, Marian noticed Widow Mary standing in the doorway of her home, watching her six children playing in front of her house. The children were all thin as boards, their cheeks sunken in rather than the plump, rosy cheeks they ought to be.

Marian slowed her steps. She and her family had enough to eat, even if it was less than they might have had before the king went on his Crusade.

Taking a deep breath, Marian walked resolutely past the children and up to Widow Mary. "Mary?"

The older woman turned her tired eyes toward Marian. "Yes?"

"I was able to get more food at the market today than my family strictly needs. Would you be able to put our extras to good use?"

Widow Mary took the basket Marian offered with tears in her eyes. "Lady Marian, you don't have to…"

"I know."

"Thank you! I didn't have the money to go to the market this week, what with the taxes and all…" Widow Mary's head lowered in shame.

Marian placed a hand under her chin, lifting her face. "Keep your chin up."

Widow Mary smiled at Marian through her tears.

Marian left Widow Mary and her children and made her way down the dirt path toward her home, empty-handed but at peace.

"That was well done."

Marian spun around at the sound of a voice she did not recognize.

A young man she'd never seen before was leaning casually against the wall of a nearby house. He was roughly the same height as Robin, but he had light brown hair and the darkest blue eyes Marian had ever seen. His hands rested lightly on a bow, and Marian could see the quiver slung over his back. The young man smiled at her and bowed. "The name's Will, ma'am. Will Scarlett."

Marian smiled, taken in by his easy manner. "I'm Marian."

Will shoved off the house in much the same manner Robin might have done, and came up to Marian. He took her hand, kissed it, and then said, "What you did for that lady and her children tells me you are a good woman."

"Is that so?"

"Yes."

"You aren't from around here, are you?"

"No," Will shook his head, a darkness settling over his face. "I'm from Middlesborough."

"That's quite a distance."

"Yes, it is…" Will studied her for a moment, seeming to consider. He glanced back toward Widow Mary's house for a moment, and then spoke, "I couldn't stand watching my people suffer at the hands of the sheriff of my district. I started to defy him and was labeled an outlaw. I fled for my life. In my travels, I met a bear of a man who'd done much the same thing in his hometown. His name is Little John. We're too well-known in our own homes to be able to do any good anymore without getting ourselves caught and killed. So we decided to come to Nottingham together."

"Why Nottingham?"

Will stepped closer and lowered his voice. "The fame of a man from around here is spreading through England. Survivors and fugitives are spreading the tales of their hero to the rest of the country. Now, Little John and I figure if we all work together we might be able to do the most good."

Marian nodded slowly.

"Well," Will continued, "Little John and I heard this famous hero is from Nottingham. He's smarter than us, we've realized. He wears a disguise so that no one knows who he is."

Marian kept her features straight with an effort. Mark's identity was still safe! "So you want to join the Hooded Rescuer?"

Will nodded, lowering his voice further. "You don't happen to know him do you?"

"I…" Marian hesitated.

Will smiled. "I don't expect you to answer that honestly, but you can trust me, Lady Marian. We're on the same side. Little John and I have been studying the events taking place in Nottingham lately, trying to locate this hero so we can offer our services…and our search led to you."

"What do you mean?"

"I mean we are fairly convinced you know who he is, that you are helping him. We just want you to arrange a meeting for us."

"I don't know what you mean." Marian turned away from Will Scarlett and began walking to her house. Will didn't follow her, but she noticed he hung around Wetherby for the rest of the day, and the next day he was there as well. Marian finally exited her house in frustration, finding Will sitting in her front yard calmly sharpening his sword. He was relaxed, and looked up with a grin. His mannerisms were so like Robin's that Marian couldn't help but be taken in by him.

"You are stubborn," she said, joining him in the grass.

"You know the man helping the innocent. I want to help him. So does Little John. We could help the people on our own, but I feel we'd do best if we all worked together for the good of the people, wouldn't you agree?"

Marian sighed. "I would, unfortunately."

"Why is that unfortunate?"

"Because I don't know you. We could use help, but I don't trust you…"

"We?" Will asked, grinning. "You do know him then. Can you arrange a meeting? You don't have to trust me, Lady Marian. The Hooded Rescuer can decide if I am worth the trouble."

Marian took a deep breath. "I could arrange a meeting."

Will grinned. "Perfect."

"We work together…" Marian hesitated, looking around the mostly empty street. "Actually, would you mind coming into my house to continue this conversation?"

"As you wish."

Marian led Will into her home, and then turned toward him. "The Hooded Rescuer does most of the fighting, I'm the brains of the operation."

Will smiled. "Well then, Lady Marian, will you consent to having Little John and myself as allies?"

"Bring Little John for dinner. My father will enjoy the company, and we can talk about a potential partnership then."

Will bowed. "We'll be there."

Aunt Lucy's face held an affectionate look. "Little John was just as Will had described him, a bear of a man. But he was as gentle as a lamb if you didn't anger him, and he loved his fellow man."

Mari-Lu's gaze never left Aunt Lucy's face. Marian wondered briefly if her daughter was still breathing, so still was the girl sitting on Aunt Lucy's knee.

"Will and Little John visited Sir Godfrey, Marian, and Mark on several occasions after that, but they lived in Sherwood forest. Yet sometimes they would stay in Nottingham at the house of a blacksmith they befriended named Marcus."

"And they're the ones who helped Marian and Mark save their father?"

Aunt Lucy nodded. "Little John was in Nottingham that night, with Marcus. Marian went to them, and together they saved Sir Godfrey while Mark distracted Lord Gisbourne."

❮❯

Marian was the first to reach home, and the minute Mark stumbled through the door she ran to his side. "Are you okay? The dagger.."

"I'm not sure…it hurt…"

49

Marian helped her brother limp over to a chair. Then she worked quickly, removing his shirt and cleaning and bandaging the wound. She wasn't a healer, but she knew enough to rinse the wound and staunch the bleeding.

Little John soon arrived with Sir Godfrey, who went to Marian and kissed her cheek, before turning to Mark. "Are you alright?"

"I'm fine, father," Mark said, rather unconvincingly as he winced in pain.

"It will likely take a few weeks to heal," Marian said. "Assuming it doesn't get infected and he dies from that."

"But I'm fine," Mark repeated.

"With your wound, you won't be much good for our group." Marian turned to Little John, "You and Will are going to have to help me more."

Little John nodded.

"There are many secrets in the castle that you will need to learn in order to help me spy on the Sheriff and Gisbourne."

"You can teach us what you know," Little John said. "But tonight, Will and I will keep watch. The Sheriff will not let Sir Godfrey off so easily."

Marian nodded. "He should go with you to the forest."

"No," Sir Godfrey interrupted. "I will not live on the run, as a fugitive."

"Father, the Sheriff will try to kill you again."

"I appreciate your help, all of you, but I will not run," Sir Godfrey repeated.

Mark looked pained. "Father—"

"My decision is final. I will face the wrath of the Sheriff rather than live on the run, or hide in the forest. I am too old for such shenanigans."

Little John was correct in his assessment. Gisbourne arrived later that morning to arrest Sir Godfrey. Marian insisted Mark remain in his bed. "You shouldn't be moving about with that wound! I'll deal with Gisbourne."

Marian met Gisbourne at the door, crossing her arms and staring up into his angry face. "What do you want?"

"If your father is here, as I suspect that he is, I am here to arrest him."

"Merely arrest him? You aren't going to hang him again?" Marian asked, unbelieving.

Gisbourne sighed. "I've already spent the entire morning being lectured and yelled at by the Sheriff for that failed attempt. I'd rather not be mocked by you. No, he is not going to be hung. The Sheriff's mood is, as ever, unpredictable. He wants your father in prison."

"For how long?"

"Until the Sheriff decides to kill him again."

"That's reassuring," Marian sarcastically responded.

Gisbourne studied Marian's face intently for a moment, and then shook his head. "Bring me your father."

"There's no need for theatrics," Sir Godfrey opened the door. "I was in bed. My daughter did not have the grace to wake me when you arrived…"

"Father, you don't have to go."

"He most definitely does have to go," Gisbourne replied.

"I'm willing to come," Sir Godfrey said.

Gisbourne marched away with Sir Godfrey, and Marian returned to Mark's bedside downcast.

"Well?" Mark asked, his brow etched with worry.

"He isn't going to be killed, at least according to Gisbourne. He's going to be locked up for now."

"That's a relief at least."

Over the following two weeks, Marian stayed home to watch over Mark. The Sheriff and Gisbourne, used to seeing her around Nottingham, assumed she was mourning her father being locked away. Will and Little John visited Mark and Marian frequently, helping Marian with her training in the bow and sword, and listening to her own instructions on how and where to sneak into the secret passageways in the castle.

Marian's wariness toward her new friends began to melt after Little John's help saving her father from Gisbourne. He'd proven himself to her in the best way, and Will's easy manners and resemblance to Robin definitely helped.

After much instruction from Marian, Will and Little John took her place in the secret passageways in the castle to spy on the Sheriff, and it was they who went out and stopped various executions from taking place, always dropping in on Marian before and after to plan and to debrief her on their actions.

When Mark's wounds had healed enough for Marian to be comfortable leaving him alone, she took up her vigil in the dark passages inside the castle walls once more. It was at this time that word came to Nottingham from the Crusade.

King Richard had been captured on his return from his Holy Crusade by the Duke of Austria who was, for reasons unknown to the people of England, angry with him. The king was being held hostage near Vienna. A ransom was needed to free him, which gave Prince John another reason to raise taxes, though the money never went to Austria. More often than not, the money raised in the name of the king ended up lining the pockets of men like the Sheriff of Nottingham.

‹‹–››

Aunt Lucy's eyes were sad. "The remainder of that year was spent in evil men stealing money and food, beating and killing innocents, and good men watching helplessly and suffering at their hands. Marian and her crew of men did what they could, but there were only so many executions the four of them could stop, and they had no strategy on how to rescue the money or food being taken from the people of England. There were many suffering and dying all across the country; England was in disarray and the people in poverty. But just after Marian turned nineteen, and new hope came for the people of England…"

Chapter 5

MARIAN HAD JUST finished restringing her bow in preparation for more practice with Will. He was still inside the house, gathering what remained of their arrows. She wasn't nearly as proficient as she would have liked to be, but Mark said he was impressed with her progress and with Will's added guidance she was growing more confident every day.

Mark and Little John were in Nottingham with Marcus, discussing an order of weapons. Marcus had begun supplying Marian's little crew with anything they required, though they had to be stealthy about it to avoid the watchful eyes of the Sheriff and Gisbourne.

Suddenly Marian felt hands on her waist and she was lifted off the ground and swung in a circle. When her feet hit the ground again, hands clasped her own and placed them over a familiar heart. "Did you miss me, Marian darling?"

Marian looked up into Robin's dancing eyes, feeling the urge to jump into his arms and ignoring it as she silently refused to answer his question. He'd abandoned them for three years for his grand adventures that she'd wanted no part of; where had Robin been when his father was murdered? When her own father was nearly executed? He'd been fighting to take someone else's land and homes. Along with the initial joy at seeing him, Marian realized she was also angry with Robin.

Will came to the open door of the house and leaned against the frame. "Who's this?"

Robin dropped Marian's hand instantly, muttering a hushed, "You didn't wait."

Marian smiled archly. Let Robin be jealous; he'd put her through enough. Robin didn't need to know she compared every man she met to him and found them all lacking.

Behind Robin stood three other people. Marian recognized Much—Robin's servant and her childhood friend, though he was far leaner than Marian remembered. The other two were strangers. One was a small blond young man and the other was a short, dark-skinned woman with her dark hair cut short.

"Will Scarlett, this is Robin of Locksley," Marian said.

"The Earl?" Will asked.

Robin bowed. "One and the same. I was sorry to hear of my father's death," Robin addressed the latter to Marian. "I wish I could have been here."

"We were sorry for it, too. And you *should* have been here." Marian remembered the grief of losing the Earl, and the pain of feeling like Robin had abandoned her. Seeing his face now, three years after he'd run off for war and glory, she was overwhelmed with a mixture of love and resentment. "Your father's death was one of the first things that spurred me into action."

"Ah," Robin grinned. "I wanted to speak to you about that. My comrades and I have heard tales of this Hooded Rescuer and the 'men of the night' in Nottinghamshire who seem to know the Sheriff's every move." Robin gestured toward his companions."You remember Much, Marian? This is Allen, a brother in arms," Robin gestured to the young man and he stepped forward.

"It is a pleasure to meet you, Lady Marian. We've heard a great deal about you," Allen glanced at Robin and winked.

Robin shoved Allen aside and laughed, and then placed a hand on the young woman's shoulder. "And this is Dusty, our master healer."

Marian ignored the beautiful young woman as well as the playful antics of Allen and Robin, and moved forward to hug Much instead. "It's good to see you."

"You, as well, Lady Marian," Much replied.

Robin turned back to Marian. "Now, about these rumors."

"Rumors?" Marian asked innocently.

"Even when he only tells his most trusted servant Sir Guy of Gisbourne in the darkest chambers of the castle, rumors say these mysterious heroes still know what the Sheriff and Gisbourne are planning and stop them. This has given rise to a belief among the superstitious that they can, in fact, read his mind." Robin winked at Marian and she couldn't help herself from smiling back at him, despite the emotions roiling her chest. "Now I know perfectly well how one might obtain such secret information, and I also know only a few people know of the castle's secrets. Now two of those people have been away from

England, which to my knowledge leaves you, Mark, and your father. Have you been helping them?"

"Helping us?" Will laughed from the doorway. "She's one of us. You, sir, are addressing the leader of these 'men of the night.'"

"Truly?" Robin asked, surprised.

"Truly," Marian said. "You doubt I could do such a thing? It wasn't as though there was anyone else around to take care of the suffering people."

"Well it is a surprise," Robin said, "but not so shocking. You've always been a protector. Who is the Hooded Rescuer then, or do you and your companion," he gestured toward Will, "take turns under the mask?"

"No, that's Mark."

"Remarkable," Robin grinned. "Where is your father?"

"In custody, as he has been for a year. I've only been able to see him for the briefest moments when spying in the castle. Mark hasn't seen him at all." *And you weren't here to protect me from any of it,* Marian thought. Robin hadn't been here to help her stop her father's execution, or to comfort her in the prolonged separation while her father was locked in the castle. He hadn't been here for any of it, and Marian could feel her frustration mounting.

"My father is ill, Robin."

"I am sorry," Robin frowned. "One of my friends has great knowledge of healing, as I said. Dusty's remarkable."

58

"I'm afraid the Sheriff isn't inclined to let my father have visitors of any nature, let alone physicians."

Before Marian could say more, she noticed Mark and Little John coming up the dirt path, returning from Nottingham with suspicious parcels, most likely containing their recently acquired arrows and swords from Marcus.

"You've all been introduced to Will Scarlett, my right hand, now meet my brother—the famed Hooded Rescuer—and the last member of our crew, Little John."

As they approached the group, Robin's eyes widened. "Little John? Why didn't you name him Mountain John?"

"We thought about it," Mark grinned, setting aside his parcels, running forward to hug Robin and then Much.

Robin re-introduced his companions to Mark and Little John and then Marian ushered everyone inside. The group had a merry dinner that night, catching up on the three years they had missed in each other's lives.

Robin was most intrigued by Will's account of their camp in Sherwood.

"There ought to be a way," Robin sat thinking, "… if we learn the secrets of Sherwood Forest the way we did of the castle, and make camp deep in its heart…"

"What are you thinking, Robin?" Marian asked.

"He's thinking," Dusty answered in his stead, "he'll help you set up a more stable camp in Sherwood."

Marian glanced at Dusty in annoyance. She didn't like that this strange woman could read Robin's mind. Dusty was beautiful, though her hair was cropped short and she wore men's clothes. Robin had said it was safest for Dusty to feign she was a man while serving as the army's healer than to let her true nature be known.

"Many caravans pass through the Sherwood road," Dusty continued, "carrying the taxes supposedly collected for the king's ransom. The Sheriff here seems to have Prince John's ear and his favor, for most of the taxes seem to gather here and line his pockets before being shipped to London. If we knew the forest well enough, we might be able to way-lay the caravans, relieve them of their unjust shipments, and escape into the thick of the woods where no one could track us."

"We'd be a flash in the night," Robin said. "They wouldn't know what hit them."

"You must let me come with you," Mark said. "I can help! I'd love to be a part of the Sherwood gang."

"I do not know, Mark…"

"You cannot now say that I am too young," Mark laughed. "I have been fighting the Sheriff's men without you."

"You seem to already have a crew here," Allen said. "Would you abandon them?"

"Wouldn't it be better if we all worked together?" Mark replied. "We know Nottingham, we know the Sheriff. If you set up camp with Will and Little John and start raiding caravans, we can work in tandem to the benefit of the people of England."

"That's a decision for our leader, isn't it?" Will said, giving Mark a sharp glance.

"He's right," Marian said. "I appreciate the loyalty, Will, but we might as well join forces. It's not different than when you and Little John came to join Mark and I."

"I will return to Locksley," Robin said. "I might be able to assist as the Earl of Locksley as much as raiding the caravans."

"So you stay in Locksley, Marian in Wetherby, and the rest of us live in the forest?" Allen sighed. "I was so looking forward to an extended stay on an actual bed."

Much laughed. "Allen is the biggest complainer you will find in the king's army."

"I like beds!" Allen protested. "There's nothing wrong with that."

The next day Robin and his gang began searching the forest for the perfect place to make camp. He and his crew seemed to have more woodcraft than Will and Little John, and had Marian not known better she might have been tempted to believe in the old tales of dryads coming out of the trees in human form.

They soon had the beginnings of a camp, and began exploring the forest to learn its secrets—the hidden paths, the animal trails, every hollow, every meadow, every boulder—in much the same way Marian, Mark, Robin, and Much had once searched out the secrets of the castle.

One clear summer night, the moon shining brightly overhead and filtering down past the branches of the trees above them, Robin led Marian through the forest toward the camp. Marian felt lost among all the trees.

"That's good," Robin said. "It means we won't be found by anyone who isn't familiar with the forest. But you will need to learn these woods, Marian."

Marian nodded. "I will do my best."

"We're planning on setting traps around the perimeter of our camp as well. We have some experience from that from the war. Some animals might trigger them at first, but eventually they'll learn to stay away from the camp."

"You have it all planned out, don't you?"

"Yes, we do. Much and I will stay in Locksley as much as we can to keep up appearances, but otherwise the camp will be the staging ground for our caravan raids."

They were quiet for a bit as Robin took her hand and led her through the maze of trees toward the camp.

"Robin?"

"Yes, darling?"

"Robin, be serious."

"I am. What did you want to ask me?"

"Why are you here? In England, I mean. Last we heard, the king was captured."

"The king sent me," Robin said simply.

"He sent you?"

"Yes," Robin stopped walking. He glanced around the dark forest and sighed. "We were in prison with him, in Austria. But Allen and I discovered a way to escape. It was risky, and if we were caught we would have been killed. The king refused to come with us, saying he would do no good for England if he was caught and killed. Dusty said I wasn't worth anything to England dead either, but we had heard rumors of what was happening in England, of what Prince John was doing."

"It certainly hasn't been easy here."

"I know. We all heard how things were going, and it wasn't good. King Richard wanted to help his people, he just didn't want to risk the escape from prison. So he told us to use our escape plan, and come in his stead. 'I'm entrusting England to you, Robin' he said to me. 'Keep my people safe.' I promised him I would do just that. So Dusty, Allen, and I made our escape, and here we are."

"I am glad you are back, Robin."

"Are you?"

"I am…"

"You don't always seem like it," Robin said, studying her face. "You are distant; not that you weren't always a little hesitant to express your emotions, but you seem far more reticent around me now. But not—well, anyway, I am glad to hear you are pleased to see me again."

"Not what, Robin? What were you going to say."

"Nothing…it's just that you aren't so reserved around Will Scarlett. I thought…well, Will Scarlett seems like a good man," Robin sighed.

Marian chuckled. "Will, Little John, and I are good friends. I don't love Will though, I don't even know him that well yet."

Robin grinned, grabbing Marian around the waist and swinging her in a circle. "You did wait, after all!"

"Robin…"

"Yes, Marian my love?"

"I didn't say I loved you."

"You don't have to," Robin winked.

"You are impossible. And I don't fully trust you, Robin."

"Why?" Robin's face lost some it's joy as he stepped closer and stared into her eyes.

"You told me you loved me, and then you disappeared for three years on some wild adventure, chasing glory as you killed people you had no business fighting in the first place."

"I'm sorry. I know I wasn't here when you needed me, but I'm back now."

"That doesn't magically fix everything."

"I know, Marian." Robin took her hands in his own, squeezing fingers gently. "I'll make it up to you. Believe me, my love, you will be able to rely on me. I promise you that."

"I wish I could believe that."

"It's alright if it takes time. I'll wait. I know you love me, and I love you."

"And what about Dusty?"

"Dusty?"

"Your beautiful, clever companion that you fought a war beside," Marian said, wishing she didn't feel so cut open and raw as she said it.

Robin shook his head with a laugh. "Dusty, for the record, is more of a sister to me than anything. We have a strong bond because we fought a war together; life and death situations will do that to a person. But there's nothing there. Marian, I promise you that. Dusty isn't anything more to me. I love you, I always have, and I have never been unfaithful to you."

Marian was quiet, wishing she could believe him.

"You're not the only one with doubts on that score," Robin said. "Mark doesn't trust me at all. He nearly punched me the other day, I swear, as he demanded to know if I had been unfaithful to you."

Marian chuckled. "He can be very protective…and so can I. He respects you and looks up to you…Robin, please take care of him."

"You mean during our raids, and such? It seems he's been up to more dangerous things under your care."

"Robin."

"I will look out for him, Marian. I'll always take care of your brother."

65

"Thank you."

Hiding in Nottingham castle later that week, Marian learned when the next shipment of the king's ransom was coming to Nottingham. She hurried to the camp, only getting lost along the way twice, to tell Robin and the others.

"Perfect!" Robin exclaimed. "Our first caravan."

"We'll just relieve the Sheriff of that burden and responsibility," Allen chuckled.

Preparations were soon begun for an ambush, and Dusty knelt in the middle of camp to pray for their safety and success.

As the caravan made its way through the green airy woods, the soldiers charged with guarding the treasure were relaxed, teasing and laughing together in no fear of an attack. But as their carts passed through the deep forest, arrows raced from behind trees and found their homes in the unsuspecting soldiers' chests. All but one soldier slumped in their saddles or fell to the ground from their horses or from up on their carts and wagons.

Robin, dressed in brown and forest green clothes to blend in with his surroundings, with a cape and hood over his head, stepped out onto the road. Taking the halter of the remaining soldier's horse as it panicked and pranced, Robin spoke to the soldier. "I thank you for your generous donation to King Richard and his subjects."

"You…you wouldn't dare," the soldier sputtered.

"Oh, but we would," Robin said, gesturing behind the soldier. The young man glanced behind to see the rest of the gang leading the horses and mules pulling carts filled with chests full of coins and jewels and other treasures away from the road.

"Who are you?" the soldier demanded.

"No one special," Robin replied. "But most people call me Robin."

"I'll remember you, Robin of the hood. You will pay for this."

Robin bowed deeply. "It was a pleasure to meet you as well. Give my regards to the Sheriff."

Robin slapped the rump of the horse and it took off down the road, hoping the soldier would relate the ambush to the Sheriff so he would know he could no longer rob the innocent without consequences.

The soldier reined in his mount as fast as he could, but when he turned back toward the place where his caravan had once been, the forest was eerily empty. There was no sign of the wagons or the enemy. With a curse, the soldier galloped toward Nottingham to inform the Sheriff of this new development.

←»

Aunt Lucy began braiding Mari-Lu's hair, closing her eyes as she thought back to the years long gone by.

"What happened next?" Mari-Lu asked, turning her head ever so slightly, though she tried not to interrupt Aunt Lucy's braiding.

"The Sheriff was furious and ranted for hours." Aunt Lucy opened her eyes and continued, as her fingers worked deftly through Mari-Lu's hair, "Gisbourne set out to investigate. He found nothing but six freshly dug graves along the side of the road. The gang left nothing undone."

"What did he think?"

"That the Hooded Rescuer had gotten far too bold. Sir Guy of Gisbourne swore he would pay this time."

"But what happened with the gang?" Mari-Lu asked.

"The morning after that first raid there were proclamations put up in every town and village under Nottingham's rule. Robin Hood, whoever he was, was declared an outlaw, a traitor to the crown, and better dead than alive. To the people, though, he was a hero…"

Chapter 6

LUCY LEANED AGAINST the stone wall, keeping her hood over her head as she leaned around the house. It was the middle of the night, and the clouds obstructed the moon, leaving the only light that which flickered from windows and doorways along the street. A few houses down from Lucy's hiding place were two soldiers, dragging a bound and gagged man down the street. Lucy could only make out their silhouettes and shadows as they moved down the street past windows of wavering light.

As they moved past another building, Lucy darted into the street, running on soft feet over the dirt path until she reached the next house over. She scampered behind the building, leaning up against the wall in much the same way she had done with the last house, leaning out into the street to watch the soldiers.

Lucy followed the soldiers and their unfortunate prisoner down the length of the street until they came to an open area in the village, a gathering place of sorts with a well in the center. Beside the well stood a gallows. Without the moon's light to guide her, Lucy could only make out the three people near the well by their shadows; they were darker than the rest of the darkness of that night. The trembling candlelight from homes nearby did little to assist Lucy, and in fact worsened her view through the darkness if she glanced at them for too long so she kept her focus on the shifting shadows.

Lucy had been traveling England since leaving Friar Tuck, helping anyone she could as she passed through. She was wayward and had no home, but that suited her. Without her parents, her life felt entirely uprooted anyway.

As the soldiers dragged the poor man toward the gallows, Lucy took a deep breath to steel herself. She slipped her bow from its secure place on her back, and grabbed an arrow from her quiver. Breathing slowly and deliberately, she nocked an arrow to the string and pulled it back towards her chin.

If the movement of their shadowed forms was any indication, the soldiers appeared to be pulling the bound man up the steps of the gallows toward the noose and the open hole where his legs would swing as he died.

Lucy took another deep breath, focusing on the shadow she thought was a soldier—praying she wasn't wrong—and let her arrow fly. He cried out in pain as her arrow hit its mark–though perhaps not as well as it might have done in daylight.

The shadow of the soldier stumbled away from the bound man and he fell to the wooden floor of the platform of the gallows with a grunt. Lucy took no time in sending another arrow toward the second soldier, and when he too cried out in pain she ran forward.

Neither was incapacitated, however, given that Lucy never shot to kill so as she ran toward the gallows, one of them jumped down to face her, sword drawn.

Lucy dropped her bow and grabbed the hilt of her sword, swinging it free of it's sheath at her waist. As the soldier came toward her, his dark silhouette all she could see, Lucy settled back into a defensive stance her father had walked her through a million times in her youth.

The soldier was limping, her arrow cutting deep into his thigh, but he came forward confidently and took the first swing.

Lucy danced around him, blocking his strikes and darting out of his reach again and again.

She heard the second soldier moving down the steps of the platform to join the fray, so she spun around and let her sword swing in a wide arc. She could barely see him, but she felt her sword connect with his flesh and she winced.

The soldier fell, and she spun around and raised her blade just before the first soldier's sword came down on her. The ring of the contact of metal on metal reverberated through the courtyard.

Lucy parried and blocked and whirled around the first soldier, keeping her distance as much as she could. He couldn't reach her, so swift as she was, but she managed to nick his arm and his shoulder.

Finally, his injured leg gave out for the briefest moment and he stumbled, thrown off his balance. Lucy took advantage of his predicament and darted forward, raising her sword and smashing the hilt into his face. He dropped to the ground unconscious.

Lucy hurried away from both soldiers on the ground, shuddering as she passed the one she'd killed, and ran up the steps of the gallows to get to the bound man.

She cut his ropes slowly and carefully despite her sense of urgency, for fear of cutting him in the darkness and her haste. She pulled the gag free of his mouth.

"Thank you," the man gasped. "You saved me."

Lucy grabbed a small pouch of money from her belt— she'd taken to splitting her money into smaller pouches so she could hand them out to people who needed it without having to go through the hassle of counting it out, or giving away her entire purse and being left with nothing.

She pressed the pouch into the man's hand.

"Are you one of them? The men of the night saving England? I'd heard the tales, but I didn't trust to hope for your rescue. I should not have doubted!"

"I am no one special," Lucy replied. "Now go. Flee to Scotland if you can, get far from here. They won't stop hunting you now you are free."

Lucy made sure the man wasn't injured, and got him on his feet and headed out of town before she returned to the scene of her crime to retrieve her arrows. She pulled the arrow from the unconscious soldier's leg slowly, hoping the pain wouldn't wake him up. She was grateful for the darkness when she went to retrieve the other arrow from the man she had killed. Death gave her no pleasure. The feel of her blade easily slicing into and then

72

getting caught inside his flesh was not something she was likely to forget soon, and she could only wonder how she would have felt if she could see the harm she had done to his body by daylight. With her arrows in hand, she returned to the wilderness outside the village.

The man she'd rescued had assumed she was one of the famed heroes saving England in the dark of night. Lucy wondered if those rumors were born of people like her, alone and friendless, but helping out regardless. Or if there was a group of people somewhere fighting the good fight.

What would it be like to have help, to have someone she could rely on in the midst of battle?

Lucy sighed as she walked along the empty fields, no stars to keep her company tonight. If the moon had been brighter, she might have found a place to sit and read the little bound book Friar Tuck had transcribed. Some of the pages of her leather-bound book were already creased and crumpled from her many readings, and more than one page was stained by her dirt encrusted fingers and her tears. She'd chosen her life alone on the run, but still she was not always happy.

All of the rumors of people like herself, rescuing innocents, seemed to point toward Nottinghamshire, so Lucy decided to head that way. If it was true, if there were others like her, perhaps they could join forces and she would not be so alone.

←»

"I'm sorry you were so lonely," Mari-Lu said softly, reaching up to hug Aunt Lucy around the neck.

"I had chosen my solitude," Aunt Lucy replied, "running from the sorrow and pain of my past. And I reaped the consequences of my decisions."

"What came next? Did you make it to Nottingham? Did you join forces with the group?"

"Not yet …"

←→

Marian sat beside the hearth in her house, listening to the silence as she mended the Hooded Rescuer outfit. Mark had not often been using it of late, so caught up was he in the raids with Robin in the forest. She missed the sound of him snoring in the next room.

She missed her father, too.

Before she could get too deep into her loneliness, Marian heard a knock at the door. Grabbing a jeweled dagger off the hearth, she went to the door and cracked it open slowly. Robin stood outside.

"Robin!"

"Can I come in?"

"Do you need something?" Marian asked, opening the door farther so Robin could come inside.

"I need advice," Robin replied.

"It's a rare day, indeed, when Robin of Locksley asks for advice," Marian teased.

"Ah, but you are forgetting, I am Robin of the Hood now."

"Or Robin Hood, rather," Marian chuckled.

"Just goes to show the true laziness of our dear Sheriff, that he can't even bother to call me by my given title earned during that first raid."

Marian rolled her eyes. "It was rather an amusing proclamation though. 'Robin Hood, whomever he may be,'" she quoted with a laugh. "What did you need advice about?"

"The ransom and other taxes we've taken from the Sheriff."

"What of it?"

"Should we keep some for the people of England?"

"I thought that was the plan all along?"

"I want to send it to Austria, to pay the king's ransom, which the Sheriff and Prince John claim the taxes are for. The sooner we pay his ransom and get him home, the sooner all the cruelty of the Sheriff and Prince John and others like them ends. Will, however, is insistent we save it for the people here, and I needed your opinion on the matter."

"I agree with Will. The people here are starving. I believe giving the people a chance to pay Prince John's outrageous taxes so they avoid imprisonment or worse, and give them a chance to afford food so they don't starve, is more than enough reason to distribute what you've confiscated to the people. The King told you to take care of his people, Robin. So do it."

"I know," Robin sighed. "But that threat of imprisonment or worse will be gone once the ransom is paid and the king is home."

"And how long will that take? How many people will die in the interim that you could have saved?"

"Alright, alright. We keep half for the people and send half to the king."

"How are you getting this treasure to the king at all?"

"Allen and I think we can find safe passage for it, passing it along from person to person among individuals that we trust until it reaches Dover, at least. From there we'd need to find a carrier for it. Dusty might have connections that we can use. And we did make powerful friends while we were away."

"Powerful like the king who is imprisoned."

"Powerful like the king's wife, and sister, and mother, and various other royals who are currently in Normandy and abroad and would help us get the money to Austria."

"You just have it all figured out don't you?" Marian crossed her arms. Something about Robin casually mentioning his friendship with the royal family rubbed her the wrong way.

"Don't be mad, Marian," Robin reached for her hands and forced her to uncross her arms. "You're right. The people do need our help; that's why I am here, why I set up camp in Sherwood at all. We'll distribute some of our booty to the people who need it, and we'll send the rest to the king. Both are possible."

"Great," Marian pulled her hands away from him, still feeling unsettled by the conversation. "Let's do that then."

As the weeks passed, the gang fell into a rhythm. Marian, Mark, Robin, and Much took turns spying inside the secret passageways inside the castle to glean information. The passages themselves were dark, no light entering the hallways encased in stone except where the chinks and cracks in the walls were located—tiny slits through which one could peer out at the rooms of the castle beyond. In this manner, they were able to keep an eye on the Sheriff; whenever an unjust execution arose, they were there to stop it, and whenever a shipment of the taxes was moving through Sherwood the gang would be there to relieve the Sheriff of his unfairly earned coin.

Robin and the gang always struck hard and fast, collecting the money for the people, and sending some off to Austria to pay the Duke in hopes of him releasing the King.

The camp itself, though originally no more than a simple perimeter of traps around a meadow with a campfire in the center, was fast becoming a home. Much erected a hut for his kitchen, with plenty of shelves for food and cookery that the gang both bought at the market and shops in Nottingham and also smuggled out of Locksley manor with the help of Robin's servants there. The campfire was a short distance from Much's hut, easy for him to reach, and it was the place where the gang would gather in the evenings to talk of their days, to plan upcoming heists, and to relax.

Each member of the gang had soon built a hut of their own with lumber they cut and shaped from nearby trees, and another storage hut was built for their excess weapons from Marcus, as well as a place to store the taxes and treasure until it was distributed among the people of England or sent to the King.

Robin and Will were often seen making new arrows, and Allen and Little John built a small forge on one side of the meadow for their use, in case working with Marcus ever became too suspicious. Dusty would spend many days gathering plants and herbs for her healing purposes. Dusty kept a pouch of such mixtures of herbs on her belt at all times in case she would need them.

Robin also spent more than one afternoon leading everyone through the forest, discussing how to move gently through the underbrush so as not to disturb the plants or dirt of the forest floor, and how to hide one's tracks if they did. Keeping the camp hidden was paramount.

To Marian's amusement and sometimes dismay, Mark could not have been more content to be living in the forest. He was in awe of Robin and his skills with the bow and begged Robin to teach him everything he knew. He was equally fascinated by Dusty's healing techniques, but he was not a quick study under her tutelage.

Marian herself continued to live alone in Wetherby, though she visited the camp often and grew more confident finding the way each time.

On one particular visit, the only person she found in the make-shift home of the gang was Will. He was seated near the center of the meadow where the fire ring was located, his sword leaned against his shoulder and down to the ground as he slowly dragged his whet stone across the edge to sharpen it. He looked up with a grin as Marian entered the camp and moved toward him.

"Find your way without getting lost for once?"

Marian pushed his shoulder playfully as she sat beside him. "Don't act like you've never gotten lost in these trees."

"What brings you to camp today?"

"Merely looking to see if I could be helpful in some fashion. Where is everyone?"

"Dusty is in Nottingham; there are several sick families that she has been tending too." As he spoke, Will continued to methodically drag his whet stone across his sword. "I'm unsure where Little John has run off to. Mark and Robin were headed to Marcus' to discuss a new sword for Mark. Robin's opinions about weaponry seem to matter a great deal to your brother."

"Robin's opinion on anything matters a great deal to Mark. It always has. He would have followed him to the Crusades when Robin left if he hadn't specifically told Mark to stay here."

Will paused his work, laying his whet stone down on his leg as he turned toward Marian. "He seems to have that effect on people. Even Little John is willing to follow his every order and command without question."

"He's charismatic," Marian shrugged.

"I understand why Allen and Dusty, and in some ways even your brother, would follow his every whim. But Little John should have more loyalty than that."

"Loyalty?" Marian's eyebrows rose.

"To you, Marian. You led our crusade against the Sheriff for years without Robin's help, and now that he's back the entire gang seems to be under the impression that he's in charge."

"He is in charge," Marian shrugged.

Will cocked his head to one side as he studied Marian, his dark blue eyes intense. "That doesn't bother you?"

"Not really. We're doing as much good—more even—together, as one crew, than we were on our own. And it isn't like Robin doesn't come to me for advice when making his decisions. I feel in some ways I still am in charge. Robin might boss you all around, but he asks my opinion first."

Will picked up his whet stone and began working on his sword again. "Knowing he takes your opinion seriously is good."

"Really, Will, I don't care that Robin has taken charge of the day-to-day running of the gang. He's not arrogant; he's willing to take my advice, and he is open to suggestions from the rest of you, too, I've noticed."

"Yes, I suppose he is. Still seems rather unfair of him to simply take over our little crew."

Marian laughed. "There's no need to be sullen about it when I don't care. Would it make you feel any better if we vote on it?"

"You're mocking me now," Will chuckled.

"Only a bit. We could vote you know…and everyone but you would vote for Robin to lead, so there you are."

Will shook his head. "It still seems presumptuous on Robin's part, and rather traitorous for Little John and Mark to go along with it so easily."

"I think you are taking it far too seriously, my friend."

"As you say," Will shrugged. "I'll drop it. Doesn't mean I'll like it."

Chapter 7

AUNT LUCY SMILED down at Mari-Lu, who grinned back at her. The little girl's eyes were dancing as Aunt Lucy continued, "After a couple months of raiding caravans, the time of Nottingham's annual Fair drew near."

Mari-Lu clapped her hands with glee. "Oh, I love the Fair!"

Aunt Lucy laughed. "I know. Many people do. Merchants from all of England come to the Fair to sell their wares, and even more people come to witness the spectacle. There are often even visitors from Scotland and France and beyond."

"I love all the singing the most!" Mari-Lu giggled. "Or the booths with all the sweet things to eat!"

"The booths are fun," Aunt Lucy agreed. "Always filling Nottingham Square from corner to corner selling all sorts of things, from scarves to weapons to spices and fruit, and cloth…"

"So many good things," Mari-Lu laughed. "Was the Fair back then as fun as ours?"

"Oh yes. All the singing and dancing, the contests and feats of arms…even back then, under Prince John's rule, the Fair was a sight to behold. For that one day people could forget their trials and hardships and simply enjoy themselves. The fine silks, the sparkling jewelry, the chance to escort or be escorted to all the entertainment by someone you admire…"

The night before the Fair, Marian had an unexpected knock on her door. She opened it to find Sir Guy of Gisbourne standing nervously before her, his dark hair a striking contrast to the red and orange in the sky behind him where the sun was setting.

"Did you need something?" Marian asked, barely managing to be polite to the man who'd imprisoned her father after nearly hanging him.

"I came to see if you would accompany me to the Fair tomorrow." Gisbourne's dark eyes were looking anywhere but at Marian, and she tried not to roll her own.

"Accompany you?" with an effort, she kept the sarcasm from her voice.

Gisbourned nodded stiffly. "Yes."

What would Robin say? He could hardly take her himself given he'd gone into hiding once it became rather suspicious and obvious to everyone—including the Sheriff—that 'Robin of the Hood' had shown up just after Robin of Locksley had returned from his travels.

The prospect of being able to pick up valuable information from the Sheriff's right hand made Marian's decision easy. Robin could think what he liked: there were bigger things at stake here.

"I'd be delighted."

Gisbourne seemed to sag with relief. He nodded briefly, and then turned to walk away. Suddenly he stopped and spun back around. "I'll…come for you in the morning."

He stood silently, staring at her, for several more moments until Marian couldn't stand it.

"Yes?"

"Would you…that is…I can take you to see your father."

Marian felt a rush of excitement at the prospect, and she could hardly stop the tears that pricked her eyelids. She hadn't spoken to her father since his imprisonment.

"You would do that?"

Gisbourne nodded. He was either being thoughtful, or he was deceptively clever in his attempts to gain her favor. Either way, Marian was not going to turn down such an offer.

"I would love that! Thank you, Sir Guy."

He nodded again, and then marched his way down the dirt path back toward the winding road to Nottingham.

What would Robin think? Marian soon had her answer. She had barely shut the door on the sight of Gisbourne walking away before she had another knock on her door.

"What did he want?" Robin demanded as Marian let him into the house. "Why was he here? Are you alright? Did he hurt you?"

"He merely asked me to accompany him to the Fair."

That gave Robin pause. He studied her for a moment, and then sighed heavily. "I should be your escort, my lady."

"You can't come. You're an outlaw."

"It would be risky. But it would be worth it, to be by your side. And to keep you away from Gisbourne; I don't trust him."

"Neither do I. But I might be able to learn something from him that we can use in our fight against the Sheriff. I'm not being watched, they don't suspect me. And Gisbourne, I believe, is strangely rather fond of me. In which case, his guard will be down and I might be able to take advantage of that for the betterment of our suffering people."

"Marian, if they knew you were the mastermind behind the Hooded Rescuer and the original gang here in Nottingham…"

"They wouldn't believe it," Marian said. "And how could they discover such a thing? You aren't going to tell them, I presume?"

"I'm just worried, Marian."

"You don't have to be. I can fight well enough given what I've learned from you, Will, Mark, and the others. I could defend myself if I needed to. But right now, I don't need to; I'm still trusted and even sought out. I'll be fine."

Robin was still morose for the rest of his visit, and he went back to camp that night in a sullen mood.

The next morning, Marian rose early. She did not know precisely when Gisbourne would call on her, but she wanted to be prepared. She was finally going to see her father and be able to talk to him!

After eating her breakfast, she gathered some of her excess—although Mark lived mostly in camp, Marian still bought for two to keep up appearances and often had more than she needed—and wandered Wetherby giving food to the various residents of the village. They'd come to expect gifts of such a nature from Marian over the years since the Crusades began, and welcomed her with gratitude.

Marian had scarcely closed her door after returning home from her errands when she heard a loud knock. Gisbourne had arrived.

Marian hurriedly put her basket away and ran a brush through her hair, deftly braiding it as she hurried toward the door.

When she exited the house, Gisbourne offered his arm and she reluctantly took it.

"You're as beautiful as ever," he said smoothly. Marian chose to ignore that comment.

"We will visit your father first if that is agreeable, and then proceed to Nottingham Square."

"I am most grateful for this visit, Sir Guy."

"You haven't seen him since his arrest," Gisbourne nodded, looking truly thoughtful and apologetic for once. "I am sorry. I don't condone keeping families apart."

"Except through death of course," Marian snapped. "You had no qualms separating me from my father the night you chose to hang him."

Gisbourne winced and did not respond.

When they passed through the gate leading into the courtyard of the castle, Marian let go of Gisbourne's arm and bounded up the stone steps, pulling open the doors and confidently making her way through the halls of the castle down to the dungeons. She went straight to her father's cell without thinking.

"Marian?" Sir Godfrey was sitting on a straw mattress, looking haggard and grey, his hair stringy and clearly falling out. His eyes were sunken in, with dark circles underneath them.

"Father! You're still ill," Marian reached her hand through the bars of the cell and her father slowly got up and limped toward her.

"I'd forgotten you would know your way around," Gisbourne said, coming along behind her. "I suppose since your father was once sheriff, this must have been your home in some fashion growing up. Yet how could you know where your father was imprisoned."

"There are only so many places to imprison someone in this castle," Marian replied. "Father, are you okay?"

"I will live."

"Will you? You don't look like it."

"I might not. But is there a reason to?"

"Father, don't talk so!" Marian glanced to Gisbourne a moment, and then back to her father. "With such high taxes, the ransom will no doubt be paid soon. And when the King is set free from his prison in Austria, perhaps he will come home and set all to rights like you used to say he would."

"I no longer believe that, child. You shouldn't either. You were right; it was naive. You are too intelligent to have turned into such a dreamer, Marian."

"It will happen," Marian insisted. She longed to tell him about her exploits with Robin and the gang, about the ways she was helping the people of Nottingham and beyond. But with Gisbourne standing so close, it was impossible. How could she give her father hope when she couldn't tell him the truth? He was right; trusting in King Richard was a fool's hope.

"Father—"

"How is Mark?" Sir Godfrey interrupted.

"He is well," Marian said. "He...yes, he is well." She had nearly said he lived with Robin, knowing her father respected Robin enough to take comfort in such news, but given that Robin was an outlaw it would not be wise to say such things.

Gisbourne cleared his throat, apparently growing impatient. "Shall we see how the Fair gets on, Marian?"

Marian sighed. "Of course. Whatever you wish." Marian placed her hand on her father's cheek. "Keep hope alive, father."

Sir Godfrey did not seem much heartened by her visit as Gisbourne led her away from the dungeons. When Marian glanced back for a last look at her father, he'd retreated to his little straw mattress, his head in his hands, looking far more defeated and dejected than Marian had ever seen him.

As Gisbourne led her back out of the castle and into the sunlight, Marian did her best to hide her tears from him, but from the furtive glances he kept giving her Marian was sure he saw them.

As they made their way toward the sounds of singing, haggling, and the general hum of a large gathering that meant they were near Nottingham Square, Gisbourne finally spoke. "I can have a physician see to him."

Marian glanced up at the strange man upon whose arm she leaned. Why would he offer such a thing? He'd once tried to kill him.

"Would you? It would ease my mind if something could be done about his illness."

"Then it will be done."

Marian stared in some disbelief as Gisbourne led her into the bustling Square. He was going to send for a physician for her father...*for her*. She knew he'd been interested in her, that much was clear, but that he would be so drastically different from his usual cruel self in order to please her was a new development, and one she might be able to make use of.

They spent the morning in Nottingham Square, watching dancers perform and walking among the booths. When Gisbourne noticed Marian fingering a silk gown of the deepest purple, he insisted on buying it for her. Marian rolled her eyes. Did he believe her affection could be so easily bought? She wouldn't care for Sir Guy of Gisbourne if he laid every jewel in England at her feet. He'd nearly killed her father, and many others besides.

He was a cruel, unjust man, and he thought a pretty dress would win her over?

That afternoon there were contests. Gisbourne and Marian followed the crowd to the fields outside of Nottingham where they enjoyed watching races, both on foot and on horse, as well as archery contests and fencing matches.

Gisbourne praised every soldier of the Sheriff's in the races, seeming to think they were of the highest quality of athlete presented.

Marian shook her head. "How can you think so when they've all been beaten by that one village boy."

Gisbourne was thoughtful. "Do you think…no, but he is too small."

Marian looked at Gisbourne for more explanation, but he shook his head and covered her hand on his arm with his own.

When the time came for the horse races, Gisbourne was among the contestants. He was a tall man on the ground, but seated upon his black stallion Victory, he looked almost regal. If he had been wearing more color than his usual black tunic and leather armor, he might have been a sight to behold.

As the nobles, villagers, and visitors from other towns and kingdoms mounted their own horses and lined up for the races, Marian could tell that Gisbourne's horse Victory was the finest one of the lot.

Victory thought so, too, apparently, as he easily outran every other beast that day. After each race, Victory would snort and throw his head back, seeming to say 'the peasants have nothing on me' and Marian would have been amused by the horse's antics if he hadn't been ridden by a man she detested so much.

"There's not a finer horse in England," Gisbourne boasted after he'd won every race.

Marian nodded politely.

"Were you cheering for me?"

"I was cheering for your horse."

That reply seemed to satisfy Gisbourne.

Marian did not pick up any valuable information for Robin as she had hoped she would by having Gisbourne as her escort. She did learn one thing though. Sir Guy of Gisbourne appeared to be sincerely attached to her. Anything Marian admired was swiftly bought, every word she spoke was hung onto like it was the brightest jewel he'd ever seen, and he even made good on his promise to send for a physician to visit Sir Godfrey.

←»

"Did he love her?" Mari-Lu asked, her face scrunched up in serious thought.

"It appeared so," Aunt Lucy replied. "As much as Sir Guy of Gisbourne was able to love anyone genuinely and honestly back in those days. But how deep was that affection, Marian wondered? How far would he go to please her? Would he even, dared she hope, join the fight against Prince John? Or perhaps at the very least, lessen his own cruelty against the people of England?"

Mari-Lu shook her head. "No. He wouldn't."

Aunt Lucy smiled knowingly before continuing, "Robin would certainly be furious if she chose to accept his attentions and court him for the sake of helping England, and Dusty would lecture her for Marian had no intention of marrying Sir Guy of

Gisbourne. She didn't love him, she wanted to use him, and Dusty could never approve of such a thing. But Marian had no intention of doing anything for the sake of pleasing Dusty, whom she still harbored some jealousy over given her close connection to Robin. And as to pleasing Robin himself, she still wasn't entirely sure she cared about that either."

"But she loves him!" Mari-Lu protested.

"She did," Aunt Lucy agreed. "But she was loath to admit such a thing, even to herself."

"I wish she would trust him," Mari-Lu said. "Robin loves her; he promised he'd be there for her and I believe him."

"You should remember he did abandon her for three years," Aunt Lucy said. "He was not there for her when her world fell apart, so her reticence was not entirely unfounded."

"Just tell me she trusts him at some point," Mari-Lu said. "I want them to be happy!"

"You'll have to wait and see…"

Chapter 8

MARIAN FEARED HER grandmother might tire from telling the long story, but Aunt Lucy seemed unaffected by the passing hours. She sat with Mari-Lu on her lap, seeming to relish the chance to share the tales of Robin Hood once more.

"The rest of Marian's nineteenth year was spent in 'confiscating'—as the gang learned to call their thieving exploits—from the Sheriff and distributing the wealth to the people of England. The rumors of Robin Hood spread far beyond the reaches of Nottinghamshire. All of England heard of his exploits, and in an attempt to help more than just his childhood home, Robin began to send the gang out on extended visits to other parts of the country—there they distributed the wealth gathered in Nottingham, stopped unlawful executions if they could, and did much the same as they were doing in Nottingham itself. Even Prince John became concerned with this 'treacherous outlaw.' The gang couldn't save everyone—every now and then there would be an execution in Nottingham they couldn't attend, having spread themselves so thin across such a distance. They couldn't be everywhere at once, after all, and some innocents slipped through the cracks."

"That's horrible."

"It was, and they all felt so."

"What else happened?"

"Robin would openly speak out against the Sheriff and Gisbourne in Nottingham until he could no longer show himself without being swarmed by the Sheriff's soldiers. Everyone from Prince John to the lowest village boy knew that Robin of

Locksley was indeed Robin Hood. It was soon dangerous for everyone in the gang, save Marian herself, to show their faces in Nottingham."

"But they still went?" Mari-Lu asked.

"Yes, but they kept a low profile. Wearing their hooded capes, keeping out of the way of the Sheriff's men. The people welcomed them, and helped them hide from the Sheriff's watchful eyes. Yet as Robin and the gang confiscated more and more, the taxes rose and rose. The people did not suffer badly for it, however, because the gang looked after everyone that they could."

"What else was happening? Just the raids?"

"Gisbourne continued to court Marian," Aunt Lucy replied. "He often brought her to meet her father, whose health was improving due to the physician that Gisbourne had brought to look after him. Robin courted Marian as well, though under cover of darkness.

Mari-Lu giggled. "Did she like that?"

"Of course she did, though she may have pretended otherwise. However much she tried to deny it or ignore it, Robin's presence was a comforting one, and his easy manners always cheered her."

"What else happened?" Mari-Lu asked, leaning forward with excitement.

"With Robin and his gang confiscating far and wide, and traveling to other districts of England to help more people, it became more and more dependent on the Hooded Rescuer to keep the people of Nottingham safe—to stop unnecessary beatings, hangings, and arrests. Mark and Marian began to work closely together again as they had before they had Will and Little John to help them, and before Robin's gang came into being. Just before Marian's twentieth birthday, another person joined the chaos in Nottingham…"

←→

Lucy stood to one side of the wide open square near the center of town. All around her booths were set up to sell wares— some tables with simple cloth awnings to shade the seller from the sun, some wagons and carts with their goods piled high.

Along the edges of the square were the shops; a butcher, a baker, a blacksmith. A number of people were milling about the market, though no one paid much attention to Lucy as they chatted about their lives and haggled over prices.

Lucy wasn't sure what she was looking for, but the city market seemed the best place to start. She had made it to Nottingham and was curious if she could locate the famous Robin Hood and his gang.

A man dressed in black entered the market, striding purposefully through the carts and booths. The crowd quieted as he marched through, their cheerful chatter falling to a soft hum. Following behind him were a dozen soldiers armed to the teeth. Once the morose looking lord and his entourage had exited the market, headed down a side street, the chatter in the market returned.

"Such a hurting soul," a voice commented. Lucy turned to see a little old lady, with a hunched back, stringy white hair, and a mouth missing most of its teeth. She had twinkling eyes though, and she smiled kindly at Lucy. "That Gisbourne," she said, gesturing the way the lord had gone. "He's a broken, hurting soul."

"Most people are," Lucy replied. "It's why we need Jesus."

The woman nodded. "True enough. I'm Tibb, little lady."

"Lucy."

"You one of Robin Hood's? I haven't seen you before now."

"I'm just visiting the city."

"Not a good city to visit perhaps," Tibb said, looking around the market. "But then, not such a bad one either."

"I came from London."

"Ah. You're a few months early for the Fair."

"I came to the Nottingham Fair when I was a girl," Lucy said. "But that isn't why I'm visiting now."

"No?"

Lucy studied the woman. She seemed kind and honest, but explaining her true purpose here didn't seem wise. And yet, Lucy had a strict personal rule against lying.

"You be careful, my lady," Tibb said when Lucy didn't respond. "This world is a dangerous place without friends to help you through it."

Tibb wandered away, zigzagging through the crowd and smiling at everyone who would bother to look her direction. One woman who stopped to speak with her had several baskets on her arm filled with food. She handed some to Tibb, and then moved down a street and disappeared from Lucy's view...

"Thank you, Lady Marian," a young woman said, accepting the loaf of bread that Marian offered her. Marian had stocked up with fresh bread at the baker's, and gotten some fruit from the market in Nottingham Square, and now she was handing out food to the citizens of Nottingham.

The young woman hugged Marian in her gratitude, and then returned to her house. Marian moved down the street toward the next house, ready to help the next person she came across.

Suddenly, she heard the Sheriff shrieking his displeasure at one thing or another. If that man wasn't insane, Marian was a horse. She moved swiftly down the street toward Nottingham Square, leaning against the side of a house and peering around the corner into the Square.

A group of children was being dragged by soldiers toward the castle. Whatever the Sheriff was saying, his shrieks made it impossible to understand. His face was purple with rage as he waved his hands about, marching out of the Square at the opposite end from Marian, on his way to the castle no doubt. The soldiers followed after him, pulling the crying, struggling children behind them. And bringing up the rear of the train was Gisbourne, clearly overseeing the arrest of the children.

The people selling goods at the booths of the market, and those buying as well, were silently watching—some looked horrified, some angry, a few were crying. But no one did anything. What could they do? If they approached the Sheriff or Gisbourne, they'd be the next ones to be arrested and threatened with death. Robin Hood and the others saved many, but they didn't save everyone. The threat of being the one person they couldn't save lingered over the people's heads, and so they watched in fear as the children were dragged toward the castle.

Dropping the baskets with the remainder of the food she had, Marian ran to Gisbourne and latched onto his arm. "What's happening?"

"Two men couldn't pay their taxes," Gisbourne replied calmly.

Marian's mind raced. How had they overlooked someone? They had been so diligent in keeping everyone from poverty. "So you are arresting their children?"

"Sheriff's orders."

"But they're only children, Sir Guy! The oldest couldn't be more than ten!"

Gisbourne shrugged.

"Will they be kept in custody until the taxes are paid?" Although Robin and the gang were away to the south confiscating, Marian knew there was money at the camp. She could get it tonight and free the children.

"No, Marian. They aren't going to rot in prison."

Marian's heart lifted.

"They're being executed at dawn."

"What? Sir Guy, you can't let that happen!"

Gisbourne studied Marian.

"Please!" Marian was desperate.

"They die at dawn."

"Bur Sir Guy!"

Though he spoke matter-of-factly, there were emotions swirling in his dark eyes that gave Marian hope that he was considering her pleas.

She had to convince him to do something. There was no way she could rescue them all tonight without help, and she didn't know when she might expect Robin back in Nottingham. "Please, Sir Guy! You have to stop this! They are only children!"

Gisbourne shrugged Marian off his arm and marched after the shrieking Sheriff and crying children. Marian sank to the ground and her head fell to her chest. It wasn't fair! Marian did not try to stop her tears from flowing. She wouldn't be able to stop this. Innocent children were going to die.

Had Marian looked up she would have seen Gisbourne stop and look back, his face a mirror of his anguish as he wrestled with his own emotions. She might have also seen another person scrutinizing the proceedings with interest, as Lucy considered her own options for stopping such a tragedy from occurring. But Marian did not look up.

Marian spent the remainder of the day in the walls of the castle, trying to plan an escape. But the children were too heavily guarded in the dungeons, so the secret passages that opened there would be of no use to her.

She spent that night pacing her home, debating the chances she had of succeeding in stopping the executions alone. But she knew it was hopeless. She couldn't fight off all of the Sheriff's men alone.

As dawn approached, Marian's feet dragged as she forced herself to Nottingham Square. She didn't want to see the sweet young bodies dangling, but she couldn't stop herself from heading that direction. Maybe there was still something she could do?

The sun had barely risen when Marian entered the Square. But the gallows were empty. Had the executions not taken place yet? But then the Sheriff's screaming voice came floating over the crisp morning breeze and Marian's heart froze in her chest.

A moment later he strode into the Square followed by a dozen soldiers dragging half a dozen bound men. What was going on?

As Marian watched, the men were hung one by one. But why?

When the deed was done the Sheriff's voice rang out again, though there was no crowd to hear his speech. "That is what will happen to anyone who dares defy me! Any traitors will be hung! How dare they? They had one duty. Guard those children."

"Yes, sir," one of the living soldiers said.

"And yet the children vanished last night into thin air! Did you help them?"

"No, sir!" All of the soldiers were shaking their heads, denying any involvement. Marian was thoroughly confused as to what was happening, but the Sheriff wasn't done.

"The money found on their person tells me these soldiers were bribed to let the children go. If you aren't loyal enough to me to withstand bribes you don't deserve to live!"

"Of course, sir."

"Should I just hang you all?"

"No, sir."

"They also refused to tell me who bribed them! The insolence!" The Sheriff's voice was rising as he spoke, his face flushed a deep red, as the soldiers stood before him with their eyes cast down, clearly unsure whether or not the Sheriff was going to order them to kill each other.

"Get back to your duties!" he snapped. The soldiers dispersed immediately, and the Sheriff made his way out of Nottingham Square.

So the children were free! Someone had paid the soldiers to let them go. But who?

Marian thought she might know the answer to that question and she was impatient to confront him. She stayed in Nottingham for most of the day for that purpose, but she never caught sight of him. Going to the castle to speak to him seemed far too dangerous; the Sheriff would be there, after all.

It wasn't until that evening that Marian was able to speak to Sir Guy of Gisbourne, when he came to her home in Wetherby.

The knock on the door surprised her, but she was relieved when she saw him standing outside her door.

"Sir Guy! Please come in."

"I can't stay," he replied. "I need your help."

"My help?"

"It's suspected you are a friend of Robin Hood's," Gisbourne said.

Marian remained silent. If he was trying to catch her in a confession, he was going to be disappointed.

"The children, Marian, they can't go home. This isn't about the outlaw, or your involvement with him. The Sheriff will kill the children if he finds them."

"If he finds them? Where are they?"

"Just inside Sherwood Forest, with my most trusted friend and soldier Andrew. He won't betray us, you can trust him, but he has nowhere to hide them. If you do know the outlaw…"

"You want me to get the children to Robin Hood?"

"Many have disappeared from executions and never been seen in Nottingham again. I don't know where he takes them, but if he can do it for so many others, surely he can do it for these children."

"I'm sure he can."

"So you'll do it? Take the children to Robin Hood, I mean?"

"Yes, I can. Thank you, Sir Guy."

"I did this for you."

"I know."

Gisbourne took Marian's hands in his. "Do you? Have you any idea how much pain you've caused me? Seeing you distressed? I could not get the image of you sitting alone in Nottingham Square weeping out of my mind, and I couldn't stop hearing my moth—" Gisboure stopped abruptly, looking horrified at whatever he'd been about to say. For a moment, several emotions warred across his face, and then he said, "Breaking faith with the Sheriff was the most difficult decision I ever made."

"But you chose to do the right thing."

"Only for you. Do you know, Marian, how much I would do for you?" His grasp on her hands tightened, his voice growing almost desperate, "Do you understand the hold you have over me?"

Suddenly he dropped to his knees on the floor of her house, and Marian backed up in surprise, though she couldn't go far with Gisbroune's tight grip on her hands.

"Marry me, Marian."

"What?" Marian shook her head, trying to pull her hands free and failing.

"Please! I'd do anything for you, Marian. Please, marry me."

Marian continued to shake her head, tugging at her hands to break them free of his grasp.

"Marian! Don't you understand? I love you more than anything. My love for you has caused me to abandon my thirst for power and wealth, things I have sought since I was a child. Things that I can get with the Sheriff, things that I cannot obtain with such acts of compassion as I showed today. But I did it anyway, *for you*. Make my sacrifice worth it; marry me."

Marian finally found her voice. "No, Sir Guy. A good deed you may have done today, and I am grateful for it. But I will never marry you."

"Marian-"

"No. You have killed and tortured the innocent, you admit power and wealth means more to you than human decency—"

"Not more than you, Marian!"

"You only helped those children to get what *you* want, not because it was the right thing, not because murdering children is an atrocious act."

"Is my love for you not a pure enough motivation for freeing those children?" Gisbourne snapped.

"You tried to kill my father!" Marian yelled back. "I wouldn't marry you if you were the last man in Nottingham."

Gisbourne jumped to his feet, his eyes flashing. "Perhaps I should give those children back to the Sheriff."

"Are you threatening the lives of those children, because I won't marry you? You realize this only solidifies my desire to never marry you? That you would kill innocent children to punish me for not loving you tells me exactly what kind of man you are."

Gisbourne's face blanched, as he opened his mouth and then closed it again, clearly at a loss for words. His face contorted in agony, he spun away from her and threw open her door, marching out into the cool air of twilight.

Marian's heart sank. Perhaps she should not have been so harsh. She could have played along until the children were securely in the camp with Robin. Now Gisbourne was likely to take them back and have them hung!

Chapter 9

MARIAN PACED HER home, wondering what to do. She could run to Sherwood, hope to find this soldier named Andrew and get the children from him before Gisbourne did. But if he was headed there now, she'd never beat him to it. If he did lock them back up to await another execution, perhaps Robin would be back in time to do something about it.

She paced and paced until long after the sun had set. When a timid knock sounded at her door, she spun around, whipping her jeweled-dagger out of her belt in surprise.

Marian opened the door a crack to see who might be visiting her at so late an hour, hoping it was Robin and she could explain her hopeless situation to him.

But when she opened the door, she wasn't met with the pleasant face of the man she loved, but rather the terrified faces of six small children.

"Are you Lady Marian?" the oldest boy asked.

"Good heavens," Marian looked them over, "are you hurt? Get inside!"

She ushered the children inside, glancing around the street to see if anyone was lurking in Wetherby at so late an hour, but saw no one. Closing the door, she turned to study the shivering, scared children.

"What happened?"

"The angry man in black came to where we were hidden by the forest," the oldest boy said. "He shouted at us to find you, and then he dragged the other man away. I liked him; he was nicer."

Perhaps she had been mistaken in Gisbourne's character after all. But no, she'd seen his cruelty in action before; Sir Guy of Gisbourne was an evil man, and she did not regret her refusal.

Marian fed the children, and then led them through the darkness to Sherwood Forest, to the camp. As they went, she spoke with William, the oldest boy who was ten years old and eager to explain the situation, and so she learned more details of what had happened.

They were cousins, it turned out. William's father was unable to pay his taxes, and so William and his little sisters Sarah and Rachel, ages eight and five respectively, were taken. Their uncle had attacked the soldiers arresting them, and after being soundly beaten by the soldiers, his children were taken as well.

"That's us," Beth, a girl of seven, piped up. "John and Peter are my brothers, they're six and four."

"Well I am glad that you are all safe. I'll pay a visit to your families tomorrow to let them know where you are. I'm afraid you'll have to stay in the camp for a while, until we can sort this out."

"We aren't going to be dead," William said, "so that's alright."

Marian settled the children down in the huts of the other gang members, as no one was currently at the camp and she wasn't going to make them sleep outside. Marian herself didn't sleep that night; she built a small fire in the pit near Much's kitchen hut, and sat beside it keeping watch.

When Robin and the others returned the next day to find their huts full of children, Marian explained the situation to them.

"Of course we can keep the children here," Robin said. The gang had gathered around the fire, seated on fallen logs that had been dragged to the firepit and circled around it for the very purpose of their gatherings. The children were still sleeping.

"I'm surprised Gisbourne rescued them at all. What a man wouldn't do for Marian," Robin kissed her cheek.

"Sir Guy may not be as vile as people believe," Dusty said. "Or at the very least, he does have a conscience, and does struggle with the choices that he makes."

"Don't count on that," Allen replied. "He did this for Marian, not for any other reason."

"You don't know that," Dusty insisted.

Will placed a hand on Dusty's shoulder, as if to calm her. "He's evil Dusty. You can't make a saint out of him."

"I don't make saints," Dusty replied. "I am only suggesting he is not fully evil, even as none of us are fully good. Only God can clothe us in any righteousness. We're all the worst of sinners before Him."

"I'd say we're better than Sir Guy of Gisbourne any day," Robin replied.

"Robin…" Dusty sighed.

Robin held up his hands to silence her. "Don't start. We all know how you feel. We don't need another lecture."

Little John steered the conversation away from Dusty. "Did Gisbourne not speak of anything else, Marian? He knows you are connected to our gang, that could mean trouble for you."

"I know," Marian said. "But he didn't say anything about it after we fought."

"He didn't mention Mark?" Little John pressed.

"Why would he ask about me?" Mark asked.

"I'm sure they've noticed you are never home," Little John replied.

"What Gisbourne will do with his information that Marian does indeed know who we are remains to be seen," Will said. "It might be too dangerous for her to continue living in Wetherby."

"We'll have to keep watch," Robin said.

The very next day, Gisbourne was at Marian's door again. This time he did not come alone; he brought soldiers. He and his men were heavily armed and several came bearing torches.

"You're under arrest," Gisbourne said tersely when Marian answered the door. She could see Widow Mary and other villagers gathering in doorways along the dusty street to see what the commotion was about.

"Why am I under arrest?" Marian demanded. "I've done nothing wrong."

"Don't bother me with your feigned innocence," Gisbourne snapped. "You admitted you were a friend of Robin Hood. Robin Hood is an outlaw and traitor, therefore you also are a traitor and no friend of the crown."

"Which crown would that be?" Marian snapped. "Since Prince John is a traitor to his brother King Richard's crown, I don't find it to be a shameful thing to be a traitor to Prince John."

"Silence! You are coming to Nottingham castle to await the Sheriff's justice."

"You can't call that mockery justice—"

"Enough!" Gisbourne grabbed her arm. "That's enough from you." Gisbourne motioned to the soldiers behind him with torches and they moved forward. "As you'll be living in Nottingham castle for the foreseeable future, you won't be needing this humble abode."

"NO!" Marian struggled against Gisbourne, but he wouldn't let go. She watched with horror as the soldiers with torches entered her house, prepared to burn it down. "Sir Guy, please! Don't do this!"

"Beg."

"What?"

Gisbourne's eyes were cold as ice. "If you don't want me to burn your home to the ground, beg for my mercy and leniency."

"Sir Guy…"

"If you'd rather not, I'll cheerfully give the order for my men to torch it."

"Please, please don't do this! Guy, I'm begging you. Don't burn my home."

"You can do better."

Marian thought of her father, of all the memories she had made growing up in Wetherby. Her father was in prison and was unlikely to ever return; all his things, all Marian's worldly possessions, it was all in that house. That house was her home.

Marian dropped to her knees and Gisbourne let go of her arm. "Please! Have mercy! Don't burn my home, Sir Guy!"

Gisbourne leaned over Marian, looking far more menacing than she'd ever seen before. "Better."

Marian held her breath.

"But still not good enough," Gisbourne snapped. He waved to the soldiers, who dropped their torches inside her home and then exited to watch the destruction unfold.

"No!" Marian leaped up, but Gisbourne grabbed her again. She struggled against him, trying to reach her home as the flames began to lick up the walls and along the floor; soon the house was full of smoke and flame, and everything Marian owned was lost.

Gisbourne dragged her away from the house as she struggled to pull away, leading her along the dirt path away from the village of Wetherby and back to the city of Nottingham.

In the bushes nearby, Robin, Much, and Mark watched in anger and horror. Mark tried to dash from their hiding place, reaching for his sword, but Much and Robin grabbed onto both of his arms and pulled him back down.

"There are too many!" Robin hissed. "Even for us. We couldn't take them, and then we'd all be killed or imprisoned with Marian. We can't save her if we do that. We need to be smart."

"My home!"

"We'll deal with the fire as soon as Gisbourne and his soldiers are away," Much said.

"And we'll find a way to rescue Marian," Robin added.

❮❯

"...and so they watched in anguish until Gisbourne and the soldiers had dragged Marian away," Aunt Lucy said. "Then they ran forward and did what they could to quench the flames. Widow Mary and the other villagers eagerly helped; they had no love of Gisbourne, but a great love for Marian and her family. But it was too late. Marian and Mark's childhood home was destroyed."

There were tears in Mari-Lu's eyes. "How could he? Why did he do it?"

"Anger can drive a person to do things they would not otherwise do," Aunt Lucy said, "which is why we must control our anger, Mari-Lu. Never let it get the best of you."

"But he burned it all down! How could he? I thought he loved her!"

"He did, in his own twisted way, but Sir Guy of Gisbourne did not know what true love was, not back then. He had a fragile ego born of his own childhood demons…but that's another story altogether. The point was that he was broken inside, and so he lashed out and broke the world around him."

"What happened to Marian?"

"She had stopped crying by the time they reached Nottingham. She was silent, grave, and determined. The people watching the procession, though confused and afraid seeing their beloved Marian arrested, were proud of her. She did not cower before Gisbourne as he led her through Nottingham to the castle.

«»

When Gisbourne pushed open the doors to the Great Hall, Marian saw the Sheriff was there, sitting on his wooden chair presumably meant to resemble a throne with its high back, though it lacked any adornments to complete the illusion. He smiled and rose as they entered.

"Ah, Marian dear, so good to see you."

"I'm sorry I can't say the same to you."

"Feisty as ever!" the Sheriff laughed. "You, my dear, are under house arrest until we can prove your connection to the outlaw Robin Hood, at which time you will be executed. In the meantime, you cannot leave this castle and you will have a guard on you at all times."

"But—"

"No objections, please, my lady. It's all arranged."

111

Marian glared at Gisbourne, but he ignored her.

The Sheriff continued, "You are free to move about in the castle, you can listen to our secret meetings all you like. It won't make a difference, Lady Marian. You won't be leaving the castle walls, so it hardly matters."

When the Sheriff was through lecturing her on the dangers of associating with outlaws, Gisbourne led her to her room, opening the door and stepping aside.

"My soldier, Andrew, will be the one watching over you," he said, motioning to the soldier who was coming down the hall towards them.

"How could you—"

"Save your breath, Marian. I. Don't. Care."

Gisbourne spun on his heel and marched away, leaving Marian alone with Andrew.

"My lady—" Andrew began, but Marian didn't care to hear what he had to say. Gisbourne had called Andrew his most trusted friend, which meant he could hardly be a good person. Marian entered her room and shut the door, leaving Andrew to stand guard outside.

Marian realized with surprise that Gisbourne had taken her to one of the nicest rooms in the castle, large and well-furnished. It also happened to have a door to the secret passageways hidden behind the tapestry along the wall, but he probably didn't know that part.

The room itself was rather dull and couldn't distract Marian; she couldn't shake the emotions of the day. Hatred for Gisbourne, grief for her home, adrenaline from the desire to fight the Sheriff.

Marian sighed, and decided to go visit her father now that she had access to the castle. Andrew was waiting outside her door. She ignored him, but she could not ignore the sounds of his footsteps following her as she made her way through the stone hallways down to the dungeons.

When Sir Godfrey saw her, his face lit with surprise. "Marian!"

"I'm under house arrest," Marian said without preamble, leaning up against the bars of her father's cell to be close to him. He came and stood beside her, brushing a stray tear from her cheek.

"What happened?"

"Gisbourne burned our home to the ground."

Sir Godfrey sighed, moving away from Marian and sinking down onto his straw mattress in defeat. "Burned to the ground?"

"Compliments of Sir Guy of Gisbourne."

"Or your outrageous dreams," Sir Godfrey sighed. "Don't you see how hopeless it is? You try to fight back, and you end up here—with nothing left in the world, if all our possessions have been burned."

"We will win, father. This is just a set back."

"How can you believe that, child?" Sir Godfrey asked. "The kingdom is doomed; our people are doomed."

"They are not," Marian insisted.

"Where is Mark?" Sir Godfrey asked, changing the subject. "Is he under arrest as well? Or is he simply homeless?"

"He's not here; he's safe though, father."

"Where is he? What have your outrageous dreams done to

my son, Marian? How many times did I tell you to protect your little brother? To set a better example for him?"

"He's safe. He's…in hiding."

"Marian—"

"I promise you he is well, father. But I can't tell you more…" Marian glared at Andrew who looked back innocently.

"Don't be foolish, Marian. You shouldn't have gotten so involved. I should have stopped you when I first found out about —"

"Father!" Marian cut him off, glancing at Andrew again. If her father let on that Mark was the Hooded Rescuer, he'd be in more danger than he already was for being associated with Robin. "And don't worry. I can't do any of the things you deem so foolish while I'm locked in the castle."

"Tell the Sheriff where Mark is."

"Father!"

"If he is brought here under house arrest with you he will be safe, rather than out there doing dangerous things he shouldn't. You aren't there to protect him now."

"He's fine. He has…" Marian wanted to say he has Robin, knowing her father would find some relief in that knowledge, but with Andrew so close she didn't risk it.

"He has what?"

"Just believe he's safe, father, because he is. For now."

Her father was unsatisfied, and Marian had no comfort for him. She soon returned to her room, Andrew following dutifully behind.

Once in her room with Andrew stationed outside her door, Marian waited on her bed. She knew Robin would come eventually, though he'd have to search every room the secret passages connected to in order to find her. The secret passages opened in the dungeons, the Great Hall, several other state rooms and chambers, and a few of the bedchambers as well—including, luckily, the one Marian now occupied.

That evening, Robin slipped through the walls of the castle to find Marian, precisely as she knew he would. He pushed the stone door carefully, letting it slide along the wall behind the tapestry, and then slipped out and moved toward Marian where she sat waiting for him.

"What's the verdict?"

Marian put a finger to her lips, glancing at the door. Robin sat beside her, and she whispered, "I'm glad to see you, but I have a personal guard." Marian rolled her eyes. "He's just outside the door."

"So it's house arrest, then?"

"The Sheriff said if he can prove I help you and the gang, I'll be executed, but for now I'm simply confined to the castle with Andrew to guard me at all times."

"I am sorry, Marian."

"I did this to myself. I chose the life of a vigilante long before you came home from the Crusades. And I spurned Gisbourne most aggressively when he asked me to marry him."

"I am glad of that, at least," Robin said. "But I am sorry your home was burned."

"So am I."

"We did try to save what we could," Robin said. "But the fire ruined most everything inside the house."

"My father is here and alive, you and Mark are safe living in the forest. The house was only that; the people I love are still safe."

"Did you just say you love me?" Robin grinned.

"Yes, Robin," Marian lay her head on his shoulder, sighing heavily. "I did say that."

Robin kissed her forehead. "I'll visit every night, Marian. You won't be alone here."

"I'm never alone," Marian said dryly. "I have Andrew."

"Very funny. You could come with me tonight, you know, leave the house arrest behind and live in the forest."

"I wouldn't want to abandon my father. If I go with you, he won't see a friendly face until...well, until the King comes home or we somehow depose the Sheriff," Marian said. "Living with you, I could spy from the secret passages, but I wouldn't be able to actually visit him, talk to him. I don't want to abandon him that way."

"Perhaps living in the castle won't be entirely pointless," Robin said. "You can learn more about the Sheriff and Gisbourne, and relay what you know when I visit you."

"How will that be any different than spying from within the walls?"

"You'll be here all the time, have access to every room in the castle, not just the ones connected to the secret passages. I'm convinced this will be a good thing, Marian."

"I suppose."

"Much is worried about you, by the way."

"Dear, sweet Much. Tell him I'm fine. How is Mark?"

"Devastated and frustrated."

"Take care of him, Robin."

"I promised you before that I always would; I meant it."

"I don't know that I can trust you."

"You can, Marian. I'm here for you, and I will look after Mark. Always."

"You're too impulsive, and so is he."

"You're one to talk."

"Just keep him out of as much trouble as you can."

"I will take care of him, Marian. I promise you that."

"I'm sorry," Marian sighed. "You know I'm just worried for both of you…and stressed from today…"

"I know," Robin wrapped his arm around her, holding her close. "You don't have to be afraid for us, Marian. I survived the Crusades, no measly Sheriff is going to get the best of me."

They were silent for a moment, Robin holding onto Marian and Marian drawing strength and comfort from the protection of his embrace.

"I understand why you don't fully trust me," Robin said quietly. "And that's okay, too. I told you before and I'll keep telling you for years to come—I'm here for you, whatever you need from me."

"I know, Robin. I'm trying…"

"You don't need to force it, Marian. I know you care for me and that's enough. We'll grow your trust one day at a time."

"If only it was so easy."

"It will be. Just…trust me," Robin chuckled, and Marian couldn't stop herself from smiling as well.

"You see, that's exactly the problem here," Marian laughed. "But I'll try."

Chapter 10

"THE FIRST WEEK Marian lived in the castle was a time of adjustment," Aunt Lucy said.

"I bet it was strange to be there all the time," Mari-Lu commented.

Aunt Lucy nodded. "It was. The Sheriff insisted they all take their meals together. He had always been amused by Marian, and now was no different. He also thought it might be rather entertaining to watch Gisbourne and Marian be stuck in a room together for several hours, given how his proposal had been spurned. Meals were strained because of this, as Gisbourne and Marian had little to say to each other and the Sheriff tried to facilitate an argument between them."

"Marian didn't like to talk to Gisbourne, did she?"

"No, she did not. When they did speak it was cold on both sides. She missed her friends very much, for though any of the gang might spend all day in the hidden passages of the castle, Marian only saw Robin and Mark, and then only at night."

"Did she get lonely?"

"A little. Andrew was a constant companion, of course, but Marian soon tired of him. He hardly ever spoke unless Marian addressed him first. He was always polite but Marian was disgusted with him regardless. He was a friend of Gisbourne's and that made him untrustworthy."

"Was he bad?"

"No," Aunt Lucy said simply. "Andrew wasn't cut out to be a villain. The only reason he was there at all was because he was Sir Guy's servant from childhood. They'd grown up together and were close friends, rather like Robin and Much. Andrew himself was good and gentle—the sorts of things Guy of Gisbourne thought weak and pathetic in most people—but Sir Guy couldn't do without him. To all appearances, Andrew fought for Prince John and the Sheriff, though in reality he only fought for Sir Guy. He was, in fact, Sir Guy's only real friend, the only person who knew what he was truly thinking and feeling. Someday I'll tell you the story of their friendship and how they got to Nottingham at all, but for now we're going to focus on Robin Hood's gang…"

"But if Andrew was good, why would he help Gisbourne at all, even if they had been friends?" Mari-Lu's forehead creased in bewilderment.

"He had a stricter, kinder sense of right and wrong than Sir Guy did…but he didn't know the Lord, Mari-Lu."

Mari-Lu did not find that answer satisfactory. "But still, if he was a good man, why would he help the Sheriff and Gisbourne hurt other good people? Marian didn't like the injustice and immediately tried to protect the people. Even you started helping people as soon as your parents died and you left Friar Tuck. If he was good, he wouldn't be on their side."

"All I can tell you is what I know," Aunt Lucy replied. "Andrew loved his friend and would do anything for him. Sir Guy loved Marian, and went so far outside of his normal behavior that he saved those children from being executed even after Marian had spurned his proposal, and yet Sir Guy was not a good man. He sometimes did good things because he loved Marian, and Andrew sometimes did bad things because of his friendship with Sir Guy."

"Oh."

"I know it's complicated, Mari-Lu, but people generally are. None of us are wholly one thing or another."

Mari-Lu still seemed bothered by the idea that Sir Guy of Gisbourne could have a friend who was a good man, so Aunt Lucy decided it was time to steer the conversation back to the story at hand.

"Marian spent every morning with her father. She wanted to revive his hope, but she could never tell him of the raids of the gang or the feats of the Hooded Rescuer or the people Robin saved because Andrew was always with her. So she had nothing but the Sheriff's complaints about these events to offer him, and he did not find it enough to hope for..."

«→»

"You're a dreamer, Marian, but sooner or later you have to face reality," Sir Godfrey told his daughter. Without the ability to tell him how much good the gang was doing, Marian could not convince Sir Godfrey that there was any hope of a positive outcome for any of them.

Near the end of Marian's second week in Nottingham, Robin brought her a surprise.

"Mark and Dusty have worked together to make this for you." Robin held up an outfit—trousers and a shirt, along with a cape and mask that looked remarkably familiar.

"Why, that looks just like..."

"The disguise you made for Mark. It's one for you, so you'll match."

"I don't understand."

"Mark figured you would be getting antsy holed up in the castle, so he came up with a plan. You can slip out at night through the secret passages and be the Hooded Rescuer alongside him and then return in the morning to be Marian. Your guard doesn't bother to check your room at night. I've been keeping an eye on him. He stays outside your door, to be sure, but he doesn't come in, so this will work perfectly."

"I have gotten tired of this castle. Now I'll be able to see you all as well, every night if I wish to. And I will be glad to be of use to the people again. This was Mark's idea?"

"Yes."

"Thank him for me."

"If you come to the camp a few nights this week I can train you."

"I know how to fight."

"I know. I've seen you practice, I know you and Mark trained together, and Will helped you, too. But since I've returned I've been teaching Mark and he's improved immensely. I think I can help you too."

"You don't think I'm good enough."

"Marian, I love you, and if anything happened to you I'd never forgive myself. I want you to be the best you can be so that you have a greater chance of survival in this violent world."

"Okay, okay. Don't get so worked up. I'll come tomorrow night. You're not wrong; I'm not great with a sword. I'm better with a bow, but it's still not impressive—certainly nothing like you."

"We'll change that." Robin said.

And so the Hooded Rescuer began to appear as though he was everywhere at once—given that there were now two of him

—on top of the rest of Robin Hood's gang foiling every plan of the Sheriff, and the Sheriff grew increasingly frustrated.

← →

"The Sheriff and Sir Guy busied themselves with plans to trap the Hooded Rescuer and Robin Hood."

"What did they do?" Mari-Lu asked breathlessly.

"They sent treasure deliberately through Sherwood with trained assassins to guard it, but still Robin Hood eluded them. They sent spies and mercenaries into the forest to root out the location of Robin Hood's hideout, but eventually they gave up sending spies because they never came back."

Mari-Lu giggled.

"As the time of Nottingham's Fair drew near once more, Marian grew pensive. A year ago she had been wondering how deep Gisbourne's love was, how far he would go for her. Now she was locked in a castle, except for her excursions as the Hooded Rescuer. She was surrounded by evil men and traitorous plots and a despairing father. How had it come to this? It was at this time Sir Godfrey became seriously ill again…"

← →

Marian sat on the stone floor of the dungeons just outside her father's cell, watching him sleep. He was restless, periodically rolling from one side to the other on his little straw mattress, sighing or groaning every few minutes. His brow was coated in sweat and he was as pale as the moon. Marian longed to put a cool cloth to his head and comfort him, but the cell remained locked as always and she had to watch from a distance as her father suffered.

"My lady," Andrew said softly from where he sat a few feet away, "would you like to speak to Guy about bringing the physician back?"

Marian tensed, unwilling to acknowledge Andrew's question. His very presence was a repulsive reminder of his master. How dare he speak that monster's name to her!

Sir Godfrey was never fully awake or coherent while Marian sat outside his cell, so she eventually returned to her room —ignoring her faithful shadow who followed behind.

Once she'd shut Andrew out in the hall, Marian moved to the window that overlooked the castle courtyard. She could see just behind the wall to the rooftops of some of the shops and homes of Nottingham. Somewhere out there her brother and Robin were saving England, but inside these walls her father was dying.

What good was all their work when her own father was dying? How could any of them claim to be heroes when they couldn't save the person she loved the most?

Marian knew that wasn't fair; the people of Nottingham and the rest of England deserved to be helped and saved despite her father's illness, but at the moment she didn't care. Her heart squeezed in her chest as tears pricked her eyes.

He was going to die.

Marian sat down on her bed and let the grief overwhelm her, sobbing her woes into her hands. Some part of her felt that it was her fault; he had been recovering until she'd angered

Gisbourne and he'd taken away the physician as a result after he'd burned her home.

Marian felt a hand on her shoulder and turned to find her brother watching her.

"Mark!"

"What has happened? What is wrong?"

"Father is worse. There's nothing I can do for him."

"Has a physician seen him yet?"

"No. I can't ask Gisbourne for that, we're barely civil as it is. He wouldn't help me."

"You have to try, Marian."

"I have no desire to owe Gisbourne anything; he wouldn't help anyway."

"Marian! Do you have some other plan to save our father from his illness? Or will you let him die because you're too prideful to talk to the man who could, in fact, help him?"

"It's not just my pride, he—"

"I know what Gisbourne is, but you have to talk to him, Marian. It's our father! You have to try."

Marian sighed. Mark was right, of course, as much as she didn't want to go anywhere near Gisbourne. Andrew had suggested the same thing and he knew Gisbourne better than anyone it seemed, so it was possible Gisbourne would agree to her request.

That night, Marian took a minute to arrange her hair and attempt to look more put together than she generally did since coming to the castle. If her only hope was what little emotion Gisbourne might feel for her, she was going to do her best to make him remember it.

When she was ready, she took several deep breaths, and then exited her room. Andrew was there, as always, politely waiting to follow her. She wondered briefly if she attempted to run away or fight him if he would actually be able to stop her. Marian had never seen him fight, though as Gisbourne's right hand it was likely he was proficient. He certainly always carried a sword at his waist. But his polite and gentle manner made her question his ability to use it.

Marian slipped through the castle with her shadow, heading for Gisbourne's apartments. When she reached them, she hesitated. What was she doing? She hated this man, and he hated her.

"He'll help," Andrew said softly from behind her. Marian glanced toward him for a moment, and then back at the door she was reluctant to knock on. Yet her father was dying, and this might be his only hope so Marian steeled herself against whatever might come and reached up to knock firmly on Gisbourne's door.

"Come in!" came a gruff shout.

Marian opened the door and took a step inside. Gisbourne was standing at his window, a map in his hand. The light from the fire in his hearth flickered and danced around the walls.

Gisbourne turned and his face mirrored his surprise at finding Marian in his room, but he quickly recovered. Throwing the map down on a nearby table, he crossed his arms. "What do you want?"

"I need to talk to you."

Gisbourne remained silent. Marian glanced over her shoulder to see Andrew waiting in the hallway. He gave her an encouraging nod, which only made Marian feel sick to the stomach. She turned back to the man who had burned down her home, the man who'd almost hung her father once before…

The man who had declared he would do anything for her, said that he loved her, and helped her father the last time he was ill.

He was as unpredictable and changeable as the Sheriff's moods, Marian realized, and she could only hope she might appeal to the better half of him.

"Please, Sir Guy. Can we not talk? We haven't had a single conversation since you burned…since I came here that hasn't ended in an argument."

Still he did not speak.

Marian walked further into the room so that the light from his fire could illuminate her more fully, moving closer until she was a few feet in front of him. "Please."

"What do you want from me?"

"I'm offering you my friendship."

Gisbourne raised a skeptical eyebrow. "I don't believe you. What are you trying to get from me?"

She couldn't tell him, not like this. She wasn't going to grovel to Gisbourne!

"Nothing. Is it so hard to believe I desire to be friends instead of always yelling at each other or refusing to speak to one another?"

Gisbourne was still skeptical. "So you're offering…"

"Friendship. Can we at least try and be civil to one another?"

Marian offered him her hand, and to her relief he slowly reached out and took it. Now she had to get around to the point, after she'd just told him she didn't want anything from him.

"Friends then?" Marian asked.

Gisbourne studied her for a moment, and then said "Alright, Marian. I'll take your offered friendship. Now tell me what this is really about, though I could guess."

"What do you mean?"

"You want me to help your father." Gisbourne dropped Marian's hand and turned to the window. "That's why you're here, isn't it? Very well. I'll send for the physician."

"Just like that?"

"Would you prefer I changed my mind?"

"No. I…thank you, Sir Guy."

He continued to stare out his window without paying her any attention, so she turned and left his room, returning to her own with Andrew following behind.

"You knew he would help me," Marian said, turning to look at him for a moment.

"Yes," Andrew replied simply, confidently.

"How could you have known? He's so unpredictable and volatile. I never know what he's going to do next."

Andrew sighed. "He's a mess, that's true. But he does care about you; I trusted that love would overcome his anger and pain eventually."

Marian scoffed at that. Gisbourne didn't know the meaning of the word love, let alone feel it for her or for anyone.

When she returned to her room Mark was waiting for her. "Well?"

"He's sending for the physician."

"That wasn't so hard, was it?" Mark kissed her cheek. "I have to go. Will you be coming out as the Hooded Rescuer tonight?"

"Of course. Give me a few hours, so I can be sure the castle is sleeping and no one will come knocking on my door. I'll meet you out there."

"Good. Robin's sending Will and Dusty on another trip to the south, and Little John's gone off eastward for a few days. There are not enough of us to cover all of England's needs. You being able to help look after Nottingham in everyone else's absence is appreciated."

Chapter 11

LUCY HELD SEVERAL arrows lightly between her fingers, dipping them into the water of the stream bubbling through the woods. Her stomach twisted inside her as she watched the blood from the tips of her arrows stain the stream a crimson red. It wasn't long, however, before the blood was floating away downstream.

Lucy was in Sherwood Forest, cleaning the arrows she'd retrieved from the arms and legs of various soldiers she'd wounded that day as she'd moved about the countryside, trying to protect farmers and villagers who were being beaten and whose food was being stolen. She'd helped a few people, always keeping her hood up. So close to Nottingham, they all seemed to expect the sort of rescue she had provided and Lucy let them believe she was part of Robin Hood's famous gang.

She wasn't, of course. She was alone in the world.

Lucy had seen Lady Marian in Nottingham on her first day, but then Gisbourne had arrested her and burned her home down. After that, Lucy had only spoken with the innkeeper with whom she'd found lodgings, and with little old Tibb, who seemed to be everywhere and know everything. She would latch herself onto Lucy whenever she wandered Nottingham, seeming determined to be her friend whether Lucy liked it or not.

Lucy shook the excess water off her arrows and set them beside her on a large smooth rock she'd pulled over, laying them out across the rock and letting the sun dry them. Grabbing another handful of bloody arrows, she dipped these in the stream as well, turning away slightly so she didn't have to see the crimson stain this time.

Lucy spent her days living in Nottingham much as she had everywhere else since leaving Friar Tuck's care. She wandered, and she helped people if she could.

Living so close to the gang who were doing precisely the same, Lucy felt a longing to join them. She didn't know where their camp was, however, and she was reluctant to approach them when they were in Nottingham.

The group was not shy about wandering Nottingham, though they would undoubtedly hide from the Sheriff's men. Lucy could recognize Robin on sight, as he was the most frequent visitor, though she'd caught glimpses of Will and Little John in Nottingham, too—the latter being the most recognizable among the gang.

She'd seen Robin on more than one occasion passing food to those who couldn't afford it, or taking Dusty to visit the sick. Being the only Palestinian woman in Nottingham, Dusty was unmistakable with her deeply tanned skin and her short dark hair.

Lucy was sorely tempted to speak to Dusty. The only women her age she'd ever known were those of the court in London, and very few of them were interested in more than gowns and gossip. The fact that she was a healer drew Lucy to her, for Lucy had learned much of that nature of work from Friar Tuck. It reminded her of home, and of the only person left in the world who knew and loved her.

But Lucy didn't approach Dusty, or any of the rest of them. She longed for connection, but she was terrified that once she found it she would lose it. Her parents had been minding their own business and they'd been killed by Prince John. The gang were always putting themselves into harm's way to help the people of England and eventually someone was going to get hurt. Lucy got as close to them as she could to satisfy her desire for friendship without actually putting her heart in danger. If she didn't know them, it wouldn't kill her when they died like her own mother had died from grief.

Lucy set aside the arrows she'd washed, and arranged them on the smooth rock beside the others. Her work was fulfilling, even if she was lonely.

Satisfied that her arrows were ready for the next time she needed them, Lucy pulled out Friar Tuck's worn little book and began to read the familiar words, relishing the dear handwriting she knew so well, and trying to hear the sound of his voice as if he was reading the Scripture to her as he so often had read to her and her parents in her youth.

«→»

"Why didn't you just talk to the gang?" Mari-Lu asked. "They all seem nice; they would have liked you."

"Undoubtedly," Aunt Lucy agreed. "And they would have been glad of the help, considering how much work there was to be done by so few people."

"So why didn't you?"

"I explained that," Aunt Lucy chuckled. "I was afraid to get too close to them, to care about them too much. So I got to know them from a safe distance."

"Without getting to know them at all," Mari-Lu said. "That's sad."

"It was," Aunt Lucy agreed. "But it was all I could manage then. I had never recovered from my father's murder and my mother succumbing to her grief. I pushed the emotions away so I could focus on helping people who were in need, but it was always there, dictating my actions. In this case, the grief led to fear that I would lose anyone else I cared about so I chose to keep myself isolated and not care, if I could help it."

Mari-Lu reached up to wrap her small arms around Aunt Lucy's neck, hugging her tightly. "I'm sorry you felt that way."

Aunt Lucy returned the hug, and then returned to her story. "While I was busy contemplating my loneliness and thinking about Friar Tuck, Marian was perched on the ramparts of the wall that surrounded the castle and courtyard, looking down over the city…"

«→»

Several of the Sheriff's soldiers were making their rounds along the wall, and they all glanced up at her sitting on the ledge above them as they passed by, but no one said anything or approached her. Andrew was sitting across from her, but he didn't speak and Marian was grateful for that. She was growing accustomed to his presence, but she was by no means interested in being his friend.

Gisbourne had gone out with several soldiers to meet the caravan of taxes that was meant to arrive that day, hoping to ensure that it did, in fact, arrive. Marian had come to the castle wall above the courtyard to wait for his return to see if he was successful.

Down in the streets of Nottingham people were going about their business; Marian saw the blacksmith Marcus walking down a street with his wife Lillian, before they disappeared behind the corner of a house and beyond her sight. Old lady Tibb was passing by, and looked up to wave and smile her nearly toothless smile at Marian. Marian grinned and waved back.

Then Gisbourne came into view, riding his black stallion Victory. He had a struggling man draped across his saddle as he galloped down the street. The soldiers on the wall near Marian shouted for the gate to be opened, and the soldiers in the courtyard below swung it wide just in time for Victory to gallop through it.

Gisbourne pulled his horse to a sudden stop, and Marian watched as the Sheriff's soldiers rushed forward to help him with the man Gisbourne was wrangling. As Gisbourne roughly handed him down off the horse into the waiting arms of the Sheriff's men, Marian could finally see his face and realized with a start that it was Allen!

Had the gang managed to get the treasure, or had their raid been a bust? If Allen was a prisoner, were the rest of them caught as well? Marian looked toward Nottingham, but no one else was coming down the street. She looked back into the courtyard and watched the Sheriff's men bind and gag Allen and drag him after Gisbourne as they all entered the castle.

Were the rest of the gang even alive?

Her heart pounding loud in her ears, Marian jumped down off the ramparts to the stone wall below, and hurried along the pathway to the tower at the corner that contained stairs down to the courtyard. Andrew hurried along behind her.

She made her way toward the Great Hall, grateful to find the door partially open. She stood outside, listening to the Sheriff and Gisbourne discuss their prisoner.

"Has it not always frustrated you that Robin Hood knows your every move? We now have Robin's right hand in our grasp. If we can get him to talk…"

"And how do you plan to do that?" the Sheriff asked sarcastically.

"Will you allow me to try?"

"How do you even know this outlaw is so well connected with Robin Hood?"

"Apart from the fact that I dragged him away from Robin Hood's ambush, I know him to be Allen of the Dale, a man who returned from the Crusades at Robin of Locksley's side and who disappeared much as Robin himself did when the outlaws first began their strikes against your caravans. Next to Robin's servant Much, who we believe is also one of the outlaws, Allen must be the closest friend that Robin has. If that is true, he would trust him with all of his secrets."

"It would be wiser not to trust anyone with your secrets," the Sheriff said.

"Indeed. But none of us can truly avoid having that one person that we confide in, I think."

"Who's yours? I'd like to know your secrets."

"That is not the point, sir."

"What is your point?"

"Allen could be useful to us. Will you allow me to try and glean information from him before you kill him?"

"Yes. And if it doesn't work, I'll kill you both!"

The conversation appeared to be over, and Marian hurried away before Gisbourne could exit the Great Hall and find her snooping. Andrew was still dutifully following along and would probably inform Gisbourne later that she'd been spying on him, but that couldn't be helped.

Marian ran to her room, shutting the door on Andrew before hurrying into the secret passage behind the tapestry on her wall. It was dark in the passage, given that there was no light within, and it was cooler than the rest of the castle—being encased in stone and with no fire to bring warmth to the darkness.

Marian put her hand along the cold wall and moved along the path with sure feet. She'd traveled this darkness more times than she could count, ever since she was a child. She knew every crack in the wall that indicated a door to a room, she knew where every twist and turn of the narrow hallways were, knew precisely when the passages would slope up or down to other floors of the castle, or even transform into stairs. The first time she'd found stairs as a child she'd fallen down them and Mark hadn't stopped laughing by the time they'd left the secret passages and gone to Sir Godfrey to patch her bleeding knee.

Marian hurried along the passages until she came to one of the exits, this one at the back of the castle, leading to the open grassy hill behind Nottingham. She slipped out, and crept along the wall of the castle until she was beyond it. The wall surrounding the city of Nottingham blocked anyone's view of her, as long as she stayed close to the wall until she was far enough away from the castle to not be seen from it's higher vantage point.

Once she felt free enough, she took off running for Sherwood and the camp.

When Marian burst into camp, she was relieved to find Robin and the others there, apparently unscathed.

"Marian!" Robin ran forward and Marian threw herself into his arms.

"I didn't know if you were alive!"

"I'm fine, we're all fine, except Allen."

"I know." Marian pulled back. "He's been captured. Gisbourne plans to torture him for information on the camp, I believe, so you have to get him out of the dungeons."

"Is that where he's being kept?"

"I didn't stay to find out, I needed to know if you were okay and let you know about Allen."

"You need to get back to the castle before you are missed," Robin said. "I don't want you getting into any more trouble. Mark says Gisbourne is softening again, and as long as you can use that to help your father, you should. I'll come by your room tonight when we are ready to rescue Allen and you can give us more information about where he's being held, if you have it."

"Then I'll see you tonight."

"Be safe getting back inside, Marian."

"I will."

That night Robin, Will, Much, Mark, and Little John successfully rescued Allen from the dungeons. They easily slipped into the dungeons through the hidden passage that opened onto that level of the castle, and one arrow from Robin killed the guard at the door before he even knew they were there. After that it was merely a matter of taking the keys from the guard's corpse and letting Allen out. He'd been in a cell beside Sir Godfrey, and Mark tried his best to convince his father to come with them to Sherwood forest and get away from the Sheriff and Gisbourne,

136

but Sir Godfrey refused to leave with them, much to Mark's dismay.

❮❯

"Why wouldn't he go?" Mari-Lu asked. "Is it because he wouldn't have a physician to see him the way Gisbourne's physician did?"

"If he'd gone to the camp, he would have had Dusty," Aunt Lucy replied. "No one has ever been a greater healer than Dusty. But Sir Godfrey didn't want to live as a fugitive in the forest. He was learning to hope, now that Allen had told him all the things about Robin Hood and the exploits of the gang that Marian had longed to share but been unable to because of Andrew's constant presence, but even learning to hope wasn't enough for him to want to live on the run."

"What happened next?"

"Marian noticed the change in her father after Allen's visit to the prison. He never spoke of it directly, likely because Andrew was always present with Marian, but the sparkle was back in his eye. Slowly, his hope was being reborn. Marian wanted to speak with Allen to figure out what he'd said that night he was in the dungeons, what he'd told her father that had finally gotten through to him."

"I'm glad he's not in despair anymore!" Mari-Lu said.

"So was Marian," Aunt Lucy replied. "But despite his rising hope, Sir Godfrey's health continued to decline. Gisbourne sent for the physician every few days, but still he faded.

"Oh no!"

"And another alarming change in the castle was the Sheriff discovering the hidden hallways. After finding the first one, he had the entire castle inspected. He closed up the passages and stationed guards at the entrances into Nottingham. Gisbourne was incredibly suspicious of the passage they found in Marian's room, but she maintained her innocence, and Andrew insisted he would have known if Marian was disappearing from her room so Gisbourne dropped the subject. Marian's way of exchanging news with Robin was gone and she could no longer sneak out as the Hooded Rescuer. Robin, being Robin, still found ways to slip past guards and visit Marian, but his visits were infrequent..."

«–»

Marian's door crept open one night, and she bolted upright in bed, reaching for her jeweled dagger which Mark had brought her weeks ago, after her home burned. She kept it under her pillow always, in case the Sheriff or Gisbourne got into a killing mood and decided to end her in her sleep. Now, as she watched her door slowly sliding open, she gripped the dagger tight in her hand.

She expected Andrew, Gisbourne, or the Sheriff perhaps, but instead Robin came slinking into the room, closing the door ever so gently behind him.

"Robin, how did you get in again?"

"The guards are foolish and ignorant creatures, and I know the castle better than anyone."

"And Andrew?"

"Is sleeping," Robin responded, tiptoeing across the room and coming to sit on the bed beside Marian. "I had to step over him; that was rather nerve wracking, but he seems a harmless enough fellow. I don't know why Gisbourne thinks highly of him, or why he thinks highly of Gisbourne. They are so different."

"Robin."

"What?"

"Focus, please. Why are you here, risking your neck? Is something wrong?"

"I'm trying to determine how the Sheriff discovered the secrets of the castle."

"He finally decided to look for them? You know that we found them as children. Surely if we could find them at such a young age, the grown Sheriff can be allowed to discover them on his own."

"Possibly. But I don't think that well of our dear Sheriff."

"Then what do you think?"

"I don't know," Robin sighed heavily, looking around the room as though looking for answers.

"Do you think he was informed?"

"I hope not."

"Robin, no one in your gang would betray you! How could you think that?"

"I don't know, Marian. I don't think that. I just don't understand…I'm just stressed."

"You've been living in the forest too long, you don't trust anyone anymore."

"You're one to talk," Robin snapped, and then shook his head. "I'm sorry. But it is suspicious, isn't it, that he just now finds them after all these years? I'm sorry, Marian, but something feels off."

"No, you're right," Marian replied, her heart sinking. "Something does seem off about the whole business. I hate the idea that one of the gang could be feeding information to the Sheriff, but if it's true I want to know who it is so we can get rid of them."

"Given everything we've all been through together...I'm not entirely sure I want to know who it is. Obviously I want to track the traitor down so we can be safe from whoever it is spilling our secrets to the Sheriff, but...Much is my oldest and dearest friend, if it's him I'd die. And Allen and Dusty and I are family—we faced so many dangers together while fighting for the King, relied on each other to save each other's lives on more than one occasion, and no one ever failed to step up in that regard. I love them, and I know they love me. If either of them are responsible..."

"I don't like the prospects either, Robin. But people..." Marian thought about her own struggle to fully trust Robin after he'd abandoned her for three years to follow the King on the Crusades, "people are almost always disappointing."

"No," Robin said quickly, taking Marian's hand and squeezing it. "Don't let this be another reason you can't trust anyone fully. I could be paranoid, Marian. Perhaps it's nothing."

Chapter 12

"WAS ROBIN RIGHT?" Mari-Lu asked, her eyes wide with worry. "Did someone tell the Sheriff? Who would betray them? Marian wouldn't. Mark wouldn't." Mari-Lu starting ticking the names off her fingers. "Much seems to do anything Robin says. Dusty seems to have strong opinions about what's right and wrong, she definitely wouldn't. Allen is Robin's brother from the war. Will is too good. Little John is Marian's friend. Who would betray the group?"

Aunt Lucy shook her head, unwilling to answer. "Robin didn't know, but he felt uneasy. Marian wished she could believe that everyone within the gang could be trusted and the Sheriff must have found the secret passages of his own accord, but if she was honest with herself she knew that it felt inevitable that someone would betray them. And then the unthinkable happened. Robin and his gang were going to waylay a caravan carrying the King's ransom. It was as well planned and thought out as Robin's raids always were…"

"What happened?"

"They were expected. The enemy was ready for them," Aunt Lucy replied. "All caravans and travelers not friendly to Robin and his crew went through Sherwood with a wary eye, ever watchful for the outlaws, but this caravan knew exactly where Robin's ambush was. The soldiers surrounding the caravan went straight for the gang's hiding places before Robin and the others had gotten their first arrows shot."

"But how did they know?"

"There was only one answer," Aunt Lucy said. "They had been informed."

"But by who?" Mari-Lu asked. "No one would betray them!"

"Robin didn't know. No one did. Relationships within the camp became strained. No one knew who the traitor was, so their trust in one another began to rust. Those that were innocent were offended and hurt that they were suspected of being the traitor. Yet they all tried to believe in one another and found it hard to imagine any of their companions as the culprit. It was too painful a thought to entertain, and yet it festered and simmered just below the surface."

"Oh no," Mari-Lu groaned. "What did Marian think?"

"When Robin informed Marian she was devastated, and yet, like Robin, she could not immediately point to any one of the gang to be the traitor. In true Marian form, she was outspoken whenever around them, voicing her displeasure at the traitor in their midst. And inwardly she held to her conviction that trusting people was not a wise option. For his part, Robin began to study his companions' every action, every word, scrutinizing everything to find out who was leaking information to the Sheriff. After two more failed ambushes, during one of which Little John received a serious wound, Robin had had enough. He came to Marian…"

❮❯

As Robin slipped into Marian's room, skirting around the sleeping Andrew, Marian hurried to him. He shut the door softly just as she reached him, grabbing his arm and whispering, "Tell

142

me Little John is alive! The soldiers who returned were boasting of killing him in the fight today."

"Little John will be alright, Dusty is seeing to him now, and she said she's healed worse. But we can't keep going like this! You have eyes and ears here among our enemies. If they are being informed they have to talk to someone. Surely they must meet up with him somewhere."

"Him?"

"I don't believe you or Dusty would do this."

"You don't believe any of the others would either."

"I don't want to believe it, but someone is feeding the Sheriff information and I need to know who it is."

"I'll try and find out, but I haven't heard the Sheriff or Gisbourne talking about a spy in your camp."

"Just keep digging, Marian. We need to root out the traitor before someone gets killed. And before the rest of the gang breaks apart because we don't trust each other anymore. The friendships of the last few years are cracking, and I can't fix it. I don't know what to do."

Marian began to spend more time stalking Gisbourne when he was in the castle. She started by keeping her distance and simply watching him, but Gisbourne noticed her and when he wasn't cold in his reception of her Marian grew confident enough to be in his company. She hated it; she hated him. But it appeared he was, indeed, softening to her again and as Mark had told her on more than one occasion, she could use that to her advantage. So whenever she could, Marian would latch onto Gisbourne's arm and chatter about nonsense as he went about his business. She didn't find anything during this charade, but she kept it up regardless.

A week after Robin had asked her to find evidence of the traitor, Marian overheard the Sheriff ask Gisbourne if they had an update on Robin. She'd been headed to the Great Hall to flirt with Gisbourne again in the hopes of him letting something slip, but this was better. Marian stopped outside the room and listened. Andrew was just behind her, but as of yet he seemed to keep her spying exploits to himself despite being proclaimed to be Gisbourne's most trusted friend.

"I'm leaving to meet my spy now," Gisbourne said.

Marian heard his boots clacking against the stone floor as he strode toward the door, so she hurriedly backed up to give the appearance she'd only just arrived as he came out of the Great Hall.

"Guy!"

"Marian?"

"Where are you going?" Marian put on her sweetest smile, moving forward to slip her arm through his.

"Out."

"May I come?"

"You're under house arrest," Gisbourne said as he began walking away from the Great Hall and toward the large oak doors that opened into the castle courtyard. "You can't leave the castle."

"Please?"

"I have important things to take care of, Marian."

"That sounds interesting," Marian smiled brightly.

Gisbourne stopped, turning toward Marian, his eyes brightening with the sort of familiar twinkle they might have held before she rejected him and he burned her home. "You can't come. It's personal business."

144

"Even more interesting," Marian said in a conspiratorial whisper, leaning in close as well.

Gisbourne frowned. "What are you up to?"

"I'm doing my best to sweet-talk you so I can spend a few hours without being followed everywhere," Marian glanced over her shoulder to give a meaningful look toward Andrew.

Gisbourne motioned to him, and Andrew moved forward. "I need you to accompany me."

Marian grinned.

Gisbourne raised a warning finger. "Stay in the castle." He turned swiftly and left with Andrew through the doors to the courtyard.

Marian nearly clapped in triumph. She peeked out the doors to watch as Gisbourne and Andrew crossed the courtyard and went through the open gate to the city of Nottingham. There were soldiers everywhere of course; those walking the ramparts on the wall above, those manning the gate below. Marian shut the door to the courtyard and made her way through the halls of the castle to another door into Nottingham she knew well; this one smaller and much less used. There was no grand courtyard or large gate; it opened from the ground floor to the street, and there was no guard attending it. Robin was right; it was rather easy to slip in and out of the castle unseen.

Marian left the castle behind and made her way to Marcus' home. She informed the blacksmith and his wife that she was onto the traitor and to tell Robin as soon as they could. Then she set out to follow Gisbourne.

She wasn't sure where he would go, so she headed for the market. Once there, she scanned the people milling about for a familiar hunched back. When she caught sight of Tibb, she hurried forward.

"Tibb!"

"Lady Marian?" Tibb grinned her toothless smile. "Out of the castle, I see."

"No, you don't see. I was never here."

Tibb chuckled and nodded.

"Have you seen Lord Gisbourne?"

"Of course. He's on his way out of town now, or so it seemed."

"Toward which gate?"

"South, Lady Marian."

"Thank you!"

Marian hurried toward the broad street that would lead her to the southern gate of the city, the very road that stretched from Nottingham to Sherwood Forest.

It took a while to find him, but eventually she caught sight of his dark hair and saw Andrew dutifully following along behind him. She kept at a discreet distance, ducking behind the corners of houses whenever the two men chanced to glance in her direction, until Gisbourne and Andrew entered a tavern near the edge of the city.

She crept up to the side of the tavern and stood by the window, not close enough to see inside–or for someone to see out and notice her–but close enough to hear what was being said inside.

Marian could hear Gisbourne speaking. "He isn't here?"

"No, sir," a man, probably the tavern keeper, replied.

Marian furtively glanced in the window. Gisbourne, Andrew and the tavern keeper were alone in the main room. The tables were empty, and no one was sitting at the bar.

"He did give me this pouch of money to give you as his pledge he's still on your side." The tavern keeper held out his hand, in which rested a small brown bag.

Gisbourne took the money and frowned. "I'll be back next week. He'd better be here."

Gisbourne and Andrew emerged from the tavern. Marian held her breath as Gisbourne sent Andrew back to the castle and walked the opposite way. He hadn't glanced her way, and she breathed easy.

Marian followed him through the streets of Nottingham, hoping to sneak back into the castle without him noticing her absence. It was likely Andrew would notice when he arrived at the castle, but it was a large building and she could argue she'd been in a different part of the castle and he'd simply missed her in his search. There was also the undeniable fact that the polite soldier had yet to inform Gisbourne she'd openly spied on him multiple times.

Suddenly she heard her name urgently whispered.

She turned and saw Robin leaning against the wall of a nearby building, his hood shadowing his face. "Robin!"

"What did you learn?"

Marian stepped off the street and moved to stand beside him. "Nothing. I followed Gisbourne to the tavern. It's where he meets his informant. But he wasn't there. The tavern keeper gave Gisbourne a pouch of money the informant left as a pledge he was still on Gisbourne's side. They mentioned no names. Only a 'he'."

Robin sighed. His face was contorted in anguish and his voice portrayed his pain. "Who would betray me, Marian?"

"I don't know. I'll keep watch. You should keep an eye on the tavern. When we find out which of your friends is feeding the Sheriff information, I'm going to kill them."

"Not before I do."

Seeing Gisbourne cross the street above them they quickly parted. Marian started for the castle.

As she slipped into a cross street she heard Gisbourne's voice behind her. "What are you doing, Marian?" Turning around, Marian saw Gisbourne was leaning against a wall much as Robin had been, his arms crossed. "I told you to stay in the castle."

Marian plastered a smile on her face and skipped over to him cheerfully. "I was out for a walk. The walls of that castle can get very boring."

"You were following me. No, don't try to deny it. I saw you near the tavern and now here. Now I ask again, what are you doing?"

Marian sighed and then smiled sweetly. "Yes, I was following you…I want to spend more time with you, Guy."

Gisbourne frowned. "How very sweet of you." He offered his arm to Marian. "But you are under house arrest and I told you I had private business."

"I believe the word you used was personal."

"Marian."

"Okay, okay. I'll behave."

Gisbourne led her back to the castle, giving her a stern look before going to meet the Sheriff. Marian did not, in fact, behave. She followed Gisbourne and waited outside the room where he spoke to the Sheriff about the informant not showing up.

148

They did not, however, name any names, and so Marian learned nothing of use.

Chapter 13

LUCY ROSE EARLY before the sun, slipping out of her room in the tavern where she was staying near the edge of Nottingham, and quietly moving down the stairs and to the kitchen where the cooks were already up and preparing food for the day. They greeted her cheerfully and let her have a bit of food for the day—she chatted with them amiably and filled her pack with their simple but mouthwatering loaves of bread and the fresh cheese they carved off the block for her. Once her pack was full she slipped out into the mostly empty streets of Nottingham in the grey light of dawn.

Lucy spent much of her time in the city getting to know the people around her, though trying to keep her identity a secret as much as she could. Old Tibb was her most constant companion, giving her a tour of Nottingham and telling her which people to avoid, as they were not as loyal to Robin Hood and the other outlaws and would be more likely to betray someone to the Sheriff for a bit of gold or food.

Lucy would spend her days talking with Tibb, and keeping an eye on the surrounding villages. She'd come across more than one soldier beating an innocent for some pretense or another, and had quietly intervened. She kept her hood up to hide her face, and always used her arrows from a distance if she could manage it—though she never shot to kill. The thought sickened her, and she avoided it if at all possible.

On this particular morning, Lucy entered the market in Nottingham Square and settled herself along one corner of the open space where she could watch the crowds comfortably. As the sun slowly rose and the crisp grey air of dawn settled over the city, the streets began to see more movement and the shopkeepers and booth owners began to open up and set out their wares for the day.

Gisbourne came striding through the market, causing more than one person to pause in their work to watch him pass by.

Whatever business he was on so early in the morning could not be good. Lucy stood and began to follow along behind him as surreptitiously as she could. The pack over one shoulder and bow over the other made her rather conspicuous, but she kept herself a good distance behind him.

Since arriving in Nottingham she'd seen him save children from an execution, burn Lady Marian's home to the ground, and then go marching around the city on his business with a sour expression. She hadn't seen any more acts of blatant cruelty after the burning in the village of Wetherby, or acts of compassion such as rescuing the children either. He was simply brooding as he went about whatever his business might have been.

He seemed much as Tibb had suggested—a hurting, broken soul. Lucy wondered what could have happened to him to make him into the man that he was, but she wasn't likely to find out. In any event, she didn't trust him not to do something as drastic as burn another person's home to the ground, so she followed him to keep an eye on him and make sure no one else crossed his path in such an unfortunate way.

His saving of the children and then burning of Lady Marian's home left Lucy with the impression that he was equally as unstable as the Sheriff, who arrested, killed, and even released prisoners on a whim and fancy with no apparent rhyme or reason.

Gisbourne made his way to the very tavern where Lucy was living. After watching him go inside, Lucy stood at the door hesitantly. Should she follow and give herself away?

Lucy pushed open the door and glanced inside. No one was in the main room, so she darted up the stairs to drop her sack full of food along with her bow and quiver on her bed before creeping back downstairs and seating herself at the bar. One of the cooks came out to ask if she needed anything, and Lucy motioned her closer so she could speak quietly.

"Did I see Lord Gisbourne come in here?"

The cook glanced around, her eyes wide, "He is here, my lady, but I wouldn't go looking for him. He's dangerous."

"I know."

"He's in the storage room back there," the cook waved her hand in the direction of a hallway, keeping her voice at a whisper. "He meets with a man sometimes, one who keeps his hood up and identity hidden. Not sure what they're up to, but it can't be anything good."

Lucy stood up, intending to spy on Lord Gisbourne and this mysterious man, but another traveler entered the tavern, drawing the cook's attention, and before Lucy could go anywhere Lord Gisbourne came striding out of the back room, his face grim as he brushed past Lucy and the other traveler and left the tavern.

Lucy waited to see the mysterious man Gisbourne supposedly met with, but no one came after him. She got up and went to investigate, finding the storage room empty except for the barrels of ale, and shelves full of food.

With nothing more to see, Lucy returned to her room to procure her weapons and her food and went back to Nottingham Square to keep an eye on things.

"Was it the traitor?" Mari-Lu clapped her hands. "You were so close! Who was it?"

"I can't just tell you," Aunt Lucy laughed. "We're not there yet."

"Oh, how much longer?" Mari-Lu groaned. "Robin is getting anxious, and Marian's not happy, and Little John almost died, and–"

"Patience, Mari-Lu," Aunt Lucy grinned at the young girl. "You will know soon enough. For it was only a week later that the Sheriff and Gisbourne were discussing the spy over dinner. The Sheriff still insisted Marian join them for meals, though the conversations were not nearly as lively and entertaining for him now that Marian and Gisbourne were on relatively good terms instead of constantly bickering…"

❮❯

"Do you know, I am feeling rather nostalgic for the old days," the Sheriff said, taking a sip of his wine.

"How so?" Marian asked.

"You used to snap at Gisbourne, and he would respond with his icy manner. It was far more amusing than this…peace," the Sheriff waved a hand at the two of them. "I am bored, Lady Marian. And when I am bored, I must do something to entertain myself."

"Such as?" Gisbourne asked.

"Kill someone, probably."

Marian shook her head, "I'll entertain you in any way you wish if it will keep you from killing an innocent person."

"Oh don't go all self-righteous," the Sheriff sighed. "That's not the entertainment I desire. Anyway, it isn't as fun if you are pretending. The natural nature of your fiery debates is what I crave. Disagree on something, will you?"

Gisbourne glanced at Marian and she stared back, unsure what to say.

The Sheriff suddenly grinned. "I know. Have you visited our friend this week, Gisbourne?"

Marian tried not to show interest as Gisbourne turned to answer him.

"No," Gisbourne said. "But I plan to meet Allen today."

Marian gasped. "Allen?"

Gisbourne glanced at Marian and she tried not to look so suspicious. "What do you know of him?"

Marian shrugged, trying to regain her composure though a fire was raging in her veins. "Nothing. He's one of the outlaws isn't he?"

The Sheriff smirked. "Yes, Marian. We have a spy in Robin Hood's camp. That outlaw won't be able to do more damage without us knowing precisely what he is up to."

Marian raised her chin. "One traitor won't stop Robin Hood."

The Sheriff laughed mirthlessly. "We'll see."

Marian's heart was burning in her chest, as hot as Marcus' blacksmith brands when he'd just pulled one out of the fire. Robin had trusted Allen as a brother, and he'd betrayed him!

Gisbourne soon left for this proposed meeting with Allen, and Marian returned to her room, trying to decide what to do about it. The one time she'd left the castle to spy on Gisbourne, he'd found her out easily. If he found her wandering the streets after the mention of who the traitor was, he'd surely be suspicious.

She could try and escape the castle to go to the camp to inform Robin who was behind the betrayals, but again the chance of being caught was too high. The door she'd used before wasn't guarded, but the streets of Nottingham were patrolled by the Sheriff's men—however poorly that might have been, she wasn't sure the risk of running into the Sheriff's soldiers was worth it.

In the end, Marian stayed in her room waiting for Robin to come to her. His visits weren't as frequent as they had been when he could go through the secret passages, but somehow or other he always found a way to slip past the guards and get to her room unseen. The fact that Andrew slept across her doorway was the only hindrance, but so far Robin hadn't woken him when he'd visited, and they'd both begun to feel more confident in his ability to visit undetected despite the absence of the secret hallways.

It was two full days after Marian had learned who the traitor was before Robin made an appearance. The minute he was inside her room and the door was shut, she was at his side, pulling him away from the door so their conversation wouldn't wake Andrew.

"Robin, I know who betrayed you!"

Robin didn't hide his surprise at her proclamation, or his reluctance for her to continue. "Do I want to know?"

"No. You don't."

Robin closed his eyes briefly and sighed. "Who is it?"

"Allen."

Robin took a step backward as though he'd been shoved. "Allen? It can't be, Marian. You must be mistaken."

"Gisbourne specifically named him. It's Allen, Robin."

Robin shook his head. "That's not possible."

"Don't you trust me, Robin? Did I not say Gisbourne specifically named him? I don't have any evidence other than Gisbourne calling him by name and saying he was going to meet with him, but that's enough. It's Allen."

Robin groaned. "How could he…"

Marian reached out, unsure how to offer comfort but not wanting Robin to feel alone in this betrayal. Robin, however, jerked out of her reach and spun around, marching toward the door.

"Robin!"

But he already had the door open and was stepping over Andrew's prone form. Marian was afraid to call out to him again or attempt to follow him without waking her guard, and soon Robin was gone.

What he would do with her information, she didn't know. Kill Allen, perhaps? Waiting in the castle and hoping for news was the worst part of house arrest and Marian longed for the days when she could escape into the night and visit the camp. She wanted to be there when he confronted Allen, wanted to confront him herself. Thanks to Mark, Will, and Robin she knew more than one way to kill a man and she was more than happy to sharpen her skills on the traitor.

Mari-Lu sighed. "Poor Robin."

"Yes, poor Robin. He wasn't sure he could trust anyone for some time after that. A good friend, and one he trusted with his life and the lives of his gang, had betrayed him. He didn't know what to think. But he was angry, that much he knew."

Mari-Lu looked wide-eyed into the face of Aunt Lucy. "Angry? Like Gisbourne was with Marian, that made him burn her house?"

"Yes, Mari-Lu, exactly like that, though Robin had a less fragile ego than Gisbourne and was more mature in his emotions in many ways. And yet the bond between Allen and Robin was so much deeper than Gisbourne and Marian, and so the betrayal hurt that much worse. He and Allen had been through a great deal together during their time following King Richard on his Crusades in the Holy Land. They were brothers, or so Robin had thought. He was furious and hurt and lashed out."

"What happened?"

←→

The next day Marian was shocked when she walked into the Great Hall. The Sheriff was seated on his wooden throne and Gisbourne was standing before him, and next to Gisbourne was the traitor.

"Allen?"

Allen spun around. "Marian!"

The Sheriff stood. "Marian, my dear. Why don't I introduce you to our newest recruit? He was apparently thrown out of Robin Hood's camp."

"Literally. Little John threw me."

"So he's taken refuge with us," the Sheriff added. "Poor fellow."

Marian wanted to scream and shout and beat her fists against the chest of this horrible man. How could he have done this to Robin? To the rest of them? She turned quickly and left the room.

Chapter 14

THAT EVENING MARIAN heard a knock on her door, and then Allen's pleading voice. "Marian?"

Marian refused to answer.

"Marian, please."

Marian glared at the door. How could he?

"Marian...I'd like to explain."

"Explain?!" Marian grabbed the door and yanked it open. "Explain? You...you...just get out, Allen!"

Marian started to slam her door but Allen jumped through the rapidly closing gap. Marian caught a glimpse of Andrew watching with fascination as the door snapped shut.

"Marian, I have to tell you. Please."

Marian crossed her arms. "Nothing you say will make me hate you any less."

Allen sighed. "I know. I can't change that, but I want to explain why I did what I did."

"There isn't a good reason, Allen. You betrayed your friend, and all of us. You nearly got Little John and the rest of them killed!"

"I know," Allen sighed. "It all got so out of hand...I was so proud to fight for England, for the King. But even more so to come home and fight for Robin here. He's like a brother to me, Marian."

"Which is why you betrayed him I suppose," Marian snapped.

"Sir Guy..."

"Offered you money."

Allen frowned and shook his head. "No. I wouldn't betray Robin for such a thing; I wouldn't take money."

"What did you take?"

"A promise."

"A promise?" Marian asked indignantly.

"The Sheriff was planning—"

"The Sheriff is always planning something, Allen!"

Allen shook his head. "This was different. When he does things in the open, we can stop him. This time was different. He was planning to kill your father."

Marian took a step back, studying Allen. Could he be telling the truth? Had her father been in danger? With the Sheriff's rapidly shifting moods, no one was ever truly safe.

"The Sheriff wasn't going to hang him," Allen said. "He was just going to have him murdered in his cell while he slept. For the brief space of time I was here, when I was captured…Sir Guy questioned me that night, offered me my life if I betrayed all of you. Sir Guy was going to kill me unless I joined him, but my own life was nothing. I would gladly die for Robin and England, and I had told Sir Guy as much. I told him I wouldn't help him, he could kill me, it didn't matter."

"Then why did you help him?"

"I had heard of the Sheriff's plan and I knew how much it would hurt you, and through you Robin. So I told Sir Guy he could kill me and I wouldn't care. He could dangle money in my face, I wouldn't care. But if he would promise to keep your father safe, I would help him. So here we are."

Marian was silent.

"Marian?"

She shook her head. "I have to think. Get out." Marian's emotions swirled around her; the fire of anger still flooded her veins, but now there was a cloud of confusion.

"Alright, I'll go. I know...I can't turn back now. I'm on the side I hate...but it is almost worth it to keep you from pain."

"Is it, Allen? I'm not proud of you. Nor am I grateful. I don't forgive you."

"If you had been hurt, it would have hurt Robin. I couldn't let that happen."

"Your betrayal hurt worse, Allen."

Allen didn't respond. Marian had nothing further to say, and so he soon exited the room and left her in peace.

Marian didn't know what to think. Allen had betrayed them, that much was still true. Little John had almost died because of it. Yet he said he'd done it all to save her father, and Marian couldn't hate him if that was true. She'd do almost anything to save her father, too.

Almost anything. But betray Robin and the others? That might be a stretch.

The next night Robin and Mark visited Marian, sneaking past castle guards and a sleeping Andrew to do so.

"Have you seen Allen?" Robin asked. He practically spat the name.

"Yes. I saw him yesterday. Did Little John actually throw him out of camp?"

"Yes. He did," Robin replied.

"And if Little John hadn't thrown him out of camp, I would have!" Mark said.

"I'm going to kill him," Robin said.

"I might kill him myself," Marian said. "But you should know what he had to say for himself." She was frustrated with Allen still, and she wasn't entirely sure of the truth of his words, but she couldn't hate him.

"I mean it, Marian. I'll never forget this."

"Neither will I. He should never have told the Sheriff about the secret places but—"

"It wasn't just that! Marian, because of Allen squealing to the Sheriff, Little John was injured terribly."

"Dusty was able to heal him," Mark put in.

"But what if she hadn't been able to?" Marian said just as Robin turned and snapped "What if Little John had died?"

"What if you die?" Robin continued, grabbing Marian's hands. "Allen could tell the Sheriff about your involvement in all of our proceedings. They know Mark is an outlaw in my gang. One word from Allen and you could be hung. I won't let that happen. I can't let that happen. I'll kill him first."

"I know what he did was terrible, but he did it to protect my father. You can't expect me to hate that. I don't trust him, but I don't hate him."

"What do you mean?" Mark asked. "How did he do this for our father?"

"He said the Sheriff was planning to kill our father, and that he extracted a promise from Gisbourne to keep our father alive. In exchange for that promise, he helped Gisbourne and the Sheriff."

Robin shook his head. "That is stupid. We could have protected your father. We could have taken him to our camp. He didn't have to help the Sheriff to protect your father."

"I didn't say it was the right choice, Robin. I just know that as misguided as his actions were, he was trying to help my father. With the secret hallways no longer available to us, you might not have been able to get to my father to save him."

"I visit you easily enough."

"I'm not locked in a cell with no available keys," Marian insisted. "I can see why Allen would think you couldn't save him, why he would imagine Gisbourne's promise to be the only way to save him."

"We got Allen out of that dungeon," Robin insisted.

"You still had the secret passages," Marian replied.

"If he spoke the truth, I can't hate him either," Mark sighed. "I want to, but I can't. He still should have told us though. We might have been able to do something—anything—rather than turn on each other."

"I agree," Robin said. "He should have come to us with his information, not Gisbourne. He's weak and pathetic, and I still want to kill him."

"Don't, Robin," Mark said. "Not yet. Find out if he spoke the truth, if my father was in danger. He was misguided, but if he spoke the truth then he was doing it for an understandable reason, at least to me. You can't kill him for trying to save my father, no matter how twisted a way he chose to do it."

"I don't forgive him and I won't trust him," Marian added, "but I can't hate him for protecting my father, however he chose to do it."

Robin sighed. "Fine. I won't kill him. But I won't trust him again either."

"Neither do we," Marian said. "I don't expect anyone could."

Mari-Lu's small face was scrunched up in concentration. "I…I don't know."

"What don't you know, little one?" Aunt Lucy asked kindly.

"I don't know if I could forgive Allen either. Even though he said he did it for Marian's father. Robin was right; he should have told the gang about the plot to kill Sir Godfrey, he shouldn't have helped Gisbourne."

Marian watched her daughter with a smile, remembering the way she had wrestled with the same question when she'd first heard the story.

"Things might have been quite different if he had told his friends, you're right," Aunt Lucy said to little Mari-Lu.

"Could you forgive him?" Mari-Lu asked.

"I didn't know him back then, at least not personally. I'd seen the tiniest glimpses of the gang in Nottingham, but I didn't know any of them. From my perspective, I was grieved for the people who suffered due to Allen's choices to help Gisbourne and the Sheriff instead of Robin Hood, and I was grieved for the broken friendship between Allen and Robin and the others, but I didn't know them or enough details of the situation to be a judge of any of it."

"But if you had been a part of the gang, would you have forgiven Allen?" Mari-Lu insisted.

"Yes, I would have," Aunt Lucy replied. "It might not have been easy, that is true, but I would have."

"How?"

"I have been forgiven for equal betrayals, Mari-Lu, and through the grace of my God I have learned to forgive in the same measure."

"That seems impossible."

"I know, little one. But if you are going to understand the rest of this story I am telling, you will need to consider the idea of the Lord's capacity for forgiveness, and how He can give you the strength and will to do the same."

"Did Marian ever forgive him?"

"That remains to be seen," Aunt Lucy smiled. "I haven't finished my story yet."

"I don't think I would," Mari-Lu said, and then she shrugged. "Go on. I want to hear the rest."

"A few days after Allen came to live at the castle and work side by side with Gisbourne and the Sheriff, the Sheriff summoned Marian to the Great Hall. He told her he considered her a 'good girl' during her stay thus far, and told her she would no longer have to have Andrew watching over her every movement. She was still required to stay in the castle, but she would not be constantly watched."

"Why?" Mari-Lu asked.

"Why did the Sheriff do anything?" Aunt Lucy chuckled. "His decisions were dictated by his moods, and they were ever changing as the wind."

"I have a question about Andrew…"

"And what is your question?"

"Why did he never tell Gisbourne that Marian was spying on him sometimes?"

"Who said he didn't tell Gisbourne?"

"But Gisbourne would have done something, would have been angry…wouldn't he?"

"Andrew had no reason to tell anyone what Marian was up to; I've told you before he was a decent man. He did not like what the Sheriff and Sir Guy did in Nottingham, did not approve of most of their actions. He did, however, approve of Robin Hood's gang, and Marian's advocacy for the people. Andrew was always pressing Sir Guy to be a better man, though Gisbourne never listened. That, in itself, was one of the reasons he wished Marian and Gisbourne would reconcile, so that Marian might join him as an influence for good over Gisbourne. That, however, is a different story altogether and someday I will tell it to you, but today we're still telling the story of Marian and myself."

"I want to hear everything!"

"I know you do, and someday you will … but first, Marian: the first few days without Andrew trailing her were pure joy. She never left the castle but she felt free nevertheless. Near the end of her first week free of Andrew, Marian overheard the Sheriff speaking to Gisbourne and Allen…"

Chapter 15

"WE HAVE TO get rid of these pests!" the Sheriff growled. "Since you are no longer in Robin Hood's camp picking up valuable information we have no clue when or where he will strike. He's getting away with my money! And ruining my executions!"

Marian stood just outside the open door to the Great Hall, as she so often did these days when spying on the three men she despised and had the misfortune of living and dining with on a daily basis.

As the Sheriff spluttered and paced in front of his throne, Gisbourne picked up the thread of conversation directed at Allen, "We need to get him once and for all. Attack him where he'll least expect it, in his own territory."

"Meaning what?" Allen asked.

"We need to attack him at the source, Allen."

"You want me to take you to the camp? I can't."

"Are you forgetting who you work for now?" the Sheriff growled.

Allen shook his head. "No. It's just that…I promised Robin…"

The Sheriff laughed. "There's no need to worry about that. No one keeps promises, and no one but a fool would expect us to."

Allen glanced at Gisbourne, and Marian thought of her father. Was Gisbourne's promise to protect her father a true one? She doubted it. He'd tried to kill her father before, and he'd burned her home in his hatred.

After a long pause Allen finally spoke. "It's quite a ride and they have an alarm, traps..."

"We'll take plenty of soldiers," Gisbourne said. "Robin only has a small band does he not?"

Allen nodded slowly, and the Sheriff insisted they begin their assault on the outlaws' camp immediately.

Marian darted away from the door and down the hallway in time to watch Gisbourne and Allen exit the Great Hall and then exit the castle altogether. Moving to a window that overlooked the courtyard, Marian watched in horror as the soldiers assembled and Gisbourne shouted orders.

Allen stood to one side, looking equally as horrified at the events unfolding as Marian felt. Even so, Marian could feel red hot anger coursing through her when she looked at him. He might feel a small measure of reluctance or remorse, but he was still about to lead Gisbourne to kill Robin and the others—people he'd professed to care for, people who had trusted him. People Marian loved.

Marian could feel a panic rising in her chest; she couldn't let her family die!

Marian ran to the great doors of the castle and shoved them open, taking the stone steps two at a time down into the courtyard. "Guy!"

Gisbourne turned. "What do you want?"

Marian scrambled for something, anything. "Uh...my... my father...he's...I'd like to send for the physician."

"Marian, I am busy."

"I know. I can go."

"Marian..."

All around them soldiers were mounting horses, sharpening weapons, and preparing to follow Allen to kill the people Marian cared for.

"Please, Sir Guy, let me go get a physician for my father."

"No. You can't leave the castle."

"Can't you make an exception, just for once?"

"No."

"Guy, please!" Marian grabbed his arm, letting the terror of losing Robin and the others overwhelm her. Tears filled her eyes, and her fingers trembled against Gisbourne's arm. "My father could be dying."

"I'll send a servant."

"I'd rather go myself."

"Marian, I can't trust you to do that."

"I'll come back to the castle. Please?"

"Promise me you will return to the castle immediately."

"I will return."

"I don't know, Marian." Gisbourne still seemed hesitant, and Marian let her guard down more than she ever had with him before. The shield dropped, and all her fear and anger swirled together. Tears stained her cheeks and her voice wavered as she pleaded with him, letting her real emotions bleed into her lies as she clung to his arm and wept. "Guy, please!"

"Fine. We'll escort you to the physician's."

"Thank you."

When the soldiers were ready, Gisbourne led them through the streets of Nottingham with Marian at his side. Allen followed closely behind.

When they reached the physician's, Gisbourne stopped. "Do you need my assistance?"

"No," Marian said, moving away from the line of soldiers. "I'll be fine."

"Go straight back to the castle, Marian."

Marian walked to the door of the house where the physician lived and watched as Gisbourne and Allen began leading the soldiers down the street, but she didn't enter. As soon as Gisbourne and his soldiers disappeared from sight, Marian ran to Marcus' home and pounded on his door.

"Marcus! Marcus, please, answer! It's Marian!"

Marcus swung open the door, his face a mask of surprise. "Lady Marian?"

"I need your horse! I have to get to Robin before Gisbourne does!"

Marcus waved toward the small stable next to his house and blacksmith shop. "Be my guest."

Marcus helped her saddle the steed, and all the while Marian could feel her fingers trembling and her legs losing their strength. She barely mounted the horse without falling off again, so weak did all her limbs feel as she thought of Gisbourne burning the camp the way he'd burned her home. She could picture his cruel sword cutting off Robin's head, and her heart nearly stopped beating.

"You're all set," Marcus said.

"Thank you!"

Marian kicked her heels into the horse, and it took off. She rode for all she was worth, taking care to stay far from the main road as she raced toward Sherwood Forest. She could see Gisbourne's group just entering the forest by the Sherwood road in the distance, and she felt the air leave her lungs.

Marian urged her mount forward, crashing through the underbrush as she entered the forest far from any path. The image of Gisbourne thrusting his sword through Mark's heart spurred her onward as trees whizzed past and her horse darted around them. They jumped a small creak and the horse nearly lost its footing on the opposite bank, making Marian's heart jump in sudden terror on top of the dull ache of horror she'd been feeling the entire ride.

She knew the way to camp like the back of her hand now, so it was easy to race through the wild trees and underbrush toward her home away from home. There was no sign of Gisbourne or Allen yet. What that meant, Marian didn't know, but she wasn't going to stop to think about it.

As soon as the first trap came into view, Marian slowed her horse slightly so as to avoid getting herself caught up in one of the traps around the camp. As she and her horse cantered into camp, she saw Robin leaning calmly against his hut, sharpening his sword, and her heart rate began to slow. Will and Little John were sitting near the fire ring, with Dusty not far away apparently mixing some of her herbs.

Will and Little John quickly stood as she hurriedly dismounted, Dusty looking up to watch, and Much emerged from his hut to see what was happening. Will ran up and grabbed the halter of the horse while Mark appeared from his hut and came hurrying over.

But Robin, still calmly leaning against his hut sharpening his sword, didn't move a muscle. "Marian."

Marian ran toward him, her lungs gasping for the air she'd deprived them of in her panic. "No time to chat, Robin. Allen's out of control. He's leading Gisbourne here. Now. With soldiers."

Dusty looked pained. "Allen? Bringing Gisbourne here?"

Marian nodded.

Robin sighed. "Get back to Nottingham before you are missed, Marian."

"What will you do? He's bringing soldiers! There's only six of you!"

"We'll do what we're best at," Robin said, setting aside his sword long enough to grab Marian's hand and give her a reassuring squeeze.

"We'll set an ambush," Will said.

"Be careful, Robin," Marian pleaded. "And work fast. They're on their way now. I don't know how I beat them here."

"Don't worry about us," Robin said. "We can handle the Sheriff's men, we aren't afraid of Gisbourne, and we need to teach Allen a lesson."

Marian grabbed Mark's hand before she mounted her horse. "Be safe, Mark."

"I'm with Robin Hood."

"That's what worries me." To the rest of the gang she called, "Good luck!"

"Pray, Marian," Dusty called back.

Marian glanced at Dusty.

"Pray." Dusty repeated. "I've always found it more effective than luck."

Marian didn't respond. She turned quickly and rode back to Nottingham as fast as she could, being sure to swing wide around Sherwood Road so as not to run into Gisbourne and the others.

Robin and the others gathered their weapons and left the camp quickly, setting up an ambush. They'd become more than

172

proficient at their job after over a year raiding the Sheriff's caravans of taxes.

Gisbourne, Allen, and the soldiers, expecting to find Robin Hood and the others unsuspecting inside their camp were completely caught off guard when arrows began to fly from behind trees and boulders long before they arrived. The soldiers quickly fell, arrows piercing their hearts.

Gisbourne shouted to Allen in the confusion. "You told me we still had a ways to go!"

"We do!"

"Someone must have warned them! The Sheriff won't like this!" he said angrily and he sped away on his stallion Victory.

Robin shot an arrow toward Allen's head. but Allen dove behind a tree in the nick of time. His years fighting in the Crusades had taught him well. He was an expert warrior and had great instincts, the same as Robin. He knew that he was far outnumbered however, and so fled the scene rather than stay and fight the gang.

Back in Nottingham, the Sheriff shrieked for over an hour when Gisbourne, Allen, and Andrew came back alone and empty-handed.

Marian had stopped by the physician's on her way back to the castle, bringing him with her to see her father and that is where she was when Gisbourne and the others arrived. After listening to the Sheriff's frustrations for some time, Gisbourne eventually made his way down to the dungeons to check on Sir Godfrey and found Marian and the physician still there.

"How is he?" Gisbourne asked Marian.

"Not well, but the physician thinks he can change that."

"Good." Gisbourne studied her for a moment and then said, "I am impressed you came back at all."

"Where else would I have gone? I am concerned for my father, I wouldn't abandon him here. I can't trust you to take care of him."

Gisbourne sighed, lingering a moment longer before exiting the dungeons and leaving Marian in peace.

In the next few weeks Sir Godfrey's health became steadily better. Marian was overjoyed to see him well again.

When her father had been well a full week and Marian was sure it would last, she spoke to Robin as soon as he visited her. How he snuck into the castle itself remained a mystery to Marian, but it was definitely less tense now that he didn't have to step over a sleeping Andrew outside her door.

"I want my father out of here, Robin. I don't trust the Sheriff or Gisbourne. The Sheriff has no rhyme or reason for anything he chooses to do, his ever changing moods dictating who he wants to kill or spare each day. And Gisbourne is spiteful; if I say the wrong thing—anger him in just the right way—he'll lose his temper and have my father killed. My father isn't safe here."

"He never was. I'm more than happy for him to come to the camp. But he's refused every other time we've tried."

"I'll convince him it's best."

"If you can get him out of his cell, we can take him from there. It will be good to have someone with the children at the camp when we go on raids and the like."

"The children! I forgot they were even at the camp. What have you been doing with them when you go on raids?"

"One of us always has to stay behind. It's usually Dusty or Much. But it's a burden to have to watch them instead of doing what we are meant to do, fighting for England."

Marian nodded. "That's a start—giving him a reason he's needed in the camp. But getting Father out of his cell seems impossible. I can't get rid of his guard by charm—I can barely control Gisbourne that way, and he claims to love me. If I try to harm the guard posted at the dungeons or kill him, I'll be in more trouble than I can easily get out of. I don't believe I'm that skilled anyway."

"Can you think of something? We can't get into his cell, or even into the dungeons, easily. The Sheriff's men aren't competent, perhaps, but there are enough of them to overwhelm us if they tried, particularly within the castle where we'd have nowhere to hide."

"I will think of something."

"Tomorrow? I can get the gang into the castle, and we can grab your father assuming he's not locked in his cell."

"Tomorrow?" Marian shook her head. "That hardly gives me the time to convince him."

"You said you wanted him out of here as soon as possible."

"I still need to figure out how exactly I'm going to do that, but alright…tomorrow it is."

Marian spent the night pacing her room, wondering how she was going to manage to get her father out of his cell. She couldn't think of a pretense to ask Gisbourne to let him out. It was possible she could attack his guard, but she hadn't been keeping up with her fighting skills since coming to the castle, particularly after the secret passages were closed and she was no longer sneaking out to assist Mark as the Hooded Rescuer.

Marian paced until dawn, but was no closer to an answer. She thought and thought over what she could do—perhaps convince Gisbourne to let her father out for a stroll around the castle to stretch his legs, perhaps kill the guards and steal the keys to free her father herself. The latter held too much of a chance of being caught and imprisoned or worse herself, and as for the former it would be difficult to separate from Gisbourne in order to pass her father over to Robin and the others.

It was afternoon when Marian finally went to visit her father.

The guard posted at the doors leading to the dungeons let her through, knowing she visited her father often. Marian considered pulling out the dagger at her waist—one Mark had brought her months before when the secret passages were still in use—and slitting their throats, but she didn't trust her own skill to be able to accomplish the deed.

When she reached her father's cell, he came to the edge to greet her, reaching through the bars to grasp her hand.

Marian leaned close, whispering, "I can get you out."

"Marian—"

"No, listen to me. Don't protest. You'll be safer in Robin's camp." Marian kept her voice low, glancing toward the guard by the door. He didn't seem to be too interested in her, suggesting he couldn't hear what she was saying. "Robin's coming for you today. All we have to do is get rid of your guard."

"How do you plan to do that?"

"I can't, father. But here," Marian slipped her father the

jeweled dagger of hers. "When he brings your dinner…or comes close to the cell for some other reason…"

Sir Godfrey shook his head. "It won't work, Marian."

"Father, please. You'll at least have the element of surprise while he's not paying as much attention."

"I can't even try. It won't succeed. Don't you have more practice with such things?"

"I don't think I could manage it," Marian said.

"What makes you think I can?"

"You were a fighter before you were the Sheriff of Nottingham," Marian responded. "And you can get close to him, catch him by surprise. He's much too big for me, he'll see my attack coming as he stands there by the door. But when he unlocks the cell and comes in with your food, you'll have the element of surprise and he'll be momentarily vulnerable. You could do it."

"Perhaps," Sir Godfrey sighed. "You could as well."

"He won't unlock the door while I'm here; I have been visiting you for a while, Father, and I've noticed the cell is only unlocked for Gisbourne or the physician."

"Either way, child, what help will I be in Robin's camp?"

"You can watch the children. You'll be a great help. It is a burden to the gang to have to take care of the children that are staying there. If you are there they can all go on the raids together and not leave anyone behind."

"That does not seem very useful, Marian. And I told you before I had no desire to live in the forest as a fugitive."

"I know but you can't stay here. Gisbourne or the Sheriff could decide to kill you at any moment—I don't trust them. And Allen betraying us only makes up my mind further. I only trust

you in Robin and Mark's care; you have to go to the camp. But…
you're afraid, aren't you?"

"It's too risky."

"Not even to ease my mind?"

"No."

"For the children in the camp?"

"No. I won't try this crazy scheme, Marian."

"Will anything convince you?"

"No!"

"I'm so ashamed of you. You're weak!"

"And you have your head in the clouds! How do you
expect to save England from all this tyranny? There are only a
handful of you rebels."

"Rebels? That's how you see us? We're the only ones truly
loyal to King Richard!"

"You are all foolish young children who do not understand
the world."

"You are a bad tempered old man who doesn't understand
anything!"

Marian spun away and marched off. She needed to think
of another plan. Robin was going to come for her father, and the
foolish old man was going to still be locked in his cell because he
was too afraid to escape and Marian was too incompetent to help
him.

Angry at her father and herself, Marian spent time in her
room fuming. But eventually, knowing time was running out
before Robin came for him, she returned to the dungeons to see
her father. The guard wasn't standing at his post, which gave
Marian some hope. But he wasn't lying dead near her father's cell

either, which meant Sir Godfrey hadn't tried to use her escape plan.

Her father was wrapped in a thin blanket on his straw mattress, his face turned toward the stone wall and away from Marian. "Father?"

He refused to answer her.

"Father, please. I'm sorry. You aren't weak. You are one of the bravest men I know. You aren't bad tempered either. You are kind and wonderful and I love you."

Still he did not answer.

Marian sighed. "I'm sorry I was angry. I just want you safe, that is all."

Still nothing.

"I love you."

Marian returned to her room downcast.

«»

"Why was he so angry with her?" Mari-Lu asked. "She was only trying to help him. She only got upset because she cared so much."

"He wasn't angry," Aunt Lucy said sadly. "He loved his daughter even more than she loved him. He was afraid, and he didn't like the idea of living in the forest, but he chose to do what she asked."

"Then why didn't he talk to her?" Mari-Lu asked.

"Because that wasn't him in the cell," Aunt Lucy said. "It was Gisbourne who—going down to visit Sir Godfrey later that day—discovered the dead guard lying in his cell in place of Marian's father."

"Oh." Mari-Lu's eyes went wide, her mouth hanging open for a moment. "He did it? He killed the guard and then put him in his own bed?"

"He did," Aunt Lucy nodded. "He did exactly what Marian had told him to do, killing his guard and then escaping the dungeons. When Gisbourne came upon the scene he'd left behind, the guard dead in Sir Godfrey's bed, he sprinted through the castle to find the Sheriff or Sir Godfrey. He didn't think Marian's father could have gotten far, and in a way, he was right. As he ran though the castle, he stumbled across two more dead bodies…"

Chapter 16

GISBOURNE PAUSED IN the hallway, studying the scene. A soldier with an arrow protruding from his chest, and an old man whose chest was bleeding profusely.

"Sir Godfrey!" Gisbourne knelt beside him. He felt for a pulse, but found nothing. Sir Godfrey was dead. "Oh no... Marian..."

Marian was sitting in her room fretting over her father's apparent anger at her when Andrew knocked on her door. Marian opened it and felt a flush of annoyance.

"I thought I was free of you."

"My lady...your father..."

"What's happened?" Marian felt a flash of excitement believing he'd escaped until Andrew continued.

"He's been found...dead."

"What?"

"I'm so sorry, Lady Marian. He's in the passage outside the Great Hall."

Marian sprinted all the way there. When she arrived, she saw a dead soldier on a litter being carried away by servants. Sir Godfrey was just being placed on another by Gisbourne.

Marian ran forward and dropped to the stone floor beside him.

"Father!" A darkness was settling around her heart as Marian struggled to see through her tears. "No, no! I'm sorry, I'm so sorry." She reached out and stroked her father's lifeless face. She'd done this; she'd told him he could escape and he'd finally listened to her.

Gisbourne knelt beside her and placed a hand on her arm, but Marian shoved his arm away, jumping to her feet and running back down the hallway toward her room—away from her dead father and her guilt.

Gisbourne followed. When he caught up to her he grabbed her arm. "Marian!"

She stopped. She couldn't see past her tears and she leaned over, overwhelmed by the searing pain in her chest.

"Marian, you're not safe."

"What?" She gasped through her tears.

"I found this dagger with the dead guard in the dungeon." Gisbourne held out Marian's dagger, scrutinizing her face with his intense dark eyes.

"So?"

"Marian, I've seen you with this dagger before; even before you came to live in the castle. I don't know how it came to be here, but I know it's yours. The Sheriff might suspect…"

Marian didn't answer.

"Marian, the Sheriff will be furious when he finds out his guard is dead and Sir Godfrey nearly escaped. He'll want to kill the culprit and he's going to look to you first."

"I didn't kill that guard."

"The Sheriff won't care who did it. It's your dagger. He'll blame you, he'll…he'll hurt you."

Marian remained silent, tears coursing down her cheeks.

"Let me help you." Gisbourne stepped closer. "I can protect you." He wrapped his arms around her shoulders. Marian remained stiff in his arms, unwilling to accept his comfort. "I can't let the Sheriff hurt you, Marian."

Marian remained still, refusing to relax into his embrace. He bent his head to kiss her forehead but she broke away from his embrace, shoving him away from her and turning to run to her room.

Once inside her room, she leaned heavily against her closed door and cried out in agony. Her legs gave out beneath her and she fell forward onto the floor. Her vision clouded from her tears and her heart felt as though a fist of iron was squeezing it slowly inside her chest, turning it to ash and dust.

"Marian?"

"Robin!" Marian looked up, letting out another strangled sob. "It's my fault, it's all my fault."

"No, Marian." Robin wrapped his arms around her and Marian sagged into him, soaking his shoulder with her tears.

"I told him…he was weak…and bad tempered…I called him an old fool!" Marian choked out the words through her sobs as Robin continued to hold her tightly to himself. "I never…get to tell him…how sorry I am…he died thinking…"

"No, Marian. I was with him when he died. He was coming to meet me when that soldier found us. I got the soldier at the same time he got your father. I'm so sorry! I should have been able to protect him. This is my fault. But, Marian, listen to me. Before he died he gave me a message for you." Robin lifted Marian's head so she was looking at him, gently wiping the tears from her eyes. "Marian. Listen. He said to tell you that you aren't foolish to dream of freeing our people from tyranny. He said to tell you to keep hope alive. You, Marian, you will set all to rights."

"What?"

"That's what he said, his last words, Marian. Your father told me that he believed you will set all to rights. Just like he used to believe King Richard would."

"Why did he have to die?" Marian collapsed into Robin's arms again, sobbing, and Robin held her close.

"I'm sorry, Marian. This is my fault. I should have been able to…I'm so sorry."

Chapter 17

"GISBOURNE ARRANGED A funeral for Sir Godfrey, despite the Sheriff's objections. People from miles around came to honor their beloved Sir Godfrey."

Tears stained Mari-Lu's small cheeks as her shoulders shook. "Why did he have to die?"

Aunt Lucy gently wiped the tears from Mari-Lu's face. "These things happen. Death is a part of life, and that was even more true during the reign of Prince John."

Mari-Lu curled into Aunt Lucy, her body shaking with silent sobs.

Aunt Lucy hugged her close. "Perhaps that is enough for one day."

"No!" Mari-Lu sat up, hastily brushing her hands across her cheeks. "What happened next? When did Robin marry Marian? We can't stop yet."

"There's more death coming," Aunt Lucy said, cupping Mari-Lu's tear-stained face in her gentle hands. "The whole story isn't a happy one."

"But some of it has to be. I know Robin marries her eventually!"

"You are certain you want to continue?"

"Please, please don't stop! I want to hear the rest."

"Very well, we'll continue."

"Thank you!"

Aunt Lucy kept her arms firmly around Mari-Lu, letting the girl's emotions settle into a quieter state before she continued.

"When the funeral for her father was over, Marian knew there was nothing left for her in Nottingham. So she slipped away from Gisbourne and the Sheriff, through the crowds, and away to Sherwood Forest."

"She and Mark must have been so sad!"

"They were. The first week after the funeral was a blur but Marian soon distracted herself by keeping busy as the Hooded Rescuer. Gisbourne had search parties out for Marian for over a month. Marian, however, never left Robin's camp except when in the Hooded Rescuer disguise so no one, except Robin's gang, could truly say they had seen Marian since the funeral…"

«»

The gang had left to raid a caravan they'd heard was coming through Sherwood that day, and Marian was left alone in the camp, surrounded by her darkened thoughts and six curious children. To distract herself, Marian grabbed her bow and pulled the string loose so that she could practice restringing it. The children gathered around to watch, their eyes wide and inquisitive.

Marian placed the bottom tip of her bow carefully against her foot, holding the top gently in her hand as she pulled the loose string up toward the top where it belonged, bracing the bow against her thigh as she pulled the tip of the bow and the string towards each other. She could hear Robin's voice in her head as she went through the motions.

"Remember, you're bringing the bow to the string, and not the string to the bow."

She remembered the way he'd demonstrated for her, standing behind her and reaching around to be her arms as he had shown her how to hold the bow and bend it against her thigh to restring it properly. The comfort found in the strength of his arms was only outweighed by her annoyance at how condescending she found him.

Robin was insistent that she get back to the basics before she could truly master archery as he had done. She knew she was improving under his tutelage, but he was a much more strict instructor than Mark or Will had ever been. He'd only gotten worse after she'd moved to the camp, insisting on training with her every day now, though Marian wondered if he didn't do that simply to keep her mind off of her father.

She felt a familiar ache in her chest, but before she could succumb to the pain, the crunching of leaves and the worried voices of the children interrupted.

Marian turned to watch as Little John rushed into camp, carrying a limp and lifeless Will in his arms.

"What happened?" Marian dropped her bow and ran forward as Little John lowered Will to the ground and the children stared on with wide, terrified eyes. "Is he…?"

Little John shook his head sharply. "No. Not yet. He's breathing. Dusty will be here soon."

Will's tunic was stained a crimson red, and Little John pressed his hands to Will's chest, trying to slow the bleeding. The children huddled together a distance away and the youngest of them began to cry.

"What happened?" Marian asked.

"Dusty was exposed too long in front of the enemy. One of those blasted soldiers shot an arrow, straight toward her heart."

"Is she okay?"

"She's fine. The arrow never hit her. This idiot pushed her out of the way and took the arrow himself, here in his chest."

Will's eyes were closed, his face ashen, and his body limp. The crimson stain was coating Little John's hands now, oozing between his fingers as he held his hands firmly to Will's chest.

"There's so much blood!"

"We need to stop the bleeding," Little John said. "Dusty will be here soon."

"Why didn't she come with you immediately?" Marian placed her own hands near Little John's, trying to stem the flow of blood leaving Will's body.

"The rest of the gang was still dealing with the soldiers. There are always more of them, every time a caravan comes through. It gets harder and harder to ambush them effectively. Dusty is coming…she's coming."

Little John's face was almost as pale as Will's, his breathing nearly as shallow.

"Little John, are you hurt?"

"No."

"Take a deep breath."

"Dusty is coming…"

"I know. She's coming," Marian nodded, reaching up to put a hand on Little John's shoulder and inadvertently staining his shirt with her bloodied hand. "She'll help Will. Robin says there's never been a greater healer. She fixed you right up when you were the one wounded in a raid, right? Will is going to be fine."

Marian felt the warm liquid trickling over her fingers as it gushed from Will's wound and doubted her own words, but Little John needed to calm down before he passed out from panic.

A moment later Dusty appeared, racing into camp and over to Will's side, knocking Marian to the side as she pushed Little John's hands off of Will and ripped his shirt over his head to get a better look at his wounds.

Dusty pressed her hands where Little John's had been a moment before, and then she bowed her head. "Lord, please use my hands to save this wonderful man. But whatever happens, your will be done."

Marian wanted to tell Dusty to hurry up, to use her hands and not her prayers, but there was no need. Once her brief prayer was over, Dusty worked quickly, ordering Little John to boil some water for her, and then cleaning the wound and applying a strange mixture of herbs before binding Will in strips of cloth.

As Dusty worked quietly, Marian held her breath. She could see her father's lifeless form sprawled across the litter in front of the Great Hall, could picture his bloodless grey face.

Marian closed her eyes as a fist of pain tightened around her heart and slowly crushed the life from within her.

Suddenly, Will groaned. Marian's eyes flew open.

Dusty was still wrapping his wound, and Will appeared to be unconscious, but Dusty's movements were not as frantic and Little John no longer looked as pale as he had.

Dusty looked up. "I think he'll be alright. Time will tell."

"How can you be sure?" Marian asked.

"I've done this many times before," Dusty replied. "I have seen death, unavoidable and insistent. And I have seen it lingering and impatient. I have also seen it shy, and ready to fly away. This time…this wound I believe it is the latter."

"That wasn't much of an answer."

"Trust me, Marian. And trust the Lord." Dusty turned toward Little John. "He'll need to stay in bed for a few weeks if he's to fully recover. He's going to protest, but it has to be done. He can't be up and about."

"I'll keep a close eye on him," Little John nodded.

"We can see to it he stays in bed," Marian agreed.

Little John gently lifted his friend and carried him over to his hut, placing him in his bed.

"We'll have to keep a close eye on him," Dusty said. "He's active and he's stubborn. He won't want to follow the order to stay in bed."

"We'll take care of him," Little John promised. He placed a hand on Dusty's shoulder, squeezing in comfort. "He'll be fine. Didn't you say so yourself?"

Dusty smiled weakly.

The children circled around Will's hut.

"Can we help?" the oldest, William, asked.

Will had gone out of his way to make their stay in the camp enjoyable. He'd spent many evenings entertaining them with stories and often bounced the smallest of them on his knee. He'd even begun teaching young William to use a bow.

Dusty turned to the children, giving them an encouraging smile. "If he needs water or just needs company in the coming weeks, I'm sure he'd love to have your help. For now, however, he needs his rest."

"Come on, everyone," Little John said, scooping the youngest toddler and leading the rest of the children away from the hut. "Let's clear some space in our storage hut for the chests of gold and jewels the rest of the gang is likely to bring to us when they're through with the raid."

The children followed Little John, though William and Beth, the oldest two, kept glancing back toward Will's hut. Dusty settled herself beside Will's bed, keeping an eye on him. Marian fetched her bow where she'd discarded it when Little John had arrived, and set about practicing restringing it again, though her eyes were drawn to Will's hut nearly as often as the children's were.

←→

"Is Will going to live? Why does Dusty pray before healing people? Did the gang get the soldier who hurt Will? Do the children ever get to go back home to their families? And when will Marian and Robin get married?!"

"So many questions," Aunt Lucy laughed. "One at a time...let's see...Dusty always prays before she heals because she knows she can only do so much as a human, and she leaves the rest up to the Lord. The gang always dealt with the soldiers they ambushed in those days, very few survived to tell tales of Robin Hood's exploits in Sherwood. It was their absence, and the absence of their treasure, that spoke of what the gang was up to. As to whether Will lives or Robin marries Marian, you will have to wait and see."

"Oh, well hurry up," Mari-Lu clapped her hands. "I need to know!"

"Alright, alright. Be patient, little one." Aunt Lucy smiled at Mari-Lu's impatience and excitement, taking her time before she spoke again. "For the next few weeks, Marian stayed in the camp to watch over Will, the children eagerly helping her. Marian hated seeing her vibrant friend reduced to such a pathetic state.

Will hardly woke up during the first few days, and after that he had very little energy when he was conscious. Young William practiced with his bow every day trying hard to please the injured Will, and managed to bring a few weak smiles to his face. Beth sat by his bed and did her best to keep him comfortable, always ready to run for anything he might need. Little Sarah tried to entertain him with stories as he had done for them. Dusty also spent a great deal of time at Will's bedside. Though she was the gang's healer and this was in itself a normal occurrence, Marian noticed how gently she'd brush Will's hair from his face, and how sweetly she would sit and watch him, and Marian began to wonder if there was more behind Will's sacrifice of taking the arrow meant for Dusty than the simple camaraderie the gang all shared."

"Ohhhh," Mari-Lu grinned. "Another love story! But we didn't get to see it. Why didn't you tell me earlier?"

"We are focused on Marian today," Aunt Lucy laughed. "I will tell you all about Will and Dusty another time."

"Fine," Mari-Lu reluctantly conceded. "What happened next? Did Robin and Marian get married yet?"

"The gang continued their raids and foiled as many executions as they could. It was harder now that they didn't have anyone in the castle and it took a great deal more risk to spy on the Sheriff. They couldn't save everyone, but they did begin to notice that more people were being saved than they themselves were responsible for…"

«»

One night, the gang was gathered around the campfire after the children had been put to bed. Given the limited amount of hut space, they still doubled up with the adults, though Will was now excluded from that duty.

Much placed another log on the fire, and Marian watched as sparks flooded the air briefly and then dissipated. Beside her, Robin draped an arm around her as he studied the other faces of the gang by the firelight. Much, Little John, and Dusty all seemed lost to their own thoughts.

"Is it possible the people are finally rising up on their own?" Robin asked.

"You mean all the good deeds we aren't responsible for?" Much asked.

"Exactly. Dusty was delivering food to the farmers outside our city walls today, as far as I am aware," Robin glanced toward her for confirmation and Dusty nodded. "Little John, you were busy distributing the Sheriff's wealth to the more deserving of his subjects, I believe."

"I was."

"I was in the castle trying to spy on the Sheriff without getting caught and killed," Much offered before Robin could ask about his whereabouts during the day.

"We were all busy, is the point," Robin said. "But someone stopped an execution at a farm some miles outside Wetherby. I didn't hear about it until it was already over, and the man was gone—safe, presumably. According to witnesses, a hooded figure saved him, exactly as we might have done. But it wasn't us."

"The Sheriff is blaming us," Much said. "He was furious judging by the conversations I overheard."

"It's a fair assumption," Mark said. "We do cause the most problems for him."

"But I know it wasn't any of us," Robin said. "Which leads me to wonder who has stepped up? I wouldn't mind if Nottingham revolted on its own; it would make our job that much easier, to be honest."

"From what witnesses have been saying," Mark said, "about this and the other incidents we weren't involved in, the man is a magnificent shot. Good enough to rival even you, Robin."

"So they say," Robin agreed. "I would like to find him, whoever he is. Since losing Allen, we could use another person in our group. And anyway, if people are fighting back, we ought to all work in tandem."

"Much like we joined forces with Marian," Little John said. "When Will and I first came here, and then when our crew added yours when you came home from the Crusade."

"Precisely," Robin said. "We should find him, if we possibly can, and see if he wouldn't be a good addition."

«–»

"But though the gang kept their eyes and ears open for any sign of the mysterious archer, they never found him."

"Him?! It's just you," Mari-Lu crossed her arms. "You can't fool me. I know it's you."

Aunt Lucy laughed. "So it is, but they didn't know that."

"Did Robin ever find you?"

"No. But the mysterious archer," Aunt Lucy winked, "eventually showed herself…"

"Oh, Aunt Lucy," Mari-Lu rolled her eyes.

"Will was soon allowed by Dusty to be out of his bed, though he was still watched closely and not yet free to help in the ambushes or any other exploits. Still, his good nature, his mind for strategy, and his overall loyalty to the gang soon made him Robin's right hand in all things, much as Allen had once been. Marian, for her part, kept an eye on both Will and Dusty and became ever more convinced that there was something there…"

"I want to hear that story!"

"Not today. Mari-Lu. Not today."

"Okay, then did Robin—"

"Marry Marian yet?" Aunt Lucy finished the question for her. "Not yet. First, the Hooded Rescuer was caught by Gisbourne when she'd been attempting to rescue a man who was being beaten in the streets of Nottingham…"

Chapter 18

MARIAN GRAPPLED WITH the soldier she'd attacked when she'd seen him kicking a young man bloody and senseless in the street. The soldier had drawn his sword, and Marian grabbed his wrist, trying to prevent him from using the blade.

The soldier's other hand curled into a fist and slammed into her stomach, but Marian held on tightly to the soldier's wrist even as she used her free hand to grab her infamous jeweled dagger from her belt and plunge it into the soldier's torso. He groaned and stumbled back a few paces, and Marian ripped the sword from his grasp.

Before she could do anything with the blade however, she felt a grip like iron wrap around her own wrist and the searing pain alone made her drop the sword.

A hand grabbed her shoulder and spun her around, pinning her to the wall of a house nearby. Gisbourne was inches from her face, his arm pressed firmly across her collar bone to hold her in place as his other hand wrapped around both her wrists in a clutch too tight for Marian to get free of, though she struggled against him.

"I've got you now," Gisbourne leered. "Let's see who you are."

Keeping his hand around her wrists, Gisbourne reached up with his other hand and ripped the mask from her face. For a moment, he was motionless, staring. Then he stumbled backwards, letting go of her entirely. "Marian?"

Marian raised her chin, preparing herself to fight Gisbourne. He was said to be one of the best swordsmen and fighters in all of England, but she would do whatever she had to to be free.

Gisbourne shook his head as if to clear it, bewilderment clouding his eyes as he stepped closer, mumbling to himself, "I should have known…the secret passages…your affiliation with Robin…"

Marian tensed as Gisbourne reached for her again, but with him towering over her and her back pressed to the wall, there was nowhere for her to go. Marian swung her knee forward, hoping to catch him off guard with a well placed kick but Gisbourne caught her knee with one hand, snatching her wrist in the other just as she went for a punch instead.

"None of that, Marian. We're friends again, remember? Though running away from Nottingham after your father's funeral has put a damper on our budding friendship, wouldn't you say?"

"Get off of me!"

"No. You're coming to the castle. The Sheriff is away on business, but he will be more than pleased to find the Hooded Rescuer has finally been caught."

Gisbourne quickly tied her wrists together, and then roughly placed the mask over her face once more, before dragging her through the streets of Nottingham to the castle. He took her to the dungeons and left her there.

Marian wasn't alone for long. She heard the thick doors of the dungeon creak open, and then saw a familiar face slink in.

"Marian," Allen greeted her sheepishly, moving to sit outside her cell. "I'm on guard duty."

"Now won't that just please Robin," Marian rolled her eyes.

Allen frowned, but said nothing.

"Allen, get me out of here."

"I can't do that."

"Why not? You told me you only joined their forces to save my father. Well guess what? He died anyway, so thanks for nothing."

"Even if I rescued you, Robin would never take me back."

"No, he won't. And I'll never trust you either, Allen. You made your choices."

"Then what would be the point?" Allen sighed.

"It's the right thing to do, you imbecile," Marian snapped.

The doors creaked open again and Gisbourne strode into the dungeons. "Marian," he stopped outside her cell, leaning against the bars and studying her, his face far more open and hopeful than Marian had seen it since the day he'd asked her to marry him. "Two and a half years ago I wounded the Hooded Rescuer…"

Marian shuddered, remembering the way Gisbourne's dagger had sunk into Mark's side, and how she'd desperately tended to his wounds, constantly worried that he would die of infection. She'd been worried for his life then, and that hadn't changed now. If Gisbourne wanted to know about Mark, he was asking the wrong person.

Marian placed her hand on her side where Mark's wound had been located. "Yes. I remember. And you'll remember you didn't see me in Nottingham for several weeks after that. You thought I was sad over my father being arrested, if I recall."

Gisbourne sighed, his open expression fading into one of darkness and doubt. He turned and left the dungeons without another word.

198

Marian knew she would die if Allen didn't help her, but all that mattered at the moment was keeping Mark safe. She turned toward the traitor and glared at him. "If he hears a word about Mark..."

"I won't say anything, Marian. Believe me, I've learned my lesson about betraying my friends. It's never happening again."

"I don't believe you. But I will haunt you from the grave if my brother comes to harm."

"He won't. Not because of me. Though if I were you I would lower my voice, or better yet not mention him at all while Gisbourne is near."

"If I were you, I'd shut up altogether," Marian said. "If I'm going to die, I hardly need my last memories to be of an idiot like you trying to give me advice."

Allen crossed her arms, frowning again, but to Marian's relief he didn't speak again. Through the evening and into the night Allen sat quietly and Marian did her best to ignore his presence. She lay on the little straw mattress in her cell, staring up at the stone ceiling above her trying to imagine how her father must have felt to live in a cell for so long.

The hours hardly seem to pass at all as Marian studied the cracks in the ceiling and wondered how Gisbourne would have her executed, but eventually morning came and with it came Andrew.

When he entered the dungeons, Marian sat up. This was it. She was going to die.

Andrew had a bundle under his arm. "Allen, you're needed upstairs. Gisbourne is in his room and expecting you."

Allen got up, rubbed his sleepy eyes, and moved out of the dungeons. Andrew pulled a key from his pocket and unlocked the cell.

Marian thought about trying to escape, but Andrew was armed and she was not, and despite her best efforts she still wasn't as proficient a fighter as other members of the gang.

Andrew held out the bundle. "You're to change into this dress and then give me that disguise," Andrew said. "Gisbourne's orders."

"What does he want with it? And why hang me in a dress? He's hanging me because I'm the Hooded Rescuer, not because I'm Lady Marian."

Andrew's eyes didn't meet hers. "Just take it, my lady."

Marian sighed and snatched the dress from Andrew, who dutifully turned around as she stripped out of the disguise and changed into the dress.

"Here's my outfit, for whatever Gisbourne needs it for," Marian rolled her eyes. Andrew took the disguise, locked Marian's cell once more, and disappeared for some minutes, but he soon returned.

"It's time."

Marian straightened her shoulders as Andrew led her out of her cell and through the castle halls. He didn't bind her, and Marian's mind began to race with possibilities. She knew this castle better than almost anyone, and Andrew was always so disturbingly polite—surely she could get away if given the opportunity.

Andrew stayed close by her side, however, and they passed too many of the Sheriff's soldiers and the prying eyes of the various nobles who called the castle their home for her to feel safe making an attempt at an escape.

Soon Andrew was leading her out of the great doors into the castle courtyard. Gisbourne was standing by a simple gallows that had been erected there, much like the one used in Nottingham Square.

As they reached the bottom of the wide stone steps, the Sheriff strode through the gate from the city beyond.

"Drat that Robin Hood!"

"Did your treasure evade you?" Gisbourne asked.

"Don't mock me Gisbourne," the Sheriff snapped. Then he seemed to collect himself as he looked about the courtyard. "But let us think of better things. We're here to hang our original nuisance today. Ah, Marian dear," the Sheriff waved to her and Andrew as they approached. "You're just in time to hang the Hooded Rescuer."

Marian held Gisbourne's gaze as the Sheriff taunted her. "I'm ready."

"As am I!" the Sheriff laughed, as Gisbourne kept eye contact with Marian, never wavering for a moment. "As you can see," the Sheriff continued, "we're hanging him here in the courtyard so that Robin Hood can't spoil it as he spoils so many of our executions. We don't need the public eye on this one, he just needs to die."

"Clever," Marian responded. Her palms were sweaty, and despite herself, her legs were shaking, but she wasn't going to let the Sheriff or Gisbourne see any weakness in her.

An arrow struck the corner of the wooden gallows with a dull thud, and Marian and everyone else in the courtyard looked up to see where it had come from. High on the wall stood a lone figure in Marian's disguise.

Marian glanced at Gisbourne but he refused to meet her gaze now.

"What's the Hooded Rescuer doing up there?" the Sheriff yelled. "You told me he was in custody!"

"He was!" Gisbourne said.

Whoever was in the disguise leaped down the outside of the wall. Gisbourne shouted at the nearby soldiers to follow him as he and Andrew ran toward the gate to go after him.

The Sheriff paced in front of the empty gallows, grumbling to himself. Marian stood still, unsure what to make of any of it. Gisbourne had specifically instructed Andrew to take the disguise and have Marian change into something else…but why? Why would he help her?

Gisbourne and the other soldiers soon returned.

"Well?" the Sheriff demanded.

"He's gone."

The Sheriff punched Gisbourne in the face. He stumbled backwards, caught off balance and wincing in pain.

"You have failed me one too many times!" The Sheriff stormed past Marian and into the castle.

Gisbourne straightened, glanced at Marian, and then marched past her into the castle as well.

"Come with me, my lady," Andrew said, taking her elbow. Andrew escorted Marian to the bedchamber she had once lived in while under house arrest in the castle.

"Wait here."

"Andrew, wait—"

But he was already gone. Marian paced the room. She could have escaped now, with no one to guard her, but her curiosity was too great to overcome. Why had Gisbourne helped her?

She didn't have to wait long to find out, as a minute later Gisbourne and Allen appeared at her door. Allen was holding her disguise.

"This belongs to you," he held it out awkwardly. Marian stared at Gisbourne as the two men entered the room and shut the door.

"You saved me?" Marian kept her gaze on Gisbourne, trying to gauge the emotions on his face and failing.

"Don't I count for something?" Allen said.

"You both saved me," Marian said, turning to stare at Allen. "Thank you…but why?"

"Get rid of that disguise, Allen," Gisbourne said, ignoring her question. "Burn it."

"Yes, sir," Allen said, giving Marian one last glance before he left the room and shut the door behind him.

Marian turned to Gisbourne. "Why didn't you let me hang?"

"Did you really believe I would?"

"After everything you've done, why would I believe anything else?"

"I'm sorry," Gisbourne ran a hand across his face, his shoulders slumping. He seemed…weary. Defeated. "I didn't mean to…Marian, can I ask…?"

"What?"

"Stay. Please. I could endure this place if only you'd stay."

Marian studied the man before her, as confused as she had ever been by him. "I…"

She wanted to rail that this one good deed wouldn't make her trust him; it was true, after all. But she knew his volatile nature too well to speak her mind this time. She would have to play along for now. And more than that, having someone in the castle would once more make spying on the Sheriff easier to do.

"I will stay."

Gisbourne simply nodded and then left the room. Marian sank onto the bed and stared at the door. It appeared Gisbourne still cared for her, and was willing to risk a great deal to protect her. And Allen, too, had lied to the Sheriff and pretended to be Marian in order to keep the blame away from her.

Marian sighed, falling backwards onto the bed and staring at the stone ceiling. Men were far too confusing and changeable. Despite what Gisbourne and Allen had done, Marian didn't believe for a moment that she could trust either of them.

That night Robin and Mark slipped into Nottingham castle to see Marian.

As Robin gently closed the door to the bedchamber, Mark bounded across the room and wrapped Marian in a tight hug. "I was so worried!"

"We were away with the Sheriff," Robin said as he moved close and claimed his own hug. "He was trying a new route for his treasure to avoid us and we weren't here when…when the message came…" Robin's arms tightened around her. "We thought you were dead for sure."

"I can't tell you how glad I am that you aren't," Mark said.

Robin pulled back from his embrace, taking Marian's hands in his own. "I couldn't live without you, Marian."

"You don't have to."

"I saw Allen. I…he…I'm so grateful."

"It's the least he could do," Mark grumbled.

"What are you going to do about him, Robin?" Marian asked.

Robin sighed. "I don't know…he wants to do right, that much I can tell. If I do let him back in our circle…I don't know that I can trust him."

"I know," Marian said. "I don't believe I can either. But he did save my life…"

"That counts for something," Mark said. "But if he comes back, Robin, we have to keep an eye on him. He can't be privy to all our meetings, our secrets."

"I agree," Robin said. "I can't believe I'm considering this…but he saved you, Marian…and that means everything to me."

"Shall the four of us leave together then?" Mark asked.

Marian shook her head. "I told Sir Guy I would stay."

"You what?!"

"He helped to rescue me. In fact, I believe he instigated my rescue. It was the least I could do. Also, who knows what he would have done if I had refused."

"Okay, so you told him in the moment you'd stay," Mark said, crossing his arms. "That doesn't mean you actually have to stay here."

Robin's brow was furrowed as he studied Marian. "You know he cares for you."

"I know."

"You—"

"No, Robin. I don't. But I owe him my life."

"Not Allen?" Mark asked. "You don't owe Allen your life?"

Marian sighed. "I can't explain it, Mark, but somehow I do think I could do some good here in the castle. I won't be under house arrest, I assume, so I could presumably come to the camp as I pleased. Yet having access to the Sheriff and Gisbourne could be invaluable. You thought so, Robin, when I was first brought here, and it's even more important now that none of you can spy from the secret passages. You sneak in here often enough, but it's far more dangerous than it used to be."

"You make a valid point," Robin sighed. "But, you don't have to stay here for him."

"I know."

"I don't trust him, and I hate that he loves you, in his own messed up way," Robin sighed.

"I don't trust him either, but we could use that messed up love to our advantage, to further help the people of Nottingham."

"You really want to stay?"

"I...I guess I do."

Mark shook his head. "This is ridiculous."

"It's my choice, Mark. I could do good here, more than sit at the camp and tend to Will or the children. We need to know what the Sheriff and Gisbourne are doing in order to stop them, don't we? We need someone on the inside now that we don't have access to the secret passages. You can visit me, or I can probably visit you if the Sheriff doesn't put me under guard, and relay whatever information I find."

"I don't like it, but I won't stop you," Robin said.

"I couldn't stop you if I wanted to," Mark sighed. "I definitely want to…but I know you too well to think I could change your mind."

"I'll be alright. For the time being, at least, Gisbourne is willing to risk everything to protect me. And Andrew is an ally of sorts. At the very least, he isn't an enemy, and he did help with my strange rescue today."

"How long will you stay?" Robin asked.

"Until today's good feelings are replaced with disgust for Gisbourne's usual antics, I suppose."

Robin grinned. "Good. That shouldn't take long at all. You're sure you aren't softening toward everyone's favorite sadist?"

Marian rolled her eyes. "No, I'm not. If someone was going to steal my heart from you it wouldn't be Sir Guy of Gisbourne."

"I'm disturbed you would suggest your heart could be stolen at all."

"You know perfectly well my heart belongs only to you, Robin. It always has."

Robin kissed her cheek. "In that case…will you marry me, Marian?"

"What?"

Mark coughed. "I think I'll wait in the hall."

"Don't leave the room, Mark!" Marian grabbed his arm. "You could get caught. I might be safe here, but you aren't!"

Robin chuckled. "Marian, I asked you a question and you are deftly ignoring it."

"Please let me leave," Mark groaned, though Marian kept a tight grip on his arm to keep him from leaving the room.

"Well?" Robin looked to Marian expectantly. "Do I get an answer?"

"This is all a bit sudden, don't you think?"

"You choosing to stay at the castle is sudden and insane," Robin replied. "My question seems tame by comparison."

"Oh just answer his question," Mark groaned again. "I don't need to be here all night…"

Marian laughed. "What do you think, Mark? Should I say yes?"

"Please," Mark rolled his eyes. "Get it over with."

Marian laughed and swatted her brother before giving Robin a swift hug. "Of course I will marry you, though how and when given the state of our lives remains to be seen."

"That is fair. We'll figure it out." Robin kissed Marian's cheek. "Be safe, Marian."

"You, too."

"At the first sign of trouble, or Gisbourne returning to his usual self, you're coming home."

"'Home' being the middle of the forest," Marian laughed.

Chapter 19

"THAT NIGHT, ALLEN disappeared from Nottingham," Aunt Lucy said. "Marian was not surprised, and neither was Gisbourne though he kept that to himself. Allen had already told him that he was fed up with working for him, and had never truly wanted to be there in the first place."

"Then why did he do it?" Mari-Lu crossed her arms. "He didn't have to betray the gang."

"I'll tell you all about why Allen did the things that he did someday," Aunt Lucy laughed. "But this story is Marian's…"

"Okay, okay. At least Robin and Marian are finally going to get married!"

"Though the gang continued to save and help as many people as they could, there were still many incidents that the Sheriff blamed them for that they knew they hadn't been a part of, though the identity of the mysterious archer remained hidden."

"It isn't hidden, Aunt Lucy. It's you."

"It was hidden to them," Aunt Lucy laughed. "Will you let me tell my story my way, or not?"

"Alright…what came next?"

"The Sheriff came up with what he thought was a brilliant plan to seize power indefinitely for himself and Prince John. Tired of waiting for the king to die in the Austrian prison, he decided to take Gisbourne and a few soldiers and go to Austria to kill the king himself."

"Oh no!"

"Marian insisted on accompanying them, and the Sheriff welcomed her along—he had always found her amusing, and this time was no different. For her part, Marian felt sure she could stall them long enough for Robin to do something, to save the king somehow. So the Sheriff's party made its way to Vienna to kill King Richard, and Robin's gang followed."

Aunt Lucy stopped speaking. Her eyes were closed and more than one tear slipped beneath her eyelids and traced a path down her cheek. Mari-Lu reached out a small hand and brushed the tears away, causing Aunt Lucy to open her eyes.

Mari-Lu placed her small hands on either side of Aunt Lucy's face. "What's wrong?"

Aunt Lucy brushed a wisp of stray hair behind Mari-Lu's ear. "This part of the story always makes me cry."

"What happened?"

"Though Robin's gang successfully rescued the king from his captors in Austria before the Sheriff could get to him, they met with some trouble…"

«→»

Marian gripped the windowsill, her knuckles white as she watched Robin in the street below, scurrying along with the rest of the gang on horseback as they attempted to slink out of the city unnoticed. The king was with them, meaning they had managed to free him from his imprisonment, but they were not free yet.

Behind Marian, the Sheriff was ranting about the impossibility of Robin Hood foiling his plans even here, so far from England.

"Something has to be done about this outlaw when we return," the Sheriff growled.

"Why wait?" Gisbourne responded, and Marian turned toward the room to watch the conversation, stepping slightly to the side to block the view from the window in case they chose to look in that direction.

"What do you mean, why wait?" Andrew asked.

"Robin Hood is clearly here," Gisbourne replied. "We could simply deal with him once and for all. He won't have the support of the people here to help him hide from us."

Marian felt her blood boiling once more as she watched Gisbourne casually discussing destroying the man that she loved.

"You truly are an imbecile."

The words were out of Marian's mouth before she knew she was going to say them. Gisbourne turned toward her with wide eyes, and Andrew watched with what appeared to be horror.

The Sheriff however, simply laughed as he walked toward Marian.

"You always did know how to speak your mind. This is precisely why we keep you around, my dear."

"I'm not your 'dear'," Marian snapped.

The Sheriff stopped in front of her, a grin on his face. But suddenly the grin froze, and a gleam hit his eye as he looked past her.

Marian forced herself not to turn and look out the window.

"Gisbourne, get my bow!" the Sheriff snapped.

Gisbourne grabbed the nearby weapon and moved toward the window. Marian stepped forward to intercept him. "What are you doing?"

"Marian, don't," Gisbourne hissed, passing the bow over her head to the Sheriff. Marian spun around, lunging toward the Sheriff, but Gisbourne grabbed her arm and restrained her.

"Don't," he hissed into her ear. "He doesn't know you're an outlaw, don't make it harder for me to protect you."

Marian jerked her arm away from Gisbourne's grasp just as the Sheriff was letting his arrow fly. She leaned out the window to see down the street, her heart pounding in her ears. Had he killed Robin?

Down in the street below, the king was slumped on the ground and Dusty was running toward him.

"Gisbourne, the soldiers!" the Sheriff snapped, spinning around.

In a moment, everyone was sprinting from the room. Gisbourne had his troops into the street and fighting Robin and the gang in a flash. Marian ran out into the dusty street and looked around at the chaos, trying to decide what to do, where to go.

Robin's sword flashed through the air quick as lightning, dropping one soldier after another. He didn't need her help.

Mark was standing over the wounded king, fighting off every attempt of the Sheriff's men to kill him. Gisbourne was headed that way with his sword drawn, likely intent on finishing the job himself.

Marian sprinted across the street, dodging around Little John in fisticuffs with two of the Sheriff's men, and Allen locked in a sword fight with another until she stood between Gisbourne and her brother.

"Guy! Stop. Look around you. You can't win."

"Marian, I have to do this." Gisbourne continued walking forward, his eyes dark.

"No." Marian held her ground, standing between Gisbourne and his prey.

"Marian!" Gisbourne gave Marian a warning swing with his sword though he wasn't yet close enough to hurt her.

Mark killed the soldier he was fighting, and as he fell to the ground with a crash of armor, he moved toward Marian.

"You can't do this, Guy," Marian said. "You can't kill the king. You can't kill England."

"No. Listen to me. I have to kill the king, but then it's over. That will be the end of it all, and you and I can leave. We can go far away; away from England and the Sheriff and all of it."

"I would rather die than be with you, Sir Guy of Gisbourne."

"What?" He stopped walking, his sword lowered slightly.

Mark was now beside her and grabbed her arm protectively, but Marian didn't stop. "I'm going to marry Robin Hood. I love him."

The next moment Marian's face crumpled in an expression of pain as a sword sliced through her. Gisbourne stumbled backwards as Mark screamed his outrage and his sword caught Gisbourne's arm as he jerked away and Marian dropped to the dirt.

"Marian!" Will's cry echoed through the street and caught the attention of the others.

"No!" Robin screamed as Marian fell to the ground, Gisbourne's sword still protruding from her chest.

"Lord help her." Dusty breathed.

Much fainted.

"Gisbourne!" the Sheriff shouted. "Let's get out of here!"

The Sheriff broke away in the moment of shock and, leaping on his horse, he pulled Gisbourne up after him and they rode away from the tragic scene.

Robin ran to Marian's side. "Marian!"

"Robin! Help the King!"

Mark sank to the ground and pulled Marian's head into his lap.

Dusty knelt beside Robin and leaned over Marian. "He's fine, Marian. I saw to his shoulder. The king will be fine."

Marian tried to take a deep breath and winced.

Robin looked at Dusty, who gave a slight shake of the head. Robin turned back to Marian and placed his hands on either side of her face. "I'm sorry, Marian love. We can't remove the sword."

"Why?" Marian looked from Robin to Dusty.

"You'll bleed out," Dusty said simply, her brow furrowed and her eyes swirling with emotions Marian couldn't concentrate on long enough to comprehend.

A look upward showed her Mark's face soaked in salty tears. "I'm so sorry, I'm so sorry."

"Mark." Marian gasped, her voice losing its strength. "This is not your fault."

"I should have stopped him. I was right beside you…"

"Mark…don't…blame…"

The entire gang circled around, Little John having revived Much, and King Richard stood beside them. Marian's eyes darted about the circle, lighting on first one face and then the next.

"Stay with me, Marian," Robin moaned, stroking her hair. "Stay with me."

"Marry…me…"

Robin couldn't stop the tears from falling. "Marian."

"Please…"

"I can't."

Mark moaned in agony and turned his face away.

Marian kept her eyes on Robin as darkness began to creep around the edges of her vision. The pain in her body was lessening, which she took as a bad sign.

"… Ro…Robin…"

Robin took a deep breath, grabbing Marian's hand and holding on tight. "I, Robin of Locksley, take you, my brave, beautiful Marian, to be my wife. To have and to hold, from this day forward, for better or for worse, for richer or for poorer, in sickness and in health. I promise to love you and cherish you… until…until death…" Robin's voice broke at the last.

Marian smiled through her tears, trying to speak but finding her voice unable to answer her needs. "I…I…"

"It's okay, Marian," Robin whispered as Mark sobbed beside him.

And I, Marian, take you, my wonderful Robin Hood, Earl of Locksley, to be my husband. To have and to hold…until death do us part.

He couldn't hear her, but looking into his blue eyes Marian knew Robin understood exactly what she was thinking.

The king knelt beside Robin, and taking his signet ring from his finger he gave it to him. "She needs a wedding band, Robin."

Robin took a shaky breath and placed it on Marian's hand.

"Kiss…me…" Marian gasped.

And so he did. Mark was not the only one sobbing in the group gathered around Marian's dying body.

"Robin," Marian closed her eyes for a moment as darkness encroached upon her mind. Gathering what little strength she had left, she looked up into his eyes and gasped out, "Promise me… you'll keep fighting."

"Marian…"

"Please…England…needs…."

The King nodded. "England does need you, Robin. Especially since I am not going back yet. I have unfinished business here. You must take care of my people."

Robin shook his head, bringing Marian's hands to his lips as tears cascaded down his cheeks, splashing onto her face.

"Robin…" Marian's voice was weak. "Promise…me…"

Finally Robin sighed. "I promise. For you, my darling Marian."

Marian's eyes suddenly filled with a vacant, distant look and Robin's shoulders shook with his sobs, as Mark let out a howl of anguish. Dusty reached over to carefully close Marian's eyes.

«→»

Marian's young namesake brushed a tear from her own cheek and sighed as she watched her daughter Mari-Lu crying in Aunt Lucy's lap. Aunt Lucy's face was also wet with tears.

"Aunt Lucy, you don't have to finish right now," the younger Marian said.

Aunt Lucy glanced toward Marian, and shook her head. "I do, Marian. We cannot end on a sad note. I will finish."

Mari-Lu sniffed. "What…what did the gang do?"

"Robin's gang departed, leaving the King behind, after they had buried Marian. Robin wanted to bury her in Sherwood or next to her father. But Dusty persuaded Robin that carrying a dead body on a long journey was not a good idea. So they buried her in

Vienna and they returned to England crestfallen." Aunt Lucy wiped Mari-Lu's tears away. "And that's when I finally made my presence known."

"And it was happy again?"

"Not at first…"

Chapter 20

"SO WHAT HAPPENED?" Mari-Lu asked. "How did you meet the gang?"

"When the Sheriff left to kill the King and then Robin's gang left as well, I had followed them. I didn't help as they rescued the king from his prison, because I was still keeping my distance, but I wanted to be near if anything went wrong...and it did."

"You were there when Marian died?"

"I saw everything," Aunt Lucy sighed. "And yet I was entirely unhelpful."

"Why? You could fight as well as any of them, and you keep saying you could shoot a bow as well as Robin ever could."

Aunt Lucy was quiet for a moment, studying Mari-Lu carefully. "I was nearby when everything went down, so I did grab my bow and move to a vantage point where I could potentially assist the gang. When Gisbourne moved for the king, I had my arrow trained on his heart...even as Marian valiantly stood up to him, my fingers were trembling with anticipation, waiting to shoot..."

"Why didn't you?"

"I was angry and scared, Mari-Lu, and I was aiming to kill him."

"So?"

"So, I don't know if you've picked up on this, but I hated killing other people. Partially because it turned my stomach and I was squeamish about it, and partially because I believed the Lord when he said 'you shall not commit murder.' I was ready to kill

Guy that day, and I stood there shaking as my desire to protect the gang I hardly knew, the anger toward Guy, and my own convictions warred within me. In the end…I did nothing."

"You did nothing?!"

"I did nothing," Aunt Lucy repeated slowly, her voice soft and gentle.

Marian kept her eyes on her daughter, wondering how she would process this part of the story. It was Marian's least favorite part, knowing Aunt Lucy could have potentially saved Lady Marian and had been unable to.

"So…what happened after that?" Mari-Lu asked, still looking up at Aunt Lucy in confusion and disbelief.

"When the gang returned, crestfallen, to England, I followed. The first few weeks back in Nottingham everything was upside down. The Sheriff was gloating over Marian's death, Sir Guy was tormented, and Robin hid in his camp. His gang still did what they could for the people, but Robin did not. I saw Dusty helping the sick, I saw Little John intimidating soldiers who had been attempting to do the same to unsuspecting villagers, I saw Will leading the gang in ambushes in the forest. But without Marian on the inside to glean information from the Sheriff and Gisbourne, it was difficult for any of us to know when innocents would be arrested or executed, and more people began to die as we failed to save them."

"Oh no," Mari-Lu frowned. "Marian was right to stay when Gisbourne asked her to, wasn't she? The gang really did need someone to spy on the Sheriff."

"Yes, Marian had made a wise decision that the gang was now feeling the absence of. The caravans through the forest was the easiest work to continue, as the gang merely had to watch the

Sherwood road and then quickly form an ambush. The Sheriff had tried a few other routes in the past and been spoiled by Marian's ability to inform the gang, so he'd given up that idea and had chosen instead to double and triple the amount of soldiers who accompanied the treasure each time."

"And you watched the ambushes?"

"Sometimes. And I'd help from a distance if I felt they needed it…"

"Still being the 'mysterious archer' instead of telling them you were there."

"Yes. They knew I was there, though. They all shot to kill, and I always wounded the enemy. Meaning if I helped from my hiding places in the trees, Will and the others absolutely noticed the difference."

"But they still couldn't find you?"

"I grew up in the trees outside London," Aunt Lucy chuckled. "Robin and Marian and the others knew the castle's every secret because of their childhood, but I knew forests. After the return from Austria, I never saw Robin. I had a vague idea where the gang's camp was located, but I had never been there and I steered clear of it as much as I could, still afraid of human connection."

"Was Robin okay?"

"Certainly not."

"And what about Mark?"

"Mark still helped in the caravan raids, but he never spoke to anyone. Not a single word. It was at that time I was finally discovered…"

«-»

Lucy let her hand slide along the thick branch beside her as her feet lightly moved across another branch below. As she moved swiftly along the length of the branch toward its end, she prepared herself for a leap and then without slowing her movements she jumped across the short distance to a tree nearby whose thick branches stretched toward the one she had been in.

She paused briefly as she landed, feeling the branch dip beneath her and quiver slightly, but when it didn't snap she moved forward toward the trunk of the tree, eyeing the surrounding branches, and the trees nearby, to chart her path forward.

Robin and his gang had been learning to cover their tracks in the forest, but Lucy found it was easier to stay hidden from the Sheriff's men and Robin's gang if she made no tracks whatsoever.

As she skipped lightly from tree to tree, Lucy had to choose her course carefully. Too small a branch and it would snap beneath her weight and she would be forced to grapple to catch herself or fall to the ground below. Trees with branches too close together presented their own problems, as her bow would snag in branches over her head, or worse there wouldn't be space for her to move quickly and easily around the tree to move on to the next one.

It was an interesting choice of travel, to be sure, but after wandering the forest for nearly a year Lucy had grown accustomed to Sherwood and had charted her own paths through much of the forest. She could travel with more speed and confidence through the woods because she already knew many of the trees and branches to use.

Lucy heard voices in the forest below, and stood still, clutching the trunk of the tree she was currently hiding in. The branches below obstructed much of her view, so Lucy began to carefully climb lower, trying to make as little noise as possible.

"Did you get him?" a gruff voice called.

"Nearly," another man responded as the sounds of a scuffle reached Lucy's ears. A few more branches down, and she could see below.

Much, someone she had never spoken to but seen a great deal of, was struggling to escape the grasp of several of the Sheriff's soldiers. Undoubtedly it was one of the search parties the Sheriff occasionally sent into the forest in search of Robin Hood's gang.

Lucy swiftly pulled her bow from her back and aimed for the soldier grappling with Much. Her arrow flew and hit his shoulder, and as he let go of Much, Lucy darted forward and leaped to the next tree over.

"Where'd it come from?" the first gruff voice asked, as both soldiers looked wildly about the trees. Lucy let more arrows fly as she danced around the treetops—one to a leg, one to an arm, another to a shoulder. In a minute both soldiers were groaning and cursing as they fell to the ground. One of them yelled for help, indicating there were more soldiers nearby.

Lucy dropped to a lower branch near Much, waited to make sure the soldiers weren't looking her way, and then dropped silently to the ground behind him. Just as another soldier became visible, running through the trees toward the sounds of the first soldiers' injured cries, Lucy grabbed Much from behind and pulled him behind her tree.

She put her hand over his mouth to keep him silent, as the soldier moved toward the injured one on the ground.

"What happened?"

"Get us back to Nottingham," the gruff soldier snapped. "We need a healer."

"What happened?" the third soldier demanded again.

"Robin Hood," one of them grunted in response, pain and annoyance coating his voice. The soldier knelt beside his comrades, and Lucy pulled Much slowly backwards, away from the soldiers and deeper into the trees. Once they were far enough away they wouldn't be heard, she removed her hand from his mouth.

"Thank you, Robin."

Lucy laughed. "You're welcome, but I'm not Robin."

Much spun around at the sound of her laughter and her voice, and then stared at her open-mouthed for a moment.

"Sorry to startle you," Lucy said. It felt strange to be talking to someone that she had watched from a distance for over a year. In many ways she felt like she knew Much, and shared his grief in losing his childhood friend Marian. And yet in truth he was a stranger.

"You're the mysterious archer, aren't you?"

Lucy laughed, and realized in an instant how grateful she was to be speaking to someone other than the tavern keeper or little old Tibb. "I don't know about 'mysterious.'"

"But you are the archer who has been helping us?" Much insisted. "We've seen your work, though we could never seem to see you. It has been you, hasn't it?"

"Yes, it has been me."

"You have to come to the camp."

"I can't." Lucy felt her breath leave her lungs in an instant, as her heart skipped several beats. Speaking to Much was one thing, but introducing herself to the rest of the gang?

"Why not?"

"Will Robin allow it?"

Much waved his hand nonchalantly. "Robin's been trying to locate you for some time. He said you would be a great addition to our team."

"Oh." Lucy told herself to breathe as Much kept talking.

"Well we should leave here in any case. Those men might wander this way and notice us in a moment, and no doubt more will come from Nottingham after they report what happened."

Lucy was still hesitant, but Much grinned at her and gestured behind her. "Come on, it's this way. You'll love the gang."

"Don't you…I mean, shouldn't you be sure you can trust me before you let me inside your camp?"

"We've never seen you do anything except help people," Much said brightly as he led Lucy in the direction of the camp. "And besides, we let Allen back in…"

"Ah, yes, I did notice that."

Much stopped walking and turned to look at her. "You… noticed?"

"I…I've been watching the gang from a distance since coming to Nottingham."

"Trying to decide if we're worth joining forces with?" Much asked, resuming his brisk walk and grinning over at Lucy.

"Something like that."

"We're definitely worth it," Much laughed.

As they neared the camp, Much pointed out the traps on the ground to avoid.

"I don't use the ground as often as the trees," Lucy replied.

Much grinned. "And Marian thought *we* might be dryads." Suddenly the smile faded from Much's face as his eyes darkened. He glanced at Lucy, then away into the trees, then silently turned back around and began walking again. Lucy followed quietly behind.

When they walked into the clearing, Will, Little John, and Allen jumped to their feet from where they'd been sitting near the fire pit. Dusty was nearby with the children gathered around her, and they all turned to look at Much and Lucy. Robin, however, barely glanced up from the bow he was restringing, and Mark was nowhere to be seen.

"Much!" Will came over, eyeing Lucy with evident curiosity. "Who's this?"

Much suddenly looked like he'd won the best prize during the tournaments at Nottingham Fair as he beamed at Will. "I've found the mysterious archer!"

Robin did look up then, though he didn't approach.

"Are you really the mysterious archer?" Little John asked as Much led Lucy and Will over toward the fire.

"Yes."

Dusty stood, leaving the children as they continued to gawk at Lucy, and came to sit beside Lucy as they all settled down on the logs around the fire. "Are you planning on joining us?"

"Well...I hadn't planned on..."

"But you must!" Allen said.

Much nodded. "You have to. All the people fighting for England have to work together."

"It does seem we can do more good when we all work in tandem," Little John agreed.

Lucy looked around the group surrounding her, all of them looking eager and welcoming. And then she glanced to the side where Robin leaned against his hut, nonchalantly ignoring the conversation.

"I…I'll pray about it," she finally said.

Dusty grinned. "Now that is a wonderful idea!"

Robin rose slowly to his feet and Will turned to him. "Robin? What do you say to another gang member?"

Robin studied Lucy for a minute and then shrugged. "What we really need is a way to get information."

"You need someone on the inside," Lucy said, remembering how Marian had been exactly that before the trip to Austria.

Judging by the darkness brewing on Robin's face, that was precisely what he was remembering, too. "Yes. We need someone with the Sheriff and…Gisbourne." The latter name came out in a strangled sort of manner, and Robin turned away from the group.

Lucy took a deep breath, trying to steady her quickly beating heart. She was not only meeting the gang, which in itself seemed overwhelming, but now she was joining their forces and agreeing to spy on the Sheriff in person.

"I don't know that I want to be on the Sheriff's good side…but I'll see what I can do."

Robin nodded briskly, and then his mouth turned up into something resembling a smile, though it may have been more of a grimace. "If you're going to stay, you'll need to know who we

226

are. I'm Robin, this is Much, Will, Dusty, Little John…and Allen. Mark is in his hut…he'll come out eventually, I'm sure."

"I'm Lucy. I've…well, to be honest, I've seen all of you in Nottingham before, and recently I've been stalking your ambushes, so I know who you are."

"We've noticed your presence in our raids," Will said. "You've definitely saved a few of us more than once. The more raids we have, the more soldiers the Sheriff and other lords send with their caravans, the more trouble we have successfully ambushing without falling to harm." Will absentmindedly rubbed his chest where his own wound had once been, and Dusty reached over to take his hand.

"We do appreciate what you've been doing," Little John said. "And it will be good to have eyes and ears in Nottingham again."

And so Lucy became a part of Robin Hood's gang.

Chapter 21

"AND WHAT ADVENTURESOME days those were!" Aunt Lucy said. "I immediately made my presence known in Nottingham, rather than staying hidden at the tavern I had been living in. I began staying with Marcus and his family, and I let word get around I was the daughter of a nobleman from London. Robin insisted we leave out the fact my father was dead, murdered by Prince John, which was probably wise."

"The Sheriff wouldn't have liked you then," Mari-Lu said.

"No, he would not have. I made a point of visiting tailors and embroiderers and recreating the sort of elegant wardrobe I had growing up as a noblewoman in court. I'd been limited to simple trousers, shirts, and my cloak since I went on the run. It was a relief in many ways to find the deepest blue silks to be fitted into form-fitting dresses with wide fluted sleeves, and soft white linen for dresses with long skirts to trail behind me. It was almost embarrassing how much I had missed the more feminine side of myself while living on the run and I relished the opportunity to work with skilled men and women to craft the perfect wardrobe."

"I love getting new dresses!" Mari-Lu clapped her hands.

"I also visited every jeweler in Nottingham to order necklaces and rings to be made. When I'd left Friar Tuck all those years ago, I had taken a small fortune with me; in the years since my departure I had given much of it away to the people I rescued, and spent some on my own necessities such as lodgings and food. But there was still enough to start my wardrobe, and on top of that I had the credit of being a noblewoman's daughter. Despite the fact that my father was killed, his estate and wealth still gave his name weight, and now that it all lawfully belonged to me I could use that to order and purchase many items that I needed without having all of the necessary money on hand. When the Sheriff heard I was in the area, he insisted I come and stay at the castle. He was always concerned about his reputation, and a noblewoman living in the tavern rather than at the castle where most of the nobles stayed when visiting Nottingham was something he wouldn't allow. And more than that, he did rather miss Marian's fiery nature and was hoping for a new companion."

"That's horrible," Mari-Lu crossed her arms. "I hate him. But did you move to the castle?"

"Yes. The Sheriff was tiring company, of course. And Sir Guy was an angry, tormented man when I first met him and hardly made for good company either, but we got what we wanted."

"You were on the inside."

"Yes. I was an honored guest so the Sheriff let me do as I pleased. I spent hours getting to know the people of Nottingham and the surrounding countryside now that I could help them in the open rather than under my hood. It was strange being able to speak openly with people, both the people of Nottingham and the gang. I was still in many ways reticent to open up fully, still fearing the loss and pain that would inevitably occur. Marian's death had only heightened my fear in that regard. But Much was too sweet and eager to remain aloof from, and Will's easy manners put me at ease before I even realized he was doing so."

"He had that effect on Marian, too," Mari-Lu commented.

"Yes, he did," Aunt Lucy said. Her face was graced with a gentle smile as she sat remembering her friendship with Will.

"What else did you do?" Mari-Lu asked when Aunt Lucy did not immediately continue.

"I went for a ride every day. I had been on my feet since I left London so riding was pure joy. The Sheriff had a full stable of horses, which had once belonged to Sir Godfrey as the previous sheriff, and I took great delight in making friends with the horses. I had been lonelier than I cared to admit during the years of my traveling, and it was easier to open up to the horses than to the gang."

"What else?"

"I spent every night sitting in Nottingham castle's dining room. One whole wall was only half there, forming a giant window or ledge along that side, and I would sit on the ledge and watch the stars."

"You always did like the stars."

"They were my favorite part of all my travels."

"What else did you do?"

"I took meals with the Sheriff and Sir Guy of course, because the Sheriff was intent on finding in me the same sort of entertainment he'd once found in Marian and so relished trying to recreate the sort of scenarios that had occurred prior to my coming to the castle."

"That makes me uncomfortable," Mari-Lu frowned.

"Which part?"

"That he missed Marian like that...he didn't know her, didn't like her, he would have killed her if Gisbourne hadn't been the one to do it."

"The Sheriff was indeed a strange man," Aunt Lucy said. "And unafraid to speak openly in front of people he deemed no threat to himself and his agenda, so I kept my eyes and ears open for any information that could be helpful to Robin. One day…"

◄—►

"We have a load of 'ransom' coming in tomorrow," the Sheriff said.

Lucy looked up from her end of the table. The Sheriff, Gisbourne, and Lucy were dining together as they often did—at the Sheriff's request—but until that moment the room had been quiet apart from the clinking of their utensils, plates, and goblets.

"But isn't the King…" Lucy began, and then paused, remembering the king's escape and Marian's subsequent death. Lucy glanced toward Sir Guy and watched the storm roiling behind his eyes.

"Out of prison?" the Sheriff finished her sentence for her. "Yes. But he could always use funds." He snickered as he said it, clearly unafraid to hide his true intentions.

"You want me to meet the caravan," Sir Guy said.

"If you will. My…that is, the King's money must be protected."

Lucy rolled her eyes. "Everyone knows the taxes are collected for you and Prince John. Why even pretend otherwise?"

The Sheriff grinned, obviously enjoying Lucy's question. "The people take it better."

"Do they?" Lucy remembered the last time she'd seen her father, and the way he'd been terrified of the Prince's assassins, and how his death had been blamed on any cause other than the truth by those in the court.

The Sheriff frowned and Lucy's eyes widened, her heart racing. She hurriedly continued, "Wouldn't you be seen as a stronger man if you didn't use petty lies everyone can see through? These people expect you to be hard but if you were entirely truthful they could come to grudgingly respect you."

The Sheriff rubbed his chin thoughtfully.

Sir Guy's chair scraped across the stone floor as he shoved back from the table and stood. "What time is the caravan passing through Sherwood?"

"Mid-day tomorrow," the Sheriff answered. "Or thereabouts."

Sir Guy nodded and quickly left the room.

"If you'll excuse me, Sheriff, I believe I'll go for a ride," Lucy said.

"You love those horses, don't you?" the Sheriff asked.

Lucy laughed. "Yes, I do."

Lucy hurried to the stables that connected to the castle courtyard on one side, and the grassy knoll outside the city and castle walls on the other. It was a spacious building with stalls all along both sides to hold the horses that belonged to the Sheriff, and the visiting nobles who called the castle home. Sir Guy's horse Victory was there, pawing the ground in his stall and snorting as she passed. Lucy admired him but went in search of a more gentle steed.

Soon enough she was on her way, riding out of Nottingham and toward Sherwood and the camp. She slackened her grip on the reins and let her mount run free the distance between Nottingham and Sherwood Forest. The sun was sinking into the treetops, the sky behind the forest filled with brilliant reds and golds.

She slowed to a trot once she entered the woods and needed to avoid bushes and undergrowth, as well as ensure she didn't run into any low hanging tree branches. When they reached the camp she nudged her horse into a gentle walk so she could keep an eye out for the gang's traps.

With the sun so slow in the sky, the light inside the meadow was low and filtered through the trees to the west, the brightest patch of light illuminating the fire ring—though no fire was yet lit for the night—where Robin and Dusty sat while the children were scattered about the meadow playing.

Lucy dismounted and hurried to the fire ring to relay her news.

"We'll plan an ambush." Dusty said.

"Will we?" Robin asked. He leaned forward heavily, his shoulders curling in as he placed his head in his hands and sat in utter dejection.

Dusty scooted over to sit beside him. "The people will need the money, Robin."

"You'll have to be careful," Lucy said. "Sir Guy is coming to guard the caravan specifically against an ambush."

Robin's head snapped up, his eyes flashing with fire. "We'll definitely plan an ambush!" His sudden passion surprised Lucy.

"Vengeance is the Lord's," Dusty said softly, as she watched him closely.

Lucy studied Robin for a moment, and then Dusty—who was still watching Robin with a sad sort of expression on her face—and then glanced back to Robin as she remembered watching Sir Guy plunge his sword into Marian. It was undoubtedly where Robin's mind was as well.

"Hatred won't do you any good," Lucy said after the silence began to stretch and her mind was filling with her own feelings of guilt for not saving Marian when she'd had the chance. "It would make you no better than your enemies."

Robin turned his fiery glare toward Lucy. "Don't tell me what to do!"

"I only meant—"

"I don't care. I don't know you, and you know *nothing* about me."

Lucy considered speaking again, but a quick shake of the head from Dusty discouraged her. With nothing more to add, she returned to Nottingham.

Night had fallen before she'd made it back to the city, and Lucy let her horse walk the whole way, keeping her eyes on the stars above. She couldn't explain why she'd always been drawn to them, but something about the night sky always gave her comfort. Perhaps because the light shining from above reminded her of where her true comfort came from.

Lucy began to pray for Robin, and she didn't stop until she'd reached her room in the castle.

The next day, Sir Guy came back from protecting the caravan—which he'd failed to do—in a sour mood. But Sir Guy was always sour in those days.

That night as Lucy made her way to the dining room ledge to watch the stars, she discovered Sir Guy had found her favorite spot. He was standing by the half wall just looking out at the darkness beyond—the only light that of the moon, and the small glimpses of firelight that could be seen in the windows of houses down below in the city.

Lucy pulled herself up onto the ledge as she always did, leaning against the wall of the castle, her knees pulled up to her chest. Sir Guy was standing only a few feet from her usual spot, and Lucy unashamedly studied him by the light of the moon.

He didn't acknowledge her.

"Do you want to talk about it?"

"What?" he barked.

Lucy's eyes widened. What would be the point in angering him further? He'd murdered the last woman who had stood up to him. And yet, Lucy couldn't stop herself. The torment written across his face reminded her of the swirling guilt in her own chest.

After a moment of silence she said, "You seem very unhappy."

He made no response.

"I've made it my personal goal in life to help everyone discover the joy that I have."

"I don't need your joy!"

"Perhaps not."

Silence.

It was clear Sir Guy wasn't in a talking mood; failing to protect the caravan and deliver the Sheriff's ill-gotten treasure had put him in quite the brooding state. "It isn't your fault you know."

"What isn't my fault?" He turned to her with blazing eyes, his face suddenly ashen as he took half a step toward her. Almost threateningly, almost hesitantly, as though he wasn't sure what he was feeling or how to act.

"The caravan. Losing the treasure," Lucy explained. "Robin Hood is renowned in these parts. He could steal money from the Sheriff with his eyes closed."

"Robin Hood." Sir Guy spat the name and turned away from Lucy. Whatever she hoped to gain from this conversation clearly wasn't happening.

"Do the stars comfort you too?"

"Comfort? Do I need comfort?" Sir Guy was angry. His voice, his eyes, everything about him suggesting he was a geyser just waiting to explode as the pressure built.

Lucy bit her lip, debating the wisdom of pushing him further. She definitely didn't want to end up like Marian. "No…I just find comfort in them."

Sir Guy relaxed, if only a little.

"Was anyone hurt in the raid?"

"Of course they were! I was the only one who left with my life."

"I don't understand that."

"What?" Sir Guy turned toward her, his eyebrow quirked in curiosity though the storm was still brewing on his face.

"The killing."

"What do you mean?" Sir Guy asked.

"I believe 'you shall not kill' is very clearly stated. Robin's such a good man, you would think…"

Sir Guy studied Lucy, his brow furrowing. "Are you a friend of Robin's?"

"I like to think I'm a friend to everyone, or at least I try to be."

He continued to study her in silence.

"At least he buries the dead, there's something in that."

The silence was made more distinct by Lucy's continued commentary on Robin's behavior, so she stopped. She turned away from her brooding companion and looked up into the night sky where the constellations were displayed. The cloudless, moonlit night was one of the most beautiful she'd seen in recent years.

"I wish he'd kill me and get it over with."

Lucy felt her heart jump in her chest at the sudden sound of his voice, and then squeeze tightly as she registered what he'd said. She could feel the involuntary tears that pricked her eyes.

"Why would you want to die?"

"I don't deserve to live."

"Not many of us do."

Sir Guy shook his head. "You don't understand."

"Then tell me," she said softly.

"It's not worth discussing." He turned and walked briskly away without another word. Lucy watched his retreating back, feeling a pull to go after him, to give him comfort of some sort. Little old Tibb was right—he was, indeed, a hurting, broken soul. It was clear he was hounded by guilt, regret...possibly remorse. And Lucy wanted to help him just as she also felt drawn to help Robin, feeling a strange connection to both of them through the guilt of the moment she'd wrestled with not killing Guy and Marian had died because of it.

And yet intermingled with that desire to help Sir Guy was a fear of his changeable and unstable emotional state—he had, after all, murdered Marian in a fit of rage.

Chapter 22

THE NEXT TIME Lucy visited the camp, Robin was alone and he was crying. It was morning, and the light from the sun lit up the meadow and reflected off of every rock and metal surface around the camp, bringing the forge and huts into sharp relief.

Lucy dismounted her horse quickly, tying its reins around a tree branch, and then hurried over to where Robin was sitting in the grass. She knelt beside him and placed a hand on his arm. "Robin?"

"I can't do it," Robin glanced up at Lucy, his eyes dark with emotion as large tears splashed down his chin. His shirt was soaked with them, and so were his hands. "I know I promised but I…I can't."

"You can't do what?" Lucy asked.

"I am so tired of doing the right thing."

"Oh, Robin."

"I want to quit, Lucy, I want to quit." Robin roughly brushed a hand across his face, trying to stop his constant flow of tears. "But first I want to kill him."

"You can't quit! These people need you."

"I can't keep going."

"Yes, you can." Lucy grabbed Robin's hand, willing him to believe her. "You are strong, Robin."

"Perhaps I'm tired of being strong."

"For Marian…you have to keep going."

He sucked in a shaky breath at the mention of Marian, but didn't reply. Seeing his distraught state of mind had Lucy flashing back to that moment in Austria when she could have shot Sir Guy and didn't. Robin's grief was her own fault, and she felt responsible for bringing him out of it.

"You promised her you'd keep fighting."

Still there was no response, as Robin closed his eyes and let his tears flow freely.

"And you can't kill Sir Guy."

"Excuse me?" His eyes snapped open and he turned toward her with a familiar fire flashing across his face.

"It would be wrong. You would be no better than him if you kill him out of your hatred."

"It's not the same! He murdered Marian!"

"And you'd be murdering him."

"You don't understand," Robin snapped, jerking his hand out of her grasp.

"Hating won't help," Lucy insisted. "Killing Sir Guy won't bring her back. You have to forgive him, Robin."

"Forgive?" Robin stood hastily. When Lucy stood as well, he backed away from her. "Had you been there, had you seen him do what he did, you would understand how impossible that is."

"I *was* there, Robin."

"What?" His eyes were wide and disbelieving. He shook his head, brushing the tears from his face again and then staring at Lucy.

"I was there," Lucy repeated, her heart dropping to her toes. How could she explain to Robin that she'd let Sir Guy kill Marian? "I watched Sir Guy plunge his sword into Marian."

Lucy shuddered at the memory, and watched as Robin stumbled backwards as though he'd been struck. Everything in her screamed not to tell him she was responsible.

"I was there. And I know he regrets it. He's tormented by the memory."

"Good."

"Good? What happened to the Robin Hood who couldn't bear to see people suffer?"

"He died with Marian."

"I don't believe that."

"Just because I care for people doesn't mean I'd feel bad for Gisbourne," Robin stormed across the camp and then back again. "I hate him! He's evil and he killed Marian."

"Robin—"

"Just get out. You don't understand. You didn't know Marian, didn't love—" Robin shuddered, his whole body trembling for a moment as he closed his eyes and sighed heavily. "Just leave."

So Lucy left, and she continued to pray. She began to spend more time in the camp after that. She didn't know what she might be able to do to help Robin through his grief, or the rest of the gang for that matter, but she wanted to help all of them. She had hidden herself away from friendship for so long, but now that she was slowly opening up again she felt an overwhelming desire to protect them. And on top of everything else, her own guilt gnawed at her and she longed to assuage it.

Robin tried to avoid her when she was in the camp, so she played with the children. She took John, Rachel, and Peter on rides on her horse and she helped Will when he was teaching William, Sarah, and Beth archery.

«»

"Will you teach me?" Mari-Lu asked.

"Aunt Lucy doesn't use a bow anymore," Marian answered her daughter's question. "She hasn't used one in years."

Aunt Lucy laughed. "Ah, Marian, it's a skill I could never forget. I could teach Mari-Lu if she wanted me to.

"Why did you help Will?" Mari-Lu asked.

"Will was a fine shot but he wasn't the best," Aunt Lucy said. "For heaven's sake, he wasn't even as good as Robin."

Mari-Lu giggled. "Robin was the best in England."

Aunt Lucy laughed. "That's beside the point. If they were going to learn to shoot they might as well be the best they could possibly be. My skills were at least equal to Will's."

Marian shook her head as Mari-Lu laughed at Aunt Lucy's comment. "They were equal to Robin's, from what I've been told."

"I never believed that," Aunt Lucy said, turning her gaze toward Marian.

"But it was proved, undeniably. I know the stories."

Aunt Lucy smiled. "You know the stories according to Mark, Ida, and Robin. And you know how they embellished the legends to suit themselves. But back to my story…"

Aunt Lucy turned to Mari-Lu, who continued to watch her with rapt attention. "Robin slowly improved. He still burned with a passion to destroy Sir Guy but he was more himself otherwise. Mark, however, still remained silent and sullen and had yet to speak to anyone since Marian's death. Sir Guy also remained as tormented as ever, but despite his denial of needing comfort, he still came to the ledge every night and we sat and talked as we watched the stars. Nearly a month had gone by since the return from Vienna and one night on the ledge…"

Lucy studied the night sky over Nottingham, trying to find all of the constellations her father and Friar Tuck had always been fond of pointing out to her. She was sitting in her usual spot at the far end of the dining room ledge, her back against the castle wall, her knees pulled up to her chest. Sir Guy stood nearby, leaning forward with his elbows resting on the stone surface of the ledge.

"I ruined everything."

"What?" Lucy shook aside memories of her father and Friar Tuck and turned toward her brooding companion, surprised that he had spoken, as he rarely did.

"I killed her, Lucy."

For a moment Lucy was transported back to Austria, watching Sir Guy's sword swing forward, feeling the rough wood of her arrow against her fingertips and knowing she could kill him if she wanted to.

"I know."

"I wish…" Sir Guy's face twisted in pain and he turned away from her. For a moment all was quiet as he wrested with his emotions. Watching him wrestle with his guilt brought Lucy's own feelings of the same to the surface once more—if she'd gone through with it, saved Marian, would she be as horrified at Sir Guy's death as he was at Marian's?

Finally Sir Guy choked out, "Why hasn't Robin killed me yet? I deserve it."

"We all deserve to die, Guy."

He shook his head.

242

Maybe it was the memories of Friar Tuck that she had been entertaining before Sir Guy spoke that brought more of the monk's teaching to mind. Maybe it was simply the truth as Lucy knew it. But whatever the reason, she felt an undeniable urge to explain to Sir Guy exactly what she believed.

"No, listen to me, Sir Guy. We really all do deserve to die. I don't know if you've ever read Scripture yourself, but I was, in many ways, raised by a monk and I carry pieces of his translated Scripture with me wherever I go. Things like 'For all have sinned and fallen short of the glory of God' and 'the wages of sin is death' speak rather eloquently of the fact that we all deserve to die."

Sir Guy was silent, but he turned to look at her. The moonlight reflecting from his dark eyes mirrored the anguish of his soul. Lucy could not begin to comprehend the turmoil inside of him, but she could see it in every expression of his face. She wanted so badly to help this man. Why she felt that way, she wasn't sure—perhaps because of her shared feelings of guilt over what had become of Marian.

"Please, Guy. Believe me. We all have failed in some way. Maybe we didn't all commit murder—" Guy shuddered and jerked away from her. "But we all do things we aren't proud of, things that displease God. We all deserve death."

Guy did not seem remotely interested in the conversation at hand, but Lucy pressed on. It was freeing in some ways to be able to talk to someone about the faith she had been raised in. Dusty understood and shared her faith, but Lucy didn't see much of Dusty or the rest of the gang on a daily basis. Sir Guy, however, was her constant shadow every night, and he was the only one who would understand her feelings of guilt—his on a deeper level, perhaps, but still…

"Our God sent Jesus so we wouldn't have to die. He loved us so much He died for us, for you. So He could take away your sin, free you from this guilt." Even as she said it, Lucy could feel her own emotions wrestling with the idea of complete forgiveness. Yet if Christ could forgive Sir Guy of Gisbourne, then surely Lucy's own guilt could be assuaged as well.

Still Sir Guy did not speak.

"He's forgiven you, Guy."

He turned to Lucy stricken. "But I can't forgive myself."

Lucy reached out to lay a comforting hand on his shoulder, understanding that pain completely. She couldn't forgive herself either. Sir Guy pulled further away from her, out of reach of her hand.

"You can't change the past," Lucy said, trying to believe what she said. "All you can do is direct the future."

Sir Guy shook his head. "You don't understand."

"I'm trying to."

As Lucy watched, the moonlight reflected off of tears slowly gliding down Sir Guy's face. He didn't say anything else, and Lucy felt she'd already said too much for one night so she kept her mouth shut. The silence stretched on, and Lucy turned back to the stars. She heard rather than saw Sir Guy's composure come back, as his gasping breaths returned to a normal steady rhythm. And before too long, he'd simply walked away.

Lucy stayed at the ledge for a while longer, thinking about Friar Tuck and wondering if she ought to write to him. She was no longer running away from connection with people, and she missed him. And he, more than anyone else in her life, would know what to say to her to assuage the ever growing feeling of guilt that wrapped around her.

Chapter 23

A FEW DAYS later, the Sheriff decided to hang a villager who had looked at him cross-eyed, or so he claimed. Lucy waited an appropriate amount of time after his declaration and then hurried to the stables to saddle a horse and ride to Robin's camp to inform him. He wasn't there when she arrived, but Dusty and Much were —quietly entertaining the children who were still confined to the camp.

"Where's Robin?"

"Everyone is busy," Dusty replied. "Little John and Will are on a trip to the west, distributing our wealth beyond the sphere of Nottingham. Robin heard there was a particularly blood-thirsty sheriff a few shires over and went to investigate, and see if there was anything to be done about it. Mark tagged along, I believe."

"What's wrong?" Much asked.

"The Sheriff, as always," Lucy replied. After she'd shared the Sheriff's plan with Dusty, she told her to pray for Sir Guy.

"Pray for Gisbourne?"

"God loves him too, Dusty."

Dusty sighed. "I suppose He does."

"He's horrible," young William piped up. "And so angry all the time."

Lucy couldn't argue with that.

To change the subject, Lucy suggested she could practice archery with those of the children who had been learning, and William and Beth eagerly agreed. So Lucy moved to one side of the open meadow to help them shoot, while Dusty stayed with the smaller children and kept them out of trouble.

Little John and Will eventually returned to the camp, so Dusty and Lucy filled them in on what the Sheriff was planning. Will wanted every detail from Lucy of the forthcoming execution, and she did not have many.

"I'll need more than 'the Sheriff wants to kill a man' in order to save him," Will said. "If you can get more information and bring it back to us so I can plan a proper rescue, that would be helpful."

"Of course," Lucy agreed. "I'll see what I can find."

Will nodded and then turned to walk away toward his hut, apparently through with the conversation, but not before Lucy heard him muttering under his breath, "Marian would not have brought such useless information."

Lucy returned to the castle and spent the afternoon shadowing the Sheriff and keeping him, as he called it, entertained until she felt she'd gleaned enough facts from him about the upcoming execution to satisfy Will. She returned to the camp that evening, and with Lucy's information the gang successfully foiled the Sheriff's hanging.

Later that week, Lucy was in the stable getting ready for a ride. She kept up a cheerful conversation with the horse to keep it at ease while she saddled it. The stables were bustling with activity, as they often were. Lords preparing to go for rides to neighboring cities for business, servants mucking out stalls or brushing down horses. So when the stable doors opened and let in a flash of sunlight from outside, Lucy thought nothing of it and continued to saddle her mount.

Sir Guy soon approached, reaching out to stroke the horse's velvety nose. "You love to ride, don't you?"

Lucy glanced at her odd companion, never quite sure what to make of him. "Yes, Sir Guy. I do."

"You ought to ride a better beast than this."

"She's wonderful, and she suits my purposes just fine."

Sir Guy shook his head. "You should ride my stallion."

Lucy tightened the last strap on the saddle and turned to him, her eyebrows raised. "Did you just offer to let me ride your magnificent mount? Sir Guy, I couldn't."

"Why not?"

"Won't you need him?"

"I'm in the castle more often than not, and if I go out it is usually on foot. Victory could use the exercise, and you seem to enjoy a ride or two daily."

"Well…"

Sir Guy patted the horse's nose one last time and then waved to a nearby stable boy. "You. Unsaddle this horse."

"Yes sir," the boy said, his eyes wide with fear as he came to care for Lucy's mount, making a wide circle around Sir Guy to do so.

Sir Guy moved away from Lucy toward Victory's stall, and was soon leading him into the middle of the stable. As the stable boy removed the saddle from the horse Lucy had intended to ride, Sir Guy took it and transferred it to Victory.

As he worked, he spoke, "You love riding, more than anyone I've met before. So you ought to have the best horse you can. Please. I would be greatly honored if you rode my horse."

How could she refuse? Besides, he was nearly done saddling Victory and it seemed rather silly to unsaddle the horse and saddle her own again. "I'll try not to be gone too long."

"Don't hurry. As I said, I rarely need him."

Lucy did find Victory to be a superior mount, though she wasn't about to tell Sir Guy such a thing. She spent an hour riding over the hills and fields surrounding Nottingham before she turned toward the forest and headed for the camp. Why Sir Guy had felt the need to share his horse, Lucy wasn't sure, but she enjoyed riding Victory more than she cared to admit.

When Lucy arrived at the camp in Sherwood, Mark was sitting in front of his hut, looking down at his hands which were open in his lap. He appeared to be alone in the camp, but that didn't surprise Lucy. The gang was often in Nottingham or traveling the rest of England to spread their heroics to the rest of the kingdom.

Lucy dismounted, tying Victory to the low hanging tree branch she usually used as a hitching post. Mark didn't look up, so Lucy moved across the meadow to sit beside him.

She realized as she sat down that it wasn't his hands he was looking at but rather a ring he was cupping in his palms, slowly letting it roll between one hand and then the other.

"That's a beautiful ring."

Mark didn't reply. His eyes were dark, his brow furrowed as he glared at the ring in his hands.

"Did it belong to someone you knew? Your mother perhaps?"

Mark looked up at Lucy briefly, but then looked down again.

"You are a silent fellow, aren't you?"

"Leave," Mark growled.

Lucy held her breath. It was the first word she had heard Mark speak since the return from Austria. It was possible he talked to the others in the gang, but Lucy doubted he was vivacious with anyone anymore.

When Mark didn't say anything else for a long time Lucy spoke again. "You are the only member of the gang that I don't know yet. Not really. I've spent time with everyone else and gotten to know them. Some more than others I suppose…" Lucy realized she was rambling to fill his silence, but she couldn't help herself. His pain only brought her own feelings of guilt back to the surface again. "Dusty is compassionate and has strong opinions, holding fast to her convictions. I respect that. Robin is a mess, but that's understandable considering…"

Mark's hands curled into fists and Lucy quickly changed course. "Allen and Will both seem full of life and mischief, and Much is just sweet. But you are rather reclusive…and silent."

Mark didn't respond, but Lucy didn't expect him to.

"I don't think it's quite healthy to never open your mouth. Your voice might forget how to work."

If Lucy had expected Mark to smile at her nonsense, she was sadly disappointed. After several more unsuccessful attempts at conversation, during which Lucy was unable to get Mark to even acknowledge her, she left for Nottingham.

The rest of her day was relatively uneventful, and that night when she watched the stars Sir Guy silently brooded beside her. He was no more communicative than Mark, but Lucy was used to him by now.

The next time Lucy visited the camp it was more lively, as several of the members of the gang were present. Lucy called a hello to Much and Dusty who were seemingly arguing over what would be best to cook for dinner. Neither of them paused to greet her as Dusty tried to sprinkle spices of some kind into the pot and

Much swatted her hand away and the children gathered around them laughed nervously.

Lucy moved to sit near Robin and Mark who were sitting by the fire ring where the gang generally gathered.

"Any news of the Sheriff?" Robin asked.

"No, nothing yet," Lucy said as she sat down. Mark didn't bother to look up at her, but Robin was watching expectantly. "I will let you know the minute I know he's planning something."

"I know you will."

"And I'll be sure to impress Will with my detailed information."

Robin quirked an eyebrow and Lucy shrugged. "He was rather unimpressed the last time, I think."

"The more details we have the easier our job is."

"I can see why," Lucy said. "And I'm working on it. I've always been working alone, you know, just finding helpless people mostly by accident or rumor. And I never had to plan anything with partners, I would just do whatever I could to help and that was that. This is all a new experience for me."

"You're doing fine," Robin said. "We're getting more information now than we were before you joined us, less people are dying because of our lack of ability to spy in the castle any longer and that's a good thing."

Lucy leaned forward to see around Robin to where Mark was sullenly watching the fire. "How are you today, Mark?"

Silence.

Robin sighed and rose, pulling Lucy up with him as he walked away from the fire and toward the outer edge of the camp.

"Don't expect him to talk to you. He hasn't spoken to any of us."

"He did speak to me."

"What? When?"

"The other day I came to the camp and only Mark was here. I tried to talk to him. He wouldn't respond to anything that I said. But finally he did say one word."

"One word isn't much. What was it?"

"Leave."

Robin sighed. "That's hardly talking to you. You had my hopes up for half a moment."

"Why is he so silent? It isn't healthy or good, you know. I realize Marian's death has been hard on you all…" Robin winced at Marian's name and Lucy trailed off.

In the silence between them that followed, Lucy could hear Dusty and Much laughing and assumed their argument over the best way to season dinner had come to a close.

"They were close, Lucy," Robin finally said. He stared at the trees, at the ground, at the sky; anywhere but at Lucy. "You wouldn't understand. You're an only child and you've also never been in love. So you can't understand the pain that Mark feels, or the pain that I feel, and you have no right to tell us what is or isn't good about the way we choose to grieve."

"Robin—"

"You can't tell me what to do."

"I thought we were talking about Mark."

Robin sighed, running a hand over his eyes for a moment. "We were."

"What did I do to make you angry?"

"I'm not angry with you."

"We were discussing Mark's inclination to remain silent and reclusive, and you suddenly snapped at me that I can't tell you what to do. Something is bothering you."

"I guess I'm still upset with you for trying to tell me I should forgive Gisbourne. That wretch!" Robin's hands curled into fists at his side and he turned away from Lucy slightly.

"I'm sorry I upset you," Lucy said. "I honestly do believe it would be wrong of you to kill Gisbourne. I think it's wrong to kill anyone—you might notice I avoid it as much as I can when I do use my weapons. I'm also very sorry about Mark. I'm sorry for all of you. Marian's death was horrible, and you're all broken in different ways from it. I get that. Even though I am an only child, Robin, I do understand pain. My parents both died when I was fifteen because of Prince John…and I still feel the sting of their deaths."

Robin turned to her with a heavy sigh. "I didn't mean to suggest you haven't had a hard life, too…it's just…Marian. You don't know what it's like for us. You didn't know her."

"I saw her. I cared for her from a distance. I wish I hadn't kept myself aloof, and hadn't been afraid of connection. But…her death just…" Lucy didn't know how to tell Robin that watching the woman that he loved die terrified her, not because she was afraid of dying but because she was afraid of loving. And then there was the fact that she could have stopped it, could have shot Sir Guy and slowed him down, maybe saved Marian…

"You ran away because of your parents, didn't you?" Robin asked. "That's how you ended up here, doing good so far from home."

"I…well, yes."

"Running was your way of dealing with the pain," Robin said, his voice growing more sure. "Well, not speaking is Mark's way and wanting to kill Gisbourne is my way. We all face our pain how we face it, Lucy. That's all there is to it. Just leave us alone about it. This is none of your business."

"I'd like to think as your friend it is my business."

"Mark's only spoken a single word to you since you met him, and I've only known you for a handful of weeks. How does that make us friends?"

"I thought—"

"Just drop it," Robin sighed. "Just…drop it."

He walked back to the fire to sit beside Mark. Lucy watched him go, unsure how she felt about the encounter. She wanted to be friends with the gang, and she wanted to ease their pain if she could. But she didn't want to force herself where she wasn't wanted. If Robin had a hard time accepting her now, how would he feel if he knew she was responsible for Marian's death?

"Are you staying for dinner?" Dusty asked, walking over to Lucy. "Much won't let me change his recipes. As sweet as he is, he can also be very stubborn."

Lucy laughed at the mock annoyance on Dusty's face as Dusty linked her arm through Lucy's and led her toward the children.

William and Beth ran forward. "Can we practice our archery? Please?"

"The light will soon be gone and we can't do it after that!"

Dusty laughed and released Lucy, "You've been summoned, it seems. I'll save you a bite to eat though."

Lucy spent the rest of the evening training with William and Beth, and then enjoying an evening meal with Dusty and

Much. Robin occasionally joined in the conversation, though Mark remained as silent as ever. Little John and Will arrived in the camp late that evening from their various exploits that day, just as Lucy was saddling Victory to return to the castle and she waved her greeting and goodbye.

When she arrived at the castle, the sun was down and the moon was high in the sky. A stableman helped her unsaddle and brush and clean Victory, and then she hurried inside. It was early spring and there were still lingering chills at night from the cold.

As she hurried up the front steps to the castle, the doors creaked open and Sir Guy held the door for her.

"You were gone awhile."

"Did you need Victory? You seemed rather insistent I could use him," Lucy said as she brushed past him and into the castle.

"Merely curious what caught your fancy for such an extended period of time."

"Visiting friends, actually."

"You have friends in Nottingham?"

"I'm making friends. Or trying to. Do you want to be one of them?" Sir Guy gave her a strange look and Lucy shrugged. "I'm rather determined you will be. But for now I'm tired and must head to bed."

"No star gazing from the ledge tonight?"

Lucy hesitated. "Did you want to?"

"It makes no difference to me," Sir Guy said sharply, taking a quick step away from her. "Good night."

"Well I didn't mean—Guy, come back!" But he was already marching off down the hall and ignored her call. Lucy sighed and returned to her own room for the night.

The Sheriff was soon in a hanging mood again. He must have had a reason, but whatever it was Lucy couldn't figure it out. Every other day he was trying to hang someone. Every other day Lucy informed Robin or another member of the gang, and they rescued the unfortunate. The Sheriff became angrier with every attack, lashing out at Sir Guy and Lucy and anyone else who was within his reach on any given day.

After this had gone on for some time, Sir Guy approached Lucy as she was saddling Victory one afternoon. "You ride a lot."

"I love it."

"I've noticed. And it doesn't seem to matter what time of day. Or how many times a day."

"I have yet to find a time of day when I don't enjoy riding," Lucy replied with a laugh.

"I'm beginning to see a pattern." Sir Guy crossed his arms, watching her closely.

"Oh?"

"Many of your rides come after the Sheriff has disclosed a new plot or spoken of treasure bound this way."

Lucy glanced around the stables, but the stablemen were busy about their work and no one was paying any attention to her conversation with Sir Guy.

"I…"

"You're helping Robin Hood," Sir Guy said simply.

"Yes, I am."

"You…what?" Sir Guy seemed taken aback by her honest reply.

"I am helping Robin," Lucy said softly.

"You do realize the danger in admitting this to me."

"There is no danger, Guy. I trust you."

He stared at Lucy silently for a long moment. She didn't know why she wasn't afraid of him, but it was true. She'd seen how tortured he was by Marian's death and believed he would never do the same again.

"I know that sounds absurd," Lucy said. "But it's true. Andrew trusts you, and he seems like a good man. And you are so tormented over Marian's death I don't think you would hurt anyone else intentionally. It's true I would have preferred no one found out because that would be safer, but since you know," Lucy shrugged. "You know. I'm not afraid of you."

Sir Guy simply stared at her for the longest time, and then finally, without a word, he turned and strode away.

«—»

Mari-Lu's eyes were wide. "But…he'd tell the Sheriff! Or arrest you! Or kill you like Marian!"

"I almost regretted my utter honesty," Aunt Lucy said. "But no. 'you shall not lie' was as deeply ingrained in my head as 'you shall not kill.' Friar Tuck had been thorough in my upbringing, and I held to his instruction like a lifeline. Even so, I lay awake that night waiting for a knock on the door, a summons to my death."

"Did it come?"

"No. It did not. It seemed, for the time being at least, that my strange feeling of trust in Sir Guy was not entirely misplaced."

"I think it is," Mari-Lu crossed her arms. "He sometimes was nice to Marian and then he killed her."

"Perhaps," Aunt Lucy said. "You'll just have to wait and see."

"What happened next?"

"About a week later, pleased with Sir Guy since he didn't betray me to the Sheriff, I decided to try something…"

"Oh no…" Mari-Lu groaned.

Chapter 24

SIR GUY WAS training soldiers in the castle courtyard when Lucy decided to approach him. Two dozen soldiers were spread out across the courtyard, sweating in the heat of the sun as Sir Guy demonstrated a particular movement with his sword and then instructed his soldiers to practice the same with each other.

Lucy's legs felt heavy and her palms were sweaty as she walked up to him, intent on her mission and yet unsure how he would respond. "Guy?"

"Yes?" He stepped aside with Lucy as his soldiers continued sparring together. "Do you need something?"

"Do you remember the children you sent to live with Robin?"

He was silent. Several emotions crossed his face one after another. Recognition, pain, shock. Finally he snapped, "What about them?"

"They need to be with their parents. Robin's camp is no place for them."

He didn't respond.

"Is the Sheriff still bent on killing them? Could they come home?"

"Come home?" Sir Guy studied her. "It has been long enough it is unlikely the Sheriff even remembers he was going to execute them…"

"Could you ask him? Or otherwise find out if it is safe for them to be returned to their families?"

"What?"

"You could always play to his weaknesses," Lucy suggested quickly. "Maybe you could suggest that the people will be more obedient to him if they see an act of kindness from him. If he leaves the children be."

"You're crazy." Sir Guy shook his head, his eyebrows raised.

"Would you try at least?"

He shrugged. "I'll see what I can do. Don't expect it to work."

He went back to training his men, and Lucy returned to the castle. It wasn't too many days before it became clear that despite Sir Guy's warnings, it did, in fact, work. The Sheriff even made a public declaration, gathering a crowd in Nottingham Square to say that he felt moved by compassion to let the children return to their parents if anyone knew their whereabouts.

Lucy saw old Tibb in the crowd, along with Marcus the blacksmith, and other residents of Nottingham that she recognized. She even saw Will and Allen off to one side, watching with disbelief written all over their faces.

Lucy stood with Sir Guy off to one side of the platform that had been erected in the Square for the Sheriff's use, listening to him wax poetic about his mercy.

"His speech is an eloquent one, I'll give him that," Lucy laughed.

Sir Guy glanced at her, and then resumed watching the Sheriff.

"Thank you, Guy."

That evening Lucy went to the camp to see the gang and collect the children to take them home. Dusty set about getting the children ready to go and Lucy moved to sit by the fire where the rest of the gang was gathered. Mark, however, was nowhere to be seen.

"How in the world did you convince the Sheriff to leave them be?" Will asked.

"I didn't. Sir Guy did."

Robin threw a stick into the fire and glared at Lucy.

"There is good in him," Allen said. "I saw it brought out by Marian."

"And that good she brought out," Robin snapped, "is, I suppose, the reason he killed her." Robin stood and stomped away from the circle. It was quiet around the fire.

"She was something else," Little John said softly.

There were murmurs of agreement.

"I don't blame Robin," Will said, glancing at Dusty as she moved into the circle around the fire, followed by six children. "I'd hate anyone who killed my love."

"But hatred will eat you up inside," Much said, watching as Robin disappeared into his hut.

"There's also the Scriptures to take into consideration," Lucy said quietly, "They tell us to love, to forgive. To do good to those who spitefully use us."

Dusty nodded mutely.

"Will Robin ever be happy?" Allen asked.

"Give him time," Dusty said. "The grief is still too near."

"I hate to see him distraught," Much said. "But Marian...I don't think any of us will move past our grief in a short time."

Will nodded. "True. Yet it would be nice to have our Robin back, rather than this brooding fellow who has taken his place."

"At least he speaks," Allen said.

Dusty sighed. "I do not know what we are going to do with Mark."

"Pray for him, Dusty," Lucy said. "That's what we can do for Mark."

"Something practical might be useful too," Little John rolled his eyes.

Lucy enlisted the help of Will and Dusty to help walk the children to their home in Nottingham. Will suggested the gang take turns keeping guard near the house for a few weeks to be certain the Sheriff would leave them alone, and so the gang made a schedule to keep watch over them. But in the days and weeks that followed, the Sheriff never so much as looked at their house.

Some days after that, Lucy visited the camp after a long gallop on Victory to find Allen alone and in a bad mood.

"They're all gone," Allen said sullenly as Lucy dismounted. "Robin has given everyone something to do today. Except me."

"This is a problem?" Lucy asked. "I imagine he is used to having to leave one person in camp to watch the children and hasn't gotten used to the idea that he doesn't have to anymore."

"He doesn't like to have me help with raids," Allen said. "And he never sends me on missions of my own like he does everyone else. He doesn't trust me. He hasn't completely forgiven me for what I did."

"Do you blame him?"

"No. But you've forgiven me."

"Your offense wasn't against me."

"No one has completely forgiven me. Not even Dusty."

"You hurt them. Forgiveness is hard, Allen."

"You don't find it so. You'd forgive any one of anything, I'm sure you would."

"I do try to be forgiving, Allen. But it isn't as easy as you think. Sometimes it is very hard. For instance, I would find it very difficult to forgive the assassins who killed my father. I don't know who they are, but if I did…if I met them, I don't know that I could be as gracious to them as I am to Sir Guy."

Allen sighed.

"Just continue to prove your worth, Allen. Keep showing how loyal and true you are. You are going to have to re-earn their trust and that will take a great deal of time."

"I know."

"I'll support you, for whatever that is worth…but Robin's opinion of me is not very high."

"Thank you, Lucy. I appreciate your friendship."

Chapter 25

THE NEXT TIME Lucy visited the camp, Mark was alone. He was sitting on a log near the fire ring, but no fire was lit. "Hello, Mark. Did Robin not have anything for you to do today?"

"No."

Lucy walked slowly over to where Mark was sitting and sat beside him. She said nothing for a few moments. She wasn't sure how to proceed. Rambling on about nonsense hadn't been helpful the last time she'd tried to bring Mark out of his silence. And she could hear Robin's voice in her head, telling her to leave Mark alone to grieve however he saw fit.

"That ring," Mark said, looking up at Lucy for what felt like the first time. "that I was holding the last time you tried to talk to me?"

"Yes, I remember," Lucy said softly, hoping her voice wouldn't startle him into silence again. She'd treated an injured doe in the woods once, stitching up a gash in it's leg that it had received from a fall. It had been skittish and every sudden movement had sent it scurrying away before she could help it. The doe had taken a lot of careful coaxing to let her near enough to heal its leg, and right now Mark was reminding her of that incident.

"That was the ring Robin was going to give my sister when he married her." Mark's hands trembled as he spoke, his voice wavering and tears escaping his eyes. "Except he wasn't able to give it to her, because it was still here in England when they had a sorry excuse for a wedding while she died."

"Oh, I'm so sorry!"

Mark's eyes were dark with pain. "I hate Gisbourne. I hate myself."

"Why would you hate yourself?"

"Because it's my fault she died."

Mark dropped his head into his hands, as the tears fell in a seemingly never ending torrent down his face. Lucy was shocked by his sudden outburst—her own feelings of guilt rising to the surface as though in answer to his—but she quickly recovered and put an arm around his shoulders. "It's alright, Mark."

"No, it isn't! I killed her."

"No, you didn't."

"I was standing right beside her…I should have been able to protect her! This is my fault. Robin should hate me…why doesn't he hate me as much as he hates Gisbourne?"

"Mark, it wasn't your fault." Lucy believed that; of course it wasn't Mark's fault, he hadn't chosen to kill Marian, he'd tried to protect her. Lucy wasn't so sure she could set aside her own guilt, though. She *could have* done something and had chosen not to; Mark had at least attempted to help Marian and wound Sir Guy. "You didn't kill Marian. You can't blame yourself."

Mark's entire frame shuddered and Lucy tightened her grip on his shoulders.

"Mark…please don't blame yourself. Marian's death was not your fault."

"It was. I'll never forgive myself."

"Mark!"

Mark sat up straighter and pushed Lucy's arm away. He roughly brushed the tears from his face, as he took a shuddering deep breath. Lucy waited, not wanting to upset him further and unsure what more to say.

After taking a moment to collect himself and brushing aside the remains of his tears, Mark said, "I didn't mean to lose it like that."

"Oh, please don't apologize! You've been through a lot."

Mark wiped his tears away angrily. "Don't tell me that, as if I don't know!"

"I'm sorry."

Mark sighed. "So am I. I don't mean to lash out at you, it's just...Marian. She was everything, you know?"

"It's okay to cry."

Mark shook his head, still attempting to stem the flow of tears. He took a few deep breaths and then shrugged. "You were right, Lucy."

"I was right...about what?"

"I think my voice almost did forget how to work." He gave her the tiniest glimpse of a wry smile and Lucy smiled back.

"I'm glad you're talking again."

Mark sighed. "I don't think talking is any better than silence."

⟨⟨⟩⟩

"Poor Mark," Mari-Lu sighed. "It's not his fault."

"No, it wasn't his fault," Aunt Lucy agreed. "He never quite believed that though. Even as the years passed and his grief grew quieter, the guilt was always simmering there somewhere."

"He told me about it once," Marian spoke up from where she sat opposite her daughter and Aunt Lucy, still leaning against the large stone in the clearing that bore an inscription. "He was very quiet about it, but Uncle Mark did tell me about what it felt

266

like to stand there, holding her arm so protectively, and somehow still not be able to protect her."

"That sounds awful," Mari-Lu said.

"It was awful to listen to," Marian agreed. "He was so downcast and depressed about it. I never heard him talk about it except that one time."

"He wasn't fond of reliving his worst memory," Aunt Lucy said. "Which is entirely understandable."

"Did Robin ever stop being angry?" Mari-Lu asked.

"Well…" Aunt Lucy said, "we haven't gotten to that part of the story yet."

"Then what happens next?" Mari-Lu asked.

«»

A week after comforting Mark in the camp, Lucy returned from a morning ride on Victory only for Sir Guy to meet her at the front door.

"You missed the Sheriff's latest scheme."

"Oh?" Lucy paused on the top step of the stone staircase leading to the front doors of the castle, Sir Guy having stepped just outside and shut them behind him.

"He's traveling to Abingdon to hang a man who's bothering him. Those are his words."

"Really?"

Sir Guy glanced behind Lucy and she looked over her shoulder. The castle courtyard was empty, though there were guards stationed at the gate into the city and up along the walls surrounding the courtyard and castle.

"He's leaving tomorrow at dawn," Sir Guy said softly.

Lucy studied Sir Guy for a moment, but he offered nothing else.

"Thank you."

Sir Guy gave her a curt nod, and then turned and entered the castle. Lucy stood dumbstruck on the castle steps for another minute and then went in search of Andrew, whom she found in the castle library tucked in a chair in a corner, quietly reading.

"Do you know what Sir Guy did today?"

"Yes." Andrew didn't look up from his book, but he was smiling. "He told me he was going to tell you."

"He does know I will tell Robin, and the gang will ruin the entire thing…doesn't he? And if he does know…is he consciously helping us?"

Andrew laughed, shutting his book and looking up at Lucy. "I can't say. It's all speculation at this point."

Lucy put her hands on her hips and frowned at him, though her eyes were sparkling. "What has he told you?"

"Nothing," Andrew held up his hands in mock surrender.

"Why would he help me, help us?"

"Out of the goodness of his heart," Andrew suggested, which caused Lucy to snort. With a grin, Andrew stood. "Come on now, he's done good things before. He freed those children from execution a year ago, and now he's helped you get them back home again."

"I still didn't expect this."

Andrew leaned in conspiratorially for a moment and whispered, "get used to it," and then cheerfully walked away, whistling as he went.

Lucy couldn't stop smiling as she rode to Robin's camp. She refrained from telling Robin how she came by her information knowing how he would respond, but he took her information about the execution and began planning with Will how best to stop the execution in Abingdon.

Lucy did pull Allen and Dusty aside the first chance she had to tell them the truth. Both were as shocked as she was, but equally as grateful and pleased with this new development.

The day the Sheriff returned from Abingdon and his failed execution, he was angry. He found Sir Guy and Lucy talking at the dining room ledge and demanded to know who had warned Robin. "I know it wasn't Gisbourne, so that leaves you, Lucy! How did you know? You weren't even here when I spoke of it!"

"I have my ways."

He glared at Lucy and marched away.

"You have your ways?" Sir Guy asked.

"I couldn't lie, and I certainly couldn't tell him the truth."

"He'll probably have you executed if he thinks you're responsible. You do have somewhere to go if you need to run?"

"Robin's camp, of course."

"Right."

Sir Guy did not seem pleased by the prospect. For the rest of the day Lucy and Sir Guy were on edge wondering what the Sheriff would do. But the Sheriff never mentioned the incident again.

≪≫

"He didn't punish you?" Mari-Lu asked.

"No, he did not. To this day I don't know why," Aunt Lucy said. "We speculated either he forgot, didn't take me

269

seriously, or he liked me too well to do anything. All options seemed unlikely."

"Well Sir Guy liked you enough to be good, so maybe the Sheriff did too."

"Perhaps. But Guy came to the light, the Sheriff never did. He was just an odd man with no consistency. Every little thing would change his opinion, first this way and then that way."

"What happened next?"

"Because I did not participate in raids, ambushes, or the rescuing of the innocent alongside the gang, and my sole purpose was to gather information I was afraid my skill would rust like a forgotten sword. So on my morning rides I always stopped by the camp and practiced archery. And if anyone in the gang was there while I was, we would spar sometimes. Robin never joined in but he was very free with his advice and criticism. 'Tuck your elbow in, Much' 'Don't pull your string so tight, Allen,' Generally following his comments would come a collective 'Shut up, Robin' from everyone else present."

Mari-Lu giggled.

"One rare day when the entire gang was gathered in the camp, Robin made a disparaging comment on my archery skills, but his voice held a teasing warmth that I hadn't heard before…"

« »

Dusty laughed and swatted Robin. "Hush, Robin. She shoots as well as you do."

"I'd say she was better," Little John said.

The group was gathered around Will and Lucy who had been playfully competing against each other, choosing various targets on the trees around the meadow to shoot at. Allen and Little John had been teasing they'd take bets on who was the better shot, and Dusty and Much had simply been watching with amusement. Mark was there, not exactly joining in the fun but present at least.

"No one is better than Robin," Much declared.

Allen laughed. "You know we'll never agree on this. We didn't call Lucy the 'mysterious archer' for nothing."

"There's only one way to settle the debate," Will winked. "We'll have to have a contest. Lucy's been showing me up all morning, so let's see how Robin can stand up against her."

"But everyone knows Robin is the best," Much insisted.

Lucy chuckled. "I see Much has no faith in me."

"Who would have faith in you when they had seen me use a bow?" Robin grinned.

"You think you're so good?" Lucy held her bow lightly in one hand, her other hand resting on her hip. "That's a lot of talk, but as Will said I have been showing him up all morning."

"Pick a target," Robin laughed.

Lucy glanced around the meadow as the rest of the gang called out options. "That tree there!" or "I think I saw a squirrel run by earlier…"

Finally Lucy settled on a choice. "You see that knot, in the tree over there?"

Robin followed Lucy's pointing finger. "You sure that's what you want as the target?"

"Too far for you?" Lucy's eyes danced.

Robin grunted, snatching Lucy's bow from her hand and grabbing an arrow from her quiver before he stepped back, drawing back the arrow and letting it fly in the same swift motion. It hit the knot, to all appearances right in the center.

Much grinned.

Mark crossed his arms and frowned.

"Nice shot," Lucy said.

"I am the best in England," Robin winked.

"He's humble, too," Dusty chuckled.

The gang gathered in a half circle around Lucy as she took her time selecting her own arrow as Robin handed back her bow.

"The...best...in...England..." Lucy repeated slowly as she deliberately drew back the arrow on the string and took her time releasing it. "Indeed."

The arrow cut through the air and hit the tree with a distinct thud. Her arrow was resting beside Robin's.

"Lucy wins again," Will said.

"I'm not so sure," Much shook his head. "How can you tell hers is in the center and not Robin's."

"And anyway, they are rather too close together to actually tell the difference," Dusty added.

Allen ran to the tree to measure the distance of the arrows from the edges of the knot and presumably find the proper center.

"I'd say Lucy's is in the center!" Allen called as he trotted back over. "Robin's was just to the left.'

Will laughed. "Did I not tell you?"

"One shot doesn't prove anything," Lucy countered.

Robin shook his head, laughing. "I'm sorry, Lucy, but you can't change it now. You've been declared the best shot in England and I'm afraid it will stay that way."

"And what will you do?" Lucy teased.

"Cry myself to sleep."

He said it so seriously, Lucy couldn't help it; she laughed. "Robin, you're absurd!"

He gave a mock bow. "Thank you, Lady Lucy. I will regard that as a compliment."

Everyone in the circle chuckled, but Mark shook his head and walked away from the merry group.

Chapter 26

A FEW DAYS later Lucy was sharing lunch with the Sheriff and Sir Guy. The meals shared with her castle hosts had become far less of a chore since her strange friendship with Sir Guy had begun to form. Lucy enjoyed conversation with him, though he was still odd and often brooding. The Sheriff was as tiresome as ever, but Lucy was growing used to ignoring his strange antics.

Before the meal was over, the Sheriff informed Sir Guy of a load of treasure coming through Sherwood.

"It will need to be met with an escort. The largest force you've yet sent to collect my treasure," the Sheriff said. "Robin Hood can't keep getting away with this. I'm going to be destitute before too long." He then turned to Lucy and pointed a finger at her nose. "Don't you dare tell anyone about this."

"Me?"

"I want a promise out of you that you won't tell!"

"Sheriff—"

"Promise!"

Lucy shrugged. "I promise I won't tell anyone that there is treasure going through Sherwood."

The Sheriff nodded approvingly. "Now we'll see if I have made out your character."

"Excuse me?"

"I've noticed your propensity for always speaking the truth. The sort of person who would, in fact, keep her promises... you heard her, Gisbourne, did you not?"

"Yes, I did."

The Sheriff grinned at Lucy. "Either you are trustworthy—an unlikely thought, but entertaining nonetheless—and my treasure will indeed arrive as it should. Or you are a liar…and I'll deal with you accordingly."

"I said I will not tell, and I will not," Lucy said firmly. "You can believe me, Sheriff."

The Sheriff soon got up from the table, and when he had left the room, Lucy leaned forward across the table. "If I get someone, say Allen, to come here…will you give them the message I promised not to?"

Sir Guy looked at Lucy for a moment, an unknown emotion seeming to cloud his face, and then suddenly he chuckled. "I should have known there was a catch. Are you sure you want to do that? The Sheriff will still suspect it was you."

"But it won't have been me, and the truth always comes out, Guy. Trust me."

Sir Guy shook his head. "This is insanity."

"Please."

"Why would you think I would help you get word to the outlaws?"

"Because you've helped me before, and Andrew said to expect you to be like that more often in the future."

"You shouldn't believe everything Andrew says."

"Will you help me?"

Sir Guy shrugged. "If you can get someone to Nottingham Square in the next hour, I'll relay the message."

Lucy skipped all the way to Marcus' home to inquire if he knew of any of the gang who were in town. To Lucy's delight, both Will and Allen were already there speaking to the blacksmith.

Marcus was leaning over his forge, his leather apron sweating from the heat as he pulled a molten piece of steel from the fire with a pair of heavy tongs. Will and Allen were watching closely.

"Learning tricks to take back to the meadow?" Lucy asked, moving into the shop.

Allen grinned. "We'll never match Marcus' skill, but yes. We're trying."

"What is your purpose here?" Marcus asked. "Need a better weapon than your flimsy bow?"

"My bow has served me well, thank you very much," Lucy laughed. "Actually, I need help from the gang."

Will and Allen both moved forward, their faces eager and expectant.

"What do you need?" Will asked.

"There's important information that Robin needs to know."

"What is the Sheriff planning now?"

"I can't tell you."

"Why not?" Allen asked.

"Because I promised the Sheriff I wouldn't."

"What?" They both stared at Lucy while Marcus shook his head and sighed heavily, returning to his work.

"Don't be so distressed. You'll still get the message."

"How?" Will asked.

"Sir Guy is in Nottingham Square. He'll tell you what you need to know. He didn't promise not to."

Will raised a skeptical eyebrow. "Can we trust him?"

"Yes."

"Robin won't like it."

276

"He'll have to get over it."

"I don't like it either," Will said, his blue eyes darkening as he stepped toward Lucy. "He cannot be trusted, whatever you and Dusty might think to the contrary."

"He can. He's helped me before, multiple times," Lucy said. "The children going home? Nothing has happened to them. And the execution in Abingdon? You were able to stop that."

Allen nodded along in agreement. "If Sir Guy is helping us, I wouldn't pass up the offer."

"Besides, how else will you get the information he has?" Lucy said.

"From you," Will said.

"I promised I wouldn't tell."

"Lucy, you're insane. You could just tell us. Don't be ridiculous."

"I am not in the habit of going back on my word. And more than that, the Sheriff is using this as some kind of test. If I can't honestly prove I didn't tell the gang the news, he might do something drastic. So no. I'm not telling you."

"If the Sheriff is testing you, then even Sir Guy giving us the news will tip him off," Will said. "Either way you'd be in trouble."

"I think I can manage the situation, so long as someone talks to Sir Guy and I'm not the one informing Robin."

"I don't think this is wise," Will said. "Apart from the nonsense of not telling us yourself, if the Sheriff is using this as a test perhaps we shouldn't use whatever information you are withholding at all, and let this incident–whatever it is–pass."

"But what if it is an innocent person dying?" Allen asked. "I'll go talk to Gisbourne."

"Thank you, Allen," Lucy said.

Allen nodded and then left Marcus' shop. After Allen walked away Will shook his head, eyeing Lucy strangely. "How do we know Gisbourne won't turn on us?"

"He won't. He won't any more than Allen would."

"Mmm. I seem to recall Allen did, in fact, betray us."

"That isn't fair, he's been faithful since coming back."

"He was faithful before his last betrayal, too. Robin doesn't trust Allen any more than Gisbourne."

"I know. But I trust him." Lucy thought for a moment. "Does Robin trust me? If I vouch for Sir Guy will Robin accept his help?"

"You and your opinion don't matter that much, Lucy. You are new to the gang. We care about you and you are becoming part of our strange little family, but your opinion of Gisbourne won't matter. Robin doesn't want anything to do with him."

"Understandably."

"And yet you insist on forgiveness?"

"It will free Robin as much as protect Guy."

"Dusty seems to think so."

"She's right."

When Lucy came to visit the camp that night, the gang gathered around the fire as usual. Will and Allen had filled Robin in on everything that had happened that day, and he threw a stick into the fire with a heavy sigh.

"We didn't have to go to him. You could have told us."

"Not after I promised I wouldn't."

"You're playing games with us, Lucy."

278

"I am not. But seriously, Robin, the Sheriff might decide to get rid of me at any moment—he's certainly suspicious—and then you never would get information from inside the castle."

"I still say you could have delivered it. We don't need Gisbourne! He's entirely untrustworthy." Robin's eyes were flashing as he glared at Lucy. "He. Murdered. My. Wife."

"And he's as tormented by it as you are! More, probably, considering…"

Robin stood and stormed away from the circle around the fire.

"You didn't expect that to go any differently I hope," Mark said, his voice full of venom as he, too, glared at Lucy. "You can't trust Gisbourne."

"I know you all think that, and I perfectly understand why —"

"Then why are you so insistent?"

"Sir Guy has helped us in the past," Dusty said. "He's made mistakes; massive, unforgivable mistakes one might argue. Yet somehow, he still helps us."

"Even so," Little John piped up, "in this scenario, Lucy could have simply told us herself, using Gisbourne was superfluous. And more than that, if this is a test, a trap, she should have been much more careful and perhaps not told us at all."

"Well next time I'll just keep my information to myself," Lucy huffed.

"If you are going to do something as stupid as tell us you can't talk to us about whatever you find out, you might as well," Mark snapped.

"Well unlike some people, I keep my promises." Robin came storming back toward the circle as Lucy lashed out at Mark.

"You're asking me to break my word like it's no big deal. But it is a big deal to me."

Robin jumped back into the argument before Mark could think of a retort. "A promise that was forced out of you—"

"It wasn't forced."

"What?"

"It wasn't forced. I didn't have to promise. I only did because I knew you could still get the information without me telling you."

"Lucy—"

"You still got the information you needed, so why does it matter?"

Robin threw up his hands in disgust and stomped away again, and Mark withdrew to his hut as a silence settled over the gang.

"That…went about as expected," Will sighed.

"Guy did give me the news without hesitation," Allen said. "Lucy's right. He is helping us."

"I almost believe it myself," Dusty agreed. "He hasn't given any indication he'd turn on Lucy."

"*Yet*," Little John growled. "There is, however, the glaring truth that he murdered Marian."

The gang continued to argue the merits of Sir Guy and the potential danger for Lucy if the Sheriff was truly using this particular caravan as a trap to ensnare her. Lucy left the camp in a sour mood, and even the starry sky couldn't cheer her as she rode back to Nottingham.

Guy was waiting in the stables when Lucy returned and quietly helped her unsaddle and cool down her horse. They made their way into the castle together, and as they passed the Great

Hall Lucy could see the Sheriff sitting in his make-shift throne, scowling at them as they walked by.

"We need a plan," Guy said softly.

"A plan?"

"When Robin Hood and the other outlaws are undoubtedly successful," Guy sighed. "Where were you, what were you doing?"

"Not telling Robin."

"Clearly," Guy sent her a glare, apparently not amused "The Sheriff will not readily believe it."

"I'm not giving him a different story; I won't lie."

"You skirted around the truth all day today."

"It's different. It's…it just is."

Guy shook his head. "You need to stay clear of the Sheriff tomorrow. He'll be in a foul mood if he loses his taxes, but give him a few days and he'll find something else to occupy his mind. He never stays on one thought or passion long."

"I can stay out of his way," Lucy agreed. "But I won't lie to him."

"Then please, don't talk to him about the outlaws at all."

Lucy kept to her room for most of the following day to avoid running into the Sheriff as Guy had suggested, but eventually she grew bored and so traversed the stone hallways toward the library.

She hadn't gone far before the Sheriff crossed her path. As soon as he saw her, his dark eyes brightened with anger. "How dare you! You are a lying, devious…" As he shouted, the Sheriff moved toward Lucy and she stood still, unsure whether she should reach for the dagger on her belt or bolt. She could fight well enough, but she had no desire to physically harm or kill a man in close combat when there wasn't an innocent life at stake to make it worth it in some fashion.

"I trusted you." The Sheriff drew his sword and Lucy took a step backwards, her muscles tensing in preparation for the fight that was surely coming. "But I should know better. No one can be trusted."

Lucy watched as his blade arced through the air, too stunned to respond immediately. He was actually trying to kill her; she wouldn't have believed it if she hadn't seen his sword cutting through the air toward her body.

The sword connected with another blade and the sound of metal striking metal bounced across the stone walls and echoed down the hallway.

Sir Guy was there, one hand holding his sword as he glared at the Sheriff, the other hand grabbing Lucy's arm and dragging her slightly behind him.

"Aw, the hero came to save the damsel in distress," the Sheriff said in a mockingly sweet voice.

"You are making a mistake," Sir Guy said. "I paid close attention to Lucy yesterday. She did not inform Robin's gang about the treasure."

"Then how did he know? Explain that to me, Gisbourne, if you wish to save your little friend."

"Robin Hood has eyes and ears in every wall, bush, and blade. He's always known our every move, even before Lady Lucy came to Nottingham. That he should have discovered another caravan traveling through Sherwood is no surprise. But Lucy did not tell. She promised she would not and she did not."

The Sheriff glared at Sir Guy, and he glared back.

"We have been through a great deal," Sir Guy said slowly, emphasizing every word. "I have always been your trusted advisor. Do you doubt me?"

With a heavy sigh the Sheriff lowered his sword. "How does he do it, Gisbourne? Answer me that! We've blocked off the secret hallways in the castle...for several weeks our caravans came, some unmolested, some through trials, but they came. We've even had successful executions without interruptions...but no, now the world has reverted back to the old days."

"I could not say," Sir Guy responded. "We will undoubtedly find the perpetrators and hang them, sir."

"No we won't," the Sheriff snapped. "We never do."

The Sheriff sheathed his blade but Sir Guy kept a firm grip on his despite lowering it to his side. His other hand was still holding Lucy's arm, and she could feel a bruise forming beneath his tight grip.

The Sheriff and Sir Guy glared at each other for a full minute before the Sheriff shrugged and walked away.

"Thank you," Lucy said softly.

Sir Guy turned to her, letting go of her arm. "You cannot ever be alone with him!" His vehemence made Lucy smile.

"I'll be more on my guard from now on. I'm sure I'll be fine."

He shook his head and silently lifted a hand to Lucy's cheek. Then he spun on his heel and passed through a door to the room he must have been in before he'd come to Lucy's aid.

❮❯

"The Sheriff just let you go? Again?!"

Aunt Lucy smiled at Mari-Lu's indignance. "I will never understand either, but it is true."

"And Gisbourne keeps helping you."

"Yes, Sir Guy did help me. He was still angry most of the time, and always brooding. But he did help me."

"I still don't like him," Mari-Lu frowned. "He killed Marian."

"He did. And it was horrible."

"But you forgave him."

"I certainly tried my best to do so."

"But it was awful!"

"It was. Yet we all do awful things to people, all the time."

"I'm never going to kill anyone!"

"I should hope not," Aunt Lucy chuckled. "You don't have to understand why I forgave him, Mari-Lu. Many who were there did not understand—the gang certainly did not. Robin and Mark were furious that I was working alongside Guy, that I would even claim to be friends in some fashion with him."

"So what happened? Did the Sheriff do anything to you?"

"Despite appearing to set a trap to ensnare me in a Robin Hood plot, the Sheriff seemed placated by Guy's assessment of the situation and he did not bring it up again. About a week after the incident with the Sheriff, another visitor came to Nottingham…"

←»

Lucy took a loaf of bread from the basket heavy on her arm and handed it to the small boy in front of her. She had gone to the castle kitchens with a large basket, filled it to the brim, and was now wandering Nottingham feeding the homeless and poor.

The boy in front of her smiled as he peeled off a piece of the bread and shoved it into his mouth. His blonde hair was dark with dirt and mud, and his hollow cheeks were stained with the same. His arms were as thin as twigs, and Lucy could count the ribs protruding from his chest as he had no shirt.

"That would taste even better with cheese, don't you think?" Lucy asked, slipping her hand into the basket again as the boy's eyes widened along with his smile.

Lucy handed him a large chunk of cheese, which he eagerly accepted. She'd seen the boy—Joseph—before. His sister Rebekah had been ill for several weeks and Lucy had tended to her because their mother could not afford to pay a physician. Rebekah was only recently on the mend.

Lucy handed Joseph another loaf. "Here, now share with your sister."

Joseph took the second loaf and then spoke around another bite of bread and cheese in his mouth, "Mama says to thank you for the food and helping Rebekah."

"I'll continue to pray for your sister's health, and I will keep visiting. If she gets sick again, be sure to let me know."

"What you did before helped," Joseph said with a grin.

"I do have some skill," Lucy smiled back. "It helps to be raised by a monk. I'll see if I can bring soup tomorrow. That will be easier for Rebekah to eat."

The little boy ran back into his house and Lucy felt a gentle hand on her shoulder. "Well done, daughter."

The familiar voice brought a flash of pain to Lucy's heart and tears to her eyes, as she dropped her basket and swung around. "Friar Tuck!"

He was standing there in his simple tunic, a smile on his face. Lucy threw her arms around his neck. "How did you find me?"

"I have searched for many years, following the trail of saved lives. It was easy to follow you, though you would not stay still long enough for me to catch up."

"You've been following me all this time?"

"As soon as you ran away, child."

Lucy picked up her basket, smiling through her tears at Friar Tuck. "How long are you staying?"

"As long as you do, child. You are as a daughter to me and I cannot leave you alone."

"I was never alone."

"Yes, your heavenly Father is always with you. But I would worry less if I could see you."

"O ye of little faith." Lucy teased, her eyes were sparkling.

"And I missed you."

"I have missed you as well."

"You are staying in Nottingham castle? I assume there is space in that castle for another soul to reside?"

"Yes! You would be welcome. But…"

"But…what, child?"

"I would prefer you stay in Robin's camp."

"Robin Hood?"

"I see you have heard of him."

"All of England knows his name. Do you know him?"

"Yes. Robin is a friend. And he is one of the reasons I would like you to stay there."

"How so?"

286

"He's bitter and full of hatred for Sir Guy. I haven't been able to get through to him, to help him heal."

"This Sir Guy…is Sir Guy of Gisbourne? Another name many know, for his cruelty and ruthlessness. I will pray…and I can do what I can at Robin's camp, if I am welcome there."

"Thank you, Friar Tuck. There's also another young man who will need your comforting hand and your wisdom."

"Who is this?"

"His name is Mark, he's part of Robin's gang. His sister died nearly six months ago and he is as bitter as Robin. But he is bitter toward himself as well as toward Sir Guy."

"I will look after this Mark as well then, as much as I am able."

"Thank you."

For the briefest moment Lucy wanted to share her own guilt and ask for Friar Tuck's advice; he had always been her comfort as a child and walked her through the times that she had done wrong and been crippled with remorse. But she couldn't bring herself to discuss it, not yet.

"Are you safe in Nottingham?" Friar Tuck asked.

"Yes. Sir Guy would never let anything happen to me."

"Sir Guy of Gisbourne wants to protect you?"

"He isn't as bad as people say."

"Is he not?"

"Well he was. But he's improving…"

"You're showing him God's love."

"I am trying. Come. I will take you to the camp and introduce you to the gang. Robin may react poorly…he doesn't like strangers waltzing into camp…but he'll get over it…"

Chapter 27

"FRIAR TUCK WAS very old by this time. His face was weathered and wrinkled—"

"Like yours?" Mari-Lu asked.

Marian snorted at her daughter's interruption to the story as Aunt Lucy laughed.

"Mari-Lu, that isn't the most flattering thing you could say to a woman. Yes, like mine. Apart from his ancient face, he was gentle and firm and always ready to smile and laugh."

"Did the gang like him?"

"Yes, they did. It was gratifying how easily they welcomed him. He was a friend of mine, and that was enough for them. Will would sit with him for hours just talking, so full of questions."

"About what?"

"About life, about Friar Tuck's faith. Dusty and I approached the world in a rather different way than Will and the rest of the gang and Will was curious as to why."

"You and Dusty don't always agree though," Mari-Lu pointed out. "You are friends with Gisbourne and she didn't want to be at first."

"That's true, but Dusty's differences with the gang had made themselves known long before I came to Nottingham. They were good people, that much is true, but her compassion stemmed from the belief that everyone around her was one of God's children, and her actions came from His love and concern for His people. The gang, on the other hand, approached compassion from a more logical standpoint. They didn't like injustice, or seeing people hurt, but their sympathy had limits as they did not have a connection to the ultimate source of mercy. They would pick and choose who deserved their forgiveness and help; while Dusty was reluctant to forgive Guy, she could more readily do so than the rest of the gang because she relied on the never-ending love of Christ."

Marian watched as her daughter stared up into Aunt Lucy's face, her brow furrowed in concentration as her blue eyes darkened slightly. What Aunt Lucy was trying to explain was a lot to take in, and Marian wasn't surprised her daughter was struggling to grasp it.

"What else happened?" Mari-Lu eventually asked, apparently hoping to change the subject.

"Well, Mark grew more hostile towards me," Aunt Lucy said. "He was still rather taciturn and would not speak to anyone much, always brooding over his grief and guilt but he'd begun to interact with the rest of the gang—yet now he reserved only the most snappish comments for me. Then one day when I visited the camp…"

«–»

As Lucy rode into camp, it appeared empty apart from Mark. He approached as she slowed Victory and prepared to dismount. It was late in the afternoon, and the sun dipped toward the treetops, sending large shadows across the meadow as the shade of both the surrounding trees and the huts within the clearing stretched long. As Lucy slid off of Victory's back, Mark took the reins and looped them around a small tree.

"Come to visit us again? You aren't planning on another archery contest are you?"

Lucy laughed. "No, I wasn't planning on it. I'm just here to train on my own. Will you practice with me?"

"No." Mark scowled at Lucy, his grey eyes stormy. "I don't like what you did."

"What I did?"

"The archery contest…" Mark crossed his arms, and then lowered them, glancing toward the sky and then back at Lucy. "Robin probably let you win."

"He might have. I don't know."

"He…" Mark sighed, seeming at a loss for words. "Just leave him alone."

"What?"

"Don't try and take her place, Lucy."

"I'm not trying to take anyone's place."

"Marian was everything; you can't replace her!"

"Mark, what are you talking about? I'm not trying to replace your sister. I know how much she means to all of you, and I'm not here to be the next Marian. I'm Lucy, okay. Just me. I want to be friends, to have my own connection with this group that is a family, but I am not trying to fill the hole that Marian left behind. I promise."

For a moment Mark continued scowling, though he said nothing. Eventually he snapped, "Go practice your archery," and then walked away from her. Lucy watched him go with some confusion. How could he think she was taking Marian's place? Robin barely liked her most days; they were not the best friends. She was in no danger of replacing Marian.

Lucy pulled her bow from where she'd lashed it to Victory's saddle and then moved to one side of the clearing to practice. She didn't hide that she owned a bow from the Sheriff, but she did think it would be safer to use it out of his sight—especially now that he had come so close to trying to kill her for her potential involvement with the outlaws. There was no need to draw his further attention.

As she picked a target on a tree near the edge of the clearing, carefully shooting her arrows toward it one by one, Lucy wondered what bothered Mark so deeply about her contest with Robin. It had been one of the only times she'd ever seen Robin not angry and brooding, and she'd taken that as a good sign that he was finally healing a bit from the horror and heartache of losing Marian—apparently Mark saw it differently. She wasn't sure what to do about that, or if she should do anything at all.

It was eerie to practice archery in the empty camp with only a brooding Mark for company, so Lucy didn't stay long.

About a fortnight later, Lucy was in Nottingham visiting the young girl—Rebekah—who had been ill. Lucy tucked the thin and patched blankets around little Rebekah as her brother Joseph watched, his eyes wide, though his mouth was full of the chunk of cheese Lucy had brought with her.

The small, dimly-lit room was cramped with two beds, a table, and a small fireplace on one side with a pitiful flickering flame in it. Due to excessive taxes the family had been forced from their larger home in the city and moved to this small hovel. The gang spread riches to the people of Nottingham as often as they confiscated it from the Sheriff, but they were also trying to feed and clothe the rest of England and the Sheriff's money could only go so far.

Rebekah coughed, the sound thin and raspy. Her mother leaned over her bed, tears in her eyes. Lucy placed a hand on her shoulder.

"She needs plenty of rest. I'm leaving these herbs." Lucy grabbed a pouch from her belt. "It's what I used to make her tea this morning, a recipe I learned from an old Friar. The tea will soothe her throat as long as you keep giving it to her."

"Thank you, my lady," the mother said.

"Lucy," Lucy said gently. "My name is just Lucy."

Will opened the front door, flooding the dim room with sunlight. "I'm sorry…Lucy? Robin wants you. He's with Marcus."

"Can he wait?" Lucy moved away from Rebekah's mother and over to the doorway to talk to Will quietly. "I always pray with the families I serve before I leave them."

"Robin is pretty urgent, but I can pray with them."

"Will you?"

"Yes, Lucy. I'm sure our God hears my prayers as well as yours."

"*Our* God." Lucy studied Will's open and earnest face, searching for an explanation to his comment. "Oh, Will!" Lucy hugged him.

Will rolled his eyes with a grin. "There's no need to be so dramatic. Go see Robin, quickly. He was rather snappish."

Lucy grabbed her bow which she'd left by the door when she came to help Rebekah, slinging her quiver over her shoulder before she hurried to Marcus' home, traversing the busy streets of Nottingham and greeting many people she knew, little old Tibb among them.

She wished she had time to speak with Will further, to get to the bottom of what he'd meant. Did he truly believe as she and Dusty did? Maybe his conversations with Friar Tuck since the monk's arrival had finally turned his mind toward the truth of God's grace.

When Lucy reached the blacksmith's home, she went to the door of his house first, rather the shop. When she knocked, Marcus' wife Lillian answered the door.

"Lady Lucy! What can I do for you?"

"Is Robin here?"

"Yes, come in." Lillian moved away from the door and Lucy entered her front room. Robin was sitting at the table, tapping his fingers against the wood. His bow was slung over his back along with a quiver full of arrows.

"Robin?"

"Lucy! Perfect." Robin rose from the table and moved toward her. "The whole gang is away from Nottingham, except for Will. We have a whole kingdom to look after, after all."

"I know."

"Well, I'd like Will to keep an eye on Nottingham and the Sheriff while I take care of something else. I couldn't trust you to keep an eye on the Sheriff and Gisbourne, as you seem so chummy with them."

"Excuse me?"

Lucy wanted to protest further, but Robin continued, "A few soldiers left the city a minute ago and it looked like trouble. I want to see what they're up to."

"And you want someone to go with you."

"Not someone. You. You're the only other member of the gang in Nottingham today, other than Will. And I already told you I trust him to stay here more than you."

"But you trust me to come with you to deal with these soldiers, whatever they're up to."

"You're brilliant in a fight."

"Alright. But I won't kill anyone."

"Fine. Marcus already saddled two horses out back."

Lucy followed Robin out the back of Marcus' home where two horses were tied to a small hitching post and pawing the ground impatiently. She secured her bow to one of the saddles before she mounted.

The two of them rode slowly out of Nottingham. "Keep your eyes on the ground," Robin said. "There will be many tracks on the road, too many to decipher where the soldiers went, but if there are tracks leading away from the main road at some point, let me know. There were three soldiers who left Nottingham, likely up to no good."

They both rode slowly, their eyes on the ground. Lucy spotted a trail first and they set out in pursuit, hoping they weren't following a farmer or merchant who'd cut across the open grassy field.

In a few minutes, a farm came into view in the distance. There appeared to be a group of people standing in front of a simple house, and Robin spurred his horse into a canter. Lucy followed suit, slipping her bow free from the saddle and grabbing an arrow from her quiver.

As they drew close to the farm house, the scene playing out before them became clear. One soldier had a sword at a man's neck—likely the farmer—while another held what appeared to be

294

the man's wife and small son who were both trying to break away from his grasp. The third soldier had a young woman in his grasp, knife to her throat.

Robin slowly reached behind him and pulled an arrow from his quiver. "I'll get the one holding the man. You shoot the one with the girl."

Two arrows flew swiftly through the air with practiced precision. One soldier dropped his sword and fell dead. The other let go of the young woman and clutched at the arrow in his shoulder.

The third soldier let go of his charges, drawing his sword as he turned toward Lucy and Robin. The woman ran to her husband and they embraced as the boy ran toward his sister.

Robin sent another arrow flying as his horse continued forward, and the soldier who'd drawn his sword fell dead. The remaining soldier—the one Lucy had wounded—yanked the arrow from his shoulder with a grunt and drew his sword.

Lucy let an arrow fly as she and Robin galloped closer and the soldier's sword dropped to the ground as the arrow ripped through his hand.

Robin brought his horse to a sudden stop, leaping down and running forward. The young woman kicked the sword out of the soldier's reach as Robin came up to him, taking hold of his bleeding hand and lashing it to his other wrist with a bit of rope he'd had on him.

As Lucy pulled her own horse to a stop, Robin looked up at her with a frown. "Now what do we do? He's seen you, your cover is blown."

"I can't help that." Lucy moved toward the farmer's daughter. "Are you alright?"

"I'm fine. But you should kill this soldier. He'll only cause you problems. You can't keep him a prisoner for life."

"I'm sorry, I don't like killing," Lucy said.

Robin sighed.

The young woman snatched up the dagger that the soldier had been holding to her throat only moments before.

"Please don't!" Lucy cried.

But it was too late. The young woman had plunged the dagger into the soldier's neck.

Robin grinned. "You have experience fighting?"

"Who doesn't, since Prince John began his rule?" the farmer's daughter retorted, watching her handiwork as the soldier gurgled and spluttered for a moment and then slumped to the ground with the dagger still in his neck. Her little brother wrapped his arms around her waist, watching with equal fascination.

"That's true enough," Robin replied.

Lucy sighed and turned away from the sight, moving toward the farmer and his wife. "Can you dig three graves?"

"Of course," the farmer's wife said quickly.

"You want to bury them?" the young woman scoffed.

"Actually, Robin started that practice," Lucy snapped, suddenly feeling defensive.

"Robin?" The little boy looked at Robin, his eyes wide. "Are you Robin Hood?"

"Yes I am," Robin grinned. "And this is Lady Lucy."

"I'm John," the boy said breathlessly.

Robin chuckled and reached out to ruffle his hair. "I believe someone is in awe."

The young woman smiled slightly. "Yes, my brother is in awe of Robin Hood. I, too, greatly admire you. I've always wanted to join your gang."

"Ida, no!" her mother wailed.

"That's not an option." her father said, moving into the circle gathered around the soldier the young woman—Ida—had stabbed. "You can help me bury these soldiers. I'm sure Robin Hood has other pressing business."

"Robin Hood…" the mother hugged Robin. "I don't know how to thank you."

"You don't have to. This is what we do."

Lucy and Robin helped the farmer and his wife dig graves. Ida looted the soldiers bodies, taking their weapons and armor, which Robin commented was rather wise. Lucy found it appalling. Once the soldiers were buried behind the farmhouse, Lucy and Robin said farewell to the farmer and his family and rode for Nottingham.

For a time they rode in complete silence. Lucy was lost in her thoughts, reliving the moment Ida had plunged the dagger into the soldier's throat. She could still hear him choking on his own blood as he struggled to breathe past the blade in his throat and the blood filling his mouth.

"Lucy?"

"Hmm?"

"Don't be so grave. If left alive, he would have had to be a prisoner in our camp and endless trouble. I would have killed him if Ida hadn't."

"I don't like killing."

"This is war, not a walk by the river. Sometimes it has to be done."

"That doesn't mean I have to like it."

"Is it the violence that disturbs you? You are brilliant with the sword and bow. You destroyed that man's hand with your arrow, and I've seen you fight in close combat before; you're phenomenal. You could probably fight just about anyone and win."

"I don't love the violence, I can't stomach it; but it's more than that. It's my faith."

"Don't commit murder and all that?" Robin shook his head. "They started it. They were going to kill that family."

"We're never going to agree on this, Robin, so there's no point arguing over it. I won't like it no matter how much you say it is worth it or necessary or whatever."

"But I want to know *why*," Robin insisted. He reached over and grabbed Lucy's reins, pulling both horses to a standstill. His blue eyes were intense as he studied Lucy's face. "Why is it so important to you not to kill people?"

"Because I grew up listening to Friar Tuck reading Scripture to me, and I believe it."

"So you won't kill because Scripture says not to…but *why*?"

"Because I believe it, Robin. I believe in the God of love who sacrificed Himself to save me—and everyone—from ourselves. We needed the Messiah, though we did not deserve Him, and He came. And if I trust Him and believe His word to be true, then I have to trust all of it. Everything He commands, everything He promises. I believe Him when He says He forgives me. I believe Him when He says murder is wrong. It's that simple."

298

"I wish the world truly was so black and white," Robin sighed. "But it isn't, Lucy."

"I told you we wouldn't agree no matter what either of us say on the subject."

"I don't need to agree with you. I just want to understand you, your motivations. You baffle me sometimes, even more than Dusty."

"The difference in my faith and Dusty's is only in presentation," Lucy said. "She shares my trust in Jesus and desire to do His will. She simply isn't as strictly disciplined in following precisely what Scripture says. There's more...gentleness to her," Lucy sighed. "I envy that in some respects, but I can't change how I approach life. I am who I am."

Robin nodded slowly, letting go of Lucy's reins and spurring his own horse into a walk again. The rest of the ride was quiet. They dropped the horses off at Marcus' home and then Robin asked if Lucy was coming to dinner at the camp. She hadn't intended to, but she agreed and so they walked quietly across the fields to the forest of Sherwood and through the trees as twilight fell.

When they entered the camp, Dusty met them with a bright smile. "We're getting married!"

"We are?" Robin asked, a grin spreading across his face.

"Not you, Robin!" Lucy laughed as Dusty playfully swatted his arm.

"Who?" Robin asked.

"Dusty and Will of course," Lucy laughed. "Where have you been, Robin, that you didn't see this coming?"

"When are you getting married?" Robin asked Dusty. "And who said I haven't noticed?"

Dusty smiled. "We haven't set a day. But Friar Tuck will marry us. And you have to be here, Lucy."

"Of course. Just tell me when and I'll come."

"Didn't he ask you before and you refused?" Robin asked.

Dusty shook her head. "No. Yes."

Robin raised an eyebrow. "No…yes?"

"He asked you to marry him and you refused?" Lucy asked, surprised at the news.

"Yes, he did ask. No, I did not refuse him exactly…I've always loved Will. He asked before Marian…" Dusty paused. Robin didn't physically react as he used to at the mention of her name, but his eyes darkened to a deeper shade of blue. Dusty hesitated and then continued. "But I couldn't marry someone who didn't believe the same as me."

"That's absurd," Robin said.

"No it isn't, Robin."

Robin glanced at Lucy, then back to Dusty, and then shrugged. "I will never understand the two of you. I am glad, however, that there will be a wedding to brighten our days. We need something cheerful to liven things up. Life has been…" Robin sighed. "Dark. It's been so dark since Austria."

"Will and I thought so, too," Dusty said. "That's why we won't wait until after all this," Dusty waved her hand in a vague manner, "to be over. We all need something good to hold onto these days."

Chapter 28

"IT WAS A glorious wedding Friar Tuck performed in the green woods of Sherwood on a beautiful day in Autumn. A gentle breeze teased our hair and softly swayed the branches overhead as Friar Tuck preformed the marriage ceremony in our little clearing. Dusty was radiant and Will had eyes only for her."

Mari-Lu sighed contentedly. "I love weddings."

"So do I," Aunt Lucy laughed. "So do I."

"What happened after that?"

"More trouble. For that one day everything was perfect but we were soon brought back to reality. The Sheriff set off to burn an entire village to the ground, inhabitants included."

"Why?"

"They bothered him."

Mari-Lu crossed her arms. "He always says that."

"Robin and the gang were away confiscating here, rescuing someone there. We were always spread so thin across England. I had no way of stopping the Sheriff on my own, certainly no way to do anything without the Sheriff noticing."

"So what did you do?"

"I went to Sir Guy. But…"

←→

"It's the Sheriff's orders, Lucy. He wants to make an example of them. And Prince John always says the best examples are written in blood."

"Guy, please." Lucy grabbed his arm as he started to walk past her. They were in the castle courtyard and she didn't want to make a scene as Sir Guy and the Sheriff gathered their soldiers and prepared to leave, but she couldn't let him get away without trying to stop the tragedy that would occur if the Sheriff was successful.

"Those people haven't done anything wrong!" Lucy hissed, trying to keep her voice low despite how desperate she was. "He's going to burn them all, the women, the children. Guy, you can't let it happen!"

He shrugged Lucy off his arm and mounted Victory without a word. Lucy watched in horror as he and the Sheriff left the castle courtyard with their soldiers following dutifully behind.

She hurried to the camp, her heart aching for the people who would undoubtedly die that day. Lucy spent much of the day in restless activity. Pacing the camp, stringing and restringing her bow, sharpening her sword and dagger, rearranging the pots and pans in Much's kitchen.

When the rest of the gang began to trickle into camp that night, returning from their various activities, Lucy tearfully informed them of what had happened.

Allen touched Lucy's arm gently. "Sir Guy won't let it happen."

"He gave me no assurance of that."

"Perhaps the Sheriff was watching?" Dusty offered.

"Or perhaps," Robin said. "He really is evil."

Allen shook his head. "He is not."

"He *is* evil." Mark said quietly.

Much lit a small fire as the gang circled around, sitting on the logs pulled around it for that purpose, each of them considering the possibilities.

"He's done so much…for both sides," Will said. "How can you even tell one way or the other?"

"But for Lucy—" Allen began.

"People said he'd do anything for Marian," Robin snapped. "And he *killed* her."

Mark winced.

"I can't believe he'd let them die," Lucy said, wringing her hands. "I don't want to believe it…"

"He won't." Allen said firmly.

"He most definitely will," Robin said. "Where was the village? We can ride there tonight, see if there are any survivors."

"I don't want to see that," Lucy sighed. But she did tell Robin where to go. As he and the rest of the gang prepared to set off to investigate, Lucy approached him.

"Somehow…I don't doubt the village is burned."

"And Gisbourne did nothing to stop it," Robin said.

"I feel like a fool."

Robin shook his head, putting a hand on her arm. "You are just too optimistic. Seeing good in people when there is none."

Much stayed with Lucy, as the rest of the gang set off for the village, preparing a small meal for the two of them and trying to keep her hopes up. Lucy spent all that night and the next morning in anguish. She wanted to believe in Sir Guy but he'd indicated he would obey the Sheriff. Had she been wrong to trust him? Robin certainly thought so.

When the Sheriff returned Lucy tried not to hope. She made her way toward the castle courtyard to see how everyone might be feeling after their expedition. She met the Sheriff in the hall but he marched silently past her. Was that good or bad? She watched the soldiers in the courtyard as they disbursed. Were they triumphant or despondent? She couldn't tell.

Sir Guy was passing Victory's reins to a stable boy, and Lucy stood on the steps leading to the courtyard, debating whether or not to approach him as soldiers filed past her into the castle.

Feeling a tap on her shoulder she turned to find Andrew beside her. "Did you believe in him or not?"

"I…"

Andrew pulled her slightly aside, away from the soldiers who were still in the courtyard. "He sent me ahead to warn them."

"What?"

"They'd all evacuated by the time the Sheriff arrived. He burned the village anyway, but the people were saved."

"You mean…he really…" Lucy spun away from Andrew, running down the steps and across the courtyard. "Guy!"

He was still standing by the stables. He turned and instead of letting Lucy barrel into him and possibly knock him over he picked her up as she ran to him and swung her in a small circle.

He set her gently on the ground, keeping his arms around her waist. "Ah Lucy. The look of disbelief in your eyes as I left…" he leaned forward, resting his forehead against hers and whispered. "But the Sheriff has spies everywhere these days and I couldn't let my guard down."

"I should have trusted you."

"I've never done anything to deserve it."

"You have, Guy. You have."

"The Sheriff is frustrated the people somehow knew…he's expecting us for lunch." Sir Guy let go of Lucy and offered her his arm. Lucy slipped her arm through his and let him lead her back across the courtyard. "He's going to be angry and suspicious. We'll need to be careful."

"He's never acted on his suspicions," Lucy said. "Even after that time he nearly killed me, nothing came of it. I'm not afraid of our dear Sheriff."

"That is precisely what makes him dangerous. You never know when he will decide to actually do harm, like the other day when he nearly killed you."

As they entered the dining room the Sheriff glared at Lucy. "I saw your little show. But you are wrong. Gisbourne didn't help you. One of my trusted men told me he refused point blank to help you when you asked."

Lucy glanced at Sir Guy as they joined the Sheriff at the table. He'd been right about the Sheriff's spies, apparently.

"That's true. He did refuse. My joy at his return was from the knowledge the people were rescued."

The Sheriff grunted. "I suppose you told Robin and I'll have to have you killed."

"There was no evidence Robin Hood was there," Sir Guy replied.

"There never is, but who else could have stopped us?" the Sheriff growled. "I'll hang your Robin Hood if it's the last thing I do."

"As is your right," Sir Guy said. "But Lady Lucy was not involved."

"So you keep saying. I am beginning to believe you might be biased in that regard, Gisbourne. You never were so blinded by Marian's involvement with the outlaws."

Sir Guy grimaced, his face contorting with agony for a moment and he fell silent, his dark eyes staring down at the table and not moving.

Lucy watched him with a pang of grief, her own guilt in Marian's death rising to the surface once more.

"If I ever catch you trying to convince my right-hand to defy me," the Sheriff snarled in Lucy's direction, "I will kill you."

The rest of their meal was a silent one, as the Sheriff glared at Lucy and Sir Guy brooded on his side of the table. Lucy left as soon as she could, wondering if or when the Sheriff would finally snap and try to kill her again. It was perhaps time to consider moving to the camp after all.

The next morning, Lucy rode to the camp in high spirits. "He did it!" she called as she entered the camp. All of the gang was there, gathered around the fire ring enjoying their breakfast. Everyone looked up as she dismounted and hurried over to them.

"Who did what?" Little John asked.

"I imagine she means the village," Dusty said. "We found it empty," Dusty added, turning to Lucy. "And later discovered the refugees. We helped them start their travel toward a safer place to live, for now at least."

"That's good," Lucy said, sitting down between Dusty and Much.

"How did they know to evacuate?" Much asked.

"Sir Guy. He sent Andrew ahead. He rescued the villagers."

Robin frowned while Allen sighed in relief. "I knew he would. Well…I hoped he would."

"I wish he hadn't," Robin said.

"Robin!" Dusty scolded. "You wish those people had died?"

"No. Of course not. But I wish someone else had rescued them."

"It's much easier to hate him when he's always doing evil," Friar Tuck observed. "If he was evil you would perhaps have grounds to hate him."

"I have perfect grounds to hate that man!"

"Hatred is never the answer, my son. And if you gave up this foolish hatred it would not sting so when he proves his worth."

"He isn't worth anything!" Robin stormed away.

Allen sighed. "He'll never change his mind."

"He shouldn't," Mark snapped. "Gisbourne isn't worth anything. He's a murderer."

Lucy didn't stay long at the camp. Her friendship with Sir Guy was scorned by Robin and Mark and confused Much. Dusty and Will were trying to see Sir Guy from a forgiving standpoint, and Allen certainly did considering his own case was not so very different. But Lucy knew whenever she spoke of Sir Guy she caused tension in the group, and that was the last thing she wanted for her friends. So she returned to the castle, eager for night to fall so she could watch the stars with Sir Guy in peace.

Late that night, before Lucy had left her room to go watch the stars, there was a knock on her door. She opened it slowly and found an unexpected visitor. "Robin?"

307

He slipped inside her room and shut the door quickly, leaning against it. "Well I haven't sneaked in here in a long while. That was fun."

"Robin, what is it? It's risky—"

"I know," Robin held up his hands to silence her. "I know. I'll probably get caught. But I wanted to apologize."

"Apologize?"

"I haven't been fair. You're performing miracles with Gisbourne and all I can do is complain."

"God's performing the miracles."

"Whatever."

Lucy was silent a moment before a teasing light filled her eyes. "You risked your neck for that?"

"I figured it would be important to you. And I am sorry if I'm ever rude to you. I don't love your friendship with him, I won't hide that. I still think he's absolutely vile and doesn't deserve the grace you give him, but I can see the good you are doing, the lives being saved because he's—at least for the moment—willing to help us."

"I do appreciate your apology, Robin. But I'm not truly the one changing him."

"So you say. I need to go." Robin pushed himself off the door.

"Wait! I'll have Sir Guy and Andrew make sure your way is clear."

"No!" Robin snarled, and then he winced. "I'm sorry. I don't want any favors from *him*."

"Regard it as a favor from me, Robin," Lucy said softly.

"I'll be fine. I got in alright, and this isn't the first time I've snuck in and out of this castle." Robin opened her door, peeking out into the hall. "Wish me luck."

"Please don't do anything stupid while you're here."

"I'll be fine," Robin winked, slipping out of her room and closing the door. Lucy could only pray he would, indeed, be fine.

The next time she visited the camp, Robin was alive and well, and it was clear the trip to Nottingham castle hadn't set off any alarms. The fact that he had risked such a trip merely to apologize for how angry he became with her whenever Gisbourne was brought up confused her, but she was gratified by it as well.

Chapter 29

LUCY URGED VICTORY into a gallop as she raced toward Sherwood, every frantic hoofbeat jarring her body. The Sheriff was plotting to murder a young woman because her father defied him and there was little time to warn the gang and get back to Nottingham.

As she entered the treeline, and slowed Victory's pace enough that she wouldn't kill herself or the horse by running afoul of a squirrel hole or low-hanging branch or some other obstacle, Lucy thought about what she would do once she reached the camp. The Sheriff had offhandedly told her not to tell Robin and Lucy had replied that she would not, which had amused Guy who'd helped her saddle Victory and told her the details of the execution while he did so. Whether or not the Sheriff meant anything by his casual comment, Lucy still felt she'd given her word. But what if Robin was the only person in the camp?

When Lucy burst into the clearing, however, the camp was empty.

Lucy swung Victory around, her eyes darting around the empty meadow. "Robin? Dusty?" She could see her breath in the cold air as she called their names but no response came, no one emerged from the empty huts.

Lucy considered for a moment. They could have left the shire altogether, on trips to other cities and villages to distribute money and stop executions; it happened frequently enough. But Lucy felt she would have been told if the entire gang was gone, and anyway Robin always liked to have at least one person watching over Nottingham. It was possible they were in

Nottingham at the market or Marcus' house, or even in the surrounding villages distributing money.

Lucy urged Victory forward again and made for the edge of the forest. Wetherby was the closest village, so Lucy headed there. It was a small village, made up of only a handful of houses on a couple small dirt streets, and even at a distance Lucy could tell that there were indeed people there. As she drew close it became clear that Mark, Will, and Robin were passing out sacks of money to Widow Mary and the other inhabitants of the village. Given the colder weather and the coming of winter, the extra food and warmth their donations would buy for the people of England were needed more than ever.

Lucy pushed Victory down the street toward them, the voice of the Sheriff demanding the head of the innocent farmer's daughter running through her mind.

"Lucy!" Will waved when he saw her. "What's up?"

"Another scheme of the Sheriff's," Lucy said as she reined Victory in.

"Well?" Mark asked.

"Robin, can you leave for a moment?"

"Excuse me?" Robin said.

Will, Mark, and the villagers nearby seemed as confused by Lucy's comment as Robin. She hopped down off of Victory's back and moved closer toward her friends, lowering her voice and hoping not to draw too much attention.

"I'm sorry. But I promised the Sheriff I wouldn't tell you. I'm going to tell Will and Mark, not you. Whether they tell you or not, is their choice."

"Lucy, you've got to stop doing this," Robin thew up his hands in exasperation.

"It keeps the Sheriff trusting me."

Robin sighed. "Does it? Or is he merely biding his time until he tries to kill you again?"

"Doesn't matter. I'm not going to tell you."

Robin sighed, reluctantly moving away from Lucy. As soon as he'd walked sufficiently far away from them, Lucy told Will and Mark of the Sheriff's plan.

"Who are they beheading?" Will asked. "We can get them to a safe location before hand, perhaps."

"It's happening now!" Lucy insisted. "And anyway, they didn't use any names."

"I guess we'll have to rescue her directly from the beheading. That's more fun anyway."

"Just don't fail."

"We won't," Mark said firmly.

«→»

"Did they save her? Did they?" Mari-Lu asked.

Aunt Lucy smiled. "Hold on. We can't skip to the end. I raced back to Nottingham on Victory, just in time to watch the Sheriff's men gathering the citizens of Nottingham in the Square to witness the execution. It had been a while since the Sheriff had attempted such a public execution, and many came not only because he insisted but also in the hopes of seeing Robin Hood and his gang rescue whoever the victim was. Two platforms had been erected in the center of the Square, facing each other. On one stood the Sheriff, Sir Guy, myself, and a handful of guards. The other was filled with several soldiers, clearly meant to be

312

guarding it against the expected rescue, and sitting amidst them was a large block of wood with a slight indention across the top."

"And indention?" Mari-Lu asked.

"Perfect for cradling a neck, the better to expose it to the blade of an axe…"

"Ohhhh…"

"More soldiers pushed people aside to form a path through the crowd leading toward a side street as several guards came forward, dragging their prisoner toward her death. I gasped when the soldiers brought the girl forward, her hands tied behind her."

"Why?"

"Because I recognized her…"

⋘⋙

The Sheriff insisted Lucy stand with him and Sir Guy on the platform, so she had a good view of the farmer's daughter as the soldiers dragged her up the steps toward the chopping block and forced her onto her knees. She was small and blond and though her eyes reflected her fear her chin was set stubbornly. It was Ida, the girl from the farm who'd killed the soldier Lucy had wounded.

A soldier pushed Ida's head forward onto the execution block.

Lucy searched the courtyard for a familiar face. She knew they were there—surely they'd followed her from Wetherby—but they had certainly done well in hiding themselves among the citizens of Nottingham for she caught sight of none of the gang.

Then one of the soldiers raised a large axe. Lucy wanted to close her eyes but she could not. Everything appeared to slow down as the axe swung first upward in an arc, and then back down again.

Ida closed her eyes and lowered her head in defeat.

There was a slight twang and then an arrow plunked into the soldier's chest. He let go of the axe and stumbled backwards and off the platform. The axe flew through the air, spinning out of control towards Ida's head. Another twang and an arrow hit the axe handle. It twisted in the air, the arrow changing its course, and sliced through the execution block, just as Ida threw herself backward and away from imminent death.

There was a collective sigh of relief from the crowd followed by shouts from the Sheriff and soldiers. The remaining soldiers reached for Ida, more arrows flew through the crowd, and the people of Nottingham began to throw stones at the Sheriff's men to take their attention off of the farmer's daughter. In the confusion that followed, Ida vanished.

As the Sheriff yelled orders and the soldiers fought off the angry crowd, pushing aside the young and old alike in their desperate search for Ida, Sir Guy bent ever so slightly toward Lucy and whispered, "I wonder how he knew."

"I didn't tell Robin."

"I suspected as much."

Sir Guy escorted Lucy back toward the castle, shielding her from the worst of the chaos as soldiers and villagers grappled —stones and shoes were being thrown, swords drawn, and everywhere there seemed to be the makings of a full-on riot—and once they were safely within the confines of the castle walls, he insisted Andrew stay near her for the rest of the day in case the Sheriff came back to the castle with any idea of vengeance.

The Sheriff, however, did not approach Lucy so the next morning she left early to saddle Victory and visit the camp. She joined the circle around the fire in the middle of a debate. The gang was all there, as well as the young woman named Ida. It was a chill morning, and as the gang spoke little puffs of frozen breath would form for a moment in front of their mouths and then dissipate into nothingness.

"Well it's certainly better than Much ever made it," Little John said playfully.

"Hey!" Much cried in outrage.

"Maybe you could be our new cook," Allen suggested to Ida.

"Wait a minute!" Much interjected.

"What's this about a new cook?" Lucy laughed.

"They're trying to steal my job!" Much complained.

"Steal?" Will asked. "We're really just giving it away."

"Confiscating," Robin corrected. "That's what we do, after all."

"Our new friend we rescued yesterday helped Much with breakfast," Dusty explained.

"Ah, I see," Lucy said. "Everyone enjoyed Ida's food more than Much's."

"I enjoyed Much's," Ida said firmly.

Robin placed a hand on her shoulder. "Lucy, you remember Ida? She can't return home because of the Sheriff so she's an unofficial member of the gang."

"It's wonderful to see you again, Ida. Though I wish our meetings would stop being under such dire circumstances."

"I feel quite honored to be a part of Robin Hood's gang," Ida said. "Though not 'unofficially' as Robin put it. I'd like to

315

help as much as I can. I'm good with a dagger." Lucy winced at the memory as Ida continued, "And until the country is back in order you'll meet a lot of people under dire circumstances."

"We wouldn't have had time to plan your rescue if Lucy hadn't told me about your execution," Will said.

"Then I am beholden to you," Ida said to Lucy.

Lucy shook her head. "That's just what we do."

"I want to help with that," Ida said.

"Then we'll find ways to include you," Robin said.

"Good."

Mark stood and moved away from the group around the breakfast fire. After a moment, Lucy followed him. "Mark! Where are you going?"

"Away from all of that foolishness." Mark gestured back toward the fire as he moved to lean against a large tree near the edge of the meadow.

"Foolishness?"

"First you, now Ida. I can't stand it."

"Oh, Mark! Robin isn't trying to replace Marian! He only just met Ida, he certainly isn't thinking about falling in love with her."

"I know, but … he could. He might."

"He won't."

Mark studied Lucy for a moment and then shook his head. Lucy, I like you. You've become one of the gang and a good friend to all of us. You even helped me out of my depression for which I shall always be grateful. But it hasn't even been a year since my sister died! Robin can't love someone already."

"He doesn't love anyone like that."

Mark raised an eyebrow. "Really?"

316

"No, of course not. Robin will never replace Marian."

"You really believe that." Mark shook his head, seemingly unconvinced.

"What?"

Mark turned away. "Nothing."

For a moment he was quiet as he watched the group at the fire, still teasing and laughing together. Eventually, Mark sighed heavily. "I still can't forgive myself."

"Oh, Mark."

"Friar Tuck has been helping; he's easy to talk to and offers a great deal of hope and comfort…but I just keep remembering that moment. I was standing right beside her. I even had my hand on her arm. I was right there! Why could I not protect her?"

The image of Guy stalking toward Marian with his sword raised flashed through Lucy's mind. She could feel the wood of her bow in her hand as she held an arrow taut to the string, tempted to simply kill him and fighting the urge to do so.

"Mark, you can't keep reliving the past. You have to let it go." Even as she said as much to Mark, Lucy wished it could be so easy to do so.

"Easy to say," Mark turned to Lucy, his grey eyes turning a darker shade. "Can you stop reliving your worst nightmares?"

"It might not be easy, but you won't be able to truly live if you keep existing in this space of guilt and pain."

"Perhaps…but is life worth living without Marian?" Tears fell from his lashes and his hands began to tremble.

"Mark…" Lucy reached out toward him and Mark collapsed into her embrace, silently shaking as his tears wet her shoulder. He didn't cry long, soon standing straight and brushing aside his tears, but he seemed in a far better mood afterward.

"Shall we join the others?" Mark said, giving her a crooked smile. "Robin will get jealous if we stay alone by ourselves for too long."

"Jealous of what?" Lucy asked, causing Mark to chuckle.

"You really don't know." Mark grabbed her arm and pulled her toward the fire. "Come on, you need to eat. Food will sharpen your senses, I'm sure."

A week later when Lucy came into the camp she found Robin alone, sitting before a small fire to keep warm. It was mid-morning, the sun high in the sky and brightening the meadow though the grass was mostly brown and dead by this point and the trees around the edge were losing all of their autumn glory.

"Where is everyone?"

"Where I sent them. Different places. Are you looking for anyone specific?"

"Not exactly. And where's Ida?" Lucy asked as she seated herself beside Robin. "Already off on missions of her own."

"With Dusty," Robin said. "You know, she's not too bad with a bow and arrow."

"Really."

Robin shook his head slowly, as though he were deeply disappointed. "She'll never reach your skill."

"And I'll never reach yours."

Robin laughed. "Now Lucy, you know you've been declared the best in England. Nothing will change that."

Lucy shook her head. "Nothing can convince your admiring people you aren't the best."

"I didn't think anything could convince my gang I'm not the best."

"How is Ida fitting in?"

"Great. She's one stubborn woman! Kind of like…"

"Marian."

"Yes." Robin sighed, throwing another stick onto the flames. "I thought I was going to grow old with her."

"I know, Robin."

"I miss her."

"I'm sorry."

"It wasn't your fault."

Lucy didn't respond. How could she possibly tell Robin that she could have saved Marian? Where did one even begin such a conversation?

"I keep wishing…wondering what I could have done differently." Robin shoved a hand through his hair and sighed. "How I could have stopped or prevented it. Maybe I should have…I don't know."

"Robin, you can't change the past. You can only direct the future."

He sighed and glared into the fire for a moment, before he shook himself slightly and gave Lucy a small smile. "You've helped, Lucy."

"I have?"

"You brought me back. When Marian died I thought life was over. I *wanted* it to be over. I would have left my people alone to suffer and die, but you wouldn't let me. And you've been showing me there's more to life yet."

"I'm just glad you aren't in despair anymore."

"Do you…do you suppose she's moved on? That she's happy wherever she's gone?"

"Who…Marian?"

"Yes. You're the one full of faith around here; do you think she's, I don't know…in heaven?"

"I…she…I don't know, Robin. You never can know what may have transpired inside her at the end. Or even before. Who knows whether she believed or not?"

"I hope…I never cared about God before."

"I know."

"But now…I'm worried about it."

"Because you want to see Marian again?"

"Because I don't want her, how would you say it? Burning in hell."

"Don't fret, Robin. 'Who of you by worrying can add a single hour to your life?' You can't change the past, and dwelling on it isn't healthy."

"I can only direct the future," Robin rolled his eyes as he repeated Lucy's phrase back to her. "Right."

"Robin…you say I've helped you …"

"Yes, you have."

"Can you do something for me?"

"Of course."

"Help Mark. He's doing the same thing you are, wondering what he could have done differently. But it's worse for him, I think, because he was right beside her. Nothing I say seems to help."

"He seems rather upset with you more often than not."

"Yes, I think he is. But then, you often are as well."

"I can't argue with that."

"But please, try to comfort him. You understand best what he's feeling, what he's going through."

"I will try. I should have been putting more effort into it already. I promised Marian a long time ago that I would always look after her brother."

Chapter 30

MARI-LU SMILED. "Is Robin happy again?"

"He was getting there. But I soon pushed him to his limit."

"Oh no. What did you do?" Mari-Lu asked, crossing her arms. "Was it about Gisbourne again?"

Aunt Lucy nodded. "It was about Sir Guy. It was a few days after my conversation with Robin that the Sheriff burned Ida's farm and killed her mother and brother. He hadn't told anyone he was going to do so—not even Gisbourne. He merely selected a troop of soldiers and left the castle on his own without a word to anyone else. I couldn't warn the gang because I didn't know about it."

"That's horrible!"

"After killing Ida's mother and brother and burning her home, he brought Ida's father to Nottingham. He was thrown in prison while the Sheriff made grand plans to execute him, and that was when Sir Guy and I realized what he'd been up to."

"Why did he do all that?"

"Because of his frustration at not finding Ida after she escaped her execution. Due to the murder of Ida's family, Sir Guy was even more paranoid that the Sheriff would turn on me, especially after he elicited another promise from me not to speak to Robin Hood. Sir Guy was sure it was a trap once more, and this time he believed the Sheriff would follow through on his threats, but even so I hurried to the camp to inform the gang. Yet when I arrived that cold morning, only one person was there…"

"Robin! Where's the gang?"

"Some of them are confiscating to the south, the rest are distributing food to the west." Robin shifted on the log bench in front of the fire so Lucy could sit but she remained standing, shifting back and forth on restless feet.

"Is Ida with them?"

"Yes."

"And Friar Tuck?"

"He went along at Mark's request."

Lucy groaned. "When will they be back?"

"Not until tomorrow or the next day." Robin stood up, moving toward Lucy. "What's up?"

"The Sheriff…"

"What?"

"I can't tell you."

"You promised not to, I imagine. Lucy—"

"I know you think it's dumb but I don't. There is a way to pass on the message, but you…"

"I'm not talking to Gisbourne."

"Robin—"

"No!" His shout caused several birds nearby to flee their warm nests.

"But—"

"I said no."

"Why are you so stubborn?"

"I could ask you the same question."

"Robin, it's happening before the gang gets back."

"So tell me."

"I can't."

"And I can't talk to Gisbourne."

"You *won't*. It's different."

"Lucy, sometimes…." Robin crossed his arms, his face reddening as he glared at her, his voice full of ice.

"Just go get the message, please? Robin…I don't understand—"

"He killed Marian, Lucy!" Robin had grabbed hold of both of Lucy's shoulders and shook her as he spoke. "He *killed* her, plunged his sword straight through her!"

Lucy was silent for a moment waiting for him to calm down. He sighed and let go of her, turning away, his shoulders slumping.

He looked defeated.

"I'm sorry," he said softly.

"Please? Do it for me."

Robin looked at Lucy silently.

She reached out and laid a hand on his shoulder. "Please? I know what he did, and I know how much he hurt all of you. I *know*, okay? But please…"

"Lucy…" Robin sighed, shoving a hand through his hair. "Fine. I'll do it. For you. But I don't forgive him."

"Thank you, Robin."

Lucy let Robin head to Nottingham on his own, choosing to slowly walk Victory back toward the city a distance behind him. She imagined he would want to be alone with his thoughts, and she also had no desire to make him angry again. That he was going to speak to Sir Guy at all was a miracle, and she didn't want to push it.

When she made it to Nottingham, she took Victory to the stables and then went to the library in the castle to distract herself with a good book from her worry over Robin and Sir Guy.

That evening when she went to watch the stars, firmly wrapped up in a fur-lined cape and hood she'd purchased from a tailor in the city, Sir Guy was absent. Lucy momentarily panicked that Robin had killed him instead of talking to him, but surely she would have heard if that was the case. All of Nottingham would be interested in such news, and the Sheriff would have certainly made a fuss over it.

The next day, Lucy went to the castle courtyard with reluctance, unsure whether or not Sir Guy had been able to pass the news along to Robin and if he'd planned a way to save Ida's father from execution. A familiar sight of the gallows in the castle courtyard greeted her, along with a dozen or more soldiers around the perimeter and up on the walls. The Sheriff was pacing in anticipation, and Sir Guy was nearby. He glanced at Lucy and smiled, and that was all Lucy needed to know.

As Lucy went down the wide stone steps into the courtyard, the Sheriff swung toward her and Sir Guy instinctively stepped forward, a hand on the hilt of his sword.

"Where have you been?"

"I haven't spoken to the outlaws, if that's what you are insinuating. As far as I am aware, they aren't even in Nottingham right now."

The Sheriff huffed, turning back to his pacing. Lucy went to stand next to Sir Guy, wishing she could talk to him without the Sheriff overhearing. She wanted to know what Robin had been like during their conversation—it had to have been difficult for both of them. Lucy studied her friend as he resolutely stared at the

Sheriff, equally unwilling to draw attention from him. Speaking to Robin had undoubtedly brought his own demons to the surface, and Lucy wished she could talk to him about it, comfort him in some way.

Suddenly two soldiers burst from the castle, bounding down the steps toward the Sheriff. One of them was limping, blood seeping from his leg and staining his trousers. The other had a gash across his face.

"What is this?" the Sheriff demanded, sending a sharp look toward Lucy. Sir Guy moved up to stand beside the Sheriff as the soldiers approached.

"Robin Hood, sir," one of the soldiers gasped, gesturing behind him toward the castle. "He's here!"

"And why aren't you with him?" Sir Guy snapped. "You let him past you?"

"He fought us off, along with the two soldiers he killed by the dungeons," one of the soldiers said.

"All of you should have fought to your last breath to stop the outlaw!" Sir Guy turned to the Sheriff, "I'll find the outlaw. He can't get out through secret passages any longer, so we should be able to get him before he gets out with our prisoner."

Sir Guy strode across the courtyard and entered the castle. The wounded soldiers hesitated and then moved to follow him.

"Oh you won't get off so easily," the Sheriff called after them. "If you're still in my castle by nightfall, I'm hanging both of you!"

The Sheriff marched into the castle as the soldiers ran after Guy as well as they could. Lucy was left in the courtyard, along with the dozen soldiers who had been meant to ensure the execution went off without a hitch.

326

Lucy had known Robin to sneak into the castle without the secret passages in the past, but to get to the dungeons and get Ida's father out, and then fight his way out again…Lucy grinned, moving toward the castle herself. He was most impressive.

Later that day Lucy rode to the camp where she found Robin and Ida's father safe and sound.

"How did you do it?" Lucy asked, moving to sit beside the roaring fire Robin had started to warm the clearing.

"With flair," Robin grinned.

Lucy shook her head. "However it happened, I am glad."

"As am I," Ida's father said, glancing toward Lucy and Robin. "Though death might have been a relief…"

"I understand that," Robin said with a sigh. "I am truly sorry for your wife and son. We should have been there…"

"You cannot be everywhere, I am sure," he replied.

"Unfortunately not."

With Ida's father present, Lucy did not find a time to talk to Robin about their argument or his conversation with Sir Guy and she returned to Nottingham feeling unsatisfied. Once she was back at the castle, she went in search of Sir Guy and found him and Andrew in his room.

Andrew winked at Lucy as he slipped out of the room. "Keep him in line, will you?"

Lucy turned to watch Andrew shut the door behind her. "What was that about?"

"Just ignore Andrew," Sir Guy said with a chuckle. "I generally do."

"Much to your detriment, I'm sure," Lucy replied.

Sir Guy moved to put another log on the fire in his hearth, though there were already several crackling there.

327

"Did you need something, Lady Lucy?" Sir Guy asked from where he knelt in front of his fire, watching the new log catch before he stood.

"I wondered if you could perhaps persuade the Sheriff to leave Ida's father in peace?"

"Like the children?" Sir Guy asked. "An act of compassion?"

"Yes."

Sir Guy shook his head. "I doubt it will work. He murdered his wife and son, and he's dead set on finding and killing him as well. Robin's untimely rescue has him on edge again, and he's unlikely to back down. More than that, he's likely going to come after you again." Sir Guy took two long strides across the room, catching Lucy's hands as his dark eyes bored into hers. "You should go to the outlaws' camp. Stop coming back here. You won't be safe."

"I can take care of myself."

"Please. I won't always be nearby when the Sheriff tries to harm you."

"Guy, honestly, I am able to take care of myself. I can use my sword with great efficiency, and there are few who can shoot better than I."

"I'm worried."

"I can tell, but I'll be fine, I'm sure. I'll be careful, of course, and try not to be alone with the Sheriff if I can help it, but you shouldn't worry so much."

Sir Guy sighed. "I wish I could convince you to leave."

"And leave you alone here with your dark thoughts? I think not."

Sir Guy smiled slightly. "I'm sure Andrew could deal with me well enough. At any rate, I will attempt to speak to the Sheriff about Ida's father, but I don't expect it to do any good. It may, in fact, anger him further."

"Thank you."

◄—»

"Did it work?" Mari-Lu asked. "Did the Sheriff let Ida's father be free?"

"Unfortunately, Sir Guy was right; the Sheriff would have none of it. So Robin kept him in the camp for a time, which was also Ida's preference. She wanted to be near her last surviving family member, and she wanted to keep him safe. But he did not appreciate staying there, isolated from the world, and consumed with his pain. He was restless and grieving his wife and young son. After a little over a week in Robin's camp, he disappeared. He left a note to Ida saying he was going to go look for the King if he could find him."

"Oh no…"

"Ida was devastated, but with the choice of following after him or staying to fight injustice with the gang, she chose the latter."

"What happened after that?"

"Well, the next time I visited the camp…"

◄—»

As soon as Lucy dismounted, Dusty wrapped her in a hug. "Robin told us what happened while we were gone, how Ida's father got to be here in the first place—although he's run off now. How did you convince Robin to seek out Gisbourne?"

"Ida's father needed saving. Robin wouldn't let him die. He'll do anything to save his people."

"Anything except talk to Gisbourne." Dusty glanced toward the fire where Robin was chatting with Allen and Ida. "Admit it, my friend. He did it for you."

"I suppose."

"Robin would have done anything for Marian. And now he'll do anything for you."

"Are you suggesting…"

"I'm not suggesting anything. I'm just telling the facts." Dusty slipped her arm through Lucy's with a grin, but Lucy did not feel the elation Dusty so clearly did.

"Oh no."

"What's wrong?" Dusty asked.

"Mark! He was right. He won't like this at all."

"Mark? He'll be happy that Robin is happy, will he not?"

"No. He won't be happy at all." Lucy stared at Dusty with wide eyes, and then glanced toward the fire and Robin. He threw back his head in a laugh at something Ida had said, his blue eyes sparkling and Lucy felt her heart twist inside her chest. "He doesn't want Robin to replace Marian."

"Well, of course not. But Robin isn't replacing Marian with anyone. It's not as though you are taking her spot. You're finding your own place in his heart."

"Try explaining that to Mark."

"Don't be so grim," Dusty said, pulling Lucy toward the group gathered at the fire. But Lucy was on edge as she sat stiffly on the log bench next to Dusty. Robin caught her eye with a grin and a wink and Lucy didn't know how to feel. Did she love him? *Should* she love him? Mark wasn't going to like it, that much was true...but what did Lucy think about the idea that Robin might care for her?

As Lucy watched Robin talked to Allen, she couldn't help but smile and relax. His easy manners and playful spirit always brought enjoyment to whomever he spent time with. And he was truly good, fighting injustice and cruelty with tenacity for years.

Even in his grief and despair, he saw to the needs of those around him.

Lucy thought perhaps she might love him, but whether he truly felt the same remained to be seen. And what Mark might do about it was another mystery...

And on top of everything else, there was still the black cloud of her own guilt in Marian's death hanging over her, like a storm biding its time to be unleashed. Robin might be starting to care for her now, but that was unlikely to remain the case once he heard the truth.

Sir Guy and Lucy continued to watch the stars together every evening. Sir Guy had taken to bringing a thick blanket with him to stretch across the ledge for Lucy to sit on, and another she could wrap around her shoulders to keep out the cold of the winter evenings. On one such night as they stared up into the dark night, admiring the pale stars overhead, he said, "I've been thinking lately."

"Oh?"

"About my life. About Marian. Like you, she always saw good where there was none."

"That's not true, Guy."

"Isn't it?"

"You were referring to yourself, but I believe there is good in you. I know so."

"Thank you." Sir Guy turned from the stars to look at Lucy, his dark eyes shining.

"So what exactly were you thinking?"

"I think God brought you to Nottingham for a purpose...to show us the light. I wouldn't have known where to look for true happiness if you hadn't come along."

"Guy, I don't offer—"

"I know. Christ does. That's what I mean."

"Oh, Guy!"

"I can barely fathom what it feels like to be forgiven...and yet here I am, drowning in the grace and mercy of our Father."

Slow tears formed and fell from Sir Guy's eyes, crystallizing on his cheeks in the cold air. "He is far too good; I don't deserve it."

"But that's the whole point, Guy. None of us do."

Sir Guy nodded with a shaky smile as more tears fell. "I know, and I am forever going to be grateful to you for pointing me toward the only person truly capable of seeing my worst and forgiving me fully and completely. I now understand the joy you have, Lucy. I have it too."

"I cannot tell you how glad I am."

"So am I."

"I just hope Robin will find it, too."

"Robin," Sir Guy sighed. "I need to ask his forgiveness."

"He's not ready."

"Will he ever be?" Sir Guy shook his head. "He won't, but I need to apologize. I know God has forgiven me and that's all I truly need. Yet I need to tell him; I am more sorry than words will ever be able express for what I did."

"I know."

"What about her brother?" Sir Guy shuddered in the darkness and Lucy was sure it was not from the cold. "I never knew Mark well; he joined Robin's gang almost as soon as Robin returned from the Crusades…but he's probably just as upset as Robin about…what I did."

Lucy sighed. "He is upset, of course he is. He lost his sister. I don't think you should talk to him though. He…I don't think he'd take that well."

Sir Guy nodded. "I don't think anyone but you would 'take it well' but I have to at least apologize."

"I understand why, Guy…I just don't think Robin or Mark would appreciate it. You have to expect they won't believe you, or even if they find you sincere, they won't care."

"I don't expect forgiveness from either of them. I do not deserve it. The mercy of God is far more than I could have asked for and I will be content with it."

Chapter 31

"I DON'T FORGIVE him," Mari-Lu crossed her arms, her tiny face a picture of her miniature wrath.

"That's okay," Aunt Lucy replied. "It isn't an easy thing to do; forgiving Guy for murder was one of the hardest things anyone in the gang ever had to face. It was impossible for those who were not making that choice with the strength of the Savior who did it first. He loved all of us while we were sinners— murderers, liars, cheats, all in open rebellion against His perfect plan for the world. Yet He *chose* to love us and forgive us all, and it was only through His wellspring of mercy that I and Dusty were able to forgive Guy and move forward."

Mari-Lu shook her head. "That's too hard."

"For you alone, absolutely. But through reliance on the unconditional love of Christ? 'I can do all things through Him.' That will hold true no matter what it is He is calling you to do, Mari-Lu. Always."

"What else happened," Mari-Lu asked, eager to move the conversation past Sir Guy once more.

"I asked Friar Tuck to come to the castle rather than live in the camp. Will enjoyed his conversation and was full of questions for him, but Robin and Mark were resistant to change and I knew Sir Guy would need his guidance more…"

❖

Lucy relished the wintry landscape of the forest as she rode to the camp—the trees dressed in crystal jewelry with skirts of fluffy white snow all around her. Every step her horse took produced a satisfying crunch in the snow. When Lucy arrived at the camp, everyone was huddled around the fire, wrapped in as many layers as they could manage, and covered in blankets.

"What brings you out of the warmth of Nottingham?" Allen asked, rubbing his hands together vigorously to keep them from freezing.

"What makes you assume the stone castle is any warmer than this camp?" Lucy laughed, joining the circle and sitting between Dusty and Robin.

"But at least you have access to more blankets," Mark said.

"We should make a run to a shop in Nottingham and get a load," Robin said. "If we're freezing, so are the poor. We can distribute blankets and food today, along with the allowance of the treasure."

"That is a good idea," Dusty said. "We should probably also stock up enough that we can travel beyond Nottingham and give warmth to whomever else in England might need it."

"There are several uprisings inspired by our own in a few other shires," Robin said. "I'm reaching out to them to coordinate as well, so perhaps we won't have to be spread so thin forever."

"Is the Sheriff up to anything lately?" Little John asked Lucy.

"No schemes that I know of," Lucy said.

"You didn't know when my family was being murdered," Ida put in, "so that hardly means he isn't scheming."

Lucy glanced at Ida, unable to form a rebuttal to her bitter comment.

"You never did answer my question," Allen broke the uncomfortable silence. "What brings you to the camp today?"

"I came to ask Friar Tuck if he'd come to live in the castle." Lucy glanced across the fire toward her oldest friend and her heart warmed as he smiled at her. "I spoke to the Sheriff about my Friar friend being in town, and he agreed to let you visit Nottingham, and stay at the castle."

"I thought you wanted me here," Friar Tuck said.

"I do, but I would also like you to visit Nottingham."

"Why?" Will asked.

"Because…" Lucy glanced at Robin. "Well…because Sir Guy has come to know the Lord as Dusty and I do, and I believe it would be best to put him in the wise hands of Friar Tuck rather than leave him alone, adrift in a stormy sea."

Robin crossed his arms but said nothing.

Dusty smiled at Lucy. "That is wonderful news for Gisbourne."

"Wonderful? Gisbourne?" Little John asked. "I do not think those two words belong together."

"Little John…" Lucy began and then stopped.

"What, Lucy?" Robin asked.

"It's just that…no one is perfect."

"We haven't murdered anyone," Little John growled.

"I beg to differ," Lucy said firmly. "What about all those soldiers you've killed?"

"They deserved it."

"One could easily argue we all deserve death and judgment," Dusty put in.

Ida rolled her eyes. "This is absurd. Gisbourne is evil, isn't he?"

336

"No." Allen said. "I don't think he is."

"Regardless of what any of you think about Sir Guy," Lucy turned to Friar Tuck, "Will you come to Nottingham sometimes, Friar Tuck?"

Friar Tuck smiled. "Of course, daughter. You need only ask."

"Thank you."

←→

"Did he come?" Mari-Lu asked.

"Yes he did. He would spend two or three days in Nottingham—brightening my days, and conversing with Sir Guy and Andrew as often as he could—and then go back and spend a few days at the camp. Sir Guy greatly benefited from his visits."

"I bet Robin didn't like that much."

"No. The gang was still divided over the whole issue of Sir Guy. Ida was angry that we would even consider befriending him at all, Robin and Mark still hated him. Dusty and I were the only ones who were truly on his side, though Will was coming around to our point of view. Allen certainly defended him more than most, as he was able to empathize with making terrible decisions."

"Of course he would defend Gisbourne." Mari-Lu rolled her eyes and crossed her arms, her little lip protruding in a pout.

"Little John was firmly in the same boat as Robin, Mark, and Ida," Aunt Lucy continued. "The idea of Sir Guy and his actions—and the intent behind them—always brought tension to our group whenever we discussed him, so I learned not to bring him up to the group as a whole unless I had to. Sir Guy was not the only one benefiting from Friar Tuck's presence. Mark was slowly becoming his old cheerful self. Very slowly, but I could see progress and healing."

"What happened after that?"

"After about a week, Sir Guy met me when I returned from one of my morning rides…"

« »

Sir Guy reached up to grab Lucy around the waist and help her dismount. Though her feet hit the pavement, he kept his arms around her. "Did you enjoy your ride?"

"Yes, I did. I stopped by the camp and practiced archery."

"You shouldn't say things like that quite so loud." Sir Guy glanced around the stables as he let go of Lucy and led Victory toward his stall to unsaddle him.

"Are you afraid of me being caught and hung?" Lucy stepped into the stall to help Sir Guy remove Victory's tack and brush him down.

"Yes." Sir Guy said simply, pulling Victory's saddle blanket off of his back. "I do fear that."

"Don't. Robin would never let it happen, and neither would you."

"I suppose you are safe then."

"Yes. I am."

"I feel such a need to protect you, Lucy, to look after you." Sir Guy patted Victory's back and turned to Lucy, watching her intently as she brushed the horse's flank.

"That's very sweet of you."

"Lucy…"

338

"What?" Lucy stopped brushing and turned to look at him.
"Nothing."

"Guy, what do you need? You can talk to me."

"I know. I just…" Sir Guy ran a hand down his face, watching Lucy with a guarded expression.

"Yes?"

"It's nothing."

"Don't lie to me, Guy," Lucy teased.

Sir Guy graced her with a wry grin. "That's one of the things I love about you. Your absolute honesty. It's rare and beautiful. Like you."

"I'm rare?"

"Yes. And beautiful. And compassionate. Lucy…"

Sir Guy gently took the brush from her hand, putting it aside and taking Lucy's hands in his, though he still seemed unable to say whatever it was he was trying to express.

"What on earth are you trying to ask me, Sir Guy of Gisbourne? You're as tongue tied as…as I don't know what."

"I'm sorry. But the last time…and I know I don't deserve…" he sighed, shaking his head. "Not that any of us deserve anything, but you deserve so much more than…"

"Guy?"

"Exactly."

"Exactly what?"

"You deserve more than me."

"I don't know about you, but I am thoroughly confused," Lucy laughed.

"Lucy…I'm trying to say that I love you. I want…would you…?" Though his words were faltering, his eyes were pleading rather eloquently. Lucy was lost in the desire she saw there for a moment.

"Guy...I..." Lucy took a deep breath. If he was trying to ask her to marry him, she knew the answer. "No."

Sir Guy's face twitched in an unmistakable grimace and he released her hands, watching her quietly as a deep sadness filled his eyes.

"What I mean is, I don't...I don't love you like that. I do care for you, Guy, so very much. You are one of my dearest friends, you have to know that. I don't quite understand how that happened, but it's true and I don't want that to change. But I don't love you the way a woman would love her husband. I'm sorry."

Sir Guy nodded. "I didn't expect anything else."

"Guy—"

"No, it's alright," Guy held up his hands to silence her. "It's alright, Lucy. It's...it's fine."

He turned and left the stall and soon exited the stables.

Victory bumped Lucy's shoulder with his nose, and she stroked it absentmindedly.

What was she going to do now?

Dusty was convinced Robin loved her, but what would she say when Lucy told her about Sir Guy's proposal? Lucy was not unaware of the predicament she found herself in and how similar it was in many ways to that of the late Lady Marian.

That night Sir Guy did not join Lucy to watch the stars.

Lucy felt awkward the next day when she and Sir Guy had their morning meal with the Sheriff, but he seemed at ease and made no mention of their conversation the day before, or his absence from star gazing and Lucy wasn't about to bring it up.

When Lucy visited the camp later that week, Robin asked her to take a walk with him.

Lucy looked at Mark who shrugged. Lucy took that to mean he wasn't going to bite her head off for taking a walk with Robin. "Alright, I'll walk with you, Robin."

They walked away from the group circled around the fire, crossing the frozen ground covered in a light dusting of snow, beyond the borders of the camp. Robin led her through the icy trees until they came to a stream Lucy knew well.

Along the snowy banks the stream was frozen, but towards the middle the cold sparkling water rushed along its path as though it were afraid to stand still.

"Did you need something, Robin?"

"Not necessarily. But I thought you would enjoy this part of the forest. It has something…something hidden and beautiful that I can't put my finger on."

"I know. It's wonderful here."

They walked along in silence for a while, the only sounds the stream running from the fear of freezing and the crunch of snow beneath their feet.

"Friar Tuck said Gisbourne asked you to marry him."

"Friar Tuck said…oh." Lucy glanced at her feet as she kept walking. It seemed she was going to find out what Robin thought after all.

"Did he?"

"Well…yes. He did."

"And you said?"

"I don't know."

"You don't know what you said?"

"I said no. I do care for him…very much. But I don't think…I mean I don't believe I really love him *that* way."

"Good."

"Good?"

"There's another caravan of treasure making its way through Sherwood tomorrow," Robin said, briskly changing the subject.

"I know."

"I'd like you to help."

"Help…how?"

"Be here. Shoot a few arrows…injure a soldier or two… that sort of thing."

"Why?"

"Because."

"Robin." Lucy stopped walking and grabbed his arm, forcing him to turn and look at her.

"Because," Robin sighed, "Ida is…she doesn't believe you are as amazing as you truly are."

"I don't mind," Lucy laughed. "Not everyone is going to think well of me—or you for that matter—I have enough confidence in my identity not to be concerned about Ida's opinion of me."

"But I do care. She's always speaking badly about you, and I can't stand it. I want you to be a part of this ambush. To prove to Ida—"

"Robin, that's ridiculous."

"Please, Lucy? It would mean a lot to me."

"Fine. But I won't—"

"Kill anyone. That's fine. I don't expect you to."

"Did you help in the raid?" Mari-Lu asked.

"I did, and several more afterward. Robin seemed to forget I had been helping in the ambushes—albeit from a distance—when I first came to Nottingham as well. But either way, relations between Ida and myself did not improve."

"She didn't like you?"

"Not much, no."

"Because you were friends with Sir Guy?"

"That, and also because of my desire not to kill anyone. Ida found me weak in that regard, and she couldn't stand weakness. There was also the fact that her family had been murdered and she was grieving them, and in her pain she could not forgive me for siding with Sir Guy when she felt he was as responsible for her family's deaths as the Sheriff was. She even blamed me in some ways for the loss of her mother and brother. Yet in an unexpected turn of events, Ida and Allen became the best of friends."

"Even though he was the traitor?"

"Even though he was the traitor," Aunt Lucy nodded. "I was confused by it, and one day I brought my confusion to Dusty…"

Chapter 32

LUCY AND DUSTY were alone in the snow-crusted camp. Drifts
had piled up against the sides of huts, and the roofs creaked under
the weight of the snow resting on top of them. The women were
huddled before the fire, as they so often were, when Lucy brought
up the unexpected friendship of Allen and Ida.

"I don't understand it," Lucy laughed.

"I know," Dusty said. "Ida hates everything to do with
anyone who has anything to do with the Sheriff or Prince John or
any of that. And though Allen is a part of our gang, and he's a
good friend of mine…he did help the Sheriff for a time."

"Maybe she's attracted to him because of that," Lucy
shrugged. "A little rebellion…"

"It's absurd, Lucy, and you know it."

"Yes, but it's sweet too. They are very sweet together."

"That's the only time Ida is ever sweet. She's a very…
prickly young woman," Dusty said quietly.

"I know. Robin respects her though."

"Don't take that personally."

"I'm not, but he's not wrong in many ways. She is strong
and brave, too. And she loves her country and her people so
much."

"And Allen too, apparently."

"Dusty!" Lucy swatted her arm.

"Well it's true."

Lucy watched the logs in their fire crackling and smoking
for a while, listening to the popping wood. Dusty put another log

on top and the whole pile shifted slightly, revealing the bright orange glow of the embers and coals on the bottom.

"Can I ask you something, Dusty?"

"Anything."

"If Will were to die…would you ever consider marrying again?"

Dusty was silent a long moment before she spoke. "I don't know, Lucy. I couldn't imagine it now, being so happily married…but I know he'd want me to move on, be happy again. Will wouldn't want me to wallow in grief forever."

Dusty looked at Lucy and smiled gently. "You aren't really asking about Will though, are you? Are you worried about Robin? He seems to be fine; he doesn't appear to be upset about falling in love with you. I know some people have tried to fight it when they fall in love for the second time because they think they are being unfair to their first loves, or betraying them somehow. But Robin doesn't seem to think that, which is good. You shouldn't worry about it either."

"It's not Robin I'm worried about, Dusty."

"Oh. You're thinking of Mark, aren't you?"

"Yes. I don't know what to do."

"You can't make everyone happy, Lucy. Besides, he's been getting better. I don't think he's quite as upset with you and Robin as he was at first."

"I hope not. I don't want to hurt him."

"It's not as though Robin is over Marian … he's still grieving." Dusty was thoughtful for a moment and then said, "He's … I don't know, I guess he's both right now—falling in love and yet still loving and missing Marian."

345

"Do they get married?" Mari-Lu interrupted Aunt Lucy's story.

"Who?"

"Allen and Ida."

"Mari-Lu you can't keep jumping to the end," Aunt Lucy laughed. "You have to listen to the story straight through."

"Well, do they?"

"You will just have to see."

"Okay…" Mari-Lu sighed. "Did Gisbourne do anything because you rejected him? You don't have a house to burn down."

"No, Sir Guy did not retaliate. He was growing into a more emotionally stable and mature man by the time I knew him, and his ever growing knowledge of and relationship with the Lord only aided in that endeavor."

"Did you and Robin ever admit you were falling for each other?"

"We'll get there," Aunt Lucy laughed again. "It was at this time a new friend came to Nottingham. Her name was Faith. She and her father Richard were merely visiting Nottingham when the Sheriff—for whatever reason seemed fit to him—decided to hang them both, which is how they came to be known to me."

"You heard about the execution?"

"Yes."

"But who was Faith?"

"Just an ordinary English girl. Faith's mother had died giving birth to her baby brother. Her father had traveled the continent after that, taking Faith and baby Richard with him. They traveled all over the known lands, learning to speak different languages and learning about other cultures. But then Richard had gotten sick when he was seven years old and had died. Faith and her father had continued traveling, though the excitement and curiosity of both had dimmed. When Faith was nineteen, they finally came back to England and found their way to Nottingham. The Sheriff did not like them for a reason likely known only to himself and decided to hang them both…"

« »

Lucy jerked her horse—not Victory today, as she felt awkward riding Sir Guy's horse after refusing his offered love—to a sudden stop in the camp, leaping off of it as she called Robin's name.

Ida looked up from her perch by the fire. "He isn't here."

Will poked his head out of his hut nearby. "Is something wrong? What is it, Lucy?"

"I'm sorry, I can't…"

"Alright, who did you promise not to tell this time?" Will chuckled as he stepped out of his hut fully and moved toward Ida's fire.

"Robin's gang," Lucy said ruefully.

"That's stupid!" Ida said. "The whole idea that you choose not to tell us is dumb in the first place, but if those are the rules you abide by, now you can't tell anyone."

"I can tell Friar Tuck. He's not technically an outlaw, or a member of the gang. He just…visits sometimes. Where is he?"

"Robin and Friar Tuck went for a walk…to talk," Will said, giving Lucy a look she didn't quite understand. "I'm not sure where."

347

"I don't suppose they went to Robin's favorite stream," Lucy suggested with a grin.

"Probably," Will replied.

"Thank you, Will."

Lucy hurried back to her horse and was soon riding in search of Robin and Friar Tuck. She made her way along the stream where Robin had taken her for a walk the day he'd been curious about her answer to Sir Guy's proposal. It wasn't long before she found them.

Robin heard the horse approaching and swung around, his bow whipped off his back and arrow notched to the string before he realized who it was and lowered his weapon. "Lucy! What's wrong?"

"I can't tell you, because you are a part of your gang. I suppose that's how that works... But I can tell Friar Tuck."

"Alright. I'll be over here when you are finished," Robin laughed and strode away.

"He's certainly changed," Lucy said thoughtfully. "Not long ago he would have been angry at my odd promises."

"I believe the gang are growing rather used to your antics," Friar Tuck chuckled. "Though I do think you might take things a bit too far at times, daughter."

"Do I?" Lucy dismounted and moved toward Friar Tuck. "I just want to be someone who keeps my word, and doesn't lie..."

"Everything we do in defense of England these days pushes the boundaries of good breeding. We cheat, we steal, we lie, all in the defense of goodness and mercy."

"But...I mean, I suppose in our case the end justifies the means."

"That is the question," Friar Tuck said, stroking his chin. "In the end, we all have to come to terms with our own inconsistencies. But what did you need, my daughter?"

"The Sheriff is going to hang this man and his daughter. I don't know who they are, really. But they haven't done anything wrong, that much is true."

"We'll see what we can do."

"Thank you."

❦

"Did they do it? Did they stop the execution?"

Aunt Lucy grinned. "What do you think?"

"I think they did!" Mari-Lu giggled.

"Faith and her father were kept in the dungeon of Nottingham castle. The Sheriff was fed up with prisoners escaping and so he charged Sir Guy—his most trusted lackey, or so he thought—with the task of guarding them. Sir Guy took that opportunity to speak with the prisoners to let them know that Robin would see to their welfare and they had nothing to fear."

"I don't understand why he switched sides."

"I will tell you his story some day, Mari-Lu, and perhaps it will make more sense. For now, just understand that he was always torn by the choices he was making for good and evil, and Marian's murder was the final blow to his shattered soul. At that point, he had only two choices. To remain fully broken forever, giving in to his more vile tendencies and never being at peace, or to accept the healing and help that came from the only source capable of taking his shattered soul and piecing it back together."

349

"You mean God."

"I do mean God," Aunt Lucy nodded, her voice filled with fervor. "No one else could have saved Sir Guy. Marian had tried to use her influence over him to bring about good, but it hadn't saved his soul. I tried, too, in my own way. Andrew had been trying for longer than any of us, but only One had the power to change Sir Guy at his core, and to Sir Guy's credit he was humble enough at the right time to let the master Healer do His work."

"That all sounds very complicated," Mari-Lu said quietly. "But I guess God can do big things."

"Yes, He can," Aunt Lucy agreed. "While Sir Guy was giving reassurance to Faith and her father—the latter of whom did not trust him at all, no matter what he said—he also shared his new-found faith with them, and discovered that Faith understood the truth as well."

"Well with a name like that, she'd have to," Mari-Lu giggled.

Aunt Lucy laughed, and then resumed her story, "Robin and his gang successfully rescued Faith and her father from their hanging—with help from Sir Guy and Andrew that they begrudgingly accepted—and the Sheriff screamed and paced in the Great Hall for hours. Sir Guy, unfortunately, had to stay and bear the brunt of the Sheriff's displeasure, but I went for a ride away from Nottingham to escape his ceaseless noise…

←»

Lucy rode for the camp, the Sheriff's threats still ringing in her ears. The snow covered knolls gently rolling toward the forest were a peaceful relief from chaos of the castle. Lucy kept

350

her horse at a slow pace, enjoying the stillness and the echoing silence that stretched across the open space between the city and the forest. The only sounds accompanying her were the crunch of the horse's hooves in the snow, and her own breathing which sounded loud in her own ears.

Sir Guy had done more than simply tell her about the Sheriff's schemes; he had actually helped Robin and the others with the escape plan. Despite her rejection of his proposal, he was still growing into a better man. Lucy was glad of that. It would have been unfortunate if he'd gone on a spree of vengeance the way he had after Marian had refused him, and more than that she would have been sorry to find her faith in his new-found character to be incorrect.

Robin, too, was impressing her. He might have been reluctant—for good reason—to work with the man who murdered his wife, but he rose to the occasion, displaying a strength and fortitude of character that Lucy found more than a little charming.

As she entered the forest and the frozen wonderland of trees encrusted in ice and snow, Lucy thought about all that Robin had been through over the last year and how far he had come already. In a few short weeks it would be a year since Marian's death, and he was pushing through his pain to fight against the Sheriff still. More than that, he was not giving in to hatred but had gone so far as to work alongside Sir Guy for the betterment of the innocent lives at stake. A lesser man would not have been able to do such things.

When Lucy trotted into camp, Dusty was speaking with the new arrivals. Faith seemed eager to learn about the ways of the camp, but her father seemed far less enthralled with his surroundings.

351

"Lucy!" Will called as she dismounted and moved toward the circle gathered around the warmth of the fire. "What are you doing here? More crazy schemes of the Sheriff's already?"

Lucy laughed. "No. He's just being very loud and giving people headaches right now."

"So you came here for a rest?" Mark asked.

"And to see Faith and her father. Sir Guy spoke highly of you," Lucy addressed her later statement toward Faith.

Faith smiled. "I had no idea he was going to be a good person. We haven't been back in England long, but we have heard many tales. Praise for Robin Hood and censure for Prince John, the Sheriff of Nottingham, and Sir Guy of Gisbourne. There are wild tales of his villainous exploits, but he was quite wonderful."

Ida groaned and rolled her eyes.

"What's going to happen now?" Lucy asked.

"We'll keep them here in the camp if they're willing to stay," Will said. "They don't have anywhere else to go."

"Can you try the Sheriff again?" Dusty asked Lucy.

Lucy shook her head. "No. I don't think we'll get the pardon we did for the children ever again. These days the Sheriff seems worse than ever."

« »

"So they stayed in the camp?" Mari-Lu asked.

"Yes, they did. Faith was fascinated by our Sherwood lives, and wanted to know if all the grand stories she had heard about Robin Hood's infamous gang of outlaws were true. The gang had too much fun sitting around the fire of an evening and

352

telling magnificent stories of all they had been doing for England."

"Did they help out with the raids and things?"

"Not exactly. Faith's father was willing to help out however he could, and Will and Allen enlisted his assistance in keeping their stock of weapons in shape—be that helping with forging their new swords, knives, or daggers should they need them, or simply keeping the existing ones sharp and ready for use. He was protective of his daughter, and wanted her to steer clear of any fighting, but he needn't have worried in that regard: Faith was a gentle soul who loathed violence far more than I did."

"Did Ida like them?"

"Ida thought Faith was weak. Faith was gentle and loving and the sweetest girl I had ever met. She wasn't a fighter like Ida, Dusty, Marian, or even I. Ida saw that as weakness. The same way she thought my refusal to kill was weakness."

"She just likes people who fight, I guess."

"She did. Ida loved Faith's father though, whose temperament was much like her own father. Ida would never admit it, of course, but she missed her father terribly and often wondered if she'd made the right choice in staying to fight at Robin's side rather than chasing after her father when he left."

"Did her father ever find King Richard?"

"That's another story altogether."

"Alright, alright. Keep going."

"Faith and Ida did find common ground in their similar tragedies. They had both lost their mothers and they had both lost their younger brothers. They did become friends, of a sort, but Ida had very little true respect for Faith."

"Did everyone else like her though?"

"Of course. Faith was sweet, and would hardly quarrel with anyone. There was very little to dislike about her."

"What happened next?

"Well the next time I came to the camp I had a rather interesting conversation with Mark…"

«–»

"What is the Sheriff doing now?" Mark asked as Lucy tied her horse's reins loosely around a tree branch and made her way across the empty meadow toward the small fire where Mark was sitting.

"Nothing. I just came for a visit. Where is everyone?"

"Distributing money to the poor, traveling across England, you know how it is…they're in many different places."

"And what are you doing?"

"Keeping watch over the camp, of course. What does it look like I'm doing?" Mark nonchalantly tossed a log toward the fire and grinned at Lucy as she sat down nearby.

"I'm sure you make a very good house…I mean, camp… keeper."

Mark laughed. "Probably not. That's Much's job."

Lucy watched the flames lick around the new log, encasing it in heat as one of the logs below shifted and cracked apart, the charred embers settling on the ground below the flames.

"Mark…can I ask you something?"

"Yes?"

"If…if I were to tell you…" Lucy hesitated, clasping her hands in her lap to keep from wringing them restlessly. She didn't know how to say what she wanted to say, but somehow Mark read her mind.

"That you were in love with Robin, what would I say to that?"

Lucy bit her lip. She wasn't always entirely certain how she felt about Robin herself, but somehow she felt she needed Mark's approval if she was going to give in to whatever feelings were growing there. "Yeah, that's what I wanted to ask."

Mark sighed, turning from Lucy to stare into the fire for a while. "I don't know. I...I still wish Robin wouldn't marry anyone. He belonged to my sister, Lucy. Ever since we were small children they belonged together. They grew up together; they were inseparable. No one who knew them expected anything different. It was always going to be Robin and Marian, even when she wouldn't admit it."

"I know."

"But..." Mark sighed, finally meeting Lucy's eyes. "But God seems to have brought the two of you together as well, in rather unexpected ways perhaps."

"Yes, He has."

"I am learning to be okay with that, Lucy. I'm trying at any rate."

"Thank you, Mark. I never wanted to upset you."

"I know."

"I tried not to like him, you know."

"Robin?"

"Yes. I didn't want to hurt you or to take Marian's place. And it's still so soon...I feel guilty sometimes."

"But you aren't taking her place. I know I've accused you of that, but it isn't true."

"I know."

"Seeing Robin at peace again is reassuring," Mark said. "It's good."

"Are you happy, Mark?"

"No. Not truly." Mark shrugged, his demeanor open and honest—unlike how he'd been when he'd first returned from Austria—yet his eyes bearing a deep well of darkness. "My sister has been gone for nearly a year…but I don't think I will ever get over her death."

"You don't still blame yourself, do you?" Lucy asked, knowing full well she had yet to approach her own guilt and shame surrounding Marian's death.

"I am trying not to, but I cannot help it. I remember the feeling of her arm under my hand, and the way it slipped out of my grip when she fell…I just keep reliving it. Friar Tuck has been helping me to see that it isn't my fault. We live in a fallen world and terrible things happen, despite our best efforts. But God's love has been the only thing keeping me from drowning in guilt some days."

"I'm so sorry, Mark. I am glad, however, that you can find comfort in the truth Friar Tuck imparts."

"I don't forgive Gisbourne," Mark said quickly, his face flushing a deep red. "I wish I had your sense of mercy, but I don't."

"I could not be as forgiving as I am without relying on the source of all grace and mercy to work in and through me."

"You sound like Friar Tuck."

Lucy laughed softly. "Well…I did learn all I know from him."

356

Chapter 33

LUCY WAS BRUSHING down her horse after a long ride across the hills and fields surrounding Nottingham. She hadn't been to the camp for companionship but for once had simply gone riding. The thrill of letting the horse run free, her hair flying behind her as they raced across the rolling hills was a joy she was coming to crave. She blamed Robin for her ever-growing adventurous side.

As Lucy stroked the brush along the horse's dark coat of hair, the sounds of shouts and cries for help echoed from the courtyard. Lucy set the brush aside and left the stall, hurrying toward the large doors of the stable that led into the courtyard—and which were currently standing open. Several stable boys were also scurrying that way to see what the commotion was about.

When Lucy reached the doorway, she shaded her hand against her eyes to block the sunlight and watched as a dozen soldiers dragged a prisoner toward the steps of the castle. More came running down the spiral staircase in the corner of the courtyard that led up to the ramparts, and several came out of the castle doors as well, all of them shouting to each other.

"We've got him!"

"Easy, he's feisty!"

The prisoner jerked free of the guards holding him, sinking his boot into the chest of one and spinning around to grab the sword from the hilt of another. But six or seven sets of hands grabbed him from behind, forcing him to drop the sword as they pushed him to his knees and forced his hands behind his back where they roughly tied them together.

As the prisoner threw his head back in defiance, glaring at his nearest captors, Lucy's heart leapt to her throat.

"Robin?!"

His blue eyes darted across the courtyard to Lucy as several soldiers turned toward the sound of her incredulous shout.

"Yes, Lady Lucy, we've caught Robin Hood at last," one of the soldiers yelled toward her as the others forced Robin to his feet and roughly dragged him toward the castle doors. Lucy hurried after them.

The Sheriff was running up the hallway as the large group entered the castle.

"Is it true? Do you have him?"

"It's Robin Hood, sir," one of the soldiers moved forward, gesturing behind him at the bound prisoner.

"The one and only," Robin called out. "Honestly, Sheriff, your famed hospitality rather leaves something to be desired, doesn't it? We ought to work on that, don't you think?"

"Someone gag him," the Sheriff said. He grinned, rubbing his hands together in his glee. "Take him to the dungeons. I need ten..no, let's say thirty guards stationed along the cells, at the door...in the hallways..."

One of the soldiers shoved a cloth into Robin's mouth as Lucy stood to one side, watching the entire nightmare unfold in disbelief. How had Robin been caught? How was she going to get him out?!

"We'll need a public execution," the Sheriff said as the soldiers pushed Robin past him and roughly led him down the hallway to take him to the dungeons. "Someone get Gisbourne! I need him in the Great Hall. I have a public spectacle to plan!"

The Sheriff skirted around the remaining soldiers following after Robin and caught sight of Lucy pressed up against the wall of the hallway, watching in horror.

"Ah, Lady Lucy… get Gisbourne, will you?" the Sheriff moved past her with a grin and Lucy took off running to Sir Guy's chambers. She knocked, but there there was no answer.

Lucy pounded on the door, unaware that her knuckles began to bleed from her vehemence, but there was no response. "Guy! Guy, I *need* you!"

She tried the door, and finding it unlocked she pushed into his room but it was empty. Lucy spun around, searching the empty room for clues. Finding nothing, she took off running again, this time toward the library where she so often found Andrew. As her feet pounded across the stone floor, Lucy could feel the panic rising in her stomach.

When she reached the library, she hit the door at a full run, shoving it open and skidding to a stop as her eyes darted around the shelves and occupants of the room.

"Lucy?" Andrew's voice drifted to her from the left and Lucy raced toward him. As he came around a table stacked with books, she collided with him, then stepped back to see his face.

"Andrew! Robin's been caught. He's in the dungeons. I need Guy! Where is he?"

"Robin's caught…right." Andrew's eyes went wide. "Guy. Wait here, Lady Lucy. I'll find him."

Andrew took off and Lucy paced along a bookshelf, ignoring the eyes of curious nobles who had been perusing the books when she'd burst in.

Andrew soon returned with Sir Guy.

"Guy!" Lucy darted toward him, but he held up a hand to silence her.

"Come with me."

He spun on his heel and marched out of the library and Lucy and Andrew hurried after him.

"Guy, please—"

"Wait, for heaven's sake," Sir Guy hissed. Lucy fell silent, and not another word passed between the three of them until they were safely in Sir Guy's chambers.

"He's too heavily guarded," Sir Guy began without preamble as soon as Andrew shut the door. "I can't get him out. The gang will have to do what they can from the execution itself. I'm needed in the Great Hall; the Sheriff has summoned me. No doubt we'll plan the execution today and have it done tomorrow morning. When I know the details, I'll tell you. You can take it to the rest of the gang."

Lucy nodded, and Andrew grabbed her hand. "Breathe, Lady Lucy."

Lucy glanced toward him and shook her head to clear it. His voice sounded far away as her heart pounded loudly in her ears, blocking all other sounds.

"Breathe," Andrew repeated, squeezing her hand.

Sir Guy put a hand on her shoulder. "Don't go near the Sheriff. I'll be back when I have more details for you and the gang. Stay with Andrew."

And with that, Sir Guy was gone, off to plan Robin's execution.

Andrew led Lucy to a chair and fetched her a glass of wine. The world was swimming around her, the room tilting on a strange axis. A few minutes of deliberate breathing under the direction of Andrew, however, brought everything back into focus.

"I need to see him."

"Guy will be back when he can be sure he's got all the information needed," Andrew replied.

"Not him," Lucy said, standing up. "I need to see Robin."

"It could be dangerous to visit the dungeons."

"I need to," Lucy repeated.

She left Sir Guy's room and resolutely made her way to the lower levels of the castle to the dungeons. When she reached the hallway leading to the dungeons, she found a dozen guards.

They let her pass without a word, though their eyes followed her every movement. The large doors leading into the first level of the dungeons were closed, but when Lucy moved to open them no one stopped her. Inside she found more guards. She moved passed them slowly, hoping they wouldn't try and stop her. There were far too many for her to fight off, and she hadn't brought her weapons with her—which limited her to her fists and the one knife she kept on her belt.

The second door to the lower dungeons was also closed, but the guards didn't stop her when she asked to go in, so Lucy kept moving. There were more guards inside the lower section, and at the farthest cell in the back, set in relative darkness as there were no torches burning nearby, sat Robin.

"Robin...what happened?"

Robin looked up, his face covered in shadow in the gloom of the cell. "Lucy?"

Lucy moved to the door of the cell, leaning against the bars. "What happened?"

"I was careless. I've gotten a little too arrogant, believing nothing can stop me. I wasn't paying enough attention to my surroundings, didn't notice the Sheriff's men until it was too late. Don't worry. I'll be more careful next time."

"Will there be a next time? Robin, I'm worried."

"Don't be. The gang will save me." Robin grinned, getting up to come stand next to Lucy, reaching through the bars to lay his hand against her cheek. "And if not…you'll look after England."

"Robin! I don't want to look after England…not without you."

Robin gently stroked Lucy's tears off her cheek with his thumb. "Lucy. There is nothing to fear. Don't you believe your God will look after me?"

Lucy's eyes darted upward, wide and incredulous "Go-… yes. I do."

"You trust Him, don't you?"

"I do," Lucy said firmly, letting that knowledge fill her with peace.

"Good. Because I do too."

"Robin!" Lucy grinned, her worry for his safety vanishing in her excitement.

"Now don't get carried away. Yes, I am beginning to share your faith. And I'm sorry I've been such a trial to you."

"Robin, you haven't been a trial."

"Now is hardly the time to start lying to me," Robin laughed.

"Well…you tried my patience."

"And you mine," Robin said. "What with your insistence on my forgiving Gisbourne, and your aggravating friendship with him."

"Aggravating?"

"Yes. You have no idea how you tortured me. I hated how you cared for him, after everything he'd done."

"I'm sorry. I never wanted to hurt you."

"Don't apologize. My problem was with Gisbourne, not you. I should not have held your grace against you."

"Robin…" Lucy's ever-present guilt rose like bile from the pit of her stomach. "There…there was always more to my friendship with Guy than simply God's forgiveness that I was trying to emulate. That was certainly part of it…but there was more…"

Robin watched her quietly in the darkness, and Lucy took a shaky breath, steeling herself to finally tell him the truth. "I felt I shared his guilt."

"Over Marian? That was in no way your fault."

"But it is, Robin."

Robin's brow furrowed, both hands cupping Lucy's face as he studied her in confusion. "I don't understand."

"I've told you before that I was there. I was in Austria at that time. I…I was in a street, watching it all happen."

Lucy could remember it all so clearly; holding her bow so tensely, aimed at Sir Guy, desperate to kill him. It was the only time she'd ever been overwhelmed with such a desire, and when she dwelled on the memory, it still frightened her.

"When Sir Guy went for the King and Marian…I saw it, Robin."

"I know."

"No, you don't. I saw what Sir Guy was going to do before he did it. I had a good view behind Marian, and I could see…I knew what he was going to do. I had my bow so I drew an arrow straight away and…"

Robin's hands dropped from her face and he crossed his arms, shaking his head as Lucy pressed on.

"But I couldn't do it. Mark had run forward and was standing beside Marian and I thought he would stop Guy…I could have done it, I wanted to, so much. I *wanted* to kill him. I could have stopped him, I could have saved Marian, Robin."

"Lucy—"

"But I couldn't do it. I would have killed Sir Guy and I just couldn't let go of that arrow. I couldn't give in to the anger and hatred, I just couldn't…"

Robin was backing away from her, slinking into the darkest corner of the cell, shaking his head.

"I'm so sorry." Lucy reached through the bars of the cell, though Robin was far out of reach at this point, slumping into the back corner and half hidden in the darkness.

"Well isn't this touching?" A familiar, unwelcome voice suddenly spoke from behind Lucy.

Lucy whirled around to see the Sheriff standing behind her, the soldiers she'd forgotten during her conversation with Robin still filling the rest of the dungeon behind him.

"Oh don't stop, dear," the Sheriff grinned. "I'm finding it quite amusing."

"Sheriff…"

"You know what the punishment for cavorting with outlaws is, don't you?"

"You can't harm her," Robin snapped, coming to the front of his cell again.

"Who is going to stop me?" the Sheriff laughed. "You? You're being beheaded at dawn. And so is this young lady." The Sheriff stepped forward to grab hold of Lucy's wrist but she danced to the side, her muscles used to slipping out of the reach of men that she fought.

The lively game of keep-away was one she played every time she fought, as she had never grown accustomed to close combat or attacking first. Defense and staying well out of reach was her strategy. But in a crowded dungeon, with no space to run away and two dozen soldiers helping the Sheriff it was not long before Lucy was surrounded, bound, and dragged into the cell beside Robin's.

"Promise me you won't tell anyone about this, Lucy," the Sheriff mocked.

When he had finished gloating over both of them, the Sheriff left, leaving his many soldiers to guard them both. There was not going to be an escape tonight.

Lucy sighed. She'd been careless, and now she was in the same predicament as Robin.

"I suppose we'll die together then," Robin commented, dropping to the floor of his cell. Lucy glanced toward him. He wasn't looking at her.

"Who says we're dying?" Lucy moved to sit along the cell wall that separated them. "The gang will figure something out."

Robin didn't respond. Lucy glanced toward the soldiers nearby and lowered her voice. "Guy is working on it."

Robin's head snapped up, his eyes flashing. He opened his mouth, but then clamped it shut again, turning around so he

365

wasn't facing Lucy anymore. Lucy pulled her knees up to her chest, wrapping her arms around herself as she watched him resolutely ignore her.

He had every right to be angry, but it still hurt.

The night stretched longer than any night Lucy had yet lived in all her life. Longer than the night she'd waited, tears streaming down her face, to hear whether or not her father had made it out of the manor when the assassins came. Longer than any night spent watching the stars.

Lucy was prepared to die, but she didn't want to.

She lowered her head, softly crying into her knees. Dying was bad enough, but now she was going to die with Robin hating her. She should never have told him…

She hoped Guy and Andrew were able to find a way to coordinate a rescue with the gang, hoped she could live long enough to make it up to Robin.

All of Nottingham, and indeed all of England, was on edge that night. News traveled quickly that the famous outlaw who'd done so much good for so many people was finally caught.

Everyone wanted to help their beloved Robin Hood, of course, but if Robin Hood himself could be caught…what good would any average man be able to do?

Chapter 34

EARLY THE NEXT morning, word came from the Sheriff to bring the prisoners to Nottingham Square, and so the soldiers came for Robin and Lucy. With their hands bound behind their backs and four soldiers surrounding them on each side—and more ahead and behind—they were led out of the castle. As they were dragged along, Lucy kept trying to catch Robin's eye but he wouldn't look at her.

There were more soldiers in the courtyard who joined the procession as they were led out of the castle courtyard and through the streets of Nottingham. People were gathered in the streets, in doorways, and hanging out of windows to see what all the commotion was about.

When they reached Nottingham Square the soldiers—now amassing about three dozen—had to push through the angry people to drag Lucy and Robin toward the platform erected for their execution. Many of the faces Lucy past were tear-stained, and all of them were wide-eyed with fear.

Robin and Lucy were led up the steps of the platform, and Lucy caught sight of two execution blocks much like the one that had been intended for Ida's beheading. Two soldiers stood beside the wooden blocks holding large axes.

Lucy held her breath, her palms sweaty and her heart pounding. Would the gang be there? Would they find a way to stop all this?

"Don't be afraid," Robin whispered as they were shoved forward toward the soldiers with axes.

"What?"

"It won't hurt. It will only be a split second and then you'll feel nothing. You will feel no pain."

"Are you speaking from experience?" Lucy glanced toward Robin, surprised to see a wry grin crossing his face.

"What if I am?"

"How ever did Dusty glue your head back on?"

"I still don't know, but I'm not sure she did it straight."

A small bit of relief seemed to fill Lucy's chest in spite of the situation; Robin might be angry with her, but at least facing down death had convinced him to talk to her before the end.

Robin and Lucy were forced onto their knees. The crowd was boisterous, people shouting at the Sheriff, yelling at the soldiers. Some of them pushed against the perimeter of soldiers that surrounded the platform. Many were crying.

"Marry me, Lucy."

"What?"

"You heard me."

"You have made a bad habit of marrying people who are dying," Lucy hissed.

Robin winced.

The Sheriff called for silence and as a hush filled the Square he said in a loud, clear voice, "Now, Robin Hood. What do you have to say?"

The Sheriff was standing on a raised wooden platform across from Robin and Lucy, exactly as he had been during Ida's failed beheading. Only this time, Lucy wasn't beside him, she was the one at the chopping block.

"The Great Robin Hood is about to die…does he have any last words?"

"A few," Robin called back, lifting his head to stare down the Sheriff.

"Do tell," the Sheriff laughed. "If you want to plead for your life, I'm listening."

"Sorry to disappoint you, Sheriff. But I don't want to plead for my life."

"Then what do you want to say, you dirty, terrible, outrageous, traitorous—"

"Alright, Sheriff. You win. You can do what you like with me. But let Lucy go."

"Proceed with the execution!" the Sheriff bellowed.

A rough hand on the back of her head shoved Lucy forward until she bent over and her neck was stretched across the execution block.

Lucy felt her heart beat slow, and her breathing seemed to relax. She could see the shadow of two axes swinging slowly upwards, hear the wood of the handles creaking under the strain of the tight grip of the soldiers' fingers.

She closed her eyes.

In the stillness and darkness that surrounded her now, she could hear her heart beating softly and steadily, hear the whispers of crying from the crowd below, the grappling of those fighting against the soldiers surrounding the platform.

And then she heard the slightest twang of a bow, followed by gasps from the crowd. There was a soft thunk, and Lucy opened her eyes. An axe lay just to her right on the platform. She sat up, and looked around, taking in the chaos around her.

There were soldiers running all over the place—likely looking for the gang who were so rudely interrupting the Sheriff's execution—the crowd doing their best to get in the soldiers' way.

People were shouting; the soldiers swords were out, slicing through the crowd as they tried to create order from the confusion.

Robin stood, glancing toward the dead soldier who had been meant to execute him, and then quickly jumped into the air, slipping his tied hands under his legs. When he landed, he knelt by the axe intended for his neck, and sliced the bonds off his wrists.

As Lucy watched him, she felt someone behind her untying her own hands. She turned and found Andrew. He gave her a small smile as he worked quickly. As soon as her hands were free, he turned and leaped off of the platform and reached up for her.

Lucy turned back but Robin seemed to have vanished, so she jumped from the platform into Andrew's arms. It was disheartening that Robin hadn't waited for her—now that they weren't dying, Lucy wondered if his anger over her declaration of guilt would become more prominent again.

Andrew set her down and then led her through the mob, ducking and dodging soldiers and villagers and swords that came their way. When they reached a corner of the Square that led off into a side street, they found Allen waiting on a horse. Andrew swiftly lifted Lucy up into the saddle behind Allen and they set off at a gallop.

Lucy wrapped her arms around Allen's waist, glancing over her shoulder at the continued pandemonium in the Square. The soldiers seemed entirely overwhelmed by the people of Nottingham and the dead and wounded from both sides began to litter the ground.

As they raced through the city and then across the grassy hills—only just beginning to green with the hope of spring—Lucy glanced behind them. There was no sign of pursuit.

As they neared camp, other horses and gang members came into view, and the group all came riding into the clearing together.

Faith stood from where she'd been sitting near the fire, running forward when they all rode in. "Is everyone alright? Thank God! I haven't stopped praying all morning."

As they all dismounted, Lucy looked around. The entire gang was present. She breathed a sigh of relief and told her heart to beat again.

"Thank you."

Will hugged Lucy. "We couldn't live without you."

"But you would have left me to the wolves I suppose," Robin laughed.

Much swung his arm over Robin's shoulders. "Oh no. We would have rescued you."

"I know you would have, Much."

"How did you plan our rescue?" Lucy asked. "How did you even know I was going to be executed at all? That wasn't a part of the Sheriff's plan until late last night."

"Sir Guy helped us, of course," Allen said.

The group began to move toward the benches around the fire ring as they answered Lucy's questions.

"And don't forget Andrew," Dusty added. "That young man is incredibly nice."

Friar Tuck sat beside Lucy, wrapping his frail arms around her. "Child…I have never been so worried."

"Friar Tuck…" Lucy relished the warmth of her dear friend's arms. "I'm safe now."

"I doubt I will ever let you go."

Robin was still asking questions. "Who shot down the executioners?"

"That was Much and Will," Dusty said.

"It was a brilliant bit of archery," Robin grinned, "if I do say so myself."

"I didn't see it," Lucy laughed, adrenaline coursing through her veins and making everything far more amusing than perhaps it would have been otherwise. "My eyes were closed."

"And who provided the horses?" Robin asked.

"Sir Guy and Marcus," Little John said. "Marcus only had access to a few, and we needed everyone present, and everyone to have an escape route so Sir Guy pulled some steeds from the castle stables."

"But Sir Guy couldn't do more than help from a distance," Dusty said. "because we don't want the Sheriff to suspect him. We still need someone on the inside to feed us information."

"That's right," Ida said, sending a glare toward Lucy. "Since Lucy no longer will be. Very clever of you to get caught like that."

Robin frowned. "I was caught off guard too, Ida."

Ida didn't respond.

"I suppose we will have to go directly to Gisbourne now," Much said, looking to Robin with wide eyes, and then to Mark.

"It's alright, Much," Robin said. "Gisbourne may be a great help. And we can go through Andrew as well; that would be more to my personal liking."

"Andrew will be more than willing to help," Lucy said. "He has already been acting as a middle man for Sir Guy, myself, and the gang when he needed to."

Mark placed a hand on her arm. "I'm glad you're safe, Lucy. I was worried for both of you. You're like family to me; everyone in the gang is like family to me."

"That's true enough," Will grinned at the group. "Let's avoid more executions though, shall we? It's becoming rather an old trick, I'd say."

Lucy smiled at Mark. "Thank you."

«»

"I thought you were going to die!" Mari-Lu cried, throwing her arms around Aunt Lucy's neck and holding on as tight as she could manage.

Aunt Lucy laughed. "Mari-Lu…how on earth could I have died then, if I am telling you this story now?"

Mari-Lu pulled back from her hug, looking at Aunt Lucy in the most serious manner. "I don't know. I'm glad you didn't die!"

Aunt Lucy laughed again. "I'm glad I didn't, too."

"What did you do after that?"

"I lived in Robin's camp. I helped in some of the raids and ambushes, but mostly I just stayed with Faith in the camp. We would walk through Sherwood picking flowers and braiding them into each other's hair. And we'd sit by the stream and let the water run over our toes. Spring filled the forest, and I relished it. Ida couldn't understand how we could be so happy and carefree when life was so hard, and the country was in uproar, and everything was so tense in Nottingham. But Faith and I, and Friar Tuck and Will and Dusty and Robin and even to some degrees Mark had found a joy in life through Jesus. No situation was too dark to find some laughter because it wasn't about the situation we were in; it wasn't about anything you could see or touch or smell. It was about the absolute knowledge that God was going to take care of us no matter what happened. He was our strength, our joy, our comfort. And He just made us want to laugh and sing and dance in spite of everything."

"What else happened?" Mari-Lu asked skeptically.

"Sir Guy and Andrew gathered lots of information for us, and I would meet Andrew at one place or another in Nottingham to collect the information he had and take it back to Robin and the gang. Andrew would also bring food from the castle to me so we could still help the people of Nottingham."

"Did you ever answer Robin's question? The one he asked during your execution?"

"To marry him you mean? Yes, I did. But not yet. You are jumping ahead again."

Mari-Lu giggled.

"Robin and I didn't talk about my confession of guilt either, but it was always present on my mind. I withdrew from him, thinking he was withdrawing from me first. We didn't fight, we didn't argue...we just never spoke on the subject and because of it, the rest of our conversations grew more distant."

"Oh no."

"After several more weeks of various raids, none of which were particularly interesting, the greatest thing that could possibly happen did."

"What?"

"The King returned to England! His army swept through England taking captive all traitors to his crown. Though Marian had never truly believed it would happen, the King did, in fact, set all to rights. Many of the traitors were brought to Nottingham and the King came also to hold trial…"

❮❯

"Why are we doing this again?" Allen asked. He looked from the flowers in his hand to the ropes of flowers hanging from every window and door along the street in Nottingham, and then glanced toward Lucy. She had a large basket full of flowers hanging off of one arm as she carefully hung a wreath in a nearby window.

"Because!" Lucy laughed. "The King will be here tomorrow, and we have to have everything dressed up. This is a grand occasion! We're celebrating."

"With flowers."

"Just put them up, Allen."

Allen sighed. "Why did you talk me into this?"

"Because everyone is helping dress up Nottingham in one way or another."

"Except Gisbourne," Allen frowned. "I can't believe they threw him in prison with all the others."

"I know," Lucy paused in her work, turning toward Allen. "But maybe…"

"The King will let him go? I doubt it. I hope so, but I doubt it."

The King rode into Nottingham later that day in a great parade—he rode on his horse in full armor, with a crimson cape blowing in the breeze behind him and a soldier beside him carrying his banner. He looked far better than he had the last time Lucy had seen him—wounded in the street in Austria, frail and thin and dirty from his time in prison. Now he was healthy, strong, his face shining with vigor and purpose.

The people gathered in Nottingham from the city, the nearby villages, the farms, and even from other cities and town across England, and everyone was cheering and laughing and singing and crying as the King rode through the city to the castle. He took up residence in the castle and prepared to hold trial against his enemies.

The next day the trials began. King Richard sat in the Great Hall with his advisors and other lords, and all of Robin's gang with him. Robin, Much, Dusty, and Allen had been a part of his Royal Guard during their part of the Crusade before the King had sent them to England, and he trusted them implicitly. He trusted Robin most of all, and wanted him present during every trial.

Hour by hour, his soldiers brought forward one after another of the soldiers, sheriffs and other lords and lowlifes who had helped Prince John against him. Prince John himself, along with many of his most trusted allies, were banished from England.

The King saved the villains of Nottingham for last. It wasn't until a few days of trials had gone by that he began to bring forward, one by one, the soldiers of the Sheriff.

All through the week of trials, Lucy had asked the King if he would grant her a favor. But he refused.

"You have done very little for this country, my lady," King Richard said one day as he took his place at the front of the Great Hall, preparing for another day of trials. "You love my people, I am sure, and are loyal to me, but I have no cause to grant you special favors."

The rest of the gang, as well as the King's other advisors, were taking their seats as Lucy stood before him, hoping to ask him to pardon Gisbourne. The King seemed resolute in refusing to even hear her request, however.

"From what I hear, you are too quick to pardon the deeds of the worst of my enemies."

Lucy glanced toward Robin, wondering what he had told King Richard. Would he ever forgive her for her part in Marian's death? They had never talked of it since the night she'd confessed her guilt and it weighed on her even more heavily now that it was out in the open between them.

On the last day of trials, the Sheriff, Sir Guy, Andrew, and the other captains of the Sheriff's garrison were brought before the King.

Lucy sat stiffly in her chair along the front of the room, the gang on either side of her, the King in the center of the group passing judgment.

The captains were found guilty and sentenced to death.

The Sheriff was found guilty and sentenced to death.

Lucy stood and left the room, for she couldn't bear to stay any longer.

Chapter 35

"I DIDN'T SEE what happened next," Aunt Lucy said softly. "But I am going to tell you what I discovered later and was told by various members of the gang."

"Please keep going! What happens?" Mari-Lu begged.

"The King tried Sir Guy and found him guilty, sentencing him to death…"

❦

The King was about to move on, soldiers approaching Sir Guy where he was on his knees before the King awaiting his judgment, when Robin stood. Ida, who was sitting next to him, grabbed his arm and shook her head.

"Robin, don't…"

Robin ignored her, strode forward, and knelt before the King, causing all the nobles present to stare. Ida continued to shake her head, though the rest of the gang merely watched quietly.

"Yes, Robin?" the King asked. "What is it?"

"Your majesty…may I ask for a favor?"

"Anything, Robin of Locksley."

"Pardon him. Sir Guy, I mean."

There were gasps from many in the room. Ida bit her lip and frowned.

The King raised an eyebrow. "This doesn't have anything to do with Lady Lucy, does it?"

Robin turned slightly and looked to his gang.

Ida was frowning, but Dusty and Will gave him encouraging nods. Friar Tuck's head was bowed in an attitude of prayer.

Robin's eyes moved along the line of his little family until they found Mark. For a moment, they merely stared at one another, a million words passing between them without a sound being uttered. And then slowly, Mark bent his head slightly in a small nod of approval.

"No." Robin turned back to the King, "this is not about Lady Lucy. Your Majesty, there is much you do not know. We would not have been able to do so much for your people without Sir Guy. There were many times when he informed us of the Sheriff's plots."

"What!" the Sheriff shrieked from nearby where he was still bound and waiting to be taken away and executed.

Robin ignored the outburst and continued. "And he helped plan the rescue of several of your subjects. He once saved an entire town from being destroyed…he has helped in many ways."

The King was thoughtful, stroking his beard as he eyed Robin skeptically. "And you believe, Robin Hood, that he deserves a pardon?"

Marian's beautiful face flashed before Robin's eyes. And her still body after her death. The pain, the grief, the anger, all flooded across his vision. And then the peace and grace he'd found in Christ, and the strength to forgive even the worst of crimes.

Robin took a deep breath. "Yes, Your Majesty."

"You really believe this, Robin?"

"Yes, Sire."

The King nodded slowly. "You have done so much for my people, and you are so dear a friend of my own…alright, Gisbourne. You have a full pardon for your past crimes. But you will not receive any special treatment should you break the law henceforth."

Sir Guy bowed his head. "I am most grateful." Though he directed his statement to the King, Sir Guy was looking at Robin.

Robin nodded tensely.

The Sheriff was yelling insults at Sir Guy, but the King's soldiers led him from the room with the rest of the prisoners awaiting execution.

Sir Guy was unbound, and he moved forward toward Robin and knelt beside him before the King. "May I ask…?"

"A favor? No. You hardly deserve that much from me. I was there when you murdered Marian, if you recall. Robin may have found a way to forgive you from the goodness of *his* heart, but I do not. What do you want?"

"Andrew, a soldier of mine, was a great help to Robin Hood and you as well, Sire." Sir Guy gestured toward where Andrew stood bound and held between two guards, awaiting his turn for judgment before the King.

King Richard looked to Robin.

Robin glanced toward Andrew and then nodded. "It is true. Andrew was a great help to us and did much for your people, Your Majesty."

"Then I grant pardon to Andrew as well. Was there anyone else?" the King asked, not unkindly but with a certain amount of exasperation.

Robin shook his head. "No, Sire."

"Very well. The Sheriff will hang at dawn. We will deal with these other traitors as time allows."

After she'd fled the room, Lucy had gone outside. She stood in the courtyard unsure of where to go. She didn't want to think about what might have been transpiring within the castle as the King judged Sir Guy. She stood on the steps, glancing toward the stables where Victory was undoubtedly content, unaware that his master might be dying soon.

Lucy sighed. There was nothing she could do for Sir Guy. Trying to evade the King's judgment and somehow rescue him from his inevitable punishment seemed too outlandish. She wouldn't have the help of the gang either, which would make it harder, not to mention it wouldn't be a fight against the incompetent Sheriff and his men but against the King himself and his highly trained guard.

Lucy heard movements and voices behind her. Today's trials must be over. Lucy didn't want to know how it had gone.

The voices beyond the door to the castle began to drift away, as people moved along the castle hallways. Lucy was too afraid to open the door and go back inside, but soon enough the doors opened anyway and Allen came outside. He walked forward quickly, pausing to stand beside her.

"Allen…?"

"It's alright, Lucy. They were both pardoned. Sir Guy and Andrew, I mean."

"How?"

"Robin spoke up for them."

"Robin?" Lucy glanced toward the castle. "Are you sure?"

"Yes. Robin. You've done wonders."

"God did that, Allen."

Before Allen could respond, Lucy ran inside. She glanced both ways past the heads of various nobles, the king's soldiers, and the members of the gang. She saw Robin down the hallway and ran toward him.

"Robin!"

Robin turned at the sound of her voice, and moved toward her, meeting her run halfway, scooping her up, and they spun in a circle together. Others in the hallways turned to stare at the spectacle.

When they stopped spinning, Robin kept his arms around Lucy's waist and Lucy reached up to wrap her arms around Robin's neck. "Robin, I'm so...I don't even know..."

"I know, Lucy. But I didn't just do it for you. Somehow it felt like the right thing to do; they did help us, after all."

Lucy hugged Robin tight, and kissed his cheek. "Oh Robin...you are wonderful!"

"No more than you are."

Lucy hid in the camp the next morning during the hanging of the Sheriff. As evil as he was and as many bad things as he had done, Lucy wished it had been otherwise. Death had never been a welcome act to her, and though the Sheriff and his cronies undoubtedly deserved the justice the King brought, Lucy could find no pleasure in it.

Chapter 36

"WHEN THE WEEK of trials was over, the King held a great archery tournament in honor of England's great hero, Robin Hood."

"Oh, fun!" Mari-Lu clapped her hands. "Did Robin win?"

"People came from all over the kingdom to participate and to watch," Aunt Lucy said, ignoring Mari-Lu's question with a wink. "There were great feasts in the evenings all week long, and at the end of the week the archery tournament was held. Everyone who wished to have a part in it was allowed to participate."

"Did you?"

"I did, through much coercion. Will and Allen were absolutely insistent that I be a part of the tournament, and Robin said he'd only enter if I did, too."

"But he had to enter, the whole tournament was for him," Mari-Lu giggled.

"That is precisely what I said," Aunt Lucy laughed. "But in the end I gave in and participated alongside him. We were not the only members of the gang who participated. Dusty, Will, and Ida all joined in the fun as well, while Little John, Much, Faith, Mark, and Allen cheered wildly from the sidelines. All day long arrows flew and crowds cheered. Slowly, one by one, men and women were knocked out of the running as they missed the targets. With every round of arrows, the targets were moved a few paces further back to increase the difficulty. Near the middle of the afternoon it was down to only Robin, myself, and two men from the King's Royal Guard."

"I bet you or Robin won," Mari-Lu said.

"Always skipping to the end," Aunt Lucy shook her head with a playful *tsk tsk* as she tapped Mari-Lu's nose. "After two more rounds, the targets being pulled farther back each time, the King's men were declared out of the running. It was only Robin and myself…"

«→»

Robin laughed. "I suppose we can call it quits now, can't we? We've been in this spot before and we both know who won."

"One shot doesn't prove anything," Lucy laughed. The crowds gathered nearby were chanting 'Robin Hood' over and over. The sun was high in the sky, and a gentle breeze brushed Lucy's hair out of her face as she laughed. "Come, Robin, there's hope to redeem yourself yet."

"You'll never change the gang's mind," Robin replied, moving to stand next to Lucy as he surveyed the targets now quite some distance away. "You were already declared the best in England."

Robin slowly drew an arrow and let it fly. It sank into the target dead center.

He turned and winked at Lucy as she drew her own arrow from her quiver, and raised her bow. She took a deep breath and then let the arrow fly. It split Robin's arrow down the middle.

The crowds cheering became more wild as Robin didn't hesitate a moment but drew another arrow and let it go in one fluid movement. Robin smirked when it split Lucy's arrow.

The cheering quieted to a suspense-filled hush as Lucy and Robin continued to spit each other's arrows, not waiting for those in charge of the tournament to move the targets further away.

The crowd was silent, watching breathlessly as arrow after arrow flew toward the target, not a single one missing its mark.

The gang was laughing and arguing over who would win. The King shouted for a pause, and Lucy and Robin reluctantly lowered their bows as the King directed the target be moved back another twenty paces.

Robin drew an arrow as soon as the target was in place and let it fly. It hit the target in the middle, which was no surprise to anyone.

Lucy drew her arrow slowly. She looked around at the watching crowd—beginning to chant Robin's name again—at the silent King, the laughing gang.

She let her fingers slide along the fletching of her arrow as she watched the gathered crowds, and then eyed the target with Robin's arrow still protruding from it.

Slowly, she let her arrow fly. It hit the target just beside Robin's.

Robin Hood had won.

The crowd erupted with shouts and laughter. There was much cheering and clapping, and the King shouted above the noise to declare Robin Hood the greatest archer in England.

The people adjourned to tables that had been set up outside Nottingham with a feast for their enjoyment. There were many long tables, piled high with food provided by the King for the people of Nottingham and other cities who were all present for the King's festivities. As for the King himself, his nobles, and Robin and the gang, they adjourned to Nottingham castle where their own feast awaited them.

"So Robin Hood is proved the best," the King laughed as they gathered around a large table in the Great Hall. "No surprise there."

Long after they had finished eating, they remained at the table laughing and telling stories of all that had transpired in the past few years. As the sun set and the stars began to appear, Lucy moved toward her familiar ledge to watch them.

Mark soon joined her, the conversations and laughter still echoing at the table behind them. "I noticed the strangest thing today, Lucy."

"Yes?"

"You let him win."

"Mark, that's ridiculous."

"Honesty, Lucy. It's your greatest virtue."

Lucy sighed. "No one was supposed to know."

"Why did you do it?" Mark asked, laughter in his voice.

"Because this is Robin Hood's day. I decided I couldn't spoil it or turn the attention elsewhere. This day is for him."

"You're a saint," Mark teased.

"Hardly."

The next few days there was partying and feasting through much of the day, and singing and dancing throughout Nottingham. The atmosphere of the entire city was exactly the opposite of what it had been for so long. The joy was palpable.

Lucy stood by a window in Nottingham castle where she could see into the streets of the city to watch the people celebrating down below. She couldn't help but smile as she watched the people below moving about with smiles on their faces and no fear left in their eyes.

Robin came to stand beside her.

"I thought you were outside enjoying the day," Lucy said.

"I was. But I thought I'd come be with you for a while."

"I'm just enjoying watching everyone. They're all so happy."

"I know," Robin leaned against the windowsill, watching the crowds below. "It's heartwarming. I thought...I mean..."

Robin hesitated, glancing at Lucy and then back down into the streets of Nottingham and the cheerful people down below. "I always wanted to stand here and watch this–the people free, and happy once more. But I always imagined I would stand here with Marian."

"I know," Lucy took his hand in hers. "I'm so sorry, Robin."

Robin sighed, and then turned toward Lucy. "It isn't your fault."

"I don't think I'll ever be able to make it up to you, but I am so, so sorry."

"Lucy." Robin cupped her face with his hands, but Lucy pulled away from him, overwhelmed with the guilt and grief that she'd carried for so long. She turned from his blue eyes, so gentle and loving, and ran.

Robin stood still by the window for a long moment, before he turned and sought out Lucy. He found her in her room. She was sitting by the window, her head in her hands, shaking with sobs.

Robin bent and removed her hands from her face. Ever so gently, he began brushing the tears from her face. "Lucy."

"I'm sorry, Robin."

"Lucy, listen to me." Robin knelt in front of her, his hands framing her face as he caught her eye and forced her to look at him. "It isn't your fault. What happened, happened."

"But, Robin—"

"No, Lucy. Don't beat yourself up. It wasn't your fault. Did you choose to kill Marian? Did you ask Sir Guy to kill her? You didn't kill her, Lucy. You always tell Mark not to blame himself, tell me not to dwell on the what-ifs. You should listen to your own advice."

Lucy leaned forward until her forehead rested against Robin's, taking a shaky deep breath.

"And whether you did or not doesn't matter either," Robin continued. "No matter what you do, you will always be forgiven, Lucy. Isn't that what you're always telling us? Isn't that the truth you helped Gisbourne believe?"

"It is," Lucy sighed.

"And haven't you been telling Mark all along not to blame himself? You can't change the past, remember? You can only direct the future."

Lucy clung to Robin and he held her gently, his own tears matching hers. "Let it go. Don't hold onto the past. You're forgiven."

Robin pulled back from the embrace so he could see her face, tilting her chin up so she'd meet his eyes once more. "Do you hear me, dearest? *I* forgive you. Just let it go."

"Thank you, Robin."

«→»

Mari-Lu sighed, leaning into Aunt Lucy's embrace. "That's so sweet."

Aunt Lucy smiled, tears glistening in her eyes. "Yes. Robin was…amazing."

"What happened after that?"

"Not too long after the King's return, Allen and Ida got married."

"Allen and Ida?!" Mari-Lu pulled away from Aunt Lucy, her eyes wide. "They did?"

"Yes, they did. That is another story I'll tell you someday."

"Why can't you tell me now?"

"Because I am growing tired," Aunt Lucy said with a smile. "And we are nearing the end of today's story."

"What else happened?"

"Robin asked me to marry him again…"

«-»

Lucy ran her hand along the wall of Much's hut—now standing empty—eyeing the meadow around her. Summer flowers were blossoming around the camp, and the trees along the border were proudly bearing their green leaves. The gang had spent the day cleaning out the camp and moving everything to Nottingham, as they would no longer be living there.

"I'm going to miss this place," Lucy said softly, walking toward the fire ring with the logs rolled around it for benches. Though she'd only half lived in the camp, it still felt more like home than anywhere else had since her parents' deaths.

"Lucy." Robin approached, coming to stand beside her. "Are you coming back to Nottingham or not?"

The rest of the gang had already left, leaving nothing but the empty huts in the meadow.

Lucy shook herself out of her nostalgic reveries and laughed. "Yes. I will. It's just hard to say goodbye."

"A new part of our lives is about to begin," Robin grinned, taking Lucy's hand in his own.

"Yes, I suppose it is. Though I doubt anything in the future will be half as exciting or harrowing as the past few years."

"Walk with me, Lucy. Down by the stream."

"Alright."

Robin and Lucy walked in silence for a time, the stream bubbling and sparkling along beside them and summer blossoms sprouting all around them.

Robin stopped walking suddenly, and took Lucy's hands in his own. "Lucy. I love you."

"I know."

"I asked you to marry me once…"

"While we were being executed. Good timing on your part."

Robin laughed, and shrugged. "You never answered me. Will you marry me? Please."

Robin's blue eyes bored into hers and she was more than ready to drown in the love she saw there.

"You don't have to answer right away. You can think about it."

"I don't need to think about it, Robin."

"No?"

"No." Lucy shook her head.

390

"Was that a 'no, I don't need to think about it' or 'no, I won't marry you.'"

Lucy's eyes began to sparkle. "What do you think, Robin Hood?"

"I can never be sure with you…"

"Yes, I'll marry you, you idiot. I love you."

Robin swept her up in a warm embrace and Lucy relished every moment of it, holding him close. Not too long ago they had nearly been executed together; Lucy had no doubt that together they could face anything life might throw at them. After all, they'd already endured the worst.

The day before their wedding Lucy went in search of Sir Guy. They hadn't had much interaction since his pardon, as Sir Guy and Andrew had kept to themselves. Many in Nottingham still had no love for Sir Guy, and the hostility that met them in the streets led them to remain cloistered in the castle most of the time.

Lucy found Sir Guy in the library with Andrew, who quietly moved away to give them space.

"Guy…" Lucy didn't know what to say; she wanted to be sure their friendship—strange as it was—wasn't going to suffer, that he wasn't going to be miserable or backslide into darkness because of her wedding, but how could she put any of that into words?

"It's alright, Lucy," Sir Guy put down the book he had been reading, smiling at her. "I imagine you're here to make sure I'm okay with tomorrow's events, considering my failed proposal."

Lucy bit her lip and nodded.

"As long as you are happy; I am okay, Lucy."

"I am happy."

"Then so am I."

⟪⟫

"And so I married Robin Hood," Aunt Lucy said.

"And they lived happily ever after," Mari-Lu said contentedly.

"For several years, yes," Aunt Lucy replied. "Until King Richard died, and more adventures took place. But that is another story altogether and I do not have the time to tell it today."

"But you still lived happily ever after, right?"

"Yes," Aunt Lucy chuckled. "I suppose we did. Robin and I soon had a daughter, and we named her Marian, in honor of Robin's first wife. We lived in peace and joy for many years. Every member of the gang remained as close as though we were family, and soon Andrew became a dear friend of ours. It was hard for the people to accept Sir Guy and Andrew at first, but they worked hard to prove their worth and loyalty, and those who truly knew them valued them."

"And then your daughter Marian grew up and got married, right?" Mari-Lu asked, clapping her hands. "And she had a son she called Robin and that's my father!"

"Yes, Mari-Lu. That's your father. And then came–"

"Me!"

Aunt Lucy laughed. "Yes, child. You."

"What else happened?"

"The rest of our adventures deserve a story of their own. There were many small trials and hardships in our lives, and several more grand adventures that I will tell you all about some other day. Everyone within the gang remained close friends for years, and we loved watching our children grow up side by side."

"And then we all lived happily ever after."

"Yes, Mari-Lu," Aunt Lucy laughed. "So you keep saying. And then we all grew old, and slowly—one by one—everyone passed on, until I became the only surviving member of our original gang."

"But we'll never forget them," Mari-Lu said firmly, her face as serious as her mother Marian had ever seen it. She hugged Aunt Lucy tightly. "We'll never forget you."

"No," Marian agreed with her daughter. "England will never forget Robin Hood and Lady Lucy and the way they saved England with only a handful of friends."

"I want to hear all the other stories!" Mari-Lu said, jumping off of Aunt Lucy's lap and dancing around the meadow where so many moments of the story she'd just been told had taken place years ago. She plucked a few flowers from the ground and glanced around. The meadow was empty, save for the tall smooth stone where her mother Marian was sitting, and in it was carved an inscription.

Mari-Lu moved to stand by her mother. "What's it say?"

Marian stood, wrapping her arms around her daughter's shoulders as she read the inscription that she knew by heart...

"Though quiet now and full of sorrow, this small meadow was once the laughter-filled home of Robin Hood and his Merry Men. To them, we say, 'we will never forget your courage and your sacrifice. May you be remembered as long as England stands.'"

Family Trees

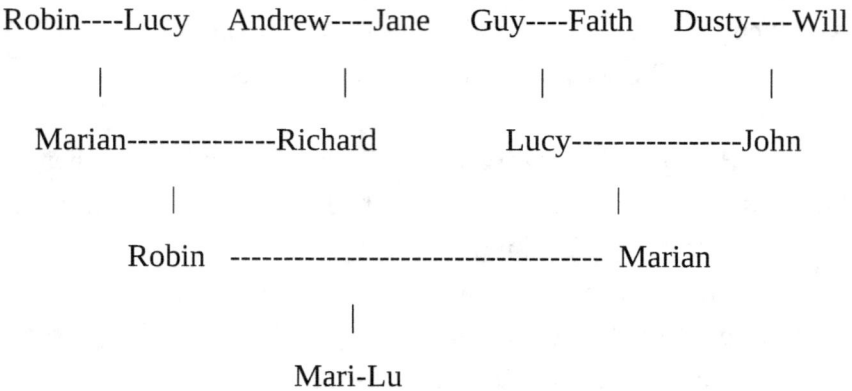

```
Robin----Lucy    Andrew----Jane    Guy----Faith    Dusty----Will
     |                  |                |                  |
Marian--------------Richard         Lucy----------------John
       |                                   |
    Robin  ---------------------------------- Marian
                      |
                   Mari-Lu
```

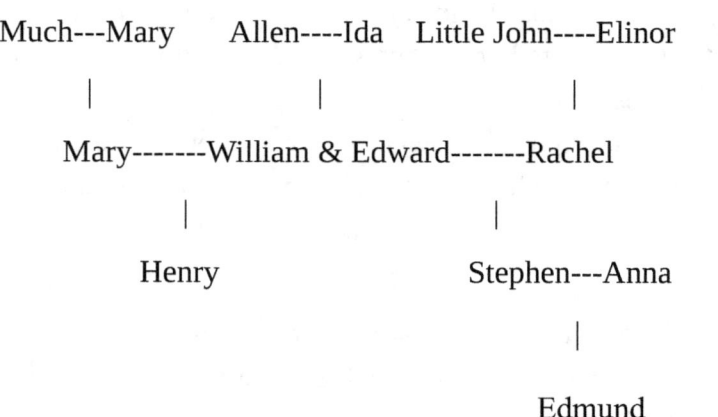

```
Much---Mary      Allen----Ida    Little John----Elinor
     |                  |                  |
Mary-------William & Edward-------Rachel
       |                              |
    Henry                    Stephen---Anna
                                   |
                               Edmund
```

Acknowledgments:

It takes a village…and this 'thank you' includes those who helped with the original 'Lucy's Legend: A Robin Hood Story' and this updated version of the book now known as The Legend of the Thief.

Rebekah–my biggest critic, biggest fan, and constant inspiration. I'm grateful for you always.

Quill and Cup, my AMAZING writing community— where to even begin? Ania, our fearless Mama Hedgie: you reaching out to ask me to join this community remains the best thing to happen in my writing career to date. Your encouragement pushed me onward even as you challenged me to 'kill my writer's ego' and hone my craft. You are an inspiration. Lillie, Lauren, Ellie, Carrie, Krysann—thank you all for your part in helping me strengthen my writing, write my pitch, and just show up every day to make progress. I most definitely could not have rewritten this book as fast as I did without all of you holding me accountable to show up to Prickles and push myself forward. To those hedgies I didn't name: you being a part of the Hedgie House is still an inspiration to me and holds me accountable so thank you for that.

And a very special thank you to my Hedgie Sister and BFF/critique partner Danni—you are the best and I love you. Your love of Will and disdain for Robin, your helpful critiques and suggestions, every comment, every conversation … this story would not be where it is without you and you deserve the biggest thank you I could possibly give.

Amy—your coaching the Hedgie House through using the enneagram to craft compelling characters and plot revolutionized everything for me, and spurred the rewrites of this book into so many meaningful and magical directions. Thank you from the bottom of my heart for that workshop and also for answering all my random DMs full of questions.

Elizabeth Hutchinson—you always catch my pesky grammar mistakes, and for that I am grateful. You deserve an award not only for editing the original book, but for being gracious enough to edit the new one as well.

Obviously I must thank my parents for their continued love and support as I pursue this crazy dream of being an author.

My sister Susannah and brother Christopher for their edits and input on the OG version (Lucy's Legend), without which there wouldn't be a Legend of the Thief.

My childhood friends (one of whom is now my sister-in-law): Sarah, Noelle, and Emily to whom teenage me would go to for advice, inspiration, and just an ear to listen to me rant about my stories.

Brittney Murphy for inspiring me to self-publish in the first place, without whom there would not have been a Lucy's Legend or any of the books to come afterward.

And finally a heartfelt thanks to my God who put this story on my heart in the first place and gave me the skill and passion to pursue it (both at age seventeen and age twenty-six)

www.ingramcontent.com/pod-product-compliance
Lightning Source LLC
Chambersburg PA
CBHW071153250626
47159CB00001B/74